Sustenance of Courage

Pioneer Women

by

JR Reynolds

[signed] JR Reynolds 03-02-2010

authorHOUSE™

1663 LIBERTY DRIVE, SUITE 200
BLOOMINGTON, INDIANA 47403
(800) 839-8640
WWW.AUTHORHOUSE.COM

First published by AuthorHouse 8/3/2006

ISBN: 1-4208-7241-9 (sc)

Library of Congress Control Number: 2005906780

Printed in the United States of America
Bloomington, Indiana

This book is printed on acid-free paper.

Dedicated to my children Peggy, Grant, Karlene, Sue
I do not ask for mighty words to leave you impressed. But grant my
story may ring true and you will be blessed.

TABLE OF CONTENTS

ILLINOIS

IOWA

NEBRASKA TERRORY

WYOMING

I am grateful to my ancestors who bravely made the difficult journey to the Pacific Northwest and to the pioneer women, who diaries I gleaned for their experiences.

My thanks to those who believed in my dream, and you know who you are. My Editors at Authorhouse, who worked my story into one I'm proud to tell.

My gratitude to my family and friends, who waited patiently for the story to unfold and who I hope will find their entertainment need fulfilled..

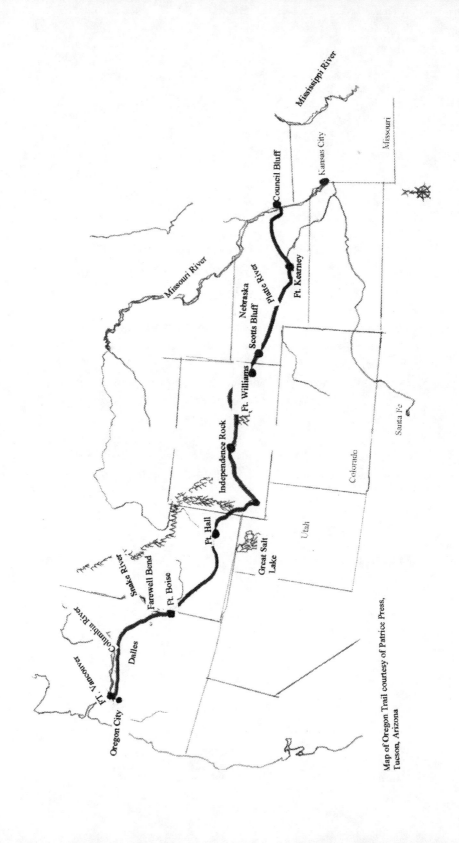

Map of Oregon Trail courtesy of Patrice Press, Tucson, Arizona

Chapter 1 Illinois

"Martha, I don't care what you say. I'm not going. You know we're never coming back. No, I've decided not to go." Thirteen-year-old Bertha Burt tossed back her long, straight, black hair.

"You might as well go, Bertha. Everything we haven't sold or given away is in the wagon. Why would you want to stay here any longer?" A wide-brimmed bonnet covered the older sister, Martha's, head as she leaned against the rough bark of an apple tree. She gazed up into branches filled with swollen buds and small green leaves, an ache heavy in her heart. Her coarse, homespun dress draped across her slender build but didn't quite reach her ankles, exposing her bare feet in the tall grass. The Burt women had thick-callused feet from walking as they did without shoes or moccasins.

"I thought the wagon looked so big when Papa brought it home. But now that it's packed, there's not enough room for us in it." Bertha sounded disgusted. She reached up to pull a branch down for a closer inspection of its delicate white flowers.

"You know, Bertha, I'm sixteen. If I were married, I'd have my own family. I'd be staying here. I wouldn't have to leave the only place I've ever known all my life. Mother and Papa weren't much older than me when they were married."

Martha couldn't help but wonder if Bertha was just scared. *It is a strange world out there we girls know so little about Savage Indians and how they treat white women. There's all kinds of ailments, so much unknown. I think I understand Bertha's feelings.*

"Martha, we've worked hard these past four years just so we can live in a cramped old wagon? This Oregon Territory is so far away! I'd like to know ... does Papa have any idea what he's doing to us?"

1

"Bertha, our grandparents had to give up everything they owned when they came to America. They came here in cramped little ships. You've heard their stories. We're not going to travel nearly as far as they did. I like the smell of the new wood and tar in the wagon, don't you?"

"It's too far, Martha." Bertha's voice was defiant. "It's just too far away. And besides, our grandparents didn't have to fight off Indians, cross rivers, or climb high mountains like I hear we're going to be doing."

"Oh Bertha, the ocean is bigger than any river."

"I don't want to leave here, Martha. Papa can move down the road a piece if he feels the need to move."

"Its nice here in the orchard. How many hours have we girls spent playing here, Bertha?" *These trees, these beautiful trees with their blossoms— they're no longer my trees. I'm never going to watch them bloom again."*

"Oh! Papa's being so selfish. I know—I shouldn't say this—even our kinfolk say Papa's too restless for his own good. He'll settle down alright, but not till he's dragged us through the wilderness and tried to drown us all. Martha, no one ever asked us if we wanted to do this. We'll have to walk, you know. Six months; that must be halfway round the world. Our legs are bound to shorten and we won't even be our full height when we get there."

"But Bertha, after we get settled out West, then we can come back together, you know. Besides, this is Grandpa's land. Papa wants his own land. Uncle Ernie told me we're going as far west as the land goes. Once Papa gets out there he can't go any farther. Come, we best get back before Papa gets angry with us for dawdling."

"I hate leaving Granny, but she insists she's through with traveling," Martha said as she followed her sister back to the empty house. "She must have so many memories of when she left her home. She never went back either."

"She frets so about Mother bringing along all those dried apricots and apples. Have you noticed? How much dried fruit do we need?" Bertha complained. "She's never been able to explain their purpose for her family; *they just did* is all she'll say."

"I know. She repeats the story so often. Why does everybody hang on her stories?" Martha looked back over her shoulder to savor a last glimpse of the little orchard.

The girls walked down the garden path, where new life would soon be sprouting but was no longer theirs to tend and care for. They walked up beside Mother, who was listening attentively to Granny, a tiny, little old lady whose deceptively bright blue eyes belied her age. Her white hair escaped the confines of a little bun atop her head and curled softly around her face.

Granny Burt, Papa's mother, was holding out a square tin the girls recognized from the numerous family occasions. "Came all the way from England, it did," she'd tell them each time she carried it with her.

"This has my potato cake for my grandchildren, from their granny, Mary. Now if I were you, I'd pour a bit of spirits over it now and again to keep it fit for a descent amount of time."

Martha knew all about Granny's coming from England with the same kind of cake and with all those dried apples and apricots she talked about. The spirits she was referring to she'd help pack away for medicinal purposes, along with the salves, potions, and herbs for the family's use along the way.

The preparations and supplies came from in a little handbook provided by the agency as a guide for settlers traveling out West by wagon train. Papa had even had his wagon built from such recommendations, as had others like him.

Papa was anxious to leave, and urged his family to board the wagon. "I was hopin' ta get started bright and early," he said, unsuccessfully attempting to hide his impatience.

Granny had insisted she come say farewell to her family this morning, and Papa couldn't refuse the little old lady.

Martha and Bertha were finding it difficult to control their emotions around Granny as they fought against tears. Granny was too old to make the journey. In their hearts they knew that if they were ever to return, Granny probably wouldn't be here to greet them.

Little sister Ruthie clung so tightly to Granny that she had had to be pulled away and handed over to one of her aunts, who tried to console the sobbing child.

Martha was unable to speak; she wiped her eyes on the sleeve of her dress as she tried to concentrate on the conversation between Mother and Granny.

"Mary, you can make it, I know you can. I made it. Our prayers are with you every step of your way from here." Granny's tears ran unchecked down her soft, wrinkled face onto her good Sunday dress as she held tight to Mother's hands. Martha felt she was witnessing something special being passed between the two women. She'd been aware of this special understanding between women before. Shed seen it when they'd gone to each other with their needs. This perhaps was such a moment, to exchange words of encouragement needed for this journey.

Mother once told her, "You'll come to understand what courage is someday. It's necessary in our lives." Martha, watching Granny and Mother, decided courage wasn't as important to men. She'd never seen men display such an exchange as she was observing between these women. Did women need more courage than men?

The emotional test for Papa came as, with his arm around Granny's shoulders, he bravely walked with her to her shay. "Now, Ma," everyone heard him say, "ya know I've always asked the good Lord ta help me when you're not around. You could change you're mind and come with us. I'd wait till ya pack your things." He helped her up onto the buggy seat and reached up for her kiss. He hesitated, quickly jerked his handkerchief from his back pocket, wiped his eyes, and blew his nose loudly.

He reached up to embrace his mother one last time before he turned away and headed for the wagon. He made a deliberate show of adjusting his hat to the jaunty angle he was accustomed to wearing it as the family watched.

He paused and faced away from the family for a few moments before turning back to face them. "Anyone comin' with me?" His voice sounded forced. "Let's get ta rollin'."

I knew it would be difficult for him, leaving all this when the time came, Martha thought. *I can't help but feel that he knows he'll never be back to see Granny again, his mother, my dear sweet, little Granny. This is the difficult time, saying good-bye. I can't—I won't let myself think about never seeing my Granny again.*

Why oh why must Papa take us so far from all we've ever known?

She turned her attention to her little brother, Stephen, who was clutched under Papa's arm, giggling and squealing, as he climbed up to the wagon seat and deposited him next to Mother.

"Come along, girls; get in so's I can lift the tailgate and secure these latches. Don't want cha' fallin' out." Uncle Joe hurried them along. "Come, give Uncle Joe one last big hug. We'll be comin' out to see ya after yur settled. Now which one of you is keeping the journal?" Uncle Joe, Papa's big brother, had come with his family all the way down from the Illinois Erie Canal he was helping to build to see them off.

I can't speak. This lump in my throat is too big to swallow. I love these people; they're my family. Oh please, Lord, let me come back. After we're settled,

Bertha and I, we'll come back. I don't want them to see me crying like this. Oh bother—what's the use? Look at us all weeping. We're acting like there's been a wake. I can't bear to look at anyone. We all look so sad, and I thought this journey was to be fun.

"That lucky Stephen, Martha, he gets to ride in front with Mother and Papa," Ruthie complained, wiping her eyes with the back of her hand. Her sobs had reduced to hiccups.

There's something to be said for bonnets with wide brims, Martha decided.

They cut off our vision from the world, like now when we women need privacy. She noticed Mother was busy tying bonnet ties with her head lowered.

Kohee, had been a constant companion to Martha and she was about to leave her beloved dog.

Papa had insisted before they left that Kohee go live with Granny and he had been right. "It'll make the separation for Kohee easier," he'd said.

She couldn't resist and walked over to fondle Kohee's neck and ears one more time before she climbed up into the wagon. Papa had insisted the journey was too hard on pets. Kohee might get lost or killed, and there was little space for extra animals.

Martha's eyes filled with tears at Kohee obediently sitting beside Granny's shay, his big, dark eyes never losing sight of his family.

He doesn't understand why he can't come with us. He doesn't know it's for his own good. Oh, I wish I could tell you how I hurt inside right now, Kohee. You've always been there for me, my faithful friend. Martha lowered her head to hide her sorrow. *He accepts this because he knows nothing more, only love. Oh Kohee, I'll never forget you.* She felt a profound sadness inside, realizing that, like Granny, Kohee probably wouldn't be here if she were ever to return.

Martha was unable to bring herself to watch as Granny's buggy with Kohee turned away from her along with the other relatives, who followed behind the big wagon, as it rattled on its way heading west. They waved and called out to each other as they parted.

Bertha and Ruthie were crying uncontrollably, and Martha felt helpless to comfort them. She glanced up to where Mother was sitting and caught sight of the little rocking chair tied securely to the hoops overhead.

She remembered Mother's smile when Papa had carried the chair out to load it into the wagon. "This goes with us; it's part of the family," he said. Papa never let the family forget how he bought Mother the little rocker to rock her babies in.

Martha revered the feelings Papa and Mother shared for each other. He always referred to Mother's coronet of gold hair as her "halo." Anyplace on earth Papa went she knew Mother was content beside him.

I hope all we're leaving behind is worth Papa's dream, she thought as she gazed out the wagon to the world she was leaving.

Granny's words suddenly came to her. "The sun up there in the sky is the same sun shining over all the world by day and the same moon by night, no matter where you are in the world." It helped to know that wherever she'd be, Granny would be under the same sun each day and the same moon come night.

Martha reached over to draw her sisters close. She felt better as excitement began to ease the pain of her departure.

The white canvas cover, stretched taut over the hoops of the wagon, glistened in the early morning sun. It billowed to its fullest, teased in a gentle breeze.

The distance between Martha and her home grew as the big wagon lumbered slowly along, pulled by Papa's yoke of four strong, sturdy oxen. They were moving westward to meet new friends at the Cross Roads Junction, and there they would become an extended family as they traveled together in search of new land out in the vast, untamed Oregon Territory.

Chapter 2

"Look! There they are!" Stephen Burt was overcome with excitement.

The three girls scrambled up behind Papa, Mother, and five-year-old Stephen to view the scene from the opening in the canvas. A good distance ahead were big canvas-covered wagons poised against a blue horizon.

"Papa, can't you make the oxen go faster? See? Look out there!" Stephen was positioned between Papa and Mother, pointing in the direction of the wagons.

Martha felt a quickening within herself at the sight. "Wonder how long they've been waiting for us?" she asked. She had pulled off her bonnet in the warm April sunshine, but now hurriedly put it on.

"They probably arrived this morning," Mother told her. "It was set up for us to meet around midday."

"That's them alright! Papa. Those are the wagons! Can't we hurry?" Stephen, impatiently shook Papa's arm.

"There's sure to be a lot of strangers!" Ruthie commented.

"Ruthie, there's only five wagons besides ours; that's not many," Bertha assured her. "This is only the first group. We'll be meeting up with a lot more at a place called Council Bluffs, remember?"

"I wish I were in Stephen's place. I'm as excited as he is about seeing those wagons," Martha conveyed in her eagerness.

"In Stephen's place?" Bertha turned to her sister. "Whatever do you mean?"

"Put yourself in Stephen's place, Bertha. Everything's a challenge, a new discovery. He's not restricted like we girls are."

"Stephen, settle down. I see them; they're not going anywhere. They need us to go with them," Papa informed the impatient boy.

Stephen, a tow-headed little fellow with big blue eyes, searched Papa's face. "How come they need us, Papa?"

7

Martha found it difficult to absorb everything around her. The fields of grass moved in a pleasant breeze, the blue sky, and white canvases. She felt like Granny often described: "almost giddy with excitement."

Stephen bounced up and down with anticipation. "Papa, make the oxen go faster."

Martha, watching her baby brother, smiled. She was brought back to the deaths of two other babies before Stephen, the only Burt male heir. *Papa and Mother are so proud of him. We girls protect him and Granny spoils him. It's a wonder he's still a sweet-natured, lovable little boy.*

"Stephen, can you tell me which way to Oregon?"

He glanced back at Martha and answered with a shrug and a grin that displayed the gap where a front tooth had been originally. "It's out there someplace," he told her "Papa knows the way; he's takin' us there, Martha, don't you worry none. Papa knows the way alright."

Big maples, hickories, and aspen trees provided shade for the wagons pulled into the circular position to form a barrier, protecting the campground on the inside.

Martha's impression of the campsite, as Papa maneuvered the wagon in beside the others, was of an active beehive. Besides the folks creating an atmosphere of excitement and festivity, it impressed her that this place and date could be so successfully organized to bring strangers together. *I'll be cooking over an open campfire, like the one over there, every day till the end of my journey .*

"Stephen, you wait now. Papa's coming to help you down." Mother reached to grab hold of him but he managed to avoid her, jumping down and sprinting across the field.

Papa helped Mother down before coming to unlatch the tailgate for the girls.

"I'm not sure I'm ready for this," Bertha whispered, holding out her hand for Papa's support before stepping down onto the footstool in front of her. She turned to see Ruthie positioning her barefoot on a wagon wheel spoke in her anxiety to get down.

"Papa, Bertha's right; there's a lot of strangers here." Martha smoothed out her skirt and straightened her bonnet. "Come along, Bertha, let's get this over with. They look friendly. Besides we need to show them we're ladies." Martha linked her arm through her sister's and followed sedately behind their parents.

Folks came with hands outstretched. Papa, with Mother by his side, extended his hand in greeting. "Well, 'pears ta me the agency did their job, pairin' us up. Name's Burt—Eli Burt. This is my wife, Mary Burt," Papa said, taking a big hand held out to him.

"Sam Emigh, Mr. Burt. Glad to welcome you and your family. My boys and I just arrived a few hours ago."

Martha, standing behind Papa, knew Papa judged a fellow by his handshake. He appeared pleased with Mr. Emigh, a man of Papa's height and stature. "Your family completes our group," Sam Emigh said. Then he introduced, "David Wilson, Mr. Burt."

"Mr. Burt, ah'm pleased to meet ya." A poised, self-assured gentleman held out his hand to Papa. "Interestin' that we're all from northern Illinois. Ya'll come from up around Dutch Chicago, or Prairie Heights, is it?" David Wilson asked in his soft, Southern drawl. "Glad to have ya here. Ah'm hoping to set ma'self up in business again in a mercantile like the one ah just sold."

"Me," Papa said, "I just want ta stake my claim and get ta farmin'. Only thing I know. Hopin' ta get a section for me and the wife. That's enough ta keep me busy."

Martha noticed Mother had slipped away from the men to mingle with the women.

She and Bertha quickly followed her. They were used to familiar gatherings where everyone knows each other. These were all strangers. She knew she needed to interact with these women, as they would be traveling together from now on like an extended family, if you will, until the journey was finished.

"I'm Alex Kenyon. Pleased to meet ya." A short, stocky man introduced himself to Papa. "The land's what I got my eye on too. I'm going fer the land," he announced.

"Gonna raise ma'self some pure breeds. There's good money in horseflesh. I'm like you, Mr. Burt—Eli, is it? I'm goin' fur the land. We're all makin' a good move, if you ask me." He grabbed Papa's hand, pumping it vigorously.

"This gentleman here, Eli, is Mr. Crawford. Comes out of Pennsylvania, ain't that what ya said, Tom?" Mr. Kenyon let go of Papa's hand to thump Tom Crawford on the back. "He come in after us last night." Tom Crawford and Papa shook hands.

The last fellow to step forward was Mr. McGraw, a big burly man with a head of unruly red hair. "Brian McGraw, Mr. Burt. Ah'm a Smithy."

"Howdy, Mr. McGraw. Bet ya travel with your tools, just like a doctor, don't ya'?"

"Ya betcha, Mr. Burt, jist like a doctor." Brian McGraw emitted such a robust laugh that the other men couldn't help but join him.

Martha turned to her sister. "Why is it our parents are so much more at ease with others? I don't know what to say."

"I feel the same," Bertha agreed. "Mother does it with such grace."

The girls watched Mother chatting with the other women, who had taken time from their work to meet the Burt family.

Martha studied the women. *We'll all be struggling though the days and months ahead. I wonder what these women fear about this journey? We're strangers to each other and we're expected to rely on and trust each other. Our lives may depend on it, but we've no choice or say about this long journey. At least we Burt women didn't.*

She reflected on something Granny once told her. "When women make up their minds to unite themselves against the odds, they're a force no man has any business reckonin' with."

She wondered if these women knew this. Her attention was drawn back to the friendliness of those inviting the Burt women into their midst.

Martha watched Papa go with the men to care for the oxen while they expressed their opinions of the journey. She glanced from one to another of the women. At the moment, they were agreed it was indeed a special occasion to celebrate. They would combine the noonday meal.

Mrs. Kenyon, though not officially appointed, had taken on the task of camp director. A large-boned, matronly woman, with prematurely gray hair she had pulled back in a severe round bun at the nape of her neck, and carried herself with dignified poise. She demanded immediate attention in her loud, commanding voice while organizing preparations for the meal.

Provisional boxes, built to carry supplies needed for daily use, were pulled from the wagons to serve as tables. Mrs. Kenyon also yelled continuously in her lusty voice for her two sons, but, much to her distress, they never materialized.

Martha discovered Mrs. Kenyon's husband was the short little man she'd observed earlier showing interest in buying land. He appeared to busy himself as much as possible out of view of his wife. "Bertha," she whispered, "that little man over there is Mr. Kenyon."

"Who?" Bertha looked in the direction Martha indicated with a nod of her head; it wouldn't have been polite to point. "Where, Martha, I don't see him?"

"He's hiding over there behind the men," Martha told her, stifling a giggle behind her hand.

"That little man, Martha? Oh, I bet he always says yes, ma'am proper-like to her, don't you?"

Mother approached the girls. "And how are you ladies doing?"

"Mother, there are so many people, how can we remember them all?" Ruthie asked as they went for their contribution to the meal.

"Don't try to remember everyone's name all at once; it comes easier with time.

Pretty soon you'll connect faces with names. Just don't forget who you are. Remember your grandmother Lane's advice. Show you have good breeding," Mother replied. "I thought you were doing a good job of conducting yourselves. Martha, listen to me, we need a big pot of coffee. Roast the beans dark, won't you? Those ladies over there will make a place on the fire rack for you. Ask nicely now."

Taking the necessary utensils, Martha headed for the campfire. The coffee would take time. Beans taken from the big bag needed to be roasted and ground before they could be added to the water in the new, big, blue-speckled coffeepot. Setting her supplies down on the ground, Martha noted the Dutch ovens in use. Cast-iron skillets or spiders of various sizes and styles all were designed for use over the open campfire. Some of the big kettles emitted delicious aromas of cooking food and baking bread.

On her way to fill the coffeepot from the stream she'd noticed when they arrived, Martha glanced up to see the sun was directly overhead. A soft breeze played through the leaves of the big trees. She stooped to fill the coffeepot from a stream meandering on its way.

Animals grazed as far as their tethers allowed, or were lying in the warm sun. It was a quiet, peaceful scene except for the campers.

The pot filled, she returned to the fireside and started the green coffee beans roasting in the skillet. They must be roasted just dark enough for the strong coffee Papa preferred. Too little roasting delivered a weak coffee but to much made it bitter. She was deep in concentration on the roasting beans and unaware of another person until an armload of wood came tumbling down.

She glanced over to a young man squatting down beside her, forcing a piece of wood into the burning fire. Smoke and ashes billowed up around Martha. Startled, she turned away, raising an arm to shield her face as she was seized by a fit of coughing.

"Oh no. I didn't mean for this ta happen. I'm sorry." The man quickly stood up.

"Are ya gonna be alright?

Martha hastily turned back to the beans; she frantically searched for something to cover the handle of the hot cast-iron skillet. The fellow quickly used the long sleeve of his shirt to pick up the skillet. Martha had the lid of the grinder open and gestured for him to pour the beans into the grinder. After he'd done as he'd been instructed, he stood awkwardly, holding the hot skillet awaiting further instruction. She glanced up to see his dilemma and gestured for him to set it down on the edge of the fire rack.

"Thank you." She hesitated; she didn't know his name.

He sensed her frustration. "Neil. My name's Neil Emigh."

"Thank you, Mr. Emigh, for saving the beans." She felt a tingling sensation creep over her as she faced up at him. *Why he has blue eyes!* She thought, *They're the same blue as Papa's.*

"Well, guess I'd best go find where I can be of further use." He turned away.

Martha was speechless as she watched after him.

Oh, I best get to grinding beans or there'll be no coffee and I'll find myself answering to Mother or Papa. She turned back to the coffee, but the blue eyes of the handsome gentleman intruded on her concentration.

Mrs. Kenyon had to announce only once that the meal was ready. Folks converged on the laden tables with their eating utensils. They bowed their heads reverently while Mr. Kenyon invoked the blessing, then everyone helped themselves to the bean dishes, along with stews, fried chicken, roasted game birds, and coleslaw. There were also breads including corn cakes, biscuits, raised biscuits, and fresh-baked bread, along with sweet butter and homemade preserves, pickles, and several pies and cakes.

"With so many good cooks, and so much good food, ya give us men a good night's rest. What more could we ask for?" Papa commented.

Folks agreed, carrying their plates away to enjoy themselves. It was decided that if this were any indication of what lay ahead, they should have a good journey.

Stephen came to sit by Papa, but ate very little before he was off again.

"Eli, I wonder if we'll be seeing much of the boy from now on?" Mother lamented. "Why, he barely ate a bite. Look at that plate of food; he barely touched it."

"Mary, he'll settle down in a few days. He's just excited now is all. I wouldn't worry if I were you."

Martha knew Mother, and she would worry; her family's welfare was important to her.

Martha found she liked the new dishes. She recalled the scene between her parents over them. Mother was proud of her few china dishes. Papa had put his arm around her, taking a china plate and setting it back in the cupboard. "When we get to our new home, I'm going to get you new china dishes, Mary."

"Now Eli, you get to take your plow. I need my dishes," Mother argued in defense of her priceless china.

"Mary, my love, my plow is not easily broken. I'm going to get you a new set of china dishes." Mother had accepted defeat. The china had gone to Granny, who offered to keep it for Mother. "Please, Granny, do with it what you will," she'd said softly, setting the dishes down on Granny's table.

Martha felt sorry for Mother. The few china dishes were precious to her, but Papa was right about their being fragile. The china had never been mentioned again. *I trust Papa; he's a man of his word. There are so many things this family has been forced to leave behind.* She found she preferred the blue enamelware to the tin herself, and they were not easily broken.

Papa requested that Martha refill his plate. Turning from the table, she collided with Neil. "Mr. Emigh, I'm so sorry. I didn't see you."

"I'm having ma'self another piece of this here cake. It's really good."

"Oh, Mother will be so pleased; I must tell her you enjoy it." Martha was proud of herself for acting just like Mother said a lady should. She was hoping Neil would notice too. She watched him cut a huge piece of cake then turn back to his family.

He'd made her feel self-conscious and uncomfortable. *What ever is the matter with me? Oh, I wonder if he thinks I'm a bold floozy. Oh dear, and I wanted him to notice me. Why did I bother to say anything? Why didn't I just smile, ladylike?*

Handing Papa his plate, she didn't share the discussion between herself and Neil with Mother.

Waiting quietly for her family to finish dinner, she found herself observing Neil across the way. She wondered where his mother was; there were only the three of them.

Neil resembled a younger version of his father. Martha, not wanting him to know she was watching him, quickly glanced over to see Stephen coming up flushed from exertion, tiny beads of perspiration dotting his forehead and nose.

"Papa, isn't it time to go yet?" he asked, dropping down to sit on Papa's knee.

"I'm ready to go. I already ate my dinner a long time ago."

Chapter 3

The Burt girls crossed the wide-open meadows with a pleasant breeze ruffling the new prairie grasses. Quick movements in the grass suggested to them it was populated with small, out-of-sight rodents. They passed an occasional abandoned trapper's shack among the groves of maples, fragrant cottonwood, massive oaks, and hickory in the warm, last-week-of-April, afternoon sun.

Beside them, the Illinois River, brown from the spring thaw, swept quietly along.

This route they were on would eventually lead them to the Mississippi River crossing.

There they would combine with more wagons, and move across the Iowa Territory to Council Bluffs to converge with yet more wagons and a Wagon Master to guide them out West.

Martha and Bertha were finding it difficult to keep stable footing while walking in the rutted grooves of the road that had been mired in deep mud after rains, and the frozen ground that thawed in the spring.

"I don't understand how Mother thinks up things like those little pockets sewed inside our canvas," Martha commented. "She amazes me, being so practical and gifted."

"I know; the pockets are so useful," Bertha agreed. "Especially the ones for the Bible and mirror. I wonder if the factory-made canvases have pockets in them."

The girls were comparing the wagon coverings of Osnaburg sheeting—made from flax or tow, durable but not very water repellent—with the ones made of heavy material called canvas that were more difficult to handle.

"I wonder if these calluses will ever go away," Bertha wondered, holding out her hands to display the thickened skin around her fingertips. "That stitching has made my hands so ugly. If only Papa could have afforded to buy our covering."

"I guess Mother thought that by making our own it would be easier to wax," Martha concluded.

"I hope I don't have to do that it again. Day after day pouring hot melted wax over every seam." Bertha sighed loudly. "The sewing, plaiting, drying, and folding the material. It was heavy, hard work, and Ruthie didn't help either. Poor Mother needed all the help she could get, and it seemed to me we'd just get started and Ruthie, the foolish girl, would fret the bees were after her and we'd have to take time to quiet her."

"Now Bertha, you know as well as me that you told her they knew who ate their honey, and the hot wax did smell like warm honey. She told us she was scared the bees would be angry if they recognized their honey."

Martha, thinking about the covering, had to smile. Papa was always challenging Mother Nature. Like the day he'd assembled the family around him to explain his idea to secure the five hickory hoops that spanned the wagon to hold the canvas.

She'd never forget how they watched him put the hoops up. "Way I figure it," he'd said, "if I hadn't come up with this idea to fasten 'em down good and tight in these brackets, the weather'd wreck these bows. So I've drilled holes into the brackets, and pushed this peg all the way through the bracket on the outside of the wagon here, right on through the bow on into the wagon. There, see how it's done?"

He stepped back, gesturing to the hoops. "Let 'er rain, let the wind try and blow my canvas off. It won't budge, and if a bracket splits, it's still pinned down. Think maybe I've got ol' Mother Nature beat for sure this time."

Martha wondered if the Crawfords' wagon up ahead would survive as it bumped and swayed along the rough trail.

Thomas Crawford, his wife Elsa, and their children, Louie and Elizabeth, in their Heavy, ankle-high, clumsy, leather shoes fascinated the Burt girls. Mrs. Crawford appeared to Martha as a tiny, white-breasted bird in her white apron, busily darting about.

Bertha said she'd heard Mr. Wilson tell Papa, "He'd bought his wagon because he didn't know nothin' about building his own. He got the biggest and best for his money to haul Mrs. Wilson's furniture in. If he hadn't gone along with his Mrs.," he said, "he'd still be sittin' at home."

"Ours is a good strong wagon, Bertha. Papa and Uncle Ernie used seasoned wood and made sure the seams were thickly coated with tar. I heard him tell all this to Mother," Martha replied.

"I like not having to use the commode inside the wagon," Bertha stated, "but I hate having to use that little extra room Mother made. I don't like folks knowin' the business I'm about, do you?"

"We could go stand behind the other women with their backs to us while they fan out their skirts, like the others do," Martha teased.

"Oh! Martha, for shame." Bertha feigned disgust.

Martha had to laugh. *Granny was right when she said my sister is vain.*

Bertha interrupted Martha's musing. "Since we're talking about calluses, let me tell you what we're gonna look like at the end of this journey. Calluses on our fingers and bigger ones on our feet. Papa's never gonna marry us off. We won't arrive lookin' much like ladies."

Martha giggled at Bertha's seriousness. However, she made sense. Walking for the next six months, what would they look like, pray tell?

"If you learn to handle the oxen, you could do as Papa does," Martha suggested.

The bright sun glaring against the dazzling white canvas forced the girls to shade their eyes with both hands when they looked up at Papa. He appeared asleep, his body moving in rhythm to the wagon's movement.

"If he gets bounced off the wagon," Martha grinned, "then you'd get your chance to take over the oxen and not have to walk."

Their laughter wakened Papa, who looked down at them, a guilty, sheepish grin across his face.

"Where does all this dust in the air come from?" Martha asked, trying to subdue a fit of coughing. "I notice our oxen don't seem to stir up the dust like the horses."

"That's because oxen have dainty feet, Martha. Look at them."

The girls had pulled on bonnets to protect their hair from the dust and weren't aware of the approaching horse and rider, but quickly stepped aside to avoid being run over.

Martha in an angry voice cried out, "Watch out! Whatever are you thinking?"

Just as she recognized Neil Emigh.

"Oh! Sorry, ladies." He apologized, touching the brim of his hat as he pulled his horse up alongside Papa. "Mr. Kenyon says they're lookin' for a campsite for tonight," he told Papa.

"That's right nice of you to come back and inform me," Papa said. "I'll be watching for a signal to stop from those in front of me. Thank you."

Neil saluted and reined about his gelding, agitating a swirl of dust around the girls.

"Whatever is the matter with him anyway?" Bertha raged. "He's so good-lookin' but he's got no good sense."

Martha was unable to keep her eyes off him as he rode away. How well he sat on his horse; he looked a the fine figure of a man. *Oh! For goodness sakes. I hope my sister doesn't see my face flush.* She was quick to cover her embarrassment with a giggle, and commented, "He's the one helped me fix coffee for dinner."

"You already know him, Martha? You didn't tell me! What's his name? You're sure, Martha?" Bertha demanded. "Oh, he is handsome."

"Too bad, Bertha," Martha told her. "He's much too old for you; after all, you're only thirteen. Papa would never abide you havin' a beau yet."

Hands on her hips, Bertha faced her sister. "He might just like me better than you. And so what if Papa doesn't approve? He can't keep me from being courted, now can he?"

Martha bit down on her lips to hold back her retort. *I musn't let myself get cross with my sister. I just met him. I don't know anything about him. And I'm so glad Bertha knows even less.*

Ahead of him, Papa saw Mr. Wilson signal a stop. He climbed down to stretch and lean his back against a wagon wheel. "Got a kink in ma' back from sittin' in the same position so long," he informed Mother as she made her way to the wagon.

"You should try walking in a road full of ruts. It's hard to keep my footing." She fanned her flushed face with her hand. "The dust is so thick. Can you still see my face?"

Mr. Kenyon called everyone to assemble under the shade of some nearby trees.

Martha, standing behind the men, sought out Neil, with his back towards her. She couldn't help but notice how his soft, deerskin shirt fit nicely over his wide shoulders. The deerskin leggings made him look so slim and tall. She found him to be far more handsome in his outfit than the men with their baggy pantaloons and long, Indian hunting shirts hanging down over their hips. The men, dressed like Papa, in homespun heavy trousers and shirts, were more appealing to her.

I like men to roll their sleeves up too. Wonder if Neil ever wears his shirts with rolled sleeves like Papa does. I wonder how I appear to Neil in my worn Lindsey Woolsey dress and dirty feet ... but then maybe he isn't even aware of me. She covered her flushed cheeks with her hands. *Why should he even think—Bertha never looks rumpled like I do, does she?* Martha put aside her thoughts to wonder, *Will we find a place to park soon, a place that's big enough for everyone?*

Mr. Kenyon and Mr. Crawford were delegated to select a campsite. Everyone returned to their wagons. Neil turned to mount his buckskin horse, and caught Martha looking at him. He winked. She quickly turned away and discovered she was standing alone in front of him. She felt a blush stain her cheeks. Quickly she lowered her head and turned towards her wagon. Passing Bertha, who was sitting on the ground, she admonished her sister, "Bertha, get up." She hadn't meant to sound so cranky.

"What's ailin' you?" Bertha asked as she stood up, smoothing out her dusty skirt.

"I just sat down for a moment. I'm flagged."

Martha, anxious to set up camp, understood water and feed would be first priority for the animals. Even now, at each stop Papa inspected the oxen for hoof problems.

She'd heard him say, "A cracked hoof on an ox is a disaster and it would have to be put down." A lot was expected of the teams; they must be strong and able to travel the two thousand miles regardless of weather and road conditions.

She'd overheard the men discussing that they hoped to make around fifteen miles a day. Martha felt sure they had gone at least that far already today. She noted the sun had moved far to the west. She found little pleasure in realizing the days would be lasting longer and that they would make use of the daylight to travel. She was weary.

Mother had climbed up beside Papa when they were on their way again. Papa remarked to her that he wondered why he found the Kenyons to be experienced travelers.

Mother recounted the story Ruth Kenyon shared with the women at dinner. "Mrs. Kenyon does come from a military background. When she was twelve," Mother told him, "her family had been ambushed by road bandits out of Fort Barnwell, North Carolina, and left for dead. She imposed on military families she knew to help her get to New York. She met Mr. Kenyon there, married, and they're now traveling out West to fulfill his dream."

Mother didn't go on to tell Papa how she'd learned to load a wagon for even balance or how Ruth Kenyon had also told the women it was important for them to learn how to care for and handle the teams. "You might be called on to manage the wagons and teams by yourselves someday," Ruth had told them.

After listening to the account of Mrs. Kenyon, Papa said, "Sounds like she's had a hard life, but she's one fine, spirited woman, if you ask me."

Papa's opinion of Mrs. Kenyon amused Mother. To her, he'd made Mrs. Kenyon out to sound like a horse. His description was of a reliable old mare, wasn't it?

Just then the Burts heard Mr. Wilson up ahead. Papa pulled his oxen to a stop but soon realized the wagons were slowly moving forward again.

"They couldn't pull their wagons off the road up there," Papa grumbled. "They're so overloaded with everything they're trying to drag along."

"Eli," Mother quietly suggested, "I just don't believe the others are as skilled as you at handling their teams."

Papa wasn't to be appeased, and grumbled on about others and their driving abilities. "Anyone plannin' on travelin' this far should be able to handle a team anywhere and anyplace."

Mother stared straight ahead spoke up, "Well, dear, Ruth Kenyon suggested we women learn to handle our teams—that it's necessary."

"Yeah, she'd be the one to say that," Papa said gruffly. "She would. I shoulda knowed she'd start something like this." Papa shook his head. "You, handle a yoke of headstrong oxen? That's the daftest idea, Mary." He paused." You listen to me. You tend to the cookin' and I'll handle the oxen. We're doing just fine now, aren't we?"

Mother decided against saying more at this time, but she was already determined she would learn to handle the oxen with or without his help. She'd keep a close watch on how he handled them from now on. They rode on in silence. She couldn't help but wonder if any of the other ladies had approached their husbands.

"Martha, how much further do we have to go today?" Ruthie whined.

"Bet you can't tell me what shape that little cloud up there makes?" Martha felt sorry for her little sister. She was done in herself. They all were.

The girls looked above them to the little, fluffy, white cloud, only to discover it was impossible to look up and keep their footing at the same time. They stumbled and bumped into each other in their endeavor to give the little cloud an image.

Mr. Wilson up ahead of Papa called back through cupped hands, "Pull off to the left, just ahead."

The Burts raised their hands in acknowledgment.

The six wagons formed a circle in a large meadow surrounded by oak, aspen, and cottonwood trees; the Illinois River was across the way.

Martha helped to unyoke the thirsty oxen, and followed along behind the other teams down to the river to quench their thirst before turning them into the inner circle of wagons for grazing and rest until morning.

Martha, as she led her ox back from the river, realized, *The pattern may change from day to day but this routine is going to be the same from this day forward. I wonder, does the walking ever get any easier?* She sighed a loud, weary sigh, but it was so pronounced it was exhaled as a groan.

Chapter 4

Martha was grateful to stop for the night. She and the sun had moved along together today and she was weary.

She helped care for the animals before she descended with her family for an invigorating encounter with the cold Illinois River.

Martha noticed Mrs. Kenyon didn't join them, but from the river's edge she nervously paced back and forth as she shouted, "Watch for the children! This river is treacherous. Keep an eye on the children."

Papa, his hair still wet, carried the provisional boxes to where Mother indicated she'd like to build her campfire. He returned to the wagon. Inside he reached into the special pocket Mother fashioned for his personal possessions, and gently lifted out his father's watch.

The watch belonged to Papa's big brother, Joseph. "Take Pa's watch with you, Eli. Your brother Ernie and I feel it's a good omen. Pa's spirit will be travelin' out West with you. Maybe you'll bring it back, or maybe I'll have to come fetch it."

Papa was speechless at first. "Tell ya what, brothers." He paused to take control of his emotions. "I'll hold it till one of ya come get it. I'll let ya know when we settle."

Papa noted the hours as he held the watch with its chain and fob. *"It's been nearly twenty-four hours since I started this journey; a good twenty—thirty miles closer to my new land.* He bounced the little watch in his hand before replacing it in with the pouch holding the money he'd saved to buy his claim.

Best go see how Mary's doing. She must be near done in. My wife's a good woman even if she does get "furhuddled," as the Dutch say. Imagining she can handle the oxen by herself. What a daft idea! He chuckled. *I'll hope she keeps busy and forgets about this foolishness.*

On their return to the fireside with their arms loaded with wood, Ruthie and Stephen discovered Mother balancing a cast-iron fire grate over several rocks. "For goodness sake, I didn't have this problem last night. I need a fire if there's to be any supper."

The Kenyon boys, Willie and Paul, arrived as the Burt family worked to manipulate the rocks and the rack. The Kenyon boys, with more experience, dug a fire pit, stacked rocks around the inside edges, then placed the grate firmly over the pit.

The fire pit dug, the children decided to investigate their new world, but Mrs. Kenyon interrupted their plans and called for Willie and Paul to fetch her more firewood.

"We'll help you," Ruthie offered. "Then we can all go exploring," she said as she and Stephen joined the boys to collect wood.

Mother had her fire burning briskly in the fire pit when she glanced over to see Mrs. Wilson, hands on her hips, appearing troubled.

After dinner today, Ruth Kenyon had assigned Mother and Abigale Wilson to carry and align the heavy, wooden, provisional boxes full of supplies necessary for everyday use in the wagons. Mother had asked Martha to help load the wagons with her. She couldn't help but wonder how long Abigale would be able to maneuver the heavy boxes in her condition. It made little difference. The women had their work cut out for them; the quicker it was done, the better off they were.

Mother insisted Abigale allow her and the girls help. "I don't care to see you lifting so much." She hoped the women around Abigale were sensitive to her condition

"Thanks, Mrs. Burt. My back's been bothering me a whole lot lately. Maybe the walking will be good for me." Mother doubted the walking would help the lady much, but she smiled and stated she wasn't looking forward to all the walking required herself.

"Would you be needin' help, Mrs. Wilson?" Mother called to her. "I happen to have a team of fire builders. Can you use them?"

"Mrs. Burt, I'm so ashamed to admit, but would you believe I don't know much about fire building. I wish I knew which direction Mr. Wilson's taken off in."

Mother sighted the children off in the direction of the river and called for them to come back.

After washing their faces, Martha and Bertha decided to pull their skirts high enough to wade out ankle deep in the cold water. Hearing their names called, they looked up to see Stephen and Ruthie with their little friends waiting on the riverbank. The girls reluctantly waded out of the water, fighting to keep their balance on the slippery rocks.

"All we do is work," Ruthie complained. "First Mrs. Kenyon needs more wood, then Mrs. Wilson needs a fire pit made. 'Will you help us? We've got so much work to do.'"

"Ohhhh! That water felt so good to my poor, weary feet," Bertha moaned.

"I can't tell." Martha drew in a quick breath as she fought to keep her balance. "My feet aren't feeling anything at the moment. Yes, Ruthie, we'll come help you."

At last the children were free to play. Mrs. Wilson had told them of a large, open meadow she'd sighted on the other side of the trees when she'd gone to answer "nature's call." The children raced beyond the trees to explore the meadow.

Martha dusted off her arms from a load of wood she'd carried for the fire and began preparations for coffee. Bertha excitedly explained to Mother how refreshed she felt from cold river-water encounter. "You have to go, Mother, if only to wash your face. Martha and I can watch supper for you."

Papa walked up just then. "Mary, I need a drink of water." He took her arm, steering her towards the river." You could use my company, couldn't you?" he asked.

While the coffee beans roasted, Martha filled the coffeepot from a bucket of river water. Bertha erected the tripod over the fire with a kettle of water hanging from it to heat for washing dishes later. "These wooden buckets are so heavy to carry; I don't like using much water from them," she commented as she ladled out water from the bucket. "And if we use water from the barrels then we have to refill them."

"We should have sent a bucket with Papa," Martha realized. From now on they must think of ways to make the water situation an easier task.

Five children arrived back in camp breathless, interrupting each other to tell excitedly about the Indians they'd just seen. "They were behind some trees, staring at us."

Willie and Paul, anxious to tell their parents, stopped only long enough to add their comments along with the others. Johnny Wilson ran straight to his wagon. As Martha and Bertha listened, a sensation of fear whispered within them. "We best go tell Papa and Mother." They ran to meet them.

"Papa, Mother, we just saw some Indians. They were spying on us." Ruthie arrived first and excitedly explained to her parents.

23

"Papa, will they hurt us?" Stephen asked, his eyes wide with fear as he grabbed a tight hold of Papa's hand.

Mother fought to keep her composure and anxiety within control. *No need to upset the children anymore than they already are,* she thought as a cold knot of fear gripped her.

"They're prob'ly just as curious of you as you are of them," Papa said, ruffling Stephen's hair. "I'd suggest you stay close to the wagons for the rest of the evening. Good idea, Mother?"

The children glanced from Mother to Papa in an attempt to understand their parents' calm reasoning. After all, Indians took little children, sold or traded them as slaves to other tribes, didn't they? Were these Indians friendly or could they be planning an attack? How could their parents act so quiet—so calm?

Martha inhaled the aroma of fresh-brewed coffee along with the pungent smell of burning wood. She'd settled down with her family to their supper of leftover boiled beans and ham. They finished the raised biscuits with sweet butter and plum preserves.

Mother voiced her worry about saving the butter. "I already miss the spring house; how ever am I going to keep things cool?"

The little squares of Granny's potato cake tasted sweet and delicious. It made them homesick for their little home and the family they'd left behind.

After supper, the women cleaned up the dishes, set dried fruit to soaking, ground wheat for breakfast mush, prepared bread starter, and set up the sleeping quarters. In good weather the men slept outside under the wagons, the women and small children inside.

Martha roasted coffee beans and ground them for breakfast, as was her habit. Papa carried the provisional boxes back to the wagon.

Passing by the fire, he picked up the coffeepot. "I've a use for this," he said on his way over to the Emigh campfire. Mr. Crawford, with Louie tagging along, came bearing a skillet. The men settled down on the ground around the campfire with their cups of coffee.

Martha saw Neil sitting on the ground, leaned against a wagon wheel, his long legs stretched out in front of him, arms crossed over his chest; he appeared to her to be intent on the conversation.

The discussion dealt with the Indians.

It's the fear, anger, frustration, and hatred these men don't understand, Papa decided as he listened to them. *Neither side will admit they're prejudiced and have little tolerance for each other.*

This issue with the Injuns is gonna plague us the whole trip; I can see that. Neil's thoughts were intent on the discussion. *It's always gonna be an unsolved problem.*

David Wilson couldn't believe Illinois had been a state since 1818, twenty-eight years. "President Poke and Governor French should be protecting us folks; aren't we encouraged to move out West? Where's the militia? These wild barbarians are free to roam. I'd like to see 'em run down an' whipped. Teach 'em some respect for us."

Sam Emigh's patient, modulated voice, acquired from his teaching vocation, interjected, "Our government has tried to establish reservations. We try to educate them; but David, it's difficult for free men to give up their freedom and culture to another man. Indians were never bought or sold to white men. I don't believe they were ever slaves in the South, were they?"

Papa wasn't for using military force. "Whatever gets solved? I sure don't want another massacre like the Black Hawk back in '32. We beat 'em, sure; we drove 'em off their land, but we're still at war with each other, far's I'm concerned."

The men grew silent but nodded their heads in agreement with Eli Burt.

Thomas Crawford thought the Indians up around Pennsylvania, where he's from, weren't as uncivilized as these savages. "These are the sneakiest, meanest, smelliest buggers I've ever seen. I guess all Indians are born savages; some just got civilized."

"Why's our government so worried about the Mexican War way down south, when we need protection here?" David Wilson asked, helping himself to a sweet bun before passing Mr. Crawford's skillet to the others.

Alex Kenyon found it interesting. "We marry up with their squaws, have young'uns with 'em, but the tribes don't want 'em sent ta our schools. We taught 'em ta use our ammunition and guns, they drink our whisky, ride our horses, half of 'em stolen, but they're still again' our ways."

"Have to agree with Alex; they're nothin' but dirty, stinkin' thieves and heathens. Why? Tell me, why do they insist on livin' their way? Can't they see how good we got it?" David Wilson's agitation was felt by the others.

Brian McGraw spoke in, "If'n we's a-staying, I kin see 'em gettin' thimsilves riled up; but we's only passin' through. We ain't gonna stay. If'n we's a-pushin' our ways on 'em, I kin see 'em gettin' thar tails in a knot. Ever notice whin one of 'em gets kilt, don't 'pear like hits 'portant. Like, they's got no feelin's like we does."

"Bet none of you have considered your wives and children are better off than you." Sam Emigh confronted them. "Those Indians—savages, you call them—and your wife get along. They use each other for trading, dealing, and swapping for necessities."

"I'd rather see ma' woman dead first!" David growled in a low voice.

"David, these Indians aren't as likely to kill women and children as they would kill you. They're valuable. You, my good man, are worth nothing compared to your horse, ammunition, and gun," Sam explained to him. The men paused to ponder his words.

"Durn redskins anyway," Neil muttered, climbing up into the wagon. "They don't know how ta use the land, and the ignorant savages don't want us ta use it either. If they'd farm and grow things, they could sell 'em, build fences, raise horses and cattle; they'd be helpin' themselves, but no, they'd rather beg, steal, and kill—and this bunch o' old men sittin' here, frettin' an' gettin' themselves stewed up over the Injun problem, and where's it gettin' 'em?"

Neil fumbled around in the dark for his bedroll. *Keep out of my way, I've got plans for my share of this earth. No wonder the savages hate us; listenin' to these old men carpin' on about 'em, I've heard enough.* Removing his boots, he crawled between the blankets and promptly fell asleep.

Stephen grew tired of tossing sap-coated twigs into the fire to explode them. "Mother, Papa said he was going to sleep outside tonight. Can I sleep with him?"

"You best go ask him," she told him. Wasting little time, he sprinted off in the direction of the Emigh campfire.

Papa reached out his arms to Stephen, cradled in a warm embrace against Papa's chest, listening to the steady rhythm of his heart and the soft drone of the voices. He was lulled to sleep before he had time to ask Papa if he could sleep outside.

Bertha and Ruthie arranged their beds up near the front of the wagon to gaze out at the stars. Removing only their dresses, they crawled under their quilts and succumbed to sleep.

Martha and Mother waited by the fireside for Papa and Stephen to return. "Why don't you go on to bed, dear?" Mother asked. Every bone in her body was weary.

"I like your company, Mother." Martha covered a yawn before going on to say, "Mother, does it seem to you we women have so little time to visit like the men do?"

"Our work is never done," Mother told her. "You'll see someday when you're a wife and mother. When your family's happy and well cared for, then so are you."

"These rules for men and women, they're so unfair, Mother."

"Why? What would this world be like without them, Martha?"

"I might have enjoyed being with the men tonight but I know better. 'A lady does not invade a man's privacy.' What a silly notion, Mother."

"Men talk rough. It's an insult to us women. We don't care to listen to that kind of talk. Men respect a gentle woman; that's why we conduct ourselves properly, so we will be respected. Besides, we women have things we need to keep private and to ourselves, you know what I mean? There are some things that are important for us to learn, like how to handle the oxen, and this has nothing to do with men's rules."

They were discussing the best method of approaching Papa with a plan, when he came toting a sleeping boy and an empty coffeepot. "He was out in a second," he said as he deposited Stephen into a bed arranged for him under the wagon, with only his blonde head peeking from under his quilt.

Martha prepared for bed. She appreciated the little room off the side of the wagon; it meant not fumbling behind a bush, or groping around inside the dark wagon for the commode.

It would have been nice if Neil had come for the coffeepot tonight. Now why, of all things, does he come to mind? I'm so weary, and I must say my prayers.

The river's even tempo, a breeze stirring through the trees, the swoop of a night hawk's wings—none of these were heard by Martha.

"You men were so serious over there, Eli."

"Yeah, it's hard dealing with the Indian problems; everyone feels different about the situation."

"Will any of you be keeping watch tonight, Eli?"

"We don't have a reason to," he told her as they bedded down. The sound of the river was heard above their breathing; their embrace was not disturbed by a call of a lonely bird in the night or the croaking frog chorus coming from the river.

The campfires cast long fingers of flames, creating shadows in the still, dark world. The weary travelers had given up their exhausted bodies to sleep. None of them were aware of the moon quietly lighting its way across the dark sky.

Chapter 5

Martha was awakened by a multitude of birds creating a din of noise in the predawn. She wondered who got up first, the birds or her parents. How can Mother and Papa get themselves up these chilly mornings? She pulled the quilt higher under her chin and burrowed deeper into the warm bed between her sleeping sisters.

These last few days had been difficult for Martha: the new routine, living like a gypsy out of the wagon, and the endless walking.

Unable to sleep anymore, Martha joined Mother by the fire. "Mother, I think I know how homesick you must have been leaving your home in England," she said as she poured herself a cup of fragrant, fresh-brewed coffee.

Mother added wood to the cheerful, warm campfire before she commented, "Yes, Martha, it was difficult coming to America. Your aunt Alice, my little sister, was only six and I was ten when we boarded the boat and crossed the ocean. We lived in miserable, cramped, filthy conditions. So many perished from deprivation."

"I suppose no one thought to bring dried apples and apricots like Granny Burt did," Martha commented.

Mother refilled her coffee cup before continuing. "I remember how frightened I was when we departed the boat. Masses of moving bodies, shoving, pushing, and shouting. So much noise and confusion. We were swept along like a giant wave on the ocean. I clung to my momma's long skirt. Alice and I didn't dare let loose or we'd have been trampled underfoot. We hung on so tight we ached. I couldn't see the sky above and I didn't understand the strange words being spoken around me." Mother sighed deeply.

"Yes, Martha I missed my home with its high, wrought-iron fenced-in garden, where my little sister and I played with our little dog. Chum, we called him. I hated this strange new place. I'm sure you feel the same, leaving your home, setting up camp each day where nothing's familiar. I was homesick for London." Mother sipped her coffee.

"I heard the words 'immigrants,'" Mother continued. "I remember straining to see who these people called immigrants were, and what they looked like. I had no idea I was one of them."

Martha interrupted. "That's when Grandfather Lane presented the letter of introduction to the Smith family, right? You told us they were friends not relatives."

"Smith's had visited the Lane Shop in London and suggested your grandfather Arthur come to the New World to work with them. They were the kindest people I'd ever known. The took us in and taught us to enjoy the culture, activities, and education in New York City. Grandfather Lane did prosper, but being independent, he wanted to move on to Chicago, a new, growing metropolis out West at this time. And it meant leaving my friends."

"You had the same feelings as I have leaving my friends." Martha gazed at the pink and purple tint of daylight slowly expanding in the east.

"Yes, I was the age you are now, Martha. I considered myself a well-educated young lady. The new business prospered because we all worked hard to help Grandfather succeed."

Bertha came to join the women around the campfire. "Oh Mother, I love this next story. You're going to tell us, aren't you? About you're meeting up with Papa? Tell us again, Mother. Martha, sit closer, will you? I'm cold." Bertha had wedged herself between Mother and Martha on the log, her voice still husky from sleep.

"It was my turn to tend shop that day, or I would never have met your papa," Mother told them. "My life changed forever when he walked in the door. I was smitten by this young gentleman with his curling, dark hair and beautiful blue eyes. I remember he asked for the best cheddar too. Cheddar takes two years to ripen, you know? Few people understand its long ripening process."

"Yes, yes, Mother, go on," the girls coaxed her.

"This handsome gentleman fascinated me, but being a lady I kept my eyes lowered as much as possible. He told me how he wouldn't dare go back home without a piece of the Lane's cheddar for his ma. He told me all this as I wrapped the piece he'd selected. My father walked in just then.

"Why Eli Burt, good to see you, and how's the family doing? What brings you to town today? Eli, you've met my daughter, Mary?"

"Your papa reached clear across the counter to take my hand. Why, I barely had time to wipe it on my apron before he grasped it. I knew he was a man of the land from the feel of his rough calluses. I remember his hand was so warm and gentle holding onto mine."

"Somehow, I've missed an opportunity to know you, Miss Lane," he told me with that roughish grin he has. Dear me, I was hoping the flutter of my heart didn't show through the thin dress I was wearing. Your papa had such good manners and was so sure of himself. I couldn't keep from staring at him. He held on to my hand all the while he told my father, "You know, Mr. Lane, my ma's tellin' everyone you're Welsh. You're cheddar is proof of it."

I could tell my father was pleased with the compliment, but he knew Mrs. Burt knew we were English and not Welsh. I quickly withdrew my hand from his to finish wrapping the cheese in paper. I took my time to tie string around the package before handing it to him, though.

"We both knew we'd be seeing each other again. Your papa says it was my blonde hair and dimples, but I tell him it was the cheddar. Oh my! Girls, I'd like nothing better than to sit here, but your papa's expecting breakfast and I've a days work ahead of me." Mother placed more wood on the fire. "Martha, I'm on my way to wash my face and bring back a bucket of water. Will you start the mush? Bertha, you could put those dried apples to stew for our dinner tonight."

Martha stood up to stretch. "What a beautiful sunrise—means another nice day. I don't mind when it rains at night. It's easier to travel, the ground has time to dry, and there's less dust."

Ruthie came stumbling out of the wagon, still groggy from sleep. She and Bertha made their way to the river to purge the sleep from their faces in the cold water.

While breakfast cooked, the girls helped Mother carry the provisional boxes to the fireside. Bertha complained how the boxes never seem to get any lighter.

"Be glad they don't, Bertha; it means we have enough food," Ruthie exclaimed.

Martha stirred a handful of dried apricots into the kettle of mush before suspending it from the tripod hook. She put more wood into the fire under it, backing away as the smoke billowed up into her face. She tried waving it away with one hand and made room for a kettle of water Bertha handed her to heat for dish washing.

Mother woke Stephen, who crawled out from his quilt under the wagon and managed to bump his head on the edge of the wagon, crying out in pain. Mother gently soothed his head and tried to comfort his yowling.

For Martha, a chain of reactions was about to impact her day from here on. It began with Stephen, then Papa coming to the fireside, his hands in his pockets, a worried frown creasing his face. Bertha and Ruthie had gone to put away the bedding.

Martha knew from his expression that Papa was upset. Mother, seeing him, knew he'd want her undivided attention. She filled his coffee cup and handed it to him. Both women knew the family would have to wait until he was ready to talk to them.

Mother reached to tuck a stray strand of hair behind her ear. "Ruthie, will you take Stephen to wash up before breakfast?" As smoke whipped into her face, she turned quickly away. "Eli, is there something bothering you, dear?" she inquired.

The family turned towards the river at the sound of a loud howling to see Ruthie returning, towing her wailing, balking brother behind her. "Mother, I can't make him wash his face. He says the water's too cold."

Martha felt as if her world had spun out of control. There was breakfast to serve, and they needed to get ready to leave. Papa had a problem and Stephen was being stubborn.

Mother picked up Stephen. "Thank you, Ruthie, you did your best. Stephen, you're a big boy now, and men wash in cold water. It toughens you up." Putting Stephen down she focused back on Papa, who was taking a sip of coffee and had eaten a bite of mush Martha prepared for him.

"One of ma' ox has a maimed shoulder; it's swollen and sensitive to touch."

No one knew what to say. Mother spoke first. "Is the skin broken or the hair gone?" "No, no outward signs; just the swelling, and she shivered when I ran my hand over her shoulder. I inspected the yokes and oxbows for signs that might indicate pressure. I don't even know for certain which bow she was wearing."

"Papa," Martha inquired, "would the liniment like we used on the horses help?"

"I'm not sure it would. Rest is the answer, but I can't spare an ox; and besides, I don't have a single yoke. I wonder if putting her in a different position might help. But it still means she's using her sore shoulder."

"I wonder if Mr. McGraw could be of advice," Mother suggested. "He has oxen."

31

Martha winced at the idea. It wasn't that they didn't like McGraws. It was that they were such a boisterous, outrageously loud family. Mr. McGraw had educated the entire wagon train with his vocabulary in the few days they'd been together.

"He's a jolly fellow," Mother was quick to explain. "A bit rough." She kept to herself, *We women don't care to listen to him or his wife, Jenny—such a thin, mousy, opinionated little women; she makes me nervous with that shrill voice of hers.* "He might have some helpful suggestions for you, dear."

After breakfast, Papa walked over to the McGraws. Later he was to tell the family, "Not only did I have to climb around all those animals, but I also found the family in various stages of bare nakedness."

Papa said he explained his problem to Mr. McGraw and apologized for being in such a hurry. He knew the wagons weren't ready to start, but the truth of the matter was, "I was afraid Mr. McGraw would go into one of his long-winded stories and I wouldn't be able to get away from the men."

Brian McGraw, his thumbs hooked in suspenders holding up worn, soiled pantaloons, let loose one of the suspenders to reach up and pull on his ear lobe. "Ya got yerself four oxen there, ain't cha?" He paused in thought. "Ya best pull with two. Ah don't like telling a gentleman life yerself what ta do, but ifn' t'was me? Ah'd be inclined ta walk two and pull with two. Rist is what hit takes ta mend a sawer shawlder. Ah known from experience. Had ma' share of sawer shawlders and ligs; don't worry none about them two. They's can be lazier than ya might be knowin' bout. Make 'em work a bit. Do 'em good, Mr. Burt. Ya understand that's if'n it were ma' problem."

Papa thanked the man and excused himself politely. "We'll be pullin' out soon I 'spect," he said as he turned to leave, trying his best not to step on animals underfoot.

"Yep, 'bout time ta roll er' out," Mr. McGraw agreed, scratching his wild red head of hair. "Now ya'll feel free ta ask fur help if'n I kin be of use to y'all, Mr. Burt." His booming voice broadcast loudly behind Papa walking back to his wagon.

After Papa left for the McGraws' Mother told the girls to get their hair combed. She requested they get out of view of everyone to tidy up. "Modesty is hard to come by the way we're traveling, but I must insist it be observed at all cost to us virtuous women." She practiced modesty and obeyed the rules of femininity, and expected her girls to do likewise.

Martha looked up to see Mrs. Kenyon coming towards them. Papa tipped his hat to the lady and Mrs. Kenyon nodded politely as they passed each other. Martha suspected trouble as the lady's swishing full-length skirt outlined her sturdy silhouette in her long strides. Strides that amazed Martha by how much area the woman so swiftly covered, her bonneted head held high. She continued to watch Mrs. Kenyon greeting each family along her route. "Howdy there, Miz Crawford; my Alex does enjoy your sweet buns. I need your recipe." On past the eighth wagon, "Mis McGraw, nice morning, ain't it?" and on she came. "Miz Wilson, you feelin' any better this mornin'?" On she came until she reached the Burts' wagon.

"Miz Burt," she stated bluntly, "you've got yourself a problem, I hear? You got a problem, you need to let us all know. We're travelin' together and we need to know what you're plannin' to do. Will you be fallin' back? Do you need our help? Don't like you mumblin' around here. I s'pose Mr. Burt will speak to the men meetin' over there," she said. Without waiting for Mother to reply, the lady turned abruptly and marched back to her wagon.

"Goodness me, I hope my hospitality won't be judged too harshly by the women," Mother whispered to the girls. "I didn't have a thing for her to sit on or a drop of coffee to offer."

Abigale Wilson waited for Mrs. Kenyon to leave before coming over. "Mary Burt, don't you let that woman upset you, you hear? Why, she intimidates me. I've told no one about my condition. Perhaps she feels I'm a problem to everyone. Maybe she feels I should drop back. Mary, she is so concerned for poor Mr. Emigh—such a lonely soul, she says, and did you hear her about Mrs. Crawford? Right out loud in front of us all too. Her Alex likes Mrs. Crawford's sweet little buns. Oh I must get back; I left baby Pearl alone."

Martha knew Mother didn't approve of gossip, but she saw her mother and sisters laugh as Mrs. Wilson mimicked Mrs. Kenyon.

Mother watched Abigale walk back to her wagon. *Abigale Wilson is a friend who is going to make this journey easier for us all.*

"Are we ready?" Papa asked as he walked up to them.

"Papa, the commode—it needs to be taken care of," Martha told him. She watched Papa react with disgust. "You mean I took the time to dig a hole for you, and now when I need your help to get things done.... I've been busy myself, you know." He slammed the tailgate with unnecessary force.

Martha grabbed the commode and the shovel. Bertha followed, carrying a bucket of water to rinse out the commode. Mother hastened to untie the extra room and fasten it up alongside the wagon bed.

"I'm sorry, Mr. Burt," she told Papa. "We've a lot to learn about how to pack up."

"Mary, let the girls finish. There's no name on the work around here. If there's a chore to be done, then everybody pitches in and gets it done."

Mother had confided in Martha earlier, "Must be the sun or perhaps the stress of this morning, but I feel one of my sick headaches coming on."

Poor Mother, she doesn't need a headache right now. But Martha knew there was little could be done to ease one of Mother's miserable headaches.

"Eli, I believe we're ready to move out." Mother heaved a weary sigh as she watched the girls put the shovel and bucket into the wagon.

Papa started to climb aboard the wagon. "The water barrels are full?"

The girls scrambled for buckets and raced to the river. The wooden buckets when full of water were difficult to carry. Water sloshed over the edges of the buckets to wet their dresses, making the wet fabric cling to their legs and run down their legs to mix with dirt that had muddied their feet.

Neil rode up to offer Papa assistance. Papa thanked him but stated loudly, "I had hoped to move out by now. The rest of you go on. Don't let us slow you down."

Martha was humiliated, her face flushed with embarrassment for Neil to see her like this. Anger welled up inside her. She abruptly flipped her head and pulled on her bonnet. *I don't care that he sees me like this.* She thought, *He's vain and arrogant; he and my sister Bertha deserve each other. She can have him.*

Mother witnessed Martha's frustration. *Oh my darling daughter, things will get better for you; maybe not here and now, but they will.* There wasn't time to tell Martha this. Papa was in a hurry to move out.

The sun warmed the travelers walking under it; a fragrance came to them from the prairie grasses and cottonwood trees. The children's voices echoed with laughter as Martha, her mother, and sisters prepared for another day of walking west behind the creaking, lumbering wagon, with two oxen plodding along.

Chapter 6

I wish we could move as fast as the river, Martha thought as she walked beside the wagon with the muddy, brown Illinois River sweeping along on the other side of her. *It's become a companion, crossing the state of Illinois and heading west with us.*

Martha and her younger sister Bertha were walking along with Mother, who was discussing her duties for the day, under an overcast sky.

"Let me see," Mother spoke aloud. "I've sourdough started for bread, biscuits, and griddle cakes for tomorrow's breakfast. We women are finally learning to prepare our meals at the discretion of travel time, but I've yet to solve my bread-rising problem. It either rises too fast inside the warm wagon or it doesn't rise properly, and it's our main food."

The girls politely listened to Mother, even though they had heard it all before—how the bread problem plagued the women daily.

They knew by heart the part Mother repeated. "The agency meant to be helpful when they recommended we women bring salted and cured meats, but with no way to keep the meat cool it's turning rancid fast." Mother always heaved a big sigh before concluding, "Thank goodness there's plenty of fresh game to be had.

"Girls, I've an idea. Let's gather some of these dandelion greens for supper. They're young and tender this time of year, and it looks like there's plenty to be had. I'll fix us some with a bit of salt pork." The girl exchanged glances; they found Mother was far too busy for their liking.

In the lead wagon, Alex Kenyon asked his wife to sight a place to pull off by the river. "Ma' team's fidgety. Won't hurt to give 'em a drink and rest 'em for a while."

Ruth Kenyon pulled off her bonnet, shading her eyes with both hands to scan the horizon "Down there," she pointed to a large open area. "It looks be a big enough place for us all."

Alex slowed his team. "It'll have to do. We've been movin' steady since we got through the mishap this mornin'."

Mrs. Kenyon crawled over on her seat, using the large white rag she'd tied to a pole for a flag. She waved it to the Crawfords behind her as the her wagon bounced unmercifully along in the rutted road.

Earlier in the morning, Stephen Burt had given his parents a frightful scare when they'd discovered him missing. The wagons were stopped while Papa retraced his steps in search of the boy.

Sam Emigh had insisted Papa ride his horse after Papa, in his anxiety to find Stephen and without having a horse to ride, was determined to take off on one of his oxen.

Not knowing what Papa might find, Sam Emigh suggested, "Neil, you ride back with Mr. Burt. I've a notion Stephen's probably where the children told us they'd last seen him. But you never know out here in this untamed land."

Stephen's disappearance brought nervous fear to the group. Danger, sickness, and death were things they understood might happen, but they weren't prepared to accept the reality of the situation so soon after starting their journey.

Martha and Bertha stood quietly, listening to an irate Mrs. Kenyon. They had already suffered the bite from her tongue when their ox developed a sore shoulder a few days earlier. "Times a-wastin' and we've a schedule to keep." Her voice sounded harsh to the girls.

"Mrs. Kenyon, ma'dear, they're havin' a bit of bad luck this mornin' is all. We'll make up the time lost," Mr. Kenyon quickly informed his wife, hoping to quiet her.

Mrs. Crawford said, "It's disgusting the way Ruth Kenyon is carrying on. Like time's more important than a little child, whose life is at stake. As for me, I just pray he's returned safely to poor little Mrs. Burt."

"Ah's a-feared somethin' like this was a-gonna happen," Jenny McGraw squawked. "Ah felt hit in ma' bones whin I woked up this mornin'."

Sam Emigh added, "I'm glad Stephen didn't come up missing when we stopped for for dinner tonight." He excused himself to get back to his Clydesdales. "I don't like leaving Nathan alone for too long with the big boys."

Abigale Wilson came to support her friend Mary Burt, who was struggling to keep her composure as she envisioned her small son snatched up by Indians, or perhaps maimed by a wild animal. She fought against the vision of him helplessly falling into the treacherous river.

Mary Burt was quiet, filled with anxiety; she waited patiently for what seemed to her to take forever for the men's return. With great difficulty, she was trying to accept what every woman she knew was ordained by fate to endure: the patience to wait for life or death.

Upon his and Neil's return, Papa told everyone how he'd found the boy "headed in the right direction." He handed down the dirty, tear-stained little Stephen to his mother.

Martha and Neil had come face to face. "Neil, how can I ever thank you and your father for helping us?" Martha looked up into blue eyes gazing down at her.

"You can't, and I happen to like it this way," Neil announced.

Martha found herself speechless and modestly lowered her head, but not before Neil caught her smile.

She can't know how much I like to make her smile, he thought. *Sometimes I wonder if she even sees me. I wish I could stop these feelings she stirs up inside me.* He gently took her arm to steer her with him as they led the horses through the surrounding crowd.

Martha allowed herself to be led. She enjoyed the thrill of his touch on her arm.

Stephen's punishment, when the train was at last ready to move on, was to ride up beside Papa for the rest of the day.

"Sure hope my oxen don't suffocate from this dust," Papa said aloud.

"What does that mean?" Stephen inquired. He was glad for Papa to talk about something besides his earlier behavior.

"They get dust in their noses and breathe it in, and then they can't get any air and die."

"Can't you wipe their noses, Papa?"

"'Fraid not, Son; we need to stop and water them to wash away the dust and dirt," Papa instructed him. "Good. Looks to me as if Mr. Kenyon's pullin' off up ahead."

Stephen, looking up at Papa, said, "What makes dust? Can I get down now?"

"No siree, I don't want ya fallin' under a wheel. I don't have time ta scrape ya up off the road. Best stay here till I'm stopped," Papa told him.

Papa's wagon wheels, as all wagon wheels, were encircled by wide steel bands to give them durability and support. The steel-banded rims were razor sharp and damaged every thing they ran over. The roads under them were being ground into a powdery dust with the passing of so many heavy wagons.

Papa thought it was necessary that the women learn about the axle size. It determined the amount of tonnage the wagon was safe to carry. However, looking at them he determined many wagons chose to ignore this fact.

Papa patiently instructed his women folk how the hub fit over the axle with spokes protruding from the hub, and how the spokes were banded on the bottom with a wide steel rim to support the inside of the wheel.

He stressed the importance of keeping the hubs and axle, where they joined, continuously greased. "Dry wheels easily break and splinter when they're not greased," he emphasized. "The screech from a dry axle is ear splitting and downright annoying."

The girls disliked the sticky, black grease kept in a bucket hanging alongside the wagon, with its rag-wrapped stick to apply the mixture of resin, tar, and tallow from cooking fat.

Papa asked Ruthie if she remembered it was her turn to grease the wheels.

"I did it already, Papa. Don't you be hittin' a big rock or fallin' into a deep hole and break a wheel now," she replied in a teasing manner.

"You're right, Ruthie. I'd hate to replace a wheel. Don't have time and I only brought one extra wheel," he informed her.

For the women, the fear of breaking a wheel would mean the wagon would have to be emptied of its entire contents in order to get the weight off the broken wheel. It would then have to be elevated somehow in order to put on the new wheel.

A broken wheel could pose a tragedy for a lone woman. A team could spook, taking off in a runaway turning the wagon over, and she'd be vulnerable to Indians.

Papa lifted the yokes while Mother and Martha freed the oxen from the oxbows. Bertha and Ruthie struggled to untie the restless oxen from the back of the wagon before they followed the family, being pulled along by the oxen to the water.

An island had been formed by a long sand bar, extending out quite a distance into the river. It had curved back to the riverbank, creating a pond.

It was into this pond that the oxen pulled the girls until they were in knee-deep water.

"Martha, the water's not the least bit cold," Bertha exclaimed, wading out with her ox.

"Oh—this is refreshing," Martha agreed. "Let's hope the buffalo don't decide to run down here for a drink of water right now."

"Martha? We haven't seen any buffalo—oh, you mean these hoof prints in the mud."

Mother, holding her oxen's rope in one hand, scooped up handfuls of water with her free hand to wash her face and neck. "I'm glad to unload some of this grit," she exclaimed.

Mrs. Kenyon was pulled out into the water by her horse. "Time for a quick bite, but no fires," she called out to the folks, who were taking advantage of the pond, churning the calm inlet into muddy water that left them feeling refreshed.

The animals were left to graze and rest after being watered, while the women hurriedly prepared cold dinners without hot coffee.

Mother hoped the beans from yesterday were still good. However, on lifting the lid from the Dutch oven, she found the beans bubbling in a frothy, foul-smelling broth.

"Oh! Oh, Mother, they smell." Martha spun away from the putrid odor.

"Phew." Bertha turned her head away, fanning the air before her with both hands.

"I need to cook a batch for supper, but it's impossible to soak beans in a bouncing wagon with all the water sloshing out," Mother told them.

Buttering thick slices of bread, Martha informed her mother, "The butter's still sweet." Next she laid slices of home-smoked ham over the bread with pieces of cheddar cheese granddad Lane sent for the journey. Along with stewed apples, they satisfied their hunger.

During dinner the families were entertained by traffic on the river. Rafts, canoes, and two big barges with wagons without wheels swept swiftly past. The folks waved to each other.

Before starting again, Mother suggested that she and Stephen lay down for a nap.

"Can't, Mother," Stephen told her. "Papa needs me; 'sides, I'm not tired yet."

Papa insisted Stephen mind his mother, who'd promised to tell him a story.

Reluctantly, protesting all the way, Stephen climbed up into the wagon.

Papa and Martha understood the cause of Mother's headache and the excuse for a nap. However, they doubted she'd get little rest in the bouncing wagon.

Martha shuddered at the thought of what females were expected to endure monthly out here in this wilderness. Mother had told

Bertha and her it was as natural as breathing. Yet it must be kept quiet, never openly discussed, out of sight, and accepted as a secret among women.

So no matter, Martha thought, *how uncomfortable we are, we're not allowed to take time from our duties; and no matter how difficult it makes our lives, we're expected to contend with it. Like Mother says, "It's a necessary part of a woman's life cycle to be endured."*

She grimaced at the thought. *I'm expected to walk thousands of miles, and one week out of each month I have to endure this without privacy or cleanliness. Oh bother!*

Martha had been walking alone behind the wagon. She paused for her sisters, who raced to catch up. They'd lagged behind to pick the brightly colored wildflowers surrounding them.

Ruthie, her nose buried in her fragrant bouquet, said she thought it was nice of Mrs. Kenyon to send over the fresh milk for their dinner.

"Why nice, Ruthie? The milk only sours if it isn't used," Bertha grumbled.

Ruthie ignored Bertha's remark. "I sure wish we'd brought our cow. I miss the milk. How come we didn't bring our cow anyway?"

"We can't afford to keep a cow and feed the oxen, Ruthie. You need to ask Papa why we don't milk the oxen." Martha tucked a blossom from Ruthie's bouquet behind her ear.

"Martha, Stephen scared Mother this morning. Is that why she's feeling bad?"

"You forget when you were five years old and had to take naps, Ruthie?" Bertha asked.

"Mother has a headache, Ruthie, you know how she feels when she has one." Martha put her arm around the little girl's shoulder. "How she's able to nap in that bouncing wagon, I'll never know."

It happened suddenly: shrieking voices, thundering hooves coming at them. The wagon train was in total surprise. Indians on horseback rapidly approached at an alarming rate of speed. They came from over the hill and right onto the families. The thick buffalo grass hid any dust they might have stirred up and muffled the sounds of their coming. The families didn't have time to prepare in defense of themselves. Children ran screaming to the nearest wagon.

In a split second the wagons were surrounded by half-naked Indians with painted faces, spears, and quivers of arrows hung about their bare chests. With bows held high over head, their eerie, ear-piercing screams filled the air.

The wagon train was utterly helpless. Through the screaming, dust, and confusion, folks fought to control their frightened teams. It was impossible to arm themselves. There wasn't time to get guns and load them. Horses in harness reared up, eyes wide in terror, nostrils dilated.

They screamed and panicked as they tried to back up and turn sideways to get away from the sudden intruders.

Oxen bawled, swinging their big bodies back and forth, trying to break from their confinement. They shook their huge heads in fright, eyes bulging. The teamsters had little control or power over the crazed teams.

The Indians formed a circle around the wagons as they continued their shrieking. A few darted between the teams and wagons, already moving in precarious positions and upsetting the animals even more.

The Burt girls flung themselves into the lurching wagon. Mother and Stephen were jolted around as they heard the shrieking Indians, the tumultuous, thundering hooves, screaming horses, and bawling oxen.

Mother looked up at Papa struggling to control the wagon seesawing back and forth. The next moment she turned to see Martha, reached to grab hold of the flap to cover the back opening, and watched in terror as a hand reached out and gripped Martha's wrist—a hand connected to a copper-colored, muscular body.

Martha stared into a red and white-painted face staring back at her. Her first reaction was to scream, and fight with all of her being, but her mind responded quickly, not allowing time for fear.

Waves of panic welled up inside her as she held on to her self-will. Her heart sent blood pounding to her head so loud it roared in her ears. "I'm going to die. He's pulling me out of the wagon. I'll fall under his horse."

His horse tossed its head, eyes wild, and hot breath came at her from its dilated nostrils. She heard the deep rumbling of breathing come from within its mighty chest like a giant bellow.

Martha was nauseous, her stomach felt hollow, and her mouth was dry with a metallic taste. A cold sweat crept over her. Her arm had to be broken, the pain was so excruciating and intense. A feeling of weakness quickly replaced itself with a sensation of strength as terror enveloped her. Breathing and thinking became difficult.

She must not let herself cry out. *Play dead—animals play dead.* The eyes of the Indian were black and piercing, never leaving her face as he watched her every move. His naked torso of well-developed muscles was taut, ready to spring into action at his command. He radiated an aura of

41

unpredictability as he anticipated her next move, his animal instinct keen. He was teasing her; she was his prey. One wrong move and she would end the struggle, finish a game he thought he would win.

She steeled herself not to struggle no matter how great her terror. She heard screaming and crying behind her but knew she must not let Mother break her concentration.

Her feet were pinned to the floor by hands gripping her ankles; she felt herself stretched beyond endurance. She wouldn't be able to endure much more before she would have to give in to the Indian's demands. Anger replaced sensibility through her pain and agony. She didn't plead, beg, or cry; she simply stated, "You're hurting my arm."

He knew he was inflicting pain by the way he sneered. His eyes stared into hers. She didn't know if he comprehended what she'd said, but maybe he understood by the tone of her voice.

He responded to her by throwing back his long, black, greasy hair held in place by a beaded headband, and laughed a loud, amused laugh. She felt the urgency to quickly snatch her hand away, but she courageously let him clutch on to her wrist. She was no longer in pain; a numbness had set in.

Abruptly as he'd grabbed onto her, he flung her backwards from him. Losing her balance, she fell to the floor of the wagon. Mother and Bertha released her ankles. She lay exhausted, her fear slowly subsided, and her mind focused on a blue stone hanging from his neck.

Pain throbbed through her arm, her body refused to function, and she was unable to give in to tears. It was over; she was still alive. Her mind refused to recall his face, but the size and shape of the blue stone were vivid to her.

Everything not fastened down shifted. Mother realized she couldn't get to Papa to rescue him. Her husband was in grave danger. She attempted to work her way to him but found it impossible to crawl forward over everything moving and falling. A sensation of futility swept through her, leaving her weak.

The family silently watched Papa stand up, trying to bring the oxen under control and away from the Wilson wagon as it turned and twisted next to him.

Mother knew better than to cry out and break his concentration. He'd fall and be trampled or crushed under his own oxen or between the wagons. She was helpless to anchor him as she had Martha. She was incapable—inadequate to do anything but pray for God in his infinite mercy to help her Eli, her soul mate. She had never felt so powerless.

Perhaps the impetuous youth of the Fox tribe became dissatisfied with their frolicking; perhaps they weren't being entertained by their antics. As quickly as they came—they left, riding off, still shrieking eerie, ear-piercing screams. The earth vibrated under the deafening hooves of the ponies. They faded across the fields and over the hills.

The wagons sat in silence and chaos. Weeping and screaming children combined with the sounds of restless, frightened animals were heard as the dust settled and the folks frozen in terror and fear came to the realization the attack was over ... for now.

Chapter 7

The women gazed at the fields where the earth displayed deep ruts gouged by the sharp hooves of the horses and wagon wheels. The wagon were poised where they had come to rest after the Indian skirmish.

"Guess we best go from wagon to wagon," Mother proposed.

The Burt girls and Mother were bravely attempting to overcome their fears, when the voices of Mrs. Kenyon, Elsa Crawford, and young Lizzy, in a loud outburst, startled them.

The three had suddenly unleashed their pent-up emotions of terror, frustration, and their vulnerability at the unwarranted Indian attack.

"Everything that can scare me has done so today," Mrs. Kenyon exclaimed. "First the Burt boy gave me a fright and now this. I'm at—"

Lizzy Crawford interrupted Mrs. Kenyon to tell of her Mother's hysteria.

"But Lizzy, dear," Elsa Crawford defended herself, "it was when I saw thy father fall backwards off the wagon seat. Goodness me! I thought he was going to lose hold of those crazed horses and them trying ta take off in a run away. What was I expected to do?"

"Yes," she continued, ignoring Mrs. Kenyon, I was a bit worried is all. Mrs. Crawford nervously twisted her bonnet ties as she struggled to keep her voice modulated and herself under control.

Mrs. Kenyon didn't bother to lower her voice but ranted on about how her wagons nearly flipped. "It took both Mr. Kenyon and myself to try and calm the horses. Can you believe this? Both of us holding on for dear life while those addle-brained savages—"

"Mother," Lizzy again interrupted Mrs. Kenyon, who was speaking loudly to make herself heard above Elsa's prattle, "you were screaming. I couldn't make out what you were saying, but you should have heard yourself."

"Only when I couldn't see thy father." Her Mother looked up with an angry scowl on her face. "Let me tell thee somethin', missy: I was sure we were all going to die and I, for one, didn't intend to die quietly. I was speakin' to the Lord, askin' him if he had any notion of what was goin' on down here."

The hostility in the women's voices attracted the men's attention, who weren't sure if it was wise to intervene at this time.

"My milk cow broke free," Mrs. Kenyon raged on. "Watched the heifer buckin' around, kickin' her back legs out behind her, 'fore she took off runnin' like the dickens. I'm still shakin' I'm so mad at those wild men."

Elsa's face flushed. "If I had my way, I'd turn around and head for home right now. My cow's been bawling, like thee hear, ever since all this happened."

"I don't care if thou knows it, I wish I'd never left home." Elsa wiped her tear-filled eyes with a corner of her apron. "I didn't want to come out here in the first place. This is no place for Lizzy; besides, I wonder if I have a single dish left. Look over yonder at my wagon, will thee? A wheel could've broken off, killin' us. Everything I own's in that wagon, and do thee think Mr. Crawford cares a hoot?"

The women, their anger spent, were quiet. Elsa's chin trembled as tears coursed down her cheeks. "Oh glory be—that cow. She'll not let her milk down tonight, thee mark my words." Her voice croaked with sobs.

Mother came to take Elsa Crawford in her arms, patting her on the back as she would a frightened child. "There, there, Elsa, I'm glad you're still alive," she whispered to the distraught little women.

"Have no idea where my cow's at," Mrs. Kenyon muttered. "S'pose they stole her. That's what them Indians do best, you know?" She sucked in a noisy breath. "Thought I'd lost ma' boys but they showed up in Sam Emigh's wagon. It's not like we weren't warned about Indians. No tellin' what they'll do to us next. We don't have a prayer of helping ourselves out here, and where're our men folks anyway? Makes me nervous with Mr. Kenyon and ma' boys out a ma' sight, but what's a body to do, I ask ya?"

Elsa, having regained herself, stated, "My goodness, we've not made it out of Illinois yet and we've been attacked by wild savages." She quickly covered her face with her apron as the tears began again. "Oh, wilt thou look at the mess around us."

"Might as well stop your bawling, Elsa," Ruth said. "Least ways you got your milk cow; they stole mine. We might as well camp here tonight," Mrs. Kenyon suggested. "Nobody's in any condition to move on."

45

"Elsa's right; it ain't the men who'll put the wagon's back together, cook supper, and tend the hurt ones." Ruth Kenyon shook her bonneted head and clucked her tongue. "Why I ever let myself be talked into comin' out here in a wagon—only the good Lord knows."

Martha could understand the fears of these women. Her aching body attested with soreness but she was managing with her frayed nerves better than Mrs. Crawford. She was relieved to hear Mother suggest, "Hadn't we best move on, ladies?"

Martha hadn't seen Neil. She didn't care to share her feelings of concern for him in front of the others. She'd mention his absence when she were alone with Mother and maybe she could ask after him.

Mr. Emigh came across the field as the women approached his wagon.

"We don't see your boys," Mother said. "Everyone alright, Mr. Emigh?"

"Nat and I were banged around a little but nothing serious. My Clydesdales can take a lot of punishment. Over there," he indicated with a nod of his head, "the fellows are repairing the broken harnesses.

"Mrs. Kenyon, I commend your boys, they made a wise decision to climb into my wagon—when," he paused, "everything happened." He was glad he'd caught himself before he had mentioned anything about the Indians.

Whew, that word would have probably set the women off again. He quickly lifted his hat and wiped his forehead on his shirt sleeve.

Martha was disappointed when Mr. Emigh didn't mention Neil.

She suddenly realized Mother was talking to her. "Oh, I'm sorry." She glanced up to see everyone was looking at her.

"I said," Mr. Emigh repeated, "you've had the daylights scared out of you."

Martha pretended to smile. "Mr. Emigh, I don't know the words to tell you how terrified I was. I have never been so scared in my life. My Mother and sister hadn't held onto my feet I'd have been pulled headfirst out of the wagon."

Mother realized, listening to Martha, how pale and drawn she looked.

"You did the right thing, Miss Burt," Mr. Emigh told her. "If you don't fight them they lose interest fast. They live for a good fight."

"If I coulda got ma' hands on ma' gun, I'd've shot one of them savages," Mrs. Kenyon snarled, listening to young Martha's dramatic rescue for the first time.

"Even if you'd gotten your gun, Mrs. Kenyon, you wouldn't have had time to load it," Mr. Emigh pointed out.

"I mighta been able ta club one of 'em upside the head, had he'd come close enough." She drew herself up in quiet dignity. "They had no call ta treat us this way."

"Glad to see you're alright, Mr. Emigh. We'd best be moving on," said Mother.

Martha waited in anticipation of Mother mentioning something about Neil, but the women were walking away.

They came upon the McGraw wagon setting at a precarious angle. The tongue and front wheels were pulled over to such an extreme position that it was ready to topple over, and if it did everything inside would be destroyed. At the sight of the wagon and restless oxen, Ruth Kenyon and Bertha hastened to summon the men.

The other women rounded the wagon just as Brian McGraw turn to face them. He was covered with blood, and an inert, headless body was sprawled at his feet. Blood stained the ground around the partially skinned carcass.

"Oh no," Elsa Crawford whispered, stunned by the grisly scene before her. She grabbed on to Mary Burt's arm for support.

"It done busted hit's neck," Mr. McGraw explained. "Node if'n Ah skinned hit right quick, I could mebbe save the meat. It was still alive when Ah found hit. Ma' young'uns done dragged the other goat inta the wagon a-fer them Injun's could see him.

Cain't save this ear hide, durn shame but this 'ere meat; we can't use it all. Thim Injun's done left hit fer dead whin they seed hit was bein' drug back o' ma' wagon."

After the start of seeing Mr. McGraw, the women quickly moved in to assist him. They were thankful the fresh meat could be saved as they peeled the hide from the goat.

"Mr. McGraw, you cut it up and I'll see it gets divided with the others," Mother assured him, wiping her soiled, bloody hands on her apron. "It won't go to waste."

Mrs. Kenyon and Bertha returned just as a glazed-eyed Jenny climbed down from the wagon.

The women exchanged quick glances at their discovery of Jenny Mc-Graw's condition. She was a thin woman in an oversized dress, so large it hadn't revealed her before. They also noted Jenny was acting peculiar.

Mr. McGraw was carrying on about his young'uns being scared to death. "But they'se managed ta git themselves inta the wagon jist in time. Hit's a wonder they didn't git one of theyselves kilt. Jist hope thim devils ain't plannin' on comin' back real soon."

Mrs. Kenyon cut him short. "We're here to help you, Mr. McGraw. You go about your business and leave us women to ours."

"Thet's right nice of ya ladies. Ah'm much obligin' to ya for comin' ta help. Ah don't mean ta be frettin' ya'll, but ma' Jinny here: ya reckon she's gonna be alright?"

"She's gonna be alright, Mr. McGraw," Mrs. Kenyon assured him.

Mother glanced over at the Wilson wagon. As soon as time permitted she must go see to Abigale. She was about to send Martha, but the men came to stabilize the wagon, and Mother was sure Mr. Wilson would have shared any problems by now.

It was decided to pull the wagons into a circle. There was an unspoken need for as much protection as possible against another assault, might there be one.

"Looky ma brood, would cha? Ya'd a niver node they's been skeert real bad." Brian Mc Graw grinned broadly at his children, who did appear as if nothing out of the ordinary had taken place.

Mother requested the girls bring containers to hold the meat while she gently coaxed Jenny McGraw into the wagon, but the woman hung back, her eyes staring vacantly.

Bertha and Virginia McGraw developed a friendship. Ginny, who was the same age as Bertha, was a pretty, redheaded girl who possessed an infectious giggle to go along with her strong-willed, independent nature.

It was beyond Ginny to associate socially with the Burts. She knew it was unacceptable or inappropriate for people of her kind. The two girls rummaged for kettles amid the clutter inside the McGraw wagon. Their social class and differences were ignored.

The women were able to work through their earlier anger, but not their fear of another assault. They put their energy in the McGraws, leaving the tantalizing odor of roasting meat cooking over a bright fire. The aroma from fresh-brewed coffee lifted the spirits of those catching its scent, and the wagon had been restored to order. Jenny, cared for, had been tucked into her bed.

Through Martha's pain and soreness, she pondered her new relationship with these women. *We women weren't prepared for the violence we faced today, but we've come out strong.*

At Mother's insistence she helped carry fresh meat to the Wilsons. The two women were startled by Abigale's appearance. Her face was ashen and she appeared in pain.

"Abigale, are you feeling alright?" Mother asked.

"I'm just a bit tired, ladies. I'm so thankful we can stop for the rest of the day. You know, I do believe it's going to rain. I feel it, don't you? The air smells different when it rains." Abigale hoped Mary and Martha didn't notice she had to lean against the wagon opening to steady herself.

"Yes," Mother admitted, "I do feel a decided chill coming on." Actually she'd had little time to be aware of the weather with the turmoil around her. "Yes, I do most certainly feel a chill, now you speak of it." She reached to tuck behind her ear loose strands of hair that were being blown across her face from a brisk freeze. "Here, let me take your bread back and bake it with mine."

"Thank you, Mary. I'm movin' a little slow. I'm so clumsy; I got bruised a bit from being bounced around, but didn't we all? I'm just thankful none of the children were hurt. None of them are, are they? Mary, dear, should I need you, I'll send one of my boys for you. My family is most grateful for the fresh meat. Mr. Wilson will enjoy a good supper."

"You know, I think Abby's right," Mother said as she headed for her wagon. "I do feel a storm coming on."

"Now to get my house in order." Martha heard mother heave a weary sigh." I'm so thankful for the meat; it's going to make a tasty supper."

Mother was pleased to see Papa had a fire burning. "I'll hurry so's I can offer him and his grizzly looking friend some fresh coffee." The girls quickly covered their mouths to keep from snickering at Mother's description of the stranger talking to Papa.

Mother set about rearranging the inside of the wagon and at the same time prepare a hearty supper of roasted meat with onions and potatoes in a savory gravy. She'd bake fresh rolls and, bless Granny, there'd be sweet cake for dessert. She wished Stephen would go play elsewhere; he insisted on clinging so tightly to her he was underfoot and tripping her.

Papa brought the stranger over to the fireside. "Mrs. Burt, Mr. Stark here's a trapper passin' through. I insisted he take supper with us." Papa introduced Mr. Stark.

Whiskers covered Mr. Stark's face, making his age questionable. A ruddy nose and two bright eyes peeked through the thick facial growth. Clad in greasy, stained buckskin clothing, Mr. Stark impressed Mother, as if there was probably a gentleman beneath his roughness.

Martha heard Mother graciously welcome him to share supper as the Wilson boys came up with Stephen. They complained they couldn't wait for supper. Mother excused herself to fix the boys thick slabs of buttered bread with sugar she scraped off the sugar cone to sprinkle over each slice before she handed them out.

The storm announced itself at first with a gusty wind lashing through the branches of nearby trees. Thunder rumbled menacingly in the distance. Lightning crackled loudly in a darkening sky as it stabbed at the earth with jagged flashes of light.

The settlers had been looking forward to a peaceful evening after their traumatic day, but were sent scurrying to fasten down and secure their wagons in anticipation of a blustery night.

The men decided against staking the livestock outside the circle of wagons to let them feed during the night. The Indians might return and steal any unattended stock. The storm with its lightning and thunder was sure to spook the herd.

To cover their fears, the men insisted they were doing this to keep their womenfolk from fretting anymore than they already were. There had been no bloodshed today, but the men confessed they hadn't been prepared and would be more alert for Indians from now on.

Papa was worried. He had no choice but to teach his women to handle the oxen. He hoped this didn't mean he was inviting grief by allowing them, with no experience, to handle a yoke of oxen during a disaster, but he needed his hands free to load and use the rifle.

The youngsters gathered around the fire gave Mr. Stark an opportunity to captivate them with stories of skin-tingling, horror-laced tales of how he crossed this here wild, uncivilized United States by himself.

They listened attentively to the account of his bravely hiding under the water with only a reed to breath through while he waited for hours in ice-cold water for the savages to leave so he could surface.

Families quickly ate their suppers and returned for the comfort of each other around the warmth of the communal campfire.

The wind blew forceful at times, whipping the flames of the fires. Thunder was heard followed by lightning tracing itself on the horizon as a reminder of the approaching storm.

The discussion continued about the Indian event. Mr. Stark recognized Eli Burt's endeavor to turn the conversation to lighter things. The man had tried several times to bring up other topics, but those around the fire continued to return to the day's event, with each vivid detail exaggerated as it was retold.

Mr. Stark began, "Anyone here know much about a young statesman name o' Abraham Lincoln? Wonder if ya'll hear tell of this young feller? Now my 'pinion of this here young buck is he's too big for his britches.

Next thing ya know he'll be thinking of runnin' for the presidency of this here United States. Young radical upstart, to my way of thinking." Mr. Stark paused waiting for reactions.

At first a pronounced silence followed Mr. Stark's speech.

"He's a Whig, and them Whigs is opposed to President Polk," Brian McGraw said.

David Wilson said he'd heard, "President Polk's busy taking care of things down 'round the Southern Territory. I hear tell there's even a war with the country of Mexico. Aren't there settlers headed that way too? I'd like to know how Lincoln feels about all this."

"Mr. Lincoln's a home state man," Papa stated. "I kinda like the notion of him runnin' for president of the United States myself. The man's worked himself up to a seat in Congress already."

"Lincoln's well liked, I've heard tell." Alex Kenyon chewed vigorously on a grass stem. "Polk's for migratin' west; he's the man for me," Tom Crawford added.

Sam Emigh thought, "Mr. Lincoln's a well-self-educated man but a poor man. I doubt he can win the presidential vote. His family isn't that well known."

The conversation ceased as imminent, deafening thunder sounded followed by lightning that flashed, cracked, and zigzagged overhead.

Families hastened to their wagons. Papa picked up few pieces of dry wood to stow under his wagon for morning. He invited Mr. Stark to bed down under the wagon, but he couldn't promise the old trapper he'd stay dry.

Mr. Stark declined. "I got my own way of handlin' my sleepin' arrangement. I once had me a bedroll and a donkey, but he took off one day while I was setting traps.

"Mrs. Burt," he told Mother. "I surely enjoyed the good cookin'. I don't get many good meals livin' by ma'self. That stew was mighty tasty; I believe I done ate myself out of a place at your table, I'm a-feared."

"Mr. Stark, Mr. Burt and I will be watching for you as we travel. The children were thrilled with your stories. We'd be honored to have you anytime."

"Well, I thank ya both. Next time I'll have ye some fresh game and new tales fer the young'uns." He reached to shake Papa's hand in a firm grasp before he turned to walk off into the night with the sounds of thunder and the crackle of lightning surrounding him.

Cramped tightly together in the wagon, the weary Burt family bedded down under the big canvas cover being buffeted and tugged by a wind so forceful that it rocked the wagon.

A curtain normally pulled to separate the parents from the children was left open to ease the girls' anxiety and fears of returning Indians.

Papa securely tired down the flaps over each end of the wagon. "There—this will keep out the wind, rain, and peepin' Indians," he assured the girls before crawling under his quilt.

"Remember the day Papa told us he thought he had Mother Nature beat when he bolted down the hoops holding up the canvas?" Bertha asked. "This riling storm sounds to me like she's pestering Papa's hoops in hopes of yanking them off."

The family agreed; they recalled Papa's challenge to Mother Nature, whom he claimed to be his adversary. However, before long, one by one, they drifted off to sleep, while outside the wagon the storm raged in all its fury as it slowly moved across the night sky.

Chapter 8

Lying next to his sleeping wife, Papa found it difficult to sleep with the wind rattling and banging containers hanging outside the wagons. He drifted off to sleep as he listened to the rain hitting against the canvas in a steady tempo, but not before he concluded the family must have a milk cow, he needed a horse, and two oxen needed replacing. One had run off during the Indian assault and the other was limping along on a maimed hoof.

He wasn't pleased with the idea of carrying more grain. It defeated his plan to travel light, and he'd been warned about the expense of buying grain from the trading posts along the way.

A man could make the journey alone. It would be cheaper, and easier, but Papa wanted his family to share the excitement and adventure. Besides, if Congress passed the Land Act he'd be allowed more land with a wife along. Maybe he should have left Mary and the children with Granny, his elder brother Joseph, or Mary's family until he settled.

He reflected back to his boyhood dream. As far back as he was able to remember, he'd dreamed of traveling out West and exploring the virgin territory.

He remembered trapping alongside his Indian friends; he'd tried to tell them of his yearning for the adventure, but they were satisfied with their land and they didn't understand.

"Eli, your traps are busy?" they'd ask him. Little Bear and Gray Wolf of the Fox tribe had shown him how to make traps and set them. They would let him go with them to where the big, soft-furred brown beaver built their dams.

This was before the Black Hawk War of '32. The Sauk and Fox tribes fought the settlers like the Burt family to keep them from settling on what they considered their land, sacred land they thought was their responsibility to protect with their lives. Without the weapons of the white settlers and military, they were defeated in the bloody massacre.

Eli Burt was twelve years old then. So many of the young warriors who died in the battle were boys his age. After the massacre, it broke the fragile trust between him and his friends.

He was never to forget the reverent dignity and respect they'd taught him concerning the souls of the animals. Everything of the animals was for their use. The meat, skin, bones, and sinews, even body fluids, influenced an Indian's way of life.

Jolted out of his sleep by a voice, Papa paused to listen before he identified it as the voice of David Wilson.

"Eli, it's David. You awake? It's your turn for watch," David loudly whispered.

Papa slowly climbed down from the wagon into the cold, wet night.

"It's miserable out here, Eli; nobody's crazy enough to bother us in this weather. The livestock's quiet. They're tired—worn out. Sorry ta leave ya but I'm froze. Oh yeah! I'm suppose ta tell ya, Alex is waiting for you over by his wagon." David ran for his wagon to get out of the drizzling rain.

Papa pulled his heavy, India rubber coat around him and shouldered his rifle, while letting his eyes adjust to the darkness, before he splashed through puddles of rainwater to circle around the wagons in search of Alex Kenyon.

"Eli, over here." Alex's voice came through the darkness.

"Sure hope this rain lets up tomorrow," Papa commented in a low voice as he neared Alex. "Travelin's been mighty hard these last three days, and I'm short two oxen as is."

"Travelin's rough alright," Alex agreed. "'Specially with the roads so mired down."

The lard-saturated torches were of little use to the sentinels standing guard in the dark, rain-filled night.

"How about we circle round the compound, Eli, get ourselves familiar in the dark. By the way, I've been meanin' ta ask ya, where did ya say yer people were from? I mean afore they come ta Chicago?" Alex asked, as the two made their way through the rain, with the wet earth squishing under their feet. Passing the McGraws' wagon, Brian's deep snores were the only disturbing sound in the darkness.

"My folks," Eli told Alex, "came from Wales, by way of England, when I was but a wee tad. Ma' pa told 'bout the fare being cheaper if the boat was full but less than half of 'em arrived alive to walk out on dry land. I'm not one to put much faith in superstitions, but there's this story my ma tells about feedin' us dried apples; that's why the family made it alive. Way I look at it, Alex, my folks were so poor they knew how to survive; that's the reason they made it."

Alex chuckled at Papa's perception. "Same way for my folks too, Eli."

Papa told Alex how he'd learned to plow "from the back of ma' pa's horses. He told me it was the only way he could keep an eye on me and keep me from being kidnapped by Indians."

"I was tied up with a rope ta a tree, myself." Alex recalled. "White young'uns and women fetched a good price. Always amazed me how they'd sell their own women and children ta each other. Never will understand them savages; they got no respect for human life whatsoever. Seems to me."

"You know, Alex, ma' pa spent his life clearin' an' plowin' to make the land produce. Then hot summers burned up the crops and frigid winter ice storms killed 'em. He died a worn-out man. The weather was hard on him."

"We always had plenty of fresh meat, though, and potatoes." Papa chuckled at the memory. "Potatoes sometimes three times a day in the winter."

"I remember the winters," Eli reminisced. "My pa traveled to Chicago to find payin' work. He'd be forced ta stay there until he could plow himself a trail home in the snow, and it might be early spring by then."

Papa paused "Whata ya say we stop by ma' wagon? The coffee's cold but it'll keep us Awake."

"Ah—coffee, I take it any way I can get it, Eli. Your speakin' of snow reminds me of how for days we packed in buckets of snow to melt it down. It was an endless job. It made so little water, but it kept us young'uns busy just gettin' enough water for the livestock."

"Yeah," Papa agreed. "We've had some bad blizzards off the Great Lakes; bitin' winds come howlin' through, freezing everything they touched. Chicago's too cold for my likin'."

Papa fumbled for cups in the big Dutch oven under the wagon. He groped in the dark for the coffeepot. The men sipped the cold, bitter coffee with their India rubber coats pulled snugly around them while they stood silently, peering into the darkness, without shadows, and only an occasional restless sound from the livestock.

"I'll sure be glad to get out of this country. I hear the weather's s'pose to be a whole lot better out West," Papa concluded as he and Alex conversed in low voices.

"That's why I'm going, Eli. I hear it's milder. Days like this sure slow us down."

"Wonder if putting up fences out West will threaten the Indians like they do here?" Papa mused before taking a sip of coffee.

"Fences do tend to rile 'em alright," Alex agreed. "Prob'ly no matter where they come from they won't like the idea of fences. You know 'em better than me, Eli."

"Ya know, Alex, They took me trappin' when I was Stephen's age. I learned a lot about their ways, and they questioned my ways too. They laughed at my idea of farmin'. I remember 'em telling me, 'We're hunters and trappers, not squaws to plant seeds.'"

Papa absentmindedly ran his thumb around the rim of his coffee cup as he gazed out into the night. "They're scared, Alex. They think they've lost control of what they were born to do: protect their Mother Earth. Now—I sympathize with the settlers being burned out and killed, but we threaten the Indians. Killing off the white folks is the only way to resolve their problem with us. They know it's not right but they do it anyway."

"Ya may be right, Eli, but that's because they're uncivilized savages. They seem ta wanna stay that way. They can't kill us all, Eli; makes no sense. We'll just keep moving west, and if we don't make it others will. Don't they understand this?"

The men paused. A silence developed between them before Alex inquired, "You leavin' much of a family behind, Eli?"

"I have an older brother, Joseph," Papa told him. "He works for the Illinois-Michigan Canal, that new extended waterway out of New York for folks comin' west."

"Oh sure, we took it ta get out here. It's faster than going overland. A real service ta the trappers, miners, and settlers. You only got the one brother?" Alex questioned out of curiosity.

"No, my other brother, Ernie, owns a sawmill in Chicago," Papa continued. "I had another brother, Brohn. He drowned trying to cross the Illinois one winter night. My ma took on something fierce. She still tells how she got him all the way here from Wales only ta lose him in the river by his back door."

Alex noticed Eli's voice took on a wistful tone as he spoke of his brother Brohn.

The men had squatted down, setting back on their heels as the rain continued to drip from the brims of their hats. Papa slowly inhaled deeply. He was able to identify the season by the smell of the air. Spring air like this brought new life, new growth. He'd met his Mary in the spring of the year.

He loved Mary from the first time he'd seen her. She was so small, gentle, and refined. He was never happier than when she chose to give up her kinder way of life to come work alongside him. Ma'd been pleased to have another woman to share the women's work. His pa had insisted they move into the big bedroom with their first baby coming.

I wish Pa could have lived long enough to see my children. Eli had always felt remorse in his memory of Pa's death. *We found him that day, leaned up against the flank of the cow he'd been milking. Ma told everyone at the funeral how "the cow cradled him next to her, never moving till I found him."*

"Ya know, Alex," Eli's voice had taken on a rugged quality, "I'll never forget the day of my pa's funeral. The Indians waited quietly, until after we buried my pa, to celebrate their ritual to his departed spirit. They honored my pa as their friend. Sure meant a lot to me."

The men still crouched down, each quiet with his own thoughts.

The rain reminded Eli of cold, crisp, autumn nights when his young'uns watched him peel apples in one long, unbroken peel, as he'd seen his pa do. Visitors stopped by now and again with news of the outside world.

This was when the restlessness, an insatiable desire, kindled within him. The vision of land stretching on for miles; rich, free soil; being able to produce crops twice the size he now planted and fought Mother Nature to keep.

In the springtime his fields had turned a soft, velvet green, with the promise of an abundant harvest. That is, if the hot summer sun didn't scorch the plants to death, the creek didn't dry up, and plant life didn't shrivel up from lack of water.

He'd watched the folks head out West, and sometimes the urgency to follow them became unbearable. He became driven to make his dream a reality.

Alex broke into their solitude. "Be glad when it's daylight. I'm starving." He stood up to resume the rounds of the wagons once again. Papa set his coffee cup aside to join him. Their feet sloshed through undetected pools of water.

"Feels like the rains lettin' up some, Alex," Papa commented. "There a-been times the rain was important to me but tonight's not one of 'em. Ma' pa came to America by ocean water and right now I feel like I'm havin' to navigate my way west in it."

"Speakin' of hunger, Alex, let me tell ya something. When we come ta the New World, I told you how my ma brought along those disgusting dried apples and stuffed them down our throats. Well, now, bless my Mary, she's doin' the same. I never liked 'em then, and for the life of me, I don't see what folks think is so great about 'em. I only tolerate 'em for the sake of ma' young'uns."

"I'd like me a nice big slab of warm dried apple pie right now," Alex sighed. "Any kind of apple pie—sounds good ta me."

The two walked on silently.

"Say, Eli, tell me, what are our chances of meetin' up with this band of Injuns?"

"Alex, who can guess? I'm 'spectin' they were just out ta stir up a little excitement for themselves the other day. I sure can't figure 'em out. We're pretty close to a settlement, which could mean if there's any military there the Indians know better than to step out of line. The Indians need the settlement for trade; they might not be so apt ta stir up trouble."

"They're a strange people. They don't understand how the earth can be divided up, then given back to them in parcels to live on, and they feel they're being given all the bad land. They told me the earth was here from the beginning of time and no one owns it. They go along for a while, toleratin' us, then they get riled up with the idea we're harnessing their spirits with fences and fear we're over trappin' their beaver.

"'Our ancestors did a better job before us,' they say. The white man won't listen to 'em and help 'em protect the earth. To them, this is the only reason they're here. Until they understand we can live together, there's gonna be a lot of bloodshed," Papa said in explanation of his concern. "Sometimes, Alex, I wonder if I'll live long enough ta see peace between us."

The men circled the wagons without any distraction to ease the long night. It became quiet but for raindrops losing their hold, dropping from where they had clung to tree branches, leaves, and wagons.

"Ever heard it said," Alex broke the silence, "that the darkest hour of the night is just before dawn?" The men paused momentarily. "Eli, it's like McGraw says: we're not stopping to claim the land, we're moving across it. We're not forcing 'em ta go with us. There's plenty here for everyone. Besides, when you ponder on it, with all these spirits and gods ta please, maybe that's what's keepin' 'em upset. Too bad they can't get down ta one god. Then maybe it wouldn't be so confusing for 'em."

The rain had ceased. Slowly darkness allowed the sky to push through a streak of silver light to announce the new day.

"Its light enough ta see. Think I'll start a fire for Mary. I need a cup of hot coffee," Papa decided aloud. "I'm starvin'. Maybe if I make enough racket I'll wake somebody up."

Alex stretched and yawned loudly. "If you don't mind, Eli, I'm gonna do the same. I need a fire ta warm me, and a good cup of coffee. Sure hope them savages had *themselves* a good night's sleep."

After Alex left for his wagon, Eli Burt, in the first light of day, gazed to the rolling hills in front of him.

We'll drop down into the settlement on the other side of these hills and get my business taken care of before movin' on. I'll head west along the Illinois River till it cuts off to head south from us. Our next stop will be Moline, then the Mississippi River crossing, and on to the Missouri River. We'll cross it into Iowa and on to Council Bluffs. Eli felt a restlessness surge within him to get on with the day as he hurried to wake his family.

Chapter 9

Mother climbed down, then returned for a warm shawl before coming to the fireside in the cold predawn. "No coffee?" she asked as she patted her hair in place and smoothed her apron to signify the beginning of another day.

Papa reached to embrace his wife with her coronet of hair, a glowing gold halo in the firelight. "No, ma'dear, I leave the coffee makin' ta you," Papa teased. "I could sure use a cup too."

The two savored the hot, fragrant coffee as they watched a steel gray light expand slowly across the sky The heat from the coffee cup helped calm Mother's shivering and warmed her hands.

She needed to retrieve the jar of bread starter she'd warmed throughout the night with her body heat. She'd need her leavening agent, saleratus, from one of the provisional boxes to finish the biscuits, but she'd wait until the girls were up and could carry the boxes to the fireside for her.

Ruthie woke and came to nestle beside Papa. "It's cold out here, Papa. Did it rain again last night?"

"If it did I didn't hear it. You slept sound too, I take it?" he inquired.

Mother glanced up to see Stephen. *He doesn't look well,* she thought, reaching to feel his forehead; but he protested, pushing her away.

Papa, who had dozed off with Ruthie cuddled next to him, was awakened when he heard Stephen's wail. "Come, Stephen, let me get you warm while Mother finishes our breakfast."

Mother passed around bowls of wheat mush, biscuits, and cups of coffee. She tried not to show her concern but noticed Stephen drank little of his coffee and didn't touch his mush, even with the extra sprinkling of sugar she'd put on it.

Bertha detested getting up so early. She was cold, she wasn't hungry, and she loathed the dirt and grime, the wet and cold, and the cramped sleeping arrangements. She wished she could find comfort living out of a wagon as her family did.

She had to force herself to eat the slimy mush. Each bite was quickly followed with bits of biscuit. A little sugar would make her bitter coffee taste better, but she wasn't about to leave the warm fire; she was too miserably cold.

"You don't look happy, Bertha," Papa said. He knew Bertha well enough to know she wasn't happy. Like her mother, she was fragile and delicate. Yet Bertha could be difficult, stubborn, and willful beyond reason.

"Papa, it's too early to be hungry," she answered in her husky voice.

"I wonder if Stephen would feel better if he slept a bit longer, Mary. I don't believe he's had his sleep out yet," Papa suggested.

Mother agreed as she set aside her bowl, and carried Stephen back to the wagon. Tucked under his quilt, she kissed his warm forehead, leaving him with instructions to call if he needed her.

"Everyone come close," Mrs. Kenyon shouted as she and Mr. Kenyon entered the circle of wagons. "We need to get movin' soon as possible."

She paused to look at everyone. "Mr. Kenyon and myself are of the notion we'd best put in a sixteen to twenty miles today if we can. This fog appears to be liftin'. We'll take a quick dinner. We've a deadline to meet, remember? A quick dinner now; no fires."

Martha glanced back to see Neil coming towards her. "Mrs. Kenyon's gettin' good at suggestin' I ride ahead and do her scoutin' for her," he confided to her. "Wish you could ride with me, Martha. You know my pa told me about that Indian. Wish I'd been here when that savage put his hands on you. I'd a killed the—"

Martha quickly interrupted him. "I'm alright, but it's nice to know you worried about me. Tell me, Neil, would you have come for me if I'd been carried off?"

She lowered her eyes modestly as she waited for his answer.

He started to speak, but just then Mrs. Kenyon beckoned and Martha found herself alone.

Martha was angered at his abruptly leaving her. *He's free to ride as he chooses. I'm just as capable of doing what he does. Didn't Mrs. Kenyon tell us women it was important we become strong and independent? I wonder if Mother ever suggested to Papa our handling the oxen?*

Martha turned her back to Neil and Mrs. Kenyon. She had work to do. She cared for Neil, more than she like to admit, but it provoked her to see him up there in front of everyone, boasting about his ride to the La Salle settlement.

Who fought off the Indians the other day? Martha fumed silently. *I work alongside Mother every day, for what? So Papa can go out West and make a name for himself in the eyes of the relatives. And wasn't Papa only too glad to have Neil accompany him the day Stephen was left behind? It should have been my mother beside Papa. Doesn't most of the responsibility for this journey fall to us women?* She threw herself into a frenzy preparing for the move out.

Neil watched Martha walk away from the group, just as Mr. Wilson, with a playful cuff to his shoulder, requested, "So tell us what's out there, young man."

"Yes, Neil," Mrs. Kenyon prompted. "Tell us, what's up ahead?"

Ginny McGraw, who had come to stand by Bertha, was gnawing on a cracker. To Bertha's understanding, Pilot crackers were emergency fare for disaster, when it was impossible to cook or the food had been ruined. The hard cracker was used mainly aboard ships and could be stored for months, even years. They had been suggested by the agency for wagon trains traveling out West, with their unpredictable circumstances and situations.

It upset Bertha to see this was all Ginny had for breakfast. She grabbed hold of Ginny's arm, dragging her back to the wagon for some descent food. Anything was better than a dry, tasteless cracker.

"But Bertha," Ginny defended herself, "Ma's still ain't fillin' good, so Pa told us ta git ourselves a cracker ta eat."

Martha was faced with a long day ahead. She had to agree the Indians and rain had slowed them down and valuable time had been lost. But she dreaded the endless walking the most.

Before they pulled out, Mother looked in on Stephen one more time only to find him asleep. She thought his breathing seemed a bit labored, and he felt feverish to her touch. It was difficult to see in the dim interior of the wagon, but he appeared flushed to her. She wished she had a little warm milk for him. Why ever had she allowed Eli to sell off her milk cows?

When at last she appeared, Papa pointed to the driver's seat beside him.

Mother wasn't a novice at handling teams of horses and quickly understood Papa's instructions. However, to operate the brake proved her greatest difficulty. She held the reins in the right hand and reached with the left hand to release the brake, but discovered she'd need both hands to pull back on the long handle holding the leather pad braced tightly against the front wagon wheel.

It required more strength than Mother had in her left arm. In order to free her hands, she tucked the reins under her and reached to release the brake. She was busy with manipulation of the brake and didn't see Papa's exasperation at her awkward maneuver.

"Mary, wrap the reins in a circle like this, then grasp them in both hands before ya reach to release the brake," he instructed. "This way, ya won't get pulled off your seat and fall onta the oxen below, or be run over by the front wheel."

They each knew there might come a time when it would be impossible to manage the brake handle with both hands, as during a stampede, or runaway, which could result in an overturned wagon. But Papa didn't allow himself worry; he'd just have to trust his teamster to handle the wagon by any means possible in such an event.

Martha and her sisters had been at odds with each other all morning. Their petty differences were aimed at everyone around them.

They were cranky and ill tempered as Ginny joined them. "What y'all squabblin' 'bout?" she asked, walking along with them in a warm sunshine trying to penetrate the fog.

"All this walking," Bertha grouched. "I don't enjoy walking all the way out West. I didn't want to come in the first place, remember, Martha?"

Martha's complaint concerned Mother. "She's worried about Stephen being sick. What can we do? We can't stop out here alone by ourselves. There's no doctor with us."

"Ain't anyone in your family ever been ailin' before?" Ginny asked. "Ya take ma' ma. She jist sleeps all tha' time whin she's ailin'. She ain't got the kind of sickness ya die from."

"How come she sleeps so much?" Ruthie was curious. "What made her sick?

Sometimes back home, she 'usta sleep fer days," Ginny replied." She just cain't seem ta git enough sleep. I don't rightly know what makes her take on this way. I don't like hit 'cause Pa 'spects me ta do all the work whin she's this way."

"Does it happen very often?" Ruthie asked as she plucked a nearby flower, adding it to her bouquet.

"Naw, jist sometimes, like whin them Indians skeered us, an' her nanny goat got itsilf kilt. Hit was her pet goat since hit was borned."

Martha wondered, *Why does Mrs. McGraw gets peculiar when she's scared? Strange, I didn't get peculiar, and I was scared bad by the Indians.*

Jenny McGraw lay quietly. She'd been terrified by the Indians from an event long ago she couldn't bring herself to talk about. Witnessing the slaughter of her pet, her mind refused to accept the situation. Instead, a state of utter helplessness invaded her. Safe and warm, buried deep in her little world, she excluded everyone. She couldn't be hurt as she slept without dreams. She couldn't know of her husband's difficulties without her. In fact, none of the others were aware of what this family was enduring, except the Burt girls.

Neil looked around for Martha but didn't see her as he made his way back to his wagon. He felt a restlessness and needed to get away and think. He mounted and urged his buckskin across the road and up into the hills.

He and his pa thought this journey would start a new life for them. They'd been living with ghost memories of a wife and mother. Their plan was to buy a claim between them. He'd run cattle. His pa thought orchards a profitable venture. They intended to build two homes and a barn between them.

Neil intended to marry someday, and he envisioned Martha as the helpmate to him, as his mother had been to his pa. But Martha could be so contrary. The woman in his dreams wasn't stubborn. His dream woman would give him children. She'd be loving, caring, and nurturing to him and their children. Still, he admired Martha's determination to endure the struggle of the journey. He just wasn't ready for the two of them. He had to make this journey before he could take on a wife and family. And what if Martha didn't wait? What if she met someone else? He had nothing to offer her but his dreams.

He hoped Martha would wait for him. He needed her to make his dream succeed. It disturbed him for her to be this important to him. He wasn't able to deal with the feelings of anxiety he felt when she came to mind.

Reining about, Neil pushed his little horse up a steep grade. He enjoyed the sensation of power and freedom, the exhilaration of speed as they raced along, shutting out the images of Martha and his dreams.

Hauling the reins, he gazed out on a world unfurled before him, its beauty beyond his wildest imagination and comprehension. He wished

Martha were here to share the warm sunshine, the blue sky, the vivid green, rolling hills blending themselves into a soft blue beyond as he inhaled deeply of the pristine air. The panorama before him made him feel at peace with himself and the world. He leaned forward to pat his gelding on the shoulder and paused a while longer to enjoy the spectacular view before turning back.

Those wagons down there are like ants, he thought, gazing down at them. *They move in a line to meet up with other wagons. Then like ants, they'll trudge along, toting their loads until they reach the home colony. The ants go underground but these folks will build their colony above ground, spread out for all to see.* He wondered if ants gave much thought to distance and time as he took his time riding down from the hills.

The wagons descended the plateau to follow beside the river. Mrs. Kenyon and her boys were briskly walking along when she sighted Neil and signaled him to her side.

"Neil, ride back and ask the folks if they want to pull off at the first place we can fit into for a quick dinner, or do they want to stop on their own. No cookin', you tell 'em. It's a cold dinner; no cookin'."

Neil pulled up alongside the Burt wagon, surprised to see Mrs. Burt in the driver's seat and Mr. Burt walking beside the wagon.

"Your first day to handle the oxen, Mrs. Burt?" he exclaimed. "Looks like she's got 'em well in hand there, doesn't it, Mr. Burt?"

Mother grinned from the compliment. "Thank you, Neil. I imagined it to be more difficult."

Neil could see she was pleased with herself. But he wondered if Mr. Burt realized he'd be giving up his seat from now on with a woman at the reins.

After he delivered the message from Mrs. Kenyon, Neil circled his horse to see Martha with her sisters and Ginny some distance behind the wagon. The girls looked weary and warm. He wished there were extra horses or a wagon for them to ride in as he waved to them.

Martha watched Neil ride up beside the wagon. *I've been traveling how many days now,* she thought, *and I've not had another person bother me like that man does. Why am I so aware of him? It's because he makes me feel—happy when he's around.* The thought caused her to smile. She had no desire to share her thoughts with the others, and quickly glanced away.

Abigale Wilson bravely tried to keep to herself the reoccurring spasms she was experiencing. She'd pleaded feeling weary so she might ride inside the wagon, but the jolting, rough ride wasn't at all pleasant. The pains came sharp at times. She hoped they'd go away, but in her heart a fear was building to tell her different.

She pulled her quilt up around her to try and shut out her fears. *I must be strong. The children—I must think of my children. They have no one but their father and me. How can he possibly manage without me? We're so far from our families. We had to leave so much behind and we have so far to go. I never realized it would be like this.*

A forceful pain gripped her once again. *Oh God, please help me. Please give me strength. Oh dear Jesus, I can't do this alone. Please help me accept your will.*

The pain passed. Abigale weakly wiped her wet brow with her dress sleeve. She felt the stirring within her womb.

Chapter 10

Martha pulled off her bonnet and lifted her face to the warm sun. She inhaled the fragrance the earth gives off as it dries, combined with the aroma of young, green prairie grass.

The blue violets, hepaticas, and redbud colors splashed against the hillsides. Feathery greens, dandelions, lamb's quarter, and tender blackberry sprouts were everywhere.

The sounds of birds came from over the hills and groves of trees as Martha followed the wagons, working themselves back and forth across the hills to the valley below and the Illinois River.

During dinner today, Mother learned from Martha and Bertha of Mrs. McGraw's peculiar sickness that made her sleep for days then Mother and Mrs. Kenyon had gone to care for her.

Mother had returned to tell of how when Mrs. Kenyon turned to leave, she stepped on a kitten; it startled her so she backed into a goat. She surprised the goat, who turned and butted her, knocking her off balance. Then poor Mr. McGraw attempted to catch her and lost his balance. They fell with Mrs. Kenyon pinned under him.

It had been difficult for Mother to relate the story and keep from laughing at how the two looked sprawled on the ground. Mother told how "Mrs. Kenyon lifted and pitched Mr. McGraw over onto his back—like he was a limp doll." Martha could still hear Papa's uproarious laughter at this part of Mother's story.

Mother continued, "Mrs. Kenyon became so flustered she picked herself up, dusted herself off, and marched away so fast her dress sailed out behind her like a sail on a sailing ship, and she wasn't even aware she'd put her bonnet on backwards."

Martha could clearly visualize Mr. McGraw rocking back and forth from heel to toe, his hands clasped behind him, as he scowled at his children. Mother said, "The children solemnly stared back at him; they wouldn't have dared move or make so much as a peep."

Mother had bitten down so hard on her knuckle to keep from laughing. Her finger was still sore, and she'd had to keep her eyes away from facing Mr. McGraw. Then, to make matters worse, she'd watched the goat contentedly munch on Mr. McGraw's dinner: his Pilot cracker.

Mother fixed cheddar cheese with bread, dried apples, and apricots for Martha and her sisters to carry to the McGraws.

Martha couldn't help but wonder if the kitten Ruthie picked up was the one Mrs. Kenyon had stepped on. As the girls were leaving the McGraws, Karl Kenyon appeared with biscuits filled with strawberry preserves.

The strawberry preserves made Martha hungry for the big, ripe, sweet berries. At home she'd helped Mother make them into preserves: put into crocks, the preserves were sealed with wax, to be enjoyed during the long cold winters.

She hadn't given any thought to next winter until now. *Wonder what we'll be eating next winter if we don't preserve this summer? But how can we? There isn't time, and how would we carry them? Mother told us she's going to try and bake dried apple pies, one for us and one for the McGraws.*

Bertha came to join Martha. "Oh Martha, hasn't this day been strange? Mrs. McGraw's sickness, and the riders. I haven't noticed the walking it's been such a busy day, with so much happening. I sure hope Stephen gets to feeling better."

It was while Mother was sponging Stephen's fevered little body that Papa saw the riders coming. The girls watched him load his flintlock, shoulder it, and join the other men with their rifles at the Kenyon wagon as they awaited the strangers.

"Here we were," Bertha said, "out in the middle of nowhere, and here comes these strangers. I was scared near to death, Martha. I didn't know what was going to happen next."

Three men dressed in cloth britches and battered felt hats rode up to the Kenyon wagon and dismounted. Two of them were wearing long-legged Indian moccasins; the other had on a pair of dusty, rugged cavalry boots.

After everyone had exchanged introductions the men said they'd come to warn the train of an Indian assault.

They told of a young man's coming into the settlement a few days earlier, telling of a small wagon train coming through, and yesterday a man from across the river came to report the assault. There'd been no killings but the Indians had destroyed the train.

68

"Tore up ticks and mattresses," the man named George Lewis said.

"Yeah, broke up their water barrels and run off the cattle and horses before settin' fire to the wagons," Zenas Charbonneau added.

The third man, Andrew Farnsworth, explained, "The fellow didn't know for sure what Indian tribe attacked. 'It all happened too unexpectedly,' was all he kept repeating."

"When you didn't show up at Fort LaSalle," Mr. Lewis said, "we decided to ride out and see if anyone was still alive."

"He asked us of we had enough ammunition and guns," Papa said, as he related the conversation to Mother. "Each of us looked at the other, then at our rifles. How could we say if we had enough of anything to defend ourselves? It takes time to load a rifle.

"We all wondered," Papa continued, "if this was the same tribe that attacked us. Sam Emigh feels we're sitting targets here in these hills. We don't know the country like the Indians do. And when Mr. Kenyon questioned them how much farther it was to Fort La Salle, we were informed, 'As the crow files, straight over those hills, but that also depends on how fast you're travelin' too.'"

"Eli," Mother was quick to say, "we're coming down into the valley. There'll be lots of other wagons, Indians, and folks using the road. We'll be alright, I'm sure."

Martha and Bertha discussed their fears as they walked along. There was no way to keep the Indians away from them. No way to prevent or punish the Indians for murder. They robbed the settlers, stole horses, kidnapped women and children, and their thirst for whiskey was insatiable.

"I don't understand how Papa thinks we can make this journey and get there alive." Martha shook her head in wonder.

The girls recalled the event of two weeks ago. They couldn't help but wonder if the others were experiencing the same fears of being as vulnerable as they were.

Martha recalled Papa's telling them of Mr. Farnsworth asking if everyone was alright. "No one's ailin'?" he asked.

"We looked at each other," Papa said, "then Mr. Kenyon asked him, what kind of ailment was he referring to.

"Mr. Charbonneau told us, 'There'd been a wagon train through with cholera and the settlement made them keep on movin'.'" Papa went on to explain how the train came from down around the Southern Territories and was going through to Iowa.

"Nothin' more was said," Papa replied, "but we all knew the deadly cholera can wipe out an entire wagon train within a matter of days. Imagine the scare when word gets around. It only serves to panic folks. It's a scare far worse than an Indian attack, I believe."

"Mrs. Kenyon offered food and drink to the men," Papa said, "but they declined. Said they needed to get back, and we all agreed with Mr. Kenyon when he told us, 'We're pressed for time. We need ta get movin'.'"

"Mrs. Kenyon asked us to push a little harder, that we might be able to make the settlement by nightfall," Papa told his family. "It's going to be difficult, grueling, and demanding for us and the teams."

Papa also explained how Mr. Kenyon turned, after the men rode off, and asked him, "Your young'un still ailin'?"

Papa said, "I wondered how the Kenyons knew about Stephen, but then it's never been a secret. So's I told him, 'You know how young'uns are: travelin's hard on 'em.'"

"Nothing more was said as we headed back to our wagons," Papa concluded.

Papa started the oxen out again, urging them along at a faster pace. Mother walked beside the girls and shared with Martha and Bertha her suspicions, the seed of fear about Stephen's ailment might already have been planted.

Martha knew from the sun's position that there were few daylight hours before darkness closed about them. She was weary and knew everyone else was, but it was necessary to keep going at this pace. Anyway, it was frightening to think the wagons might travel after dark.

Mrs. Kenyon, to her way of thinking, was a caretaker, and the Burt's sick child became an issue with her.

"Alex, I feel I'm right in what I've got to do. I'm going to ask the Burts to fall back and stay away from us until their boy is better. Now I don't expect you to understand, but we mothers have children to protect, and as a mother, I don't want mine around that boy, or until—"

"Or until what, Ruth?"

"You know as well as me. We could lose every family in this wagon train. It's just best to be cautious rather than be careless, I always say."

"But Ruth, you don't know the boy's ailment. You're for leavin' 'em out here, easy prey to Indians or any other disaster. You want that on your conscience?" Alex asked. He heaved a resigned sign when he recognized from the set of her head and shoulders that she'd made up her mind.

"We'll be stopping to water the teams soon, won't we?" she inquired. "I'll go back then and have a little talk with the Burts."

Martha remembered Mrs. Kenyons coming to them.

"You folks will have to fall back and keep to yourselves," Ruth Kenyon bluntly stated. "Our children will be forbidden to come near you. We're going to consider your family contagious, Mr. Burt, until the boy shows signs of improvement. I feel justified in speaking for all of us."

Martha remembered her parents' reaction. In the name of fear, her family was being discriminated against. They quietly watched after Mrs. Kenyon returning to her wagon, and observed other members of the train either turning away or lowering their heads as she passed by.

Martha remembered how her family recoiled in anger at first against Mrs. Kenyon's demand that they be expelled from the train and the injustice of it. They agreed, however, that if it were one of the others, they would have harbored the same fears. They had no way of knowing the outcome of Stephen's ailment,

Martha had watched helplessly as her mother's shoulders drooped.

Mary Burt's stomach knotted in fear that her little one might have a dreaded disease, that her family was in danger of something she had no power over. Out here in the wilderness, without a doctor or Granny Burt to help her, an outcast to her friends. What was she to do? She choked back her tears of frustration.

Papa attempted to be jovial and lighten the mood. "We won't have to fight the dust. I look at it this way—there have been hundreds travel these roads. They made it; so will we. We haven't met up with any problems we couldn't handle, now have we?"

"We haven't been through a real Indian attack either, Papa," Bertha quietly stated.

"It doesn't bother you, Papa, that we're out here alone from now on?" Martha asked.

Papa reached for a blade of grass. Martha remembered watching him put it in his mouth and belabor it with his teeth as he squinted up at the sky. He removed his hat and wiped his brow with the sleeve of his shirt before replacing his hat. At the same time, he rotated the grass stem into the other corner of his mouth. "It's gettin' late," was his only comment.

Mother had gone to look in on Stephen. "How's the boy doin'?" Papa asked when she returned.

Mother leaned against the wagon wheel and covered her face with both hands. Martha remembered how she and Papa had collided in their rush to Mother's side.

"Mary, you alright?" Papa's voice was gruff with concern. "You're doing too much. I can't have you down. Here, you take over the oxen for a while."

"Oh for goodness sakes! What's the matter with you all?" Mother sounded stern but she wasn't able to hide her weariness or worry from them.

Martha had suggested she ride inside and stay with Stephen to spell Mother.

Mother had been grateful for the break from Stephen and a breath of fresh air. "Eli, am I the only one going to handle the oxen today?"

To Martha, the sun setting on the edge of the horizon displayed itself as a huge red fireball. The other wagons were barely visible in the far distance. Soon would come the twilight, then night and darkness. She dreaded the thought of the family being out there alone in a strange land with perhaps Indians around them, and her little brother sick.

Papa, determined not to worry, had settled back. He intended to stop at the first place he could water the oxen and maybe stay the night. He might as well relax. He too hoped his little son would get better.

Cresting a hill with the sun in his eyes, Papa noted a rider coming his way. He reached back to ensure his rifle was handy as he watched the rider moving closer. He didn't feel right with the women so far behind. He pulled the oxen to a stop, jumped down, and yelled around the side of the wagon to them.

Mother glanced ahead to see that the oxen weren't moving; she heard Eli shout but couldn't make out his words.

Stephen! Something is wrong with Stephen. She gathered her skirt to run when she saw the rider. "Get to the wagon!" she screamed back to Bertha and Ruthie. The girls raced to crawl aboard the wagon.

Martha, unaware of the commotion outside, had been sponging Stephen. She looked up in surprise as her sisters scrambled into the wagon. "What's going on?"

Mother and the girls, though breathless, tried to explain all at the same time.

"Mother?" Martha interrupted them. "Stephen's fussing; he says he's thirsty for milk. What should I do?"

"Water, Martha, mix a bit of sugar in water and see if he'll drink it." Mother pushed her way to Stephen. His face was flushed, his eyes swollen, and his lips were crusty and dry.

Mother accepted the water as she gently lifted Stephen's head, enticing him to drink.

"No, Mother!" He tasted the water and pushed the cup away. "I don't want no water. I'm sirsty for milk."

Mother patiently coaxed him into taking a sip; through he protested, he took a swallow then greedily gulped down the contents of the cup. He licked his lips, sighed contentedly, and rolled away from her.

"Girls, I think he's feeling better. Did you see him drink the water?" Mother was elated as she hastily pulled herself up to the canvas opening. "Eli?"

Papa held up his hand to silence her. She backed up inside the opening to watch a horse and rider stop some distance away.

The tired, restless oxen shook their heads, rattling their chains; the sun was in Papa's face, making it difficult to recognize the rider.

A voice shouted, "Mr. Burt, I've a message for you."

Martha recognized Neil's voice and heard Papa tell him to come closer if he wasn't afraid.

Riding up beside the wagon, Neil informed them, "Mr. Kenyon doesn't want you folks out here alone after dark. Says to tell you he'll save you a place but to keep some distance from the others."

Papa was reluctant to accept the offer; he felt he'd been insulted and humiliated, but Mary and the family would feel safer near the others. He thanked Neil for coming back to deliver the message.

Neil had barely inquired as to how Stephen was doing when Mother stuck her head out the wagon. "Stephen's so much better, Neil. Why, he even drank a little water. You tell the folks we appreciate their saving us a place. And Neil? Thank you for coming all the way back to bring us such good news."

Martha watched Mother quickly turn her back to Neil as she wiped away tears. She felt sorry for Mother, trying desperately to be brave and courageous, accepting whatever came to her. Her faith was her strength, like now when she was scared of Stephen's sickness.

"Yoah, Martha, see you in camp!" Neil waved as he turned to ride away.

"Yes, Neil, thank you for coming," Martha called as she waved to him.

"I'm not about to push these tired beasts," Papa informed the family. "Instead I'm gonna enjoy this sunset."

"You know, Martha?" Papa didn't take his eyes from the road. "To worry only shows my lack of faith. I believe your little brother is strong enough to pull through whatever he's dealing with. He's not very big but he's like I was; he's a strong lil' feller."

Papa didn't see Mother, her face buried in her hands, her shoulders shaking with sobs as she wept silently, but Martha did.

Martha and Bertha walked along, enjoying the spectacular splendor of colors painted across the evening sky.

Martha sensed that Papa and Mother were happier knowing the others were waiting for them.

"You know, Martha," Bertha spoke up, "I was afraid earlier this afternoon we were going to be walking all night. I'll be so glad we're going to stop—but when?

Chapter 11

Martha awakened from a sound sleep to whispered voices. She pulled herself up on one elbow to better hear what was being said. It wasn't Papa's voice, he couldn't whisper; then she recognized Mr. Wilson's voice and the urgency with which he spoke.

"She's had this pain for some time, but it's getting worse. If you could come over, Mary, I don't know what to do for her."

Martha lay back down quietly as Papa and Mother shuffled around in the dark. She was awake, as they made their way to the Wilson's wagon, she was unable to sleep.

Mother climbed up the steps but once inside the dark wagon, she couldn't see, however, she heard Abigale moan.

"Abby, it's me, Mary. David, I need some light in here. I can't see a thing." Mother wondered why she bothered to whisper, everyone must be awake.

"Children, can you make your way to me?" She called out to them.

A small voice came out of the darkness. "Is my Momma going to be alright, Mrs. Burt?"

"I'm here to take care of your Momma, but I need your help right now. Can you come to me in the dark?"

First she had to move the children someplace else before she could take care of Abby.

Martha heard Papa return. "Is everything alright?" She whispered. "What's the matter with Mrs. Wilson, Papa?" Papa in the darkness of the wagon reached out to feel his way around. He lifted his arm in an attempt to locate the lantern and managed to strike several metal objects in his way setting off a percussion of sounds. "Where's the damn lantern anyway?" Martha knew he intended his oath to be a whisper, but Papa couldn't whisper.

She tried not to step on Bertha as she too reached into space for the lantern, but she managed to collide with papa upsetting them both.

Bertha was awakened by the commotion, but didn't know which way to elude the moving bodies above her. Her only defense was to yell, "Watch out, I'm down here."

"Then move, Bertha." Papa was able to right Martha and himself. "I'm in a hurry, give me some candles."

"What's going on anyway?" An irritated Bertha demanded to know, but Papa was gone.

"Something's wrong with Mrs. Wilson, Mother and Papa left with Mr. Wilson and I'm not sure what's happening." The words were barely out of Martha's mouth than Papa returned, carrying baby Pearl with Homer and Johnny tagging behind him.

"Martha, take these children and make them comfortable. I need to help your Mother." He handed baby Pearl, wrapped in her quilt, up to Martha.

"Papa! You can't do this. Papa, we best not." But again Papa was gone.

"And just what are we expected to do with them?" Bertha snapped at her sister. "Bertha, quit being nasty, we wouldn't be asked to do this if it weren't something important . Here, take baby Pearl. Here's my hand boys." She helped them onto the nearest tick mattress and covered them with a quilt. "I know you can't see, but I don't think you're going to be here for long."

"Not when Mrs. Kenyon finds out what Papa's just done. We won't be here for very long either," Bertha grumbled.

The children were cold, afraid, and confused. They silently followed Martha's directions. Her gesture of kindness was the first since their Daddy told them their Mother was sick and needed them to be quiet.

Sleep had been impossible for them listening to Momma moan and cry out in a pain they didn't understand, but that something was hurting her.

To leave her was difficult but coming to the Burt's wagon was worse. It had something to do with Stephen.

Earlier the grownups had talked about him in loud voices that frightened them. What was going to happen to them when they were found in the Burt wagon?

Martha drew back the flap to see light from the candles illuminate the Wilson Canvas as silhouetted figures moved around inside the wagon.

A small voice distracted her. "Martha, can I have a drink of water? I can't sleep no more. Why is Johnny and Homer here?" "Stephen, is that you? You're feeling better?" Martha desperately wished Mother was here. What if Stephen has the plague? I'm never going to keep everyone separated. Maybe Papa will come and take the Wilson children back to their own beds.

She stepped outside to fill his cup from the water barrel and returned to find Stephen sitting up.

"I feel just fine, Martha," he told her. "Johnny are you asleep?"

Suddenly laughter filled the dark Burt wagon, the tension was broke as the wide-awake children excitedly talked back and forth to each other.

After the children had been cared for, candles and a lantern lit, Mary Burt was able to concentrate on Abby and her condition. The first thing on Mother's plan of action was for hot water. "David, I need some hot water, if you please." Had Mother been able to observe the men's faces, she'd have noticed the surprised exchange of glances. A fire? When they were trying to keep out of sight of the Indians. They'd traveled late into the night hoping to make the LaSalle settlement, however, darkness closed in on them so it was decided to quietly camp where they were, and travel into the Settlement early in the morning. And here Mary was requesting a fire!

Papa shrugged his shoulders. "So we attract the Indians. Maybe they can loan us a Medicine Man and a couple of extra horses and wagons to help out here. They might as well make themselves useful."

David chuckled at Papa's remark, the chuckle turned into laughter and if he didn't get hold of himself, David knew he'd be crying next. Eli's remark wasn't all that humorous but the idea struck his fancy and amused him. He wiped his eyes and caught his breath. He'd done the best possible thing to go for Eli and Mary Burt. He knew Abby was grateful and she'd be better soon with Mary in charge. He was glad he'd stood his ground today when the issue came up of bringing the Burt's within safety of other wagons for the night. The fire started as a twinkle in the dark night, but soon gave way to a bright, blazing signal. Eli and David busily filled every kettle they could find, and put the water over the flames to heat as Mary had requested.

The noisy voices of the children drifted out to the men. "Eli, I knew your little boy wasn't contagious, that was Mrs. Kenyon's idea. She's like all women, they get these peculiar notions at times." David laughed quietly. "Everyone knows young'uns can get to ailin' easy. Wonder it wasn't one of mine."

77

Papa when he heard Stephen's laughter had to agree with David. He'd never thought of Stephen as bad off in the first place.

"David, come close," Mary Burt called from the wagon. "I need you."

"Mary, is Abby alright? My wife's, she's alright?"

"David, go get Mrs. Kenyon, I need help." She disappeared back inside the wagon.

He'd heard authority like this before, from women, when his other babies were born. He lost little time in running to wake the Kenyon's.

The flap covering the rear opening had been pulled down, securing the canvas. Slapping his hand against it, and at the same time calling, "Mrs. Kenyon, Mrs. Kenyon can you hear me? It's David Wilson." Above the racket he made, he heard stirring inside the wagon.

"Yeah, whata ya want?" Alex Kenyon's grumpy voice answered. "Quit hittin' the canvas 'fore ya tear a hole in it."

"David, what's the matter, whata ya want?" Ruth Kenyon's muffled voice inquired.

It's my wife, she needs help and Mary Burt says ta tell you, she needs ya right now."

"I'll be right there, David. Tell Mary, I'll be right there."

David decided to wait for her. Gazing heavenward to a sky full of stars and a slice of moon, he paused to send up a silent prayer.

Please, God, I try not to ask for much. I try to deal with my trials and not complain, but my Abby, Lord. Please spare her for the children's sake and for me. Please be merciful to us, Lord.

How will I come to terms with you, Lord, if something happens to Abby. I'm not strong, Lord, not to live alone with out her. Please don't ask this of me.

Ruth Kenyon appeared and David helped her down from her wagon. They walked silently across to his wagon in the light from the bright campfire.

There was plenty Ruth Kenyon would have liked to say, but she felt pity for the family. Out here in this wilderness without a doctor. It was going to take a miracle, she reasoned, to save this lady and her baby.

Papa had gone to retrieve some support for his friend. "David, you need a good dose of this medicine. It's the best, Doctor Burt recommends it at a time like this." He handed David a whisky jug.

David tipped the jug up and swallowed a couple of big swigs before handing it back. Eli guessed David needed a couple more doses to help along his cure. It amazed him the patient didn't choke on the first drink. "Here, my friend, that was only your first dose. You need to follow it with another."

"Eli, I've never been this scared as I am right now." David had squatted down on his heels before the fire as he unfolded his tale of woe.

There, Papa thought, the patient's showing signs of getting better already. "Eli, the life long legacy of the Wilson men has been, 'we men don't show fear, and we aren't permitted to cry.' It would be an exposure of our weakness, and that we've lost our self-control. Now we believe in lettin' our womenfolk cry and show fear, because by nature they're weak. We men are their superiors, protectors. We're responsible for them. A man is born strong by nature and must show it to qualify for the benefits of men." David shifted his position to put his head in his hands. "But right now Eli, I'm tellin you, I'm scared. I'm scared for my Abby."

Eli handed David the bottle. "You better wet your whistle after that little speech, my good man."

Once again David tilted the jug and swallowed noisily a few gulps. "Eli," he said, wiping his mouth with the back of his hand, "my Father-in-Law is known as a Gentleman, he's well known and respected. Manages a large plantation with cotton and slaves. He's big in political circles and I stole his daughter from him."

"When Homer, our first born came, I even named him after the old man. I vowed, my son would never face the discrimination I went through coming from a Cherokee Rose. I never knew my Mother, I was raised by my Father's people, who reminded me, with their back-handed insinuations, who I was. I brought my darlin' bride out here, thinkin' a new start would be good for us and look what I've done to her. How much is a man expected to endure?" His voice had dwindled to a whisper.

Eli didn't much care to see his friend, with his elbows resting on his knees and hands covering his head, appear defeated.

David reached for the whisky jug. "Have I destroyed the most precious things I've ever had by my selfishness? What a fool I am to think I could do better."

"You know, David, you take my oxen."

"Sorry, Eli, sir--- now you show me a horse and I'll tell you blindfolded how old it is, if it's been abused or injured, but an ox? I have to confess I don't know the animal, Eli, sir."

"Like I was sayin', David, we men, we mean well, but sometimes we do harm. The easy part is we have to learn the hard way."

"Sure we do, Eli, sir. Yes, sir, Eli sir."

Papa decided things were going to get a mite unpleasant if Mrs. Kenyon and Mary found out he'd gotten David drunk. It only took a couple of swallows. That was all they had." Elsa Crawford had awakened and was aware of what was taking place. She decided to get up and make coffee for everyone. She hoped she had enough sweet buns to go around. Poor Mrs. Wilson, she had no business to come out here in this rough wilderness. It wasn't a journey for such a lovely lady.

Elsa's opinion was that, God, being a man, did he know about birthin' and death like a woman did? She reasoned that God got himself so busy at times, was why women slipped away. We women understand these things even though we might rank pretty low when it comes to importance, like doing the Lord's work for him.

We try, she thought, we try, and we go right on creatin' don't we?

Elsa shook her head, hadn't she been through it herself. She was fortunate that God hadn't been busy during her time. By the time my Lizzy grows up, I hope things will have changed. She didn't see how it could be, though, considering all babies came out the same way. She was so thankful it wasn't her child over there in that wagon fightin' to birth a baby and keep hold of her own life. What a shame for them both. What if one should lose the fight to survive?

On her way to the fire she prayed. Please, God, have time to be with Abby tonight.

The men, who were wakened by the commotion taking place outside their wagons, came in support of David. Each arrived with his whisky. The bottle and jugs were as important as the water always necessary at birthings. They agreed, they never could understand why so much water was needed. But it was a man's duty to stand with a kettle of boiling water in one hand and their bottle of fortification in the other and they better have whichever was needed handy and right there.

The fellows became a happy relaxed group, while the women silently hurried back and forth between their wagons.

The women were bonded together in assisting the one needing care, as the one receiving care put her trust in her providers.

United, the women realized Abby's fears were their burden to bear. Her hopes were theirs also. There was neither bias nor prejudice, only gentle coaxing, and encouragement at dawn's first light when Abby was delivered of a tiny lifeless boy child, who needed to be hastily buried. He would never be known or know love.

Folks gathered around the fire, silently bowed their heads after being told of the tragedy. In sympathy, in grief and out of respect for the Wilson's, these people felt as if they were leaving a part of themselves out here in this wilderness. A baby boy forever lost to them. There was never a bigger campfire as a beacon. Its flames caressed the dark sky for everyone to see. No one questioned its size. It simply blazed up quickly and burned itself out. A mound of ashes was all that was left to tell of its existence in the dark night.

Mother mentally listed her needs to ready Abby for traveling. She needed some good broth to replace the blood loss and for strength. Her breasts would need to be bound as soon as possible and she needed laudanum for pain.

Standing up, Mother felt a wave of light-headedness pass over her, but suddenly remembered, she hadn't had time to think about Stephen. Surely someone would have come to tell her if he were worse off.

After the tragedy of tonight, he was more precious to her than ever before. She longed to take him in her arms. As soon as David came to sit with his wife, she'd go to her little son.

The wagon train families, out of respect, allowed David and his Abby a brief time alone.

Mother, on return to her wagon, couldn't have been more pleased or grateful than to see Stephen. He appeared a little pale, but he was beautiful in her eyes. Eli was right, it must have been a touch of Summer, she decided, as she busied herself with placing cold vinegar compresses to Papa's head and seeing to the breakfast preparation.

The Burt girls were aware of how tired Mother was, and Papa must be too, the way he complained of a headache and refused breakfast. They discussed the idea between them; he might have the same ailment Stephen suffered with. However, they didn't want to upset Mother, so kept their thoughts to themselves.

Before the wagons moved out, everyone gathered around a little mound of hastily dug earth. It was marked with a pile of stones, placed atop the little grave to keep it safe. Sam Emigh spoke a few words and Alex Kenyon said a prayer.

David Wilson's head was bowed with grief. He knelt to place a hand atop the little mound. His two sons, Homer and Johnny, were by his side. It was a somber group turned back for their wagons. Abby, asleep, was unaware of the burial for her baby boy. The folks were a weary group from a difficult night of lost labor. They were grieving for the Wilson family. Yea, though they had walked through the shadow of death, they were now in the valley and it was without fear. They would follow the road to the Settlement ahead.

Chapter 12

In the late afternoon the last of April, the Burts joined with covered wagons, buggies, and buckboards entering the busy town of LaSalle, Illinois, a trading post settlement with the remains of the original fort built in the 1600s by the French explorer and trader Robert De LaSalle still visible. Their journey had brought them one hundred and fifty miles from Chicago, with two thousand miles ahead of them to travel.

Mr. Emigh told Martha and her family how Indians from the Iowa, Otos, Fox, Osage, Kansas, and Great Plains tribes shared the settlement with inhabitants attending mission schools set up by the early Jesuit priests.

The Illinois River to the south was busy as pack boats with supplies and passengers, keelboats, canoes, and pirogues loaded with furs made their way to the settlement.

Papa's restless oxen, forced to walk at a slow pace, were thirsty and impatient, tossing their heads in protest and irritation with the scourge of flies pestering them.

Inside the wagon, Stephen and the Wilson boys peered out at the surroundings. They and the children passing by in other wagons silently stared at each other.

"Johnny! Look over there—that dog—he's got on a harness." Stephen jumped up to point out the dog. "He looks funny pulling those sticks behind him."

"Martha, I've never seen so many handsome fellows," Bertha exclaimed. "And they look to be our age too. Oh—don't you hope they're all going west?" She and her sister found it difficult to stay modestly back inside the wagon.

Mr. Kenyon pulled off to one side of the dirt road. Mrs. Kenyon signaled for everyone to line up behind her wagon.

Martha glimpsed across a nearby bare field to where Indians had erected their conical, animal skin tepees with outside campfires smoking. Noisy, swarthy-skinned children, some lighter in color, but all with big, expressive, liquid dark eyes, came with their mongrel dogs to stare at the settlers or to beg.

"What tribe do those Indians belong to?" Martha pointed them out to Papa.

"From the looks of their tepees, I'd say they belong to the Plains Indians. They're great hunters, I've heard," Papa replied.

The exhausted members of the wagon train were eager to find a camp area and settle in for the night. Mr. Kenyon suggested, "Sam, you and Neil can ride into the settlement faster than we can get these wagon through. Find out where it's recommended we park. I'll watch you're team while your gone."

Papa waited until the two rode off before returning to his family. "Best stay in the wagon until we're settled," he told them. "There's too much confusion going on around us."

While waiting for the men to return, Papa studied the fort's impressive structure. At each end of the circular, high, thick wooden walls were two wide, tall, wooden gates, which could be closed during an Indian raid. The fort presided before him was still and unused.

Mother used the time to look in on Abby. It was amazing to her how fast Stephen had come out of his fever, but Abby's condition disturbed her.

Mr. Emigh and Neil reported back. "We're to work our wagons around back of the fort. There's plenty of space for camping down by the river."

The wagons were unable to form their customary circle and had to pull up side by side, facing the river gently lapping at its banks. Tall pines and leafy maples provided shade. However, the livestock would have to be tethered beside the wagons. There wasn't enough room to make a corral for them.

"I'm not lettin' my livestock out of my sight," Tom Crawford commented. The others agreed. They too were uneasy with so many Indians milling around.

"That's fine with me." Neil was heard as he expressed his anger and disgust. "I don't want them savages even close ta me."

In a terse voice his pa retorted, "Don't invite trouble, Neil."

Stephen and Johnny nearby heard the conversation between the two. The little boys glanced around them. "Who's trouble?" Johnny asked. They didn't wait to find out who trouble was. They were anxious to be off and investigate their new world.

Papa called the boys to come help him. While he waited for them he gazed at the well-grazed fields around him. He wasn't happy having to feed the oxen from his coveted grain supply.

When the boys arrived he explained, "It's a bit of a walk to the river to water the oxen and Mr. Wilson's horses. Whata ya say we fill Mother's washtubs here with water for 'em?" He and the boys worked up a sweat as they carried buckets of water until the tubs were filled and the livestock were satisfied.

Mother was grateful the Kenyon boys had taught her to build a fire pit as she piled twigs into hers. She then took a Lucifer with a small square of sandpaper from a tight-lidded jar and, deftly holding the Lucifer away from her, scratched it against the rough paper. She was experienced enough to know the matches were unpredictable; when lit they exploded, shooting sparks randomly, and emitted a nasty sulfur odor.

Mother commented to Papa as he walked by, "There doesn't appear to be much wood around."

Earlier Papa had spied an Indian with his dog harnessed, pulling two wooden shafts toting a load of wood. He, with the boys at his heels, went in search of the Indian. When they found him, Papa with the help of hand signals interpreted his desire to buy the wood. He reached into his pocket and extracted two pennies to offer the Indian.

The boys watched the two barter, with Papa finally handing the Indian twenty-five cents for wood, and it was to be unloaded at Mother's campsite. It surprised the boys as they were leaving to hear the Indian grunt to himself, then he turned to thank Papa in fluent English for his business.

Mother, exhausted from a sleepless night and miles of walking, asked the girls to decide on supper for her just as Mr. Emigh walked up with some dried apples he'd had soaking but didn't want to fuss with. Mother thanked him and insisted he and his boys take supper with them before she turned to ask Martha to stir up an apple pan dowdy. "Oh, and Martha, use a bit of cinnamon to spice them nicely, won't you?"

Bertha had requested cornbread. "But Mother, how do you expect me to make it without milk or eggs?"

"You use a teacup of starter in your ground cornmeal, a little water, a bit of sugar and salt, and pour a little melted lard into the batter. It'll come out just fine," Mother instructed her.

Ruthie filled the big coffeepot with water and set it to boil before she started the coffee beans roasting.

"Make a big pot, Ruthie. We're going to need it with the Emigh and Wilsons sharing our supper."

Martha prepared ham gravy the way Papa liked it. She slowly browned the flour and lard together to make a rich, brown roux before adding the water and ham. The camp area soon filled with the tantalizing odors of cooking food.

Papa stopped by to caution his family, "Easy on the wood; that's all we have."

"I hope it lasts, Papa. We'll need wood to bake bread later this evening," Martha stated.

The little boys were sent out to tell the men when supper was ready. Everyone assembled around the provisional box tables. Papa asked a blessing before plates were laden with the tasty food.

As they were eating, a young Sioux woman appeared, dressed in a well-worn, deerskin dress with long-legged, beaded moccasins. She carried a papoose in a blanket tied on her back and held a little dark-eyed child by its hand.

Everyone paused to watch as she held out two wooden bowls to Mother, who accepted the dishes and scooped up cornbread, ladled gravy over it, and handed them to the young mother.

The Indian woman, as must have been her custom, backed up several steps and lowered her head with its two long, black braids before she turned to sit down by the Burts' wagon with her children.

The Burt girls watched quietly. Neil's neck and ears burned a fiery red as he looked on. Mr. Wilson continued eating. Papa and Sam Emigh admired Mother's quiet dignity. The boys stopped eating to watch the silent exchange between the women.

After the Indian women had been served, it was as if nothing unusual had taken place. The families went about consuming the contents of the big Dutch kettles.

"Cured the bacon yourself, Eli?" Mr. Emigh asked as he dug into a big slab of corn bread covered with the smoke-flavored ham gravy.

"Yep, sure did—you call it bacon?"

"Ham, bacon, it's all smoke-cured pork, isn't it?" Sam asked.

"You're right there. We brought along both kinds. Happen to like the smoky-flavored ham best in gravy like this; not as salty as ma' bacon."

After the cornbread and ham gravy, the families went on to feast on the warm, spicy, sweet apple pan dowdy served with cups of hot, strong coffee.

"You women make coffee like ma' ma used to make it," Neil stated.

"Thank you, Neil, but it's like all pot coffee, isn't it?" Mother inquired.

"Oh no, not the way Pa makes it."

"How's that, Neil?" Papa asked.

"Well, Pa pours water in the coffeepot, adds the beans, and then boils it till the water turns brown." Everyone had a laugh at Neil's explanation. Mr. Emigh quickly interrupted to exclaim. "I sure did a good job with this delicious pan dowdy, if I do say so myself."

"Pa," Nathan shyly reproached him, "we all know you didn't make this."

"Nathan, I only help a little. Without your pa, we wouldn't have any." Martha carried the big coffeepot over to offer Mr. Wilson more coffee.

Poor David, he looks so wretched, Mother thought, looking over at him. "Think I'll go sit with Abby for a while, Mr. Wilson." She thought he looked pleased with the idea.

"Thanks, Mrs. Burt. She was sleeping when I came over here. Mrs. McGraw brought over some broth but she wasn't feeling up ta eating such. I'm kind of worried about her. She's been through so much, and the journey is difficult for her."

"You men enjoy your coffee. I'll go freshen Abby; she'll feel better." Mother hoped to reassure David and kept herself busy besides. She was likely to fall asleep on her feet.

The girls had cleaned away supper when Mother returned. She set the bread to bake, grateful for the work to ease her worried concern for Abby. She thought Abby appeared weaker than when she'd previously seen her.

The Kenyons and Crawfords came to sit by the Burts' fire. Brian and Jenny McGraw joined the group and took part in the lively discussion concerning tomorrow's plans.

Ruth Kenyon inquired, "So you're suggesting we take only one wagon at a time, or one wagon and we all go in it?"

"I ain't leavin' my wagon unattended," Alex Kenyon sputtered.

"I can walk over to the trading post and leave Mr. Kenyon here with his wagon," Mrs. Kenyon offered.

"Now I ask you, Mrs. Kenyon?" Alex inquired disgustedly. "How'er you expectin' to carry your supplies back? In a sack on your back?" he guffawed.

"Mr. Kenyon, you don't know how to shop for me. You haven't a notion what I need."

Neil sensed an argument coming on between the Kenyons and quickly interrupted. "When they're ready I can escort the girls. We'll need to double up and make a couple of trips back and forth—but is this alright with everyone?"

Mr. McGraw's opinion was, "Sam's got the smaller wagon an' Ah'm obliged ta help tote supplies fur ya, ladies; that's if'n we's decide ta take one wagon."

"What'd ya think of this idea, Sam?" Papa asked.

Mother glanced up in time to see David Wilson silently slip away from the group.

"I've too much to do afore noon," Elsa Crawford stated. "I'll be here to keep an eye on the wagons for them that wants to go early in the day. Mr. Crawford can pick up my supplies."

Martha looked up to see Mother beckoning to her. "I think it's a good night for poppin' corn, how about you?"

The big Dutch kettles were set over the fire, and Mother melted some bacon grease before adding a handful of dried yellow corn kernels to the big kettle. She covered it with a lid only until the kernels started to explode and filled the air with a fragrant aroma.

Papa came to pour the fluffy white kernels into another big kettle. Mother sprinkled a bit of salt over the popcorn before inviting everyone to help themselves to a handful of crisp, crunchy, bacon-flavored popcorn. Martha and Mother repeated the procedure three times before everyone was satisfied.

Martha watched as Mother carried to the Indian woman, sitting beside the wagon, a bowl full of popcorn for her and the children. Again, as the young woman silently accepted the popcorn from Mother, she stood up then backed away several steps with her head lowered in a show of gratitude. The group continued to eat their popcorn as they witnessed the ritual. Mother's smile and nod was the only response between the two women. The young woman sat back down on her blanket beside her babies after Mother turned to leave.

Mr. McGraw sent Junior for his Jew's harp. The boy returned with not only his pa's instrument but an empty liquor jug. The two commenced to entertain with irresistible, toe-tapping music. The McGraw family demonstrated their knowledge of clog dancing, and before long the others were executing the steps to the twang of the Jew's harp and the "thug thug" from Junior's jug.

Neil danced with all the ladies and girls. However, his greatest enjoyment was with Martha. He held as her close as was permissible, swinging her about until she was breathless, her long dark hair swept out behind her and her color heightened from the exertion.

The riverside took on a festive atmosphere during the evening as some distance down from them another group was heard clapping and singing to the sounds of fiddlers.

The fire died down, the coffeepot was empty, and the music, dancing, and popcorn became memories as the folks made their way back to their wagons.

Mrs. Crawford and Lizzy carried baby Pearl, Abby's sweet-natured little girl, away with them, over the protests of the Burts.

Papa questioned Mother, "What do you suggest I do with our guest? She's wrapped up her young'uns and herself in that blanket of hers and she's asleep under our wagon."

"Shouldn't we let her sleep there, dear? What are you suggesting?"

"Mary, must you always answer me with a question? I thought it bein' a nice night and all, our young'uns bedded down, you and me might sleep under our own wagon."

"Shall I pull out the ticks?" Mother asked.

"See, there you go again. I asked you a simple question and you question me back. Ah—let's get ta bed. But tomorrow, Mary?" Papa grumbled. "I suggest you take care of this problem. You insisted on feeding her—next thing, she'll be wantin' ta make the entire trip with us."

Before drifting off to sleep, Martha gave thought to Mrs. Wilson. She'd been missed this evening. Martha liked Mrs. Wilson. She was a lady like Mother was. Mr. Wilson was such a handsome gentleman, but he was certainly showing signs of his worry. He was so quiet around everyone. She'd go with Mother to visit Mrs. Wilson tomorrow.

Martha in her prayers requested God in his infinite love to heal Mrs. Wilson quickly for her family's sake. She couldn't imagine life for Mr. Wilson without his gracious wife, nor the children their Mother, nor the rest of the wagon train members.

An occasional restless movement was heard from the livestock, as well as the sound of the river, and coyotes up in the hills sang throughout the night, but the exhausted travelers were oblivious.

Chapter 13

To a seasoned farmer like Papa, as he climbed down from the wagon and hurried to start a fire, the chill in the air forecasted stormy weather ahead. He vigorously rubbed his hands together to warm them while he waited for the hungry flames to chew into the dry kindling and produce some heat.

Mother crawled out of her warm bed to face a cold, dark morning. She hurried towards the warmth of the fire. She was thankful Eli had a fire burning; she'd make him a pot of coffee before she started the breakfast mush, and there were cinnamon rolls to go along with their Sunday breakfast.

Papa returned shortly with a bucket of warm milk from the cow he'd purchased. "Mary, good-lookin' bucketful, wouldn't you say?"

"I heard you talking to my little cow," Mother coquettishly teased him. "You just have a way with the ladies is all. You didn't sleep well last night?"

"I'm itchin' ta get movin' again." he set the bucket down to embrace his wife.

"Here, Eli, fresh coffee." She disengaged herself from his arms to pour the coffee. Silently they toasted each other before they savored the fragrant, hot, bitter brew and watch the night sky give up to steel gray daylight.

One by one the girls came to cuddle around the brisk, crackling, warm fire and brush away wafts of irritating smoke.

"I'll never get used to this smoke." Ruthie hugged herself to keep warm. "I think it's going to snow. Papa, could it still snow this time of year?" she asked.

"Something tells me there's a rain storm brewin'," he replied.

The boys descended to push their way between the girls and get near their share of the heat.

"Papa, do we leave today?" Stephen asked through chattering teeth.

Mother announced, "Breakfast is nearly ready, and then everyone needs to prepare for church. We can walk to the settlement; it isn't a far a walk."

"Oh no, not church. We don't like church do we, Johnny?" Stephen protested. "It takes all day and we was plannin' on playin' down by the river."

"It's only for a little while," Mother assured him as she dished up bowls of mush to hand around. "We have so much to be thankful for, Stephen. You and I of all people need to give thanks."

"I'll go with you, Mrs. Burt," Johnny said as he accepted his bowl of ground wheat mush covered with fresh milk.

Papa, overhearing the boy's plans to play by the river, warned them about its swiftness. "It'll carry you away before we can get to you fellows. Best stay away from it."

"One day my momma took us to church," Homer spoke up, "and the preacher man said Jesus told his friend to walk on the water. I sure wished I'd been there. I'd a liked tryin' ta do that."

A cry, an animal wail of agony unlike any on earth, as man complains in his helplessness which he feels is an injustice dealt to him by God—so was David Wilson's cry heard throughout the campsites.

Families came down from their wagons. They stopped whatever they were doing and hurried to the Wilsons' wagon. Papa, first to reach the wagon, flung aside the flap to witness David holding the inert body of his Abby clutched to his chest.

He turned to those congregated around the wagon and held up his hand to signal them that Mr. Wilson should be left alone in his grief with his beloved wife, Abby, the mother of his children.

Without her apron or bonnet Mrs. Kenyon arrived out of breath, her hair disheveled. She immediately assigned and delegated chores to those clustered around the wagon, with their whispered concerns for Mr. Wilson and his family.

Neil was dispatched to summon the minister. Men were ordered to bring out the pine boards carried with them to build the coffin. Women, without hesitation, began the preparation for Abby's burial.

Ruth Kenyon's opinion was that "Abigale Wilson was delivered of an unnatural birth, and from the odor, I do believe there were complications that caused her passing."

Jenny McGraw, who was put in charge of food preparation for those able to stop and eat, had come to suggest the women take time for a cup of coffee. She waited for Elsa Crawford, with her arms full of soiled linen, to pass, and noticed the children gathered around the wagon.

"You young'uns got nothin' better to do than get underfoot? Go play somewhere's else," she yelled at them. "Cain't ya see we's busy here?"

Martha came to rescue the children and guide them away from the wagon. She could see concerned expressions on their little faces. None of the grown-ups had taken time to explain Mrs. Wilson's passing to them.

"Let's give the women room to work. We'll be close here by the fire if they need us."

Martha glanced over to see Homer was sitting by himself, his little shoulders hunched forward and his arms folded over his drawn-up knees. He looked so pitiful and forlorn as he lifted his head now and again to look over at his wagon, then buried his head again in his arms.

Martha started for Homer to comfort him when Johnny tugged on her skirt. "Martha, what happened to my momma?" His eyes were big and round in his thin, elfin face. "Why won't they let me see my momma?"

Martha was inexperienced in explaining death and felt hopelessly inadequate. Here were two little boys, their lives disrupted as well as those of the other children. But these children were not her family. There were proper ways families explained death to their children, but there weren't any family members around to answer their questions.

Martha was at a loss for words and wished for her Granny. *Granny would know how to talk to Johnny and the others. She knows about these things.*

"Johnny, I wish I knew why God took your momma to heaven, but I don't," was all Martha could tell him "My momma's gone forever?" he asked in a forlorn-sounding, small voice.

"Your daddy's still here, and you have us. Your mommy will never be far away. You'll see her in your dreams and you'll remember the things she loved and shared with you."

Martha watched his little chin tremble as he gave way to deep sobs. "She's left us all alone hasn't she? She left me." Martha held him close and let him cry. He wiped at tear-filled eyes with his little fists. "I want my momma back," he wailed.

"Shush, little one. You're going to be alright, Johnny. We'll take good care of you. Hush, little one," Martha crooned, holding him in her arms.

Back from his errand, Neil was in time to catch Martha's gesture toward Homer. He turned to see the boy with his head down on his knee, the little shoulders heaving in silent sobs.

Neil, with as much cheerfulness as he was able to exhibit, exclaimed, "We're gonna need us a mess of fresh fish fer supper, everyone."

The children, who were sided in support of the Wilson boys, found Homer ignored them, and Johnny halfheartedly allowed them, in their compassion, to cheer him up.

"Neil," Stephen shrugged, "we don't got any fishin' poles to fish with."

"Oh, you will. I'm fixin' lines, but you have to handle the poles."

"Neil, you must be starved; you haven't eaten yet," Martha exclaimed. "Mrs. McGraw is in charge of breakfast but we have some cinnamons rolls." Martha was thankful for the excuse to busy herself. "Who knows when we'll eat again?" she prattled on. "I know, everyone, let's have cinnamon rolls with Neil." All the while she was busy, she was aware of Johnny's sad little face, watching her every move as he picked listlessly at his roll.

Ginny McGraw came looking for Bertha and Ruthie. Lizzy Crawford, with baby Pearl on her hip, handed Martha a pan of sweet buns. "Mother says these are to go with coffee," she said before she set off in search of the other girls.

Martha decided that even though she'd been brought up to believe death was natural, there just wasn't anyway out of its pain. There were no easy answers. No simple way to take away the heartache and sorrow for the little Wilson brothers.

Nothing she could say or do would help them. She wasn't looking forward to enduring anymore agony like this for the rest of her journey.

Mother needed a breath of fresh air. She'd walked a short distance to get away by herself when she discovered the plant with a little golden flower. *It's so magnificent in such a harsh place*, she thought as she gazed down at it. *Like Abby, so magnificent but so out of place.*

She stooped down and plucked the little blossom. She was impressed that it could survive.

Abby had been laid out in her hastily built coffin, dressed in the nicest dress the women could find. Between her folded hands Mary Burt placed the delicate, golden dandelion.

The church services were attended by more travelers than local citizens. The Burt family recognized Mr. Goodman, whom they'd met earlier, and concluded the short, plump little lady with him was Mrs. Goodman.

After the service introductions were exchanged, Mrs. Goodman, when told the details of the young mother and wife's death, wiped away tears. "This journey is so difficult. It's mean. Its demands take so much out of us women and our babies."

Papa held David's arm to steady him. *When has this man eaten last and had a decent night's sleep? Now he has this heavy grief to bear up under. How much can a man take?* Papa couldn't help but wonder.

The pastor assembled the quiet, solemn group and gave them instructions to follow the horse and buggy bearing Abby in the pine box to her final resting place amid the soft, rolling green hills overlooking the busy valley. The river below mirrored the reflection of a steel gray sky.

At the newly dug gravesite, the reverend told how Abigale Carrie Wilson lost first her stillborn son and then her own life, "far from her desired destiny and far from her tiny baby." He went on to explain, "Her dreams of a new start in life would never be realized here on earth; they were never meant to be. For these two, the greatest journey had been completed, and she with her little son is now resting safely in the hands of their Creator."

Abby's friends watched her family drop a handful of dirt over the coffin. They were leaving her behind as they'd done her infant son.

A little wooden cross inscribed with her name and date was erected to mark the spot of her final destination.

Each man and woman assembled around Abby understood from the beginning of this journey that there would be difficulties and miseries. They had been told the road leading west was already decorated with numerous markers as the only remaining evidence to the person's existence. But to them the challenge of going out West was a worthwhile endeavor they were willing to take.

Mrs. Kenyon began a hymn. To those around her, it came as a surprise to hear her beautiful contralto lift in the song "Blest Be the Tie that Binds," a grand old hymn familiar to everyone as they joined in with her. At the end of the hymn, one by one a silent farewell was said to Abby before the families turned back for their wagons.

Martha was behind her parents and heard Mother softly say, "Oh Eli, David's had to suffer so much lately, and those poor little children." Martha and Mother wiped at tears from the profound sorrow they felt for the Wilson family.

Martha glanced back over her shoulder to see Mr. Wilson with his two little boys. They held on to each other; three heads were bowed under a monstrous grief as David said good-bye to his beloved wife and the children to their mother.

Martha arrived at an unbelievable perception. The men—why there wasn't a wet eye among them. She realized she hadn't seen one man take time to openly comfort Mr. Wilson.

Men's control and restraint of themselves mystified her. Even Neil had excused himself to stay at the campsite and "protect things," he'd told her.

It bothered Martha that a decent time to mourn wasn't being observed. They'd not only hastily buried Mrs. Wilson, but now everyone was in a hurry to move on.

Martha found it difficult to accept this situation. In fact, she was homesick for Granny and the way things used to be done.

The sky darkened, a cold wind whipped up, and the chirps and songs from the birds heard earlier had ceased as the storm signaled its approach.

Everyone gathered to share supper. A big, center fire burned energetically, and clean clothes flapped nosily on a clothesline as they were buffeted with gusts from a brisk wind.

"Well, David?" Papa turned to him. "What can we do to help you get ready for tomorrow, or what are your plans?"

David wasn't sure what he should do; he hadn't planned to make the journey alone, and with small youngsters. They were but babies. "What happens to them," his voice grew husky and broke, "if something happens to me?"

Sam Emigh explained, "There's only my two boys and me. You get used to cooking and dish washing; and besides, I've learned you're never alone, David, unless you choose to be."

"Your boys are older than mine, Sam; they can take care of themselves."

"If you take time to notice, David, these good women around you have had your youngsters, allowing you time to care for your wife," Sam reminded him.

David looked up in surprise. "Your right, Sam. Ladies," he looked around, "I thank you. I—I wasn't aware … I didn't realize."

Ruth Kenyon explained, "No child would ever be abandoned while with this group. If you decide to turn back, David. You're certainly going to be alone." Everyone nodded in silent agreement.

"I don't want to pose a hindrance is all. I'd like, for the sake of my youngsters, to go on. I'll learn women's work if you women'll show me.

I'm willin' to carry my share of the load, if you'll accept my travelin' on with ya'll." David passed a hand quickly over his eyes, lifted his head skyward for a brief moment, and blinked rapidly several times before he could face those around him.

From somewhere a jug appeared and was passed from man to man. "Just a wee swaller?" Mr. McGraw inquired of his wife. The women continued their conversations and politely ignored the men.

Martha dreamily poked at the bright embers of the fire with a stick. "I love the orange color of the fire," she commented.

Bertha gazed into the quivering flames and remarked, "Papa once told me that the Indians believe you can see spirits dancing in the flames if you look for them."

Martha glanced over to Neil. "Have you ever seen faces or forms in the flames?" she asked.

"Naw," he said disgustedly. "Ain't got time fer such nonsense."

"I have, Martha," Homer spoke up. "I like to watch the fire dancers."

"Come on, fellows," Mr. Wilson called. "It's time we settled down for the night."

"Can't we sleep with Stephen again to night?" the boys pleaded.

"Not tonight. I need your company. Look—see that lightnin' over yonder? You best sleep with me tonight." Two little boys reluctantly left the fireside.

After the others departed for the night, Martha and Neil stayed beside the fire.

His knees drawn up with his arms wrapped around them for his chin to rest on, he watched the firelight play across Martha's face as she stirred hot coals with her stick. He wondered what she was thinking. He felt the need to be included in her thoughts, but just then he was interrupted.

"Martha, come on ta bed. I wanna turn in," Papa called.

She tossed the remains of her stick into the flickering flames and turned to see firelight mirrored in Neil's eyes. "Tomorrow, would you mind if I rode with you for a while now that we have a horse of our own? But of course, I'll need to ask Papa first."

"Martha, you know very well I'd like nothing better, but what if it rains?"

"Oh, I'm on my way to pray it doesn't."

They laughed at her show of confidence as Neil stood up and reached to help her stand. She allowed herself to be pulled into his arms before they walked hand in hand to her wagon.

Chapter 14

A heavy rain fell throughout the night, and a fierce wind buffeted the big canvases with such force it rocked the wagons. It rained so hard the campground became islands surrounded by miniature lakes

Under the steady rain and wind, Mother's Lucifer refused to light the kindling. "Eli, I simply can't get a fire going," she complained, tossing aside another spent match.

Papa's attempts were unsuccessful. "Looks like we'll have to do without a fire this morning." They looked around to see others had given up in despair.

"Mornin', David," Papa called to him. "My wife sent over these vittles for your breakfast. Ya have ta do with a cold breakfast; we can't get a fire started. What can I do ta help ya get out of here this morning? We're in for a hard time getting' outta here, I'm afraid." Papa handed the food up to David.

"I don't know about you, Eli, but I didn't get much sleep with this storm."

"No fire, no coffee. Mighty poor way to start a day," Papa said, turning away to his wagon with his head held down against the pelting rain.

The camp quickly turned into a quagmire. The wet earth gave off a swamp water stench. Footwear became caked with the sticky mud. The bonnet brims hung limp over the faces of the women, and the hems of their dresses were soaked. Steam evaporated off the backs of livestock as they shivered in the cold rain.

Mother prepared a hasty breakfast of buttered bread, meat, and cheese along with leftover stewed fruit and fresh, warm milk. "Wish I had a cup of hot coffee for you, Eli."

"I'll settle for milk, Mary," Papa replied as he scraped mud from his boots before he climbed up into the wagon's cramped quarters. "Sure be glad when this rain quits."

Vacating camp became a laborious undertaking. The wagons swayed precariously and slid sideways, and the horses struggled for sure footing to gain enough momentum to pull the overloaded wagons out of the semi-liquid earth. The oxen, their feet mired deep in the sticky muck, strained in their yokes to haul their heavy wagons up the incline and onto the road.

"Ruth, keep movin'. Once you're past the fort I'll catch up with ya later," Alex Kenyon shouted to his wife wrapped in her India rubber cape.

Every head turned in a farewell glance to the little cemetery as they passed by Abigale Wilson. It was a sad moment leaving her behind, but their destiny lay ahead.

###

Martha was weary of the constant rain. They'd left Fort LaSalle three days ago, and she was frustrated with their slow progress. The wagons and horses using the road coming and going from the settlement had turned it into deep ruts and mud. She and her sisters were finding it difficult to walk through the wet, grassy fields beside the wagons to avoid walking in the road.

Martha and Ruthie had laughed at Bertha's notion that they resembled wet, ragged, dirty witches. They did look bedraggled in their wet clothes and water-soaked moccasins under a rain that showed little pity.

"I've had my fill of this rain," Elsa Crawford complained. "I've turned my straw ticks over and now both sides 'er wet."

Mother agreed. "The wagon canvases were never made to stand up under this much rain. I too hate to have my children sleep in wet beds."

"I know. I'm so tired of fighting mud morning, noon, and night." Ruth Kenyon had come to join the ladies assembled under umbrellas.

"The hem of my dress feels like its weighted down with lead, and my feet are cold all the time," whined Jenny McGraw.

"I think every one of thy young'uns has a runny nose," Elsa said with concern. "It bothers me to hear the little ones cough at night."

"Ah'm tired all the time too," Jenny McGraw whimpered.

The women were worried about Jenny and her condition, but they had little to offer her but sympathy.

"I'm glad we've been movin' right along. I think it helps David keep his mind off his misery," Ruth Kenyon expressed. "My Paul complained of an earache, so I got up and warmed a bit of sweet oil to put in it. Must have helped; he went back to sleep."

"Warmed the oil, Ruth? How did thee warm the oil? Speaking of warm. Oh, what wouldn't I give for a cup of hot coffee," Elsa moaned.

"Warmed the spoon over a Lucifer stick, Elsa."

"Thou didn't worry about getting the oil too hot fiddlin' around in the dark?"

"I guess it didn't," Ruth replied. "As I said, he went right back to sleep afterwards."

"I wonder," Mother commented, "do you suppose if I soaked ground coffee in cold water I might get something that tasted like coffee?"

Ruth agreed. "We soak tea leaves in cold water for compresses, why not coffee?"

"Oh no, thou has to have water good and hot to make decent coffee," Elsa adamantly stated.

"Did anyone else hear the men talking about our coming to a Rock River? Sam pointed it out to us on his little map," Mother commented. "In this rain, I wonder what kind of crossing we can expect."

"Oh, there's bound to be a bridge," Ruth Kenyon stated.

I do so hope this rain wears itself out by the time we camp tonight," Elsa sighed. She found the women to be in harmonious agreement with her.

"Ladies," Mary Burt excused herself, "I really must get back and see if the men have pulled our wagon out of the mud yet."

Martha's sympathy was with the children. She was surprised their spirits had remained high, confined to their wagons as they were with the flaps pulled down against the driving rain. She watched them burst out of the wagons when they were able to get free, and charge wildly about.

She glanced up to see Mother grab on to Stephen's arm to get his attention. "I insist you settle down, young man; every thread on you is sopping wet from running through these wet bushes."

Suddenly Mother shrieked, "What? Oh my goodness. Your arm—lift your shirt. Oh no! Stephen, you're covered with bugs. Martha, run tell Mrs. McGraw to look her children over for ticks. Bring the Wilson boys to me at once."

"Mary, get their heads. A tick's head'll burrow under the skin. If you break 'em off from their bodies," Papa emphasized, "they'll make bad sores. You gotta get their beaks."

Stephen screamed hysterically, "Get 'em off me, Mother, get 'em off!"

Everyone came to investigate the commotion and found that Junior and lil' Joe McGraw were picking the parasites off each other, but they were dismembering the bodies from the tiny black beaks.

Jenny McGraw noticed what they were doing and forgot her problems and yelled in her shrill voice, "Turpentine spirits! Douse 'em with turpentine spirits."

Mr. McGraw rummaged for the bottle of turpentine spirits he carried as part of his smithy supplies. He might need the heat from a small twig or a Lucifer stick to keep a beak from burrowing. He'd used this method on animals before when he'd removed ticks. He hoped he wouldn't be forced to touch the site with the direct heat, but if he didn't the sores would never heal, and the fever from them could kill a body.

Ruth Kenyon's concern, while she inspected her boys, was whether these were hard or softshell ticks. She knew one kind carried the deadly fever. She wondered how the folks knew one from the other. Everyone seemed more worried about tick sores than the deadly fever.

Brian McGraw explained the difference as he showed her. "These are the safe kind. They's a big soft and round."

Martha rolled up her sleeves to help wipe down the children with turpentine spirits before handing them off to their mothers, who lathered them with strong homemade soap. Women turned their backs inward and fanned out their wet skirts to provide a curtain of privacy around the naked youngsters, screaming in protest at being bathed in cold water in the pouring rain.

They emerged chilled, with their teeth chattering, as they were again carefully inspected before being wrapped in damp cloths and sent to their wagons to dress.

"We'll have to stay clear of bushes and grass until we're out of this area," Mrs. Kenyon cautioned everyone.

The children found themselves once again confined to the wagons, but they accepted their restrictions quietly after what they'd just come through.

To walk on the edge of the slippery muddy road posed a difficult problem for Martha and the other girls, and though they didn't complain aloud, they became sullen as they tried to skirt the mud and found themselves lagging far behind the wagons.

A company of blue-coated cavalrymen overtook them and passed by so close Martha could hear the squeak of saddle leather and harnesses. The girls tried to duck away from the mud slung at them from the horses' hooves as they cantered past. The men saluted respectfully and acknowledged the settlers but were unaware of the anger they were creating among the young ladies.

At any other time, Martha and her friends would have been enchanted to see men in uniforms, but today they kept their heads lowered in embarrassment of their muddy, wet appearance and out of anger at the clods of mud being hurled at them as the formation quickly rode their horses out and around the wagons.

After they'd passed, Ruthie told Martha, "I hope they get bitten real good with ticks for lettin' their horses throw mud at us like this."

The rain subsided and the sun appeared in such brilliance it was blinding. The heat, though welcome, seemed unduly warm after the last three days of constant chilling rain and dark skies. Attitudes were uplifted with the thoughts of the road drying out to make traveling faster and easier.

The wagons arrived on the banks of the Rock River, swollen from the recent rains; a dirty, brown, foreboding river raced swiftly before them

Off to one side of the wagons was an Indian camp. A band of Indian men, wrapped in red, green, and white striped–blankets, with red-painted, shaved heads and many long, colored strings of beads hung about their necks, walked from their tepees to the wagon train.

Mr. Kenyon asked Papa and David to parley with them. The Indians stopped a few feet from the wagons and paused before they gave a silent, head-bowed greeting. Papa hoped they could understand his English. "This is the place to cross the water?"

One of the Indian men stepped forward and nodded his head. "Four dollars for wagon to cross."

Papa walked back to the men. "You heard? They want four dollars to cross." "We're not crossing a bridge," Tom Crawford argued. "Tell 'em we might pay for help, but they don't own the river."

Mr. McGraw muttered, "Offer 'em two dollars; thet's the bottom offer. Ya tell 'em thet's all we's offerin'."

Papa and Mr. Wilson returned to the Indians. "There's no bridge. We could lose our wagons, our families, and our livestock in the fast water. We offer two dollars."

The Indians walked away to discuss the issue among themselves. After some time one of them returned. "Two dollar fifty cents and we help you cross the river."

Papa carried the offer back to the others. "They want two dollars and fifty cents?"

"Wonder if this is as good a deal as we can make?" Tom Crawford said nervously. "I wanna get out of here before they think of somethin' else to charge us for."

"We can do better than this, can't we?" Neil challenged with a smirk. "Like ya say, they don't own this river."

Alex Kenyon suggested, "Best take 'em up on it. Times a-wastin'."

Papa commented, "They are experienced and we could use the help."

The men returned to accept the Indian's offer. They and the Indians shook hands to signify the parley agreeable. The Indians collected their money and returned to their tepees.

"We shoulda told them redskins we'd pay after we cross," Neil grumbled.

"It don't work that way, son; we pay first. We need ta keep peace with 'em. They got this fool notion we're trespassing," Alex Kenyon said, heading back to his wagon.

It was decided to transport the children across by horseback first, as a precaution against a wagon tipping and their being thrown into the fast current and carried away.

Mrs. Kenyon suggested they scout the river as to depth, rocks, and holes. The men decided to make the crossing at various points. The wagons could stir up the river bottom, moving the boulders and creating deep, unseen holes if using the same path.

The river already testified to its turbulence with carcasses of dead animals lying about on either side and debris swiftly washing past them.

Several muscular, bare-chested Indian youth rode up quietly on strong ponies and positioned themselves beside the Kenyon wagon first to lead off. The milk cow was tied on the side of the wagon away from the direct current.

Mrs. Kenyon held tight to the reins as she urged her four horses into the water. The wagon rolled forward slowly. Mr. Kenyon rode along one side to encourage his team into deeper water as they contended with the heavy wagon behind them. The Indians silently guided the nervous horses, who lost their footing and floundered at intervals. However, they made the crossing and came out unscathed.

Tom Crawford didn't trust his wife to handle their four horses. Everyone watched the big, overloaded wagon sway precariously in the middle of the rapid river. The horses were reluctant and became nervous when they were forced to struggle for footing.

Everyone sighed with relief as they watched the wagon pulled safely out onto the riverbank.

Mr. McGraw, at the suggestion of the Indians, crossed his oxen further upriver. Papa waded his horse out to show that the water depth came halfway up his boot as he sat in the saddle and beckoned Mr. McGraw to follow.

Mr. McGraw cautiously waded his oxen out into the river; they were frightened and struggled to turn back. Brian cracked his whip to force them forward, but they slipped, became confused, and balked. Mr. McGraw knew the longer his wagon sat in the soft river silt the deeper the wheels would sink. Neither the crack of his whip nor his cursing would make them move. They began thrashing about in the water and sinking into the soft silt under them. The big wagon began to slowly list into the current.

Papa and the Indians quickly swam their horses out to fasten ropes onto the horns of the agitated oxen and tow them along. The oxen's eyes bulged with fear; they bawled in protest and tossed their heads about in the water. The big wagon lurched and listed to such a degree that Mr. McGraw nearly slid off his seat.

Those along the river's edge held their breath as they watched Papa and Neil, who were having difficulty, keep from becoming tangled in the debris floating past them and keep their ropes taut in the swift water. By keeping a few feet ahead of the oxen, they were able to maneuver them to pull the heavy wagon over the undetected underwater rocks and out onto dry land.

Mr. McGraw was bounced about when the wagon wheels hit the big boulders, but he managed to hang onto the reins. Those along the river-bank hadn't realized until the wagon was out of the water they had been holding their breath.

The men assisting were exhausted and there were three wagons yet to cross over.

Sam Emigh, without hesitation, slipped his big Clydesdales into the water, with a "ya, ya!" the light wagon bounced its way across to climb out onto the other side. Folks on both sides of the shores laughed and clapped as they watched Sam cross so quickly and effortlessly.

David Wilson, not to be outdone by Sam, commanded his horses with skilled expertise. Though the horses slipped and fought for secure footing, they pulled his heavy wagon though the river, over the big rocks, and through the soft silt, safely up onto the riverbank. Those watching David thought him fortunate not to have suffered his horses' broken legs or his wagon a cracked wheel.

Papa was last. He dreaded the move. Oxen's legs are shorter than horses'; their hooves were splayed, making it easier for them to slip. Horses had halters, oxen didn't.

He instructed Mother and Martha, "Let the reins out as much as possible and we'll guide them. Watch closely for my signals."

It surprised Papa to discover the river was deeper where he started than he'd thought, even though he picked the widest part of the river from where the others crossed.

Mother urged the oxen into the water and watched her husband for his signals. Martha, sitting beside Mother, fought hysteria that threatened to consume her as they moved into the middle of the rapid river.

She held her breath and closed her eyes, but when she opened them the sight of land seemed far away.

Suddenly the big wagon dove down as if it had fallen off a ledge. The oxen floundered and Mother was helpless. She and Martha were nearly flung face forward onto the backs of the oxen and into the swirling water beneath them.

Papa saw the terrified faces of the women. The oxen were bobbing like corks in the water; they were unable to protest in their terror and were furiously blowing water from their nostrils.

Papa instantly let out rope, and forced his horse out as fast as was possible into the turbulent water, yelling at the same time for Neil to do the same. The Indians on horses swam along beside the oxen and grabbed onto their massive heads to keep them above water until they were able to get their feet onto solid ground.

Once the oxen found solid footing, as fast as they were able, they made it through the water and came out onto dry land, with Mother and Martha dripping water as well as the wagon and its contents.

Those on shore observed that one ox was being dragged and ran to free it to enable the one next to it to climb up off its knees. The sides of the oxen heaved as they shook their heads, coughed, and blew water. The dead ox was released from the oxbow, while people pushed and pulled the wagon out of the mud and water.

The little milk cow, with her head hung down, trembled but otherwise she seemed little worse for her swim.

After the pandemonium, the settlers glanced up to see the young Indians, who had finished their part of the bargain and were quickly and quietly crossing back over the river. They didn't stay to be told how grateful the settlers were that no lives had been lost because of their skilled assistance.

Martha, standing back from the others, silently overcame her horror of the ordeal.She and Mother were fortunate the wagon didn't tip over, or a wheel hadn't been broken, and that everyone had made the crossing but the one poor ox.

She remembered when Papa brought the new wagon home and told the family that having the wagon's bed tarred, as he'd done, the wagon would be able to ford rivers and any supplies weren't likely get wet. *I feel fortunate to be alive,* she decided as her trembling subsided.

"Looks like I'm not meant to make the trip with four oxen," Papa lamented, looking down at his dead ox. It would join the carcasses of the others along the riverbank.

"Eli, we're coming to the Mississippi; you can pick up another ox there."

"Mary, I don't have the money to keep buying oxen." Papa's abruptness startled her. She knew the loss of the ox was painful to him. It had been at his mercy. It didn't seem right somehow to leave it here beside the river to rot, but there wasn't time to prepare it for food; the meat might well be tainted from its fright.

"Eli, if you'll find me a campsite, I'm going to make you a good, hot cup of coffee. It's about time you had one."

"Mary, I almost lost you—and Martha. It happened so fast. How much luck does a fellow get in a lifetime with other people's lives?"

"Eli, I'm glad it's over; we're safe here beside you and we need to keep moving."

Mother couldn't bring herself to look down at the great ox. *What a waste of a beautiful animal. I've never dealt with as much death as I have lately.* Papa didn't see the tears she quickly wiped away. "Come, Eli, find me a campsite, You need that cup of coffee."

Mrs. Kenyon suggested, "We've traveled far enough for one day. It's going to take some time and patience as it is to get fires started with wet wood. That grove of trees over yonder looks like a likely place to make camp for tonight."

The travelers assembled into the customary circle for a well-earned rest, a good hot dinner, and to take inventory of any wet supplies.

Neil wished there was some way he could spend time with Martha. He hadn't spoken with her since the crossing. He would never forget the look of terror on her face and how helpless he'd felt and outright scared at the thought of losing her.

Maybe they could use his help to unload the wet supplies. "Pa, I'm gonna mosey over an' see if the Burts could use an extra hand."

Sam Emigh watched after this son. *You've got the right idea, ma' boy: make yourself useful. That's the way I did It too once long ago,* he chuckled. *No matter how disastrous our lives are today, it will be our youngsters with their dreams and determination that keep our future alive tomorrow.*

Chapter 15

An ocean of grass was fanned by a gentle breeze. Cottonwoods and oaks dotted the rounded hills and dense, green shrubbery grew along the riverbank. Martha lifted her face to the warm, late afternoon sun and drew in a slow breath. The sunshine had restored her soul, leaving her feeling renewed after the many days of rain and her harrowing experience of the river crossing today.

She, along with her sisters and Neil, had been busy helping Mother discard their water-soaked supplies. Mother had refused to use the muddy river water and insisted the water barrels be emptied and filled with fresh water from a nearby stream.

The trunks had been taken out of the wagon and opened to ensure everything inside was dry. "If the clothes or quilts are damp," Mother insisted, "they take on a foul smell, and I've no time to wash."

"Mother, is it too early to start cooking? I'm starved," Martha complained. "Did you have something in mind for supper? We didn't have time for dinner, after all."

"I haven't had time to think about supper," Mother confessed, dragging another heavy trunk back inside the wagon.

"I'll fry up some bacon and make some biscuits with gravy," Martha proposed.

"Fine, that will be fine, Martha. I'm not sure how you'll cook with wet wood."

Martha used a handful of damp wood shavings to find they weren't beneficial for producing a hot fire. The wet wood smoldered weakly, refused to catch fire, and sent up a plume of blue smoke. She glanced up, glad to see Neil coming towards her. *Oh good, he'll help me with this lifeless fire.*

She watched him stop abruptly and then turn back for his wagon. He yelled something to her but his words were lost in the sudden piercing cries coming from the river behind her. Martha froze in terror. *This can't be happening—not Indians again!*

Men ran for their guns. Terrified women and children, before they scrambled into the wagons, caught sight of the half-naked Indians on horseback thundering towards the wagons, their shrill screams rending the air.

Neil quickly aimed his single-shot rifle and pulled the trigger, but in his haste his shot went awry of his target.

The Indians heard the crack of the rifle and hauled their ponies to a stop. The racket from their screams ceased.

Panic welled up inside Martha, who was peeking out from behind the rear flap and recognized the Indian leader was none other than the one with the blue stone hanging from his bare chest. Cold fear gripped her. *Why was he here? What did he want? What were they going to do to her people this time?*

Mother and Bertha were behind Martha and shared her view. Ruthie and Stephen were laying on their stomachs, peeking out from under the canvas flap.

"Martha!" Bertha whispered excitedly. "It's him, it's that Indian. Where's Papa? I can't see Papa! I heard a rifle shot. Who fired the gun?"

"Bertha, hush," Martha murmured. "Don't let them hear us in here."

The young Indian with the blue stone, sitting bareback astride his powerful, black stallion, appeared to be the leader of the band. He gazed slowly around him before he leaped from his horse and made his way to the Burts' wagon.

He snatched the canvas flap from Martha's grasp and peered inside the wagon at the four terrified, speechless women.

He gestured for Martha to climb down, but she was paralyzed with fear and unable to make her body move.

Neil had quickly reloaded his gun; the click from the firing pin sounded loud in the stillness around him. Just as he was about to squeeze off the shot, his pa reached over and lifted his arm.

"We're in their territory; leave them alone, Neil. We need to talk, find out what they want."

"What's the matter with ya, Pa? They got no right ta do this ta us. Let me teach 'em some manners."

Eli Burt gestured for the men to remain where they were as he walked towards the Indian.

"I'm gonna protect Mr. Burt if no one else will," Neil exclaimed loudly, lifting his rifle to his shoulder.

"Neil, put the gun down. Don't threaten them; don't give them reason to attack us," Sam cautioned his son.

"You speak English?" Papa shouted. The warrior didn't move. Papa repeated the question. He used the upturned palm of his hand in the universal Indian greeting of peace, as he'd done with his friends the Sauk, Fox, and Kickapoo tribes, when coming up to each other.

The young Indian remained motionless with a fixated stare at Papa, who stood waiting to be acknowledged, aware that any move he made could be misinterpreted.

There was silence as the people watched the two men.

The warrior at last very slowly lifted his hand to exchange the greeting. The folks observing the two men exhaled with relief.

"You speak English?" Papa repeated as he and the Indian stared at one another.

"I come for woman and gun," the young Indian demanded aggressively.

Papa wished at that moment he had some beaver pelts to give in a friendship trade. "My horse is a good one—fine saddle—valuable to you," Papa offered.

"No horse. I come for woman and gun," the Indian stated emphatically.

"Daughter is mine," Papa said calmly. "We are many men." He indicated the men with their guns in sight.

The Indian's face was devoid of expression. His bright black eyes glared at Papa as he sneered, "You have many women." He gestured to Martha. "I take woman and gun."

"We have many guns." Papa paused then asked loudly, "You would die for a woman? You would break the friendship between the Fox tribe and my people for a woman?" Papa hoped his voice conveyed the scorn and disgust as he intended. He realized the young warrior wasn't in any position to back down. He must decide between facing shame from his men or the wrath of the white men.

They stood their ground before each other until Papa made the first gesture. He slowly lifted his gun and handed it to the young brave. "Gift in friendship between us. Tell your chief Eli Burt honors the Fox tribe."

The warrior seized the gun, made a running leap onto his horse, and rode back to his comrades.

The members of the wagon train were unable understand and watched horrified as Eli Burt gave his gun to an Indian.

They all watched as the young Indian hesitated. He had the gun; why was he pausing? The band of Indians wondered at their leader's actions also, as they nervously wheeled their horses in circles, anxious to be off.

The young Indian had accepted the gun in the name of friendship. He suddenly realized he was obligated by Fox tribal law to present a gift in return. It was important that he and his men to stay on good terms with the Fox tribe; he needed to present a gift to the father of the young women for whom he'd announced his intentions.

He turned and rode back to Papa and lifted the blue stone from his neck. He glanced over to make sure the white woman he'd failed to capture observed him making the gesture on her behalf before he handed the blue stone to her father. "Soon I come for my woman," he stated loudly. He then reined his horse about sharply and with the gun held high over his head, he cried out in a victorious cry that signified his conquest. The band of followers joined him riding back across the river.

Neil watched them retreat and vowed, *If I ever meet up with any of 'em again, Pa got in my way this time but it won't happen again. Nothin' galls me more than lettin' these ignorant, thieving redskins get away with treatin' us bad, and they're still alive ta do it again.*

Papa watched the young warrior ride away with his gun. *These people lead two lives. We teach them our ways—yet they insist on preserving their traditions, using our words and ways to get what they want. Why must peace be so difficult between us?*

Papa studied the blue stone; it had to be valuable. He decided it could be used to fetch enough money to replace his gun and buy a new ox. He tossed it up and caught it expertly in one hand before he turned to his family.

"Give ya quite a scare did they, Mary?" he asked.

"Of course not, Eli, I know you'll take care of us. You always have." She turned to finish her chores.

What's to happen next? she sighed. *Goodness knows it will surely be something I could easily do without.*

Martha wasn't able to explain her impulse to feel the blue stone and smell the leather thong that had held it around the Indian's neck. "Papa, may I hold the stone?"

"Sure is beautiful, isn't it, Martha?" Papa handed it to her.

She held it to her cheek. *It's so smooth and warm—is it from Papa's hand or the body of the Indian?* She smelled the leather thong for a scent of his body, but it disappointed her to find it smelled like leather. She surprised herself that she was deathly afraid of him, yet she was curious about him at the same time.

"This is the largest stone I've ever seen," Papa explained. "You've seen stones like this before in the jewelry they make, haven't you? I've never seen one so large. It has to be worth a lot of money. Wonder how he came by such a big one?"

"Papa, I saw him gesture towards me. Does that mean he'll come back?" Papa judged her feelings to be of fear. "I honestly don't know, Martha, but we'll be across the Mississippi River by tomorrow. He was just showing off in front of the others is all. They have these foolish games they play ta challenge their bravery. I think he's happy, now he has ma' gun.

"They're strange people, Martha. They have a reverence for the earth spirits and will die for 'em, but for the life of me, I don't understand their reasonin' for killin' the spirits in each other and us. No, Martha, I don't believe we have ta worry. We're not apt ta be seein' that Indian ever again."

Martha leaned against the tailgate of the wagon. *No wonder I'm so tired. I've crossed a raging river, been through an Indian scare, and I'm slowly dying of starvation.*

"Martha, please move yourself. We need to put these sacks of grain back in the wagon." Mother and Bertha hoisted a sack up onto the tailgate.

Martha yearned to say, "Please step over my dying body, I'm too weak to move." Instead she helped Mother lift the remaining sacks of the grain supply into the wagon.

Loud voices from the Emigh wagon drew Martha and Mother's attention. The distance between the two wagons didn't permit the women to clearly hear the words, but they could see the display of anger between Sam and his son and knew the two were about to come to blows.

Mother gathered her skirt, running for Papa, who was busy greasing a wagon wheel. "Eli, stop Sam and Neil before they hurt each other."

"Mary, they're father and son; I have no right to interfere."

"But they're going to hurt each other. Please, Eli, do something, will you?"

"Mrs. Burt, I'm hungry. Will my supper be ready soon?" He glared at Mother.

"Yes, dear, you're right. I have work to do."

Martha watched Neil balanced on his toes, inches from his pa's face. His arms were rigid at his sides and his hands balled into fists. Mr. Emigh was eye level with his son, and his hands were clenched into fists at his sides before he abruptly turned away. With one hand on his hip, and without saying a word, the other hand he used to casually remove his hat and scratch his head before replacing the hat.

Neil, red faced, continued to shout. He suddenly turned away from his pa, stomped off, flung himself onto his horse, and rode bareback out across the plains.

"Martha?" Mother called, "it's not proper or polite to stare, dear."

"This wet wood doesn't do anything but make a lot of irritating smoke, and there's no heat coming from it," Bertha yelled in exasperation at her sister. "You want me to eat this bacon raw?"

"Why don't you try a Pilot cracker instead?" Martha calmly suggested. Just then Stephen appeared. "When're we gonna we eat? I'm hungry."

"As fast as we can get this wet wood to put out heat and—Oh, this smoke!" Martha choked, fanning the smoke as she faced away from it.

"Why won't the wood burn faster?" Stephen wanted to know as he squatted down and attempted to blow at the feeble fire.

"It needs dry wood, Stephen, that's why," Bertha grumbled. "Like maybe some boards off the side of the wagon?"

"They're probably still wet, Bertha." Martha had to laugh at her sister's notion.

"You have any better ideas or you just gonna sit there in that smoke all night?"

"My, tempers are certainly short tonight, Bertha," Martha said as she turned the bacon and probed the smoking fire with the same fork she was cooking with. "Bertha, give everyone a Pilot cracker and be thankful they came through the ordeal fit to eat."

The sun sent a splash of vibrant colors across the prairie sky. The meal was eventually cooked over a fire with little heat and billowed with dense smoke.

The clear night sky filled with stars with the promise of a nice tomorrow. But to the weary travelers, regardless of the weather they must travel on.

Later, as Martha and Bertha cuddled under their quilts, Martha whispered to her sister, "The Indian who gave Papa that blue stone? I know he meant it for me."

"It was between Papa and the Indian, Martha."

"I know, but Papa gets to keep the stone. I'd accept it if he'd offer it to me. I wonder why the Indian gestured like he wanted me to have it?"

"Papa needs the money for a new gun. Besides, who can understand these savages. I'd think you'd be scared to death of him. Best let Papa handle things. Now go ta sleep will ya?" Bertha positioned her pillow away from Martha and heaved a tired sigh.

Martha still pondered the issue. *Papa's a fair man. It's his responsibility to take care of us. I know his decisions are for my own good. I don't feel comfortable speaking my mind. It would be most disrespectful, but I still wonder.*

Sam Emigh's thoughts revolved around coming to terms with his son. The boy is a man. He had to accept this, but he didn't understand Neil's unjust prejudices towards the Indians? He had a right to his opinion. *It's his attitude I can't accept. I don't feel I was too hard on him today. He has to learn tolerance if he's to make this journey and come out live.*

Neil returned to camp sullen and quiet. He still felt the sharp sting from the words of conflict that had passed between him and his pa.

How can Pa be so blind as not to see how these savages push us around? They make unacceptable demands and they're constantly begging from us. It bothered Neil that none of the folks seemed concerned for Martha.

Mr. Burt accepted whatever it was they gave for her, didn't he? He same as traded off his own flesh and blood, his own daughter, to those uncivilized heathens. How must she have felt watching him trade her off like that? Maybe he's scared of the Indians. What kinda fool gives his gun to some savage to use against us? Neil slept fitfully.

Mother Burt had difficulty sleeping also. *We've lost so much precious food today. There's going to be a trail from here to the Oregon Territory filled with rancid and spoiled food, isn't there? I've witnessed the bones picked clean and gnawed by scavengers, the remains of food left by others before us. Wild animals may end up eating better than my family.*

Papa's mind was on the Mississippi crossing ahead. It gave him courage after the despair he'd experienced today. What he needed right now, he decided, was sleep. *I'll be able to face tomorrow after I've had a good night's rest.*

The Indians, after they stopped for the night, roasted meat over an open fire. They wiped the grease from their hands into their braids before they crawled under blankets beside the fire to sleep.

They taunted their friend for giving away his blue stone. "For a worthless white woman's favors?" they'd laughed at him.

He sat, lost in thought before the dying embers of the campfire. *The white man does not know my hopes and dreams. He does not know my mother died trying to save me during an Indian attack on the white people she lived among. Revenge burns in my spirit with white-hot coals of fire. The blue stone my mother's father gave me will buy the young white woman. She must not be frightened or forced, or she will run like the deer and antelope. I must be kind with her. I gave the stone to her father as my wish to trade for her. I will take her for my woman and then will I be accepted back into my father's world. I will once again claim my rightful name of John. I will forever give up the name of my mother's people, who call me Ouxe, the Fox. I will refuse to ever say it again. I will forget it when I become one with the white people.*

Selecting a stick lying nearby, he hurled it onto the dying fire. *My brothers here we are born half-breeds—outcasts. We protect each other; we live and fight to survive as we can in either world.* He paused to listen to the lonely howls of coyotes as they called out to each other in the night.

These wagons traveling away from me are taking the white woman I must have. I need not make my plan known to anyone; only my heart must know, my eyes to watch for the right time.

He placed more wood on the fire, pulled his blanket up around him, and settled down to sleep.

Chapter 16

Martha and her sisters enjoyed walking in the warm morning sun, with the gentle breeze moving the green prairie grass to expose the delicate little spring violets. Inquisitive cardinals, with red flashes of color, darted from one grove of oaks to another as they squawked and scolded the intruders.

Martha had learned the state of Illinois was not known for its lofty mountains as they'd see in the great northwest. These rounded hills and shadowed valleys around her continued for as far as she could see. The Illinois River flowed beside her in its ever-changing mode of deep blues and greens to rich browns.

This morning the girls watched large barges slowly glide through the river carrying soft coal from the coal mines north of them to ports upriver.

Papa had announced at breakfast they'd be leaving the Illinois River as it turned south and they would continue on west. This had brought about a nostalgic moment for Martha. The river had been a constant companion since leaving home. She wondered if, like her family she'd left behind, she'd ever see it again.

She was disturbed from her reverie by the children's shouts. "A peddler, a peddler's coming!"

Up over the hill came the peddler with his house-style wagon painted a bright red with a vivid blue stripe. Its smokestack protruded from a steeply pitched roof. The metal wares hung about the wagon clanged loudly in a profusion of sound long before it reached the wagons.

The peddlers were solitary figures to the pioneers. These men scavenged through piles of discards left from abandoned, demolished, and overloaded wagons. These men were a source of information, political

113

and regional. Papa had told Martha their medicinal remedies made them trusted friends with the Indians. It intrigued her that every remedy imaginable was covered as they plied their wares.

This peddler was a colorful little man in garish attire; black kinky curls escaped a bright red bandana, and a gold ring adorned his left ear. Gold bracelets and necklaces hung about his neck and wrists. A black patch covered the right eye.

"The result of a battle with bandits," he claimed, and enjoyed being encouraged to tell of his escapade. The other eye twinkled in his creased, tanned, leathery face, making it difficult to judge the man's age.

Papa whispered to Mother, only Papa was unable to whisper, "Wonder what keeps those pitiful-lookin' old nags alive?" The two emaciated old horses stomped impatiently as flies collected about their bony structures.

"Bet you folks're travelin' West," the peddler stated, squinting his good eye.

"You're right," Sam Emigh replied.

"Lots of settlers movin', some west, some south. I hear folks refer to Californy as west, but I'll venture you're headin' to the far northwest. Right?" The children were fascinated, and stared in amazement that he knew so much about them.

"They's only Indians up north. Now, you talkin' them poor devils going south? They's got them Mexicans and unpredictable Indians to contend with. Man needs a whole lot of gunpowder ta get there alive. President Polk maybe outta run them Mexican's back to their own pasture afore they get the idee' there's free territory for 'em to take a likin' to."

"We'd like to think the northwest ain't so mean, but you're right," Alex agreed. "Them Indians sure know how to make life miserable if they ain't been civilized."

The peddler charmed the young girls with his quick smile. Ruthie and Ginny giggled behind hands held over their mouths.

He asked the boys, "Ya young'uns know what the Indian word Illinois means to an Indian? Superior Man—but ya already know'd thet, didn't cha?" He laughed to expose a mouth full of white teeth.

He turned a serious face to the men. "There's a road to the left of your comin' down into the township," he informed them. "Moline's rough. Ya'don't wanta park your wagons in Moline. Its a dirty, stinkin', rough-talking, crowded place. Ain't fit fur the ladies, gentlemen. You'll be comin' to a well-formed stream crossin' the road; after the stream ya hang a left.

Say—kin I interest ya ladies in any of ma' fine wares? Maybe some tonics fer fevers an' itches an' the like? I got somethin' here to cure every sickness known to man."

The women graciously declined but thanked him as they bid good-bye.

The road coming down off the hills into the city of Moline was busy with wagons, buggies, and herds of "pokey cows," as Stephen referred to them.

The families paused on the limestone cliffs high above the town to observe Moline, Illinois, and the great Mississippi River, sparkling like a bed of diamonds below them in the bright morning sun. Wooden bridges and waterways on three sides gave the town an island appearance.

The wagons turned left as the peddler suggested and into a large meadow.

"Looks like there's plenty o' good eatin' fur the livestock, Pa," Neil commented at the abundance of lush grass surrounding them.

The teams were unhitched and watered before the women set up camps. The men decided this was a good time to investigate their Mississippi River crossing.

They rode down into Moline to find it crowded with a multitude of humanity. They heard strange dialects and languages. Hawkers and peddlers cried out their wares. Bawling cattle and braying donkeys and mules mingled with the noisy clamor of wagons. The clang of metal being pounded against a smithy's anvil. Wagons continuously moved back and forth, creating dust that hung in the air. The men felt caught up in the element of perpetual motion.

Eli Burt, Sam Emigh, and Alex Kenyon jostled their way down to the waterfront, through crowds attired in every conceivable style. The odors of body sweat, animal urine, the stench of raw sewage, and rotting refuse assaulted their nostrils, combined with the smell of tar and acrid wood smoke.

"Looks to me like we got ourselves a couple of choices here," Alex Kenyon commented, as the men watched a paddle wheeler docked down from them and another in the middle of the river. "Those barges don't look too bad; only thing is, we'll have to swim our stock across."

"It's being done." Sam gestured to cattle tied alongside barges slowly making their way across the water.

"I'm takin' mine across by boat," Papa insisted. "After the river crossing the other day? I don't care to swim 'em if I can help it."

The men approached a man dressed in a blue naval uniform. His attention, at the moment, was with a paddle wheeler filling with passengers and freight. The three waited until he was free to inquire about the Mississippi River crossing.

A boat leaves every hour," he informed them. "It's necessary to get one's name on the roster along with your livestock count. The ferries are in service twelve hours a day, seven to seven, except Sunday or when they're down for repair. The passenger lists are long, and today we're experiencing trouble with one of the ships. It's likely we'll need to pull it out for repairs. Those barges down there," he gestured, "go oftener, but you'll need to remove your wagon wheels, and some of them limit the head of livestock crossing at one time. Usually a return trip is necessary to collect all your goods too. The barges are cheaper, I might add, but they can only pull up near the riverbank, so you have to wade out and carry your supplies to dry land. They don't have slips like our steam boats do."

Just then a paddle wheeler belched black smoke and blew a deafening whistle blast to announce its arrival and warn small river craft to get out of its path. Whenever a boat slipped into the berth, the activities on the waterfront increased as everyone pushed forward in hopes of boarding.

The lower deck of the big boat accommodated livestock, the deck above was filled with wagons and cargo, and on the upper deck passengers walked about or leaned against the bright white railings to view the sights below.

Armed with the information, the three men decided in favor of boarding the steam ship.

The sight of livestock packed in so tightly surprised them; it left little room for them to move, especially when the big ship emitted a deafening whistle blast as it slowly pulled away from its slip with fifty or more frightened animals. "Wonder they don't all try to stampede," Eli said in amazement.

"Let's get our names on the list," Alex Kenyon suggested as they worked their way though the masses around them.

"Can't imagine bringing the women into this," Papa shouted above the deafening noise.

"Some of them words sound purty raw, even for me," Alex laughed

The men passed saloons with the sound of pianos and women's laughter coming from behind the swinging wooden doors. Wagons passed so close the men worried about being pinned between them or run over in the cattle herds.

They pulled up outside the ticket office. "There's too many mean, hungry-lookin' fellers hanging 'round here for my likin'." Papa proposed to stay with the horses.

"But Eli, you know what'd happen to a horse thief?" Alex stated.

"In this mob? How'd we ever catch up with one? I'm fine here with the horses." While he waited, Papa was entertained by several conversations.

"Once we get across the river, we gotta outride these greenhorn farmers and their wagons. They're too durn slow and we gotta push fer Council Bluffs," one man told another.

"Ain't them greenhorns, hits them cattle that slows ya down. Don't dare tangle with one of them ornery drovers neither," commented his companion.

On the other side of him Papa heard a gentleman explain, "Way I see it, we can travel with our group and follow at a distance behind the train out of Council Bluffs. There's safety in numbers from Injuns that way."

"I'm more skeert of them bison than Injuns. Heard tell of a stampede once. There wasn't enough left to set up housekeepin' after fifty 'er more stone weights plummetin' from all di-rections hit me, this feller told me. Said he was 'bout ta give up right then and thar, but 'twere the sickness what brung 'im back"

Alex Kenyon appeared. "Looks like we got us a wait. Ticket agent suggested we stop in to check the passenger list a couple a times a day and see where our names place."

"You miss the boat, ya get back on the list. A boat breaks down, ya get back on the list." David laughed. "That's the reason so many run for the boats coming in; they hope some poor bugger mighta missed his turn."

Sam shared his appreciation of the ticket master. "This fellow, all dressed up dandy, has himself a big fancy buggy, a cook's wagon, lots of women, and hired hands with two other wagons full of supplies. He wanted to reserve a whole paddle wheeler for his outfit. 'You'll wait your turn like everyone else, sir,' he was told. The agent even pushed away the bills the gentleman shoved at him as a bribe."

"I heard him, Sam," Alex said. " The feller isn't too happy about having to wait in this fleabag town, he called it. He's got that much money, why don't he buy his own boat and sell it on the other side?"

Papa related what he'd overhead for the amusement of the others.

"Unbelievable," Sam sputtered. "Those wagons are unbelievable!" He'd just caught sight of two huge wagons designed like ships, maneuvering their way through traffic.

"They look like big boats. Wonder how much a rig like that costs?" Papa questioned.

"You fellers never seen a Pennsylvanian Conestoga before? Built like big ships on purpose. They got more room than our wagons. Can ya picture tryin' ta cross the prairie in one of those during a bad windstorm, say, with the wind blowin' 'round a hundred miles an hour? Ya wouldn't stand much of a chance a-comin' through it, but folks travel in 'em anyways. Makes our wagons look small in comparison, don't they?"

"Eight head of oxen! They must carry a lotta feed," Papa commented.

"I wasn't expecting to see the river looking so brown," Sam said. "It's downright muddy-looking for being so big. Our business finished here?" he questioned, as he mounted up for the ride back to camp, back through the little town with its dirt streets and neighborhood homes prevalent in a busy town.

"Girls, help me get these ticks outside. Shake them as hard as you can. Maybe we can move the straw inside and get them to dry out here in the sun. I know they smell moldy and I know they should all be redone, but we haven't clean straw or the time."

"Mother, these mosquitoes—they're eating me alive," Bertha whined as she violently fanned her arm at the insects swarming around her.

"I know, dear; it would seem the smoke from the fire and our moving around that they'd be discouraged, but between them and these gnats it's miserable, I have to agree with you." Mother was busy protecting her own exposed areas.

"Oh, Mother!" Martha exclaimed. "There's nothing but nasty, rotten straw in these ticks. They stink."

"That's why I suggested we lay them out and turn them in the sun. They might sweeten a little if they dry out," Mother explained.

"Martha, I remember when all the canvases were so white and shiny," Bertha said. "Look at what a dingy brown they are now."

Mother wondered, as she glanced up from her scrub board to the dirty-looking Canvases, if she'd ever see anything white again.

Tom Crawford, Brian McGraw, and Neil had stayed behind to assist each other with wagon repairs. When the men returned from town the three paused long enough to listen to them tell of their booking everyone passage on the paddle wheeler and of the encounters they'd witnessed while in town.

Papa told Sam and Mother he was riding back into town later to check the passenger list and to ask an assessor about the blue stone. "I need to replace my rifle and buy a new ox."

"Eli, I wonder if we might replace our provisions. I'd like to ride with you, if you don't have an objection to taking the wagon," Mother suggested. "Girls, dinner's ready. Where's your brother?"

"He's wherever the Kenyon and Wilson boys are," Bertha grumbled.

Ginny McGraw had come looking for her brothers and overheard Mrs. Burt ask about Stephen. "He'll be wherever the McGraw boys are," she said as she passed.

"Anyone seen Louie?" Lizzy Crawford called over to the Burts.

The boys were located some distance down the road in a big field. They sat tailor fashion in a circle with several Indian boys in elaborately beaded buckskins with matching headbands, who were busy trading the boys out of their leather shoes and shirts for bows, arrows, beads, and trinkets.

Papa herded the half-naked children back to camp. They had removed their heavy long johns after the tick episode. "I knew you women would be upset with 'em, so I didn't say anything to 'em when I found 'em this way."

Angry voices of the mothers could be heard throughout camp as they scolded their irresponsible sons for trading away valuable shoes and clothes.

David Wilson appeared with a bare-chested boy in each hand. "I'd like to whale the daylights out of 'em for giving away their shoes," he bellowed.

Mother bit her tongue to keep from laughing. "Life is going to be miserable enough with these mosquitoes and their tender bodies, I do believe, Mr. Wilson. They will get their just reward dressed as they are."

The two families gathered for the midday meal. A delicious hash of chopped meat; potatoes and onions; fresh biscuits; sweet, dried fruit cobbler; and good, strong, hot coffee satisfied their hunger.

Three little boys sat slapping at their heads, sides, and necks when they weren't scratching furiously at the areas where the insects feasted on their succulent little bodies.

The day became uncomfortably warm and the humidity oppressive. These conditions along with the irritating insects made tempers short.

Martha had asked permission to ride into town with Neil. However, Bertha and Elizabeth thought it more important to ride out and find greens for supper. Harsh words passed between the sisters, making Papa cranky. Stephen whined with discomfort from his mosquito bites, and Mother found herself nursing a miserable headache.

Papa stated he was taking the horse and going to town. "I've business to take care of, and Neil, you're welcome to ride in with me."

Papa would take the horse so Martha wouldn't be able to go with Neil. Papa's business, he'd stated, was to sell the precious blue stone. Martha was disappointed to see it sold, but Bertha was right: the stone's ownership was between Papa and the Indian.

Why is this so difficult for me to accept? Who am I to be heard? My place is to be be silent and obedient, even if it's not by permission of my spirit. Martha watched Papa ride away with the blue stone.

Papa returned sometime later to show off his new gun. Martha with a heavy heart knew how it had been purchased. She overheard Papa telling Mr. Wilson and Mother, "I got a fair price for the turquoise, enough to purchase a gun and money left over for a new ox."

Papa suggested to Neil that they take Nathan and Stephen with them to break in the new gun and bring back some fresh game for supper.

On their return the men carried a fair-sized antelope and several rabbits to share with the others in camp.

Ruthie, when she saw the soft fur bodies of the rabbits with their wide-open, lifeless eyes, was unable to bring herself to eat the supper with its tantalizing smell and delicious roasted meat. Her quietness during the evening remained unnoticed by the others.

Martha couldn't bring her mind to rest over the fate of the blue stone, she found it difficult to concentrate on evening chores.

Papa's gun might be valuable to him, but the blue stone was worth more than money to me. Why had the Indian traded something so valuable as his blue stone for a gun? Was killing that important to him? Was there something about giving it to Papa I don't understand? Was the stone of so little value to the Indian? The thoughts tumbled through her mind. There was something in her woman's nature that told her there had to be more to the blue stone than she'd ever know.

What if the Indian decided to retrieve it? Would he kill them all when he found out Papa had sold it? Would he capture her and take her away with him, sell or trade her, take her for himself? Was there evil connected to it? She must make herself stop thinking these silly thoughts. It was an even trade. Papa even said the Indian seemed happy with the gun.

Her thoughts were hers to keep within her heart. *What if I'd been carried away by the young brave? Would he have been kind and tender to me? Would he have been gentle, or were these men all rough, mean, crude, and brutal as I've been told. I've never known anyone taken by Indians and returned. I heard this band of Indians are called half-breeds too. This means they are undesirable people, but I don't understand why? It has something to do with their blood. I've heard folks say half-breeds take on undesirable Indian ways of acting, and I didn't understand this either. I don't think he's one of those kind. All I understand for certain is that the stone from the young brave has gone from my life forever.*

The young boys continued to court disaster. They discovered that the flaming ends of small sticks, when released from bows, traveled straight up into the night sky to fell back, trailing sparks behind them. No one knew for certain whose lighted stick fell onto the Emigh wagon. Though the fire was quickly extinguished there remained a gaping hole in the canvas.

Bows were quickly collected and the children sent to bed. They accepted their punishment. However, there remained a certain adventurous excitement over the ordeal.

Papa decided to turn in for the night. "Coming, Mary?" He paused to wait for her. "Mary, what's the matter? Is there a problem?" He sounded testy.

"Eli, you go on to bed, dear. I'll come soon." Mother sat rubbing her aching forehead.

"I'd appreciate it if you'd come now, Mary."

"Eli." She hesitated—her hands balled into fist to keep from lashing out at him.

"Eli, I'll be there directly. I just want to sit here in the fresh air and quiet a bit."

"Suit yourself, lady. Whatever pleases you." Papa bedded down under the wagon.

It distressed Mother even more to know Eli was upset with her. *I'm making this journey to the best of my ability for my husband and the children. I'm feeling no better than a hired hand. Do the other women feel this way? I doubt slaves work as hard as we women are expected to. I know the effort and work I put into this journey will only benefit me. My union with Eli is so difficult. It's one long compromise, but we have our children. Dear God, I know enjoyment isn't what you put me here on earth for. Let me be more patient and grateful. Forgive me my selfishness.*

Mother slipped quietly under her quilt. She listened to her sleeping family and the incessant noisy whine of the mosquitoes. A cool breeze rustled the big canvas overhead.

Martha sighed deeply in her sleep. The day had been unduly trying for everyone, and tomorrow there was another river to cross.

Chapter 17

Sam Emigh gratefully accepted a cup of coffee from Martha. "First cup of morning coffee is always the best, I say." He gingerly took a sip of the bitter, hot black brew. "This place is going to be hotter than Hades pretty soon. I didn't sleep too soundly with these bloodsucking, whining mosquitoes pestering me."

Martha poured a cup of coffee for Neil as he approached the fireside. "Wonder if ya'd like ta ride into town with me this morning, Martha?" he asked, accepting the cup.

She quickly looked over to Papa for approval.

"Think ya best stay here for your mother; she may need ya."

" The missus not feeling good, Eli?" Sam asked.

"One of her misery headaches, Sam," Papa replied, taking a drink from his cup.

Earlier, when Papa had gone to wake Mother, she'd moaned in pain, "Oh Eli, it can't be morning. I've such a headache."

Papa had awakened Martha. "I've built a fire so you can start our breakfast."

"Martha's fixin' breakfast for us, Sam. I'm hungry for a mess of griddle cakes. We got eggs, Martha? With some bacon, that'll fill us up. Mary's been lookin' out for David and his boys. They'll be here directly."

Martha smoothed her apron and averted her eyes from Papa. She was disappointed she wouldn't be riding into town with Neil. Her sisters were quite capable of watching Mother, but she knew better than to sass Papa. Any other time, she would have enjoyed taking over Mother's responsibilities.

Breakfast over, Neil and Mr. Wilson decided to ride into town. Ruthie was delegated to keeping cool vinegar and water compresses on Mother's head. Martha put the beans Mother had soaking from the night before to cooking. There were enough for several meals along with the bread she'd baked. Bertha had the last of the breakfast dishes washed and put away as a band of ragged, grubby Indian men, women, and children walked up looking for food.

Martha sent Bertha for Papa as she silently watched them lift pot lids and poke at her baking bread. One of them stuck his finger into the hot liquid of the bean kettle to dig out a piece of meat and nearly knocked the kettle from the grate as he jerked back his hand.

A tall Indian in worn, tattered buckskins offered Papa a pair of moccasins and a string of beads. Everyone's attention was on a woman who had plucked a chunk of meat from the bean kettle, but it was hot and slipped from her fingers onto the ground. Before she could retrieve it, a small child stooped down and quickly shoved the hot piece into his mouth.

"You have bowls?" Papa asked. A thin, haggard woman handed him a clay bowl with intricate designs painted on it. Papa handed it to Martha to fill with meat and beans. The other Indians offered the peace sign as Papa handed back the filled bowl. One of the men shoved a pair of moccasins at Papa as he hurried the women and children away with him.

The Burts noticed similar groups were begging at the other wagons.

"Papa," Martha whispered, "the beans weren't nearly finished cooking."

"Don't worry about 'em, Martha. These people are so hungry they'll eat 'em anyway they can get 'em." He shook his head as he watched after the pathetic group.

"The Sauks are not meat hunters. Nut hunters we called 'em. Shame their lives are so difficult. We've encouraged them ta settle and develop their land but they refuse, and they're slowly starving ta death. They've no strength ta fight anymore."

Martha was stirred with compassion for these people as she listened to Papa.

The children had gathered by the stream's undergrowth to watch a snake in the process of ingesting a frog feet first. They'd been fascinated for sometime, but were growing restless. The bigger boys ruled in the snake's favor, but the younger ones were for retrieving the frog.

"His back legs won't ever work again if we save him." Louie Crawford explained.

"Oh, what do you know, Louis? You think you know so much; I say we save the frog." Lil' Joe looked around for support from the other boys.

"What if we kill the frog? Then he won't suffer none," Paul Kenyon suggested.

"Then the snake won't eat him," Louie replied.

"See! What'd I tell you? Louie here knows everything, don't cha, Louis? Ya think ya knows everything," lil' Joe taunted.

"That's 'cause maybe I've seen it happen before." Louie's face and neck reddened as he towers over lil' Joe.

At the sound of horses coming, the boys left the snake to its meal.

Everyone crowded around the two riders. "By the time we get packed up and down the road," Mr. Wilson exclaimed, "it'll be our turn to board the boat."

"Yeah," Neil affirmed, "we're on the afternoon postin'. Whew! It's gettin' warm." He took off his hat to wipe his flushed face on his shirt sleeve.

"You girls dish up dinner. I'm gettin' your mother up right now.

"Mary, you can't rest in this heat." Papa smoothed a strand of damp hair back from her flushed face. "You'll feel better outside in the fresh air. We're gettin' ready ta leave for the river crossin' in a bit."

"Eli, the bright sun only makes my head hurt worse." Mother weakly protested. However, she allowed her husband to help her down from the wagon.

Elsa Crawford appeared with a slice of her *Apfel Kuchen*. "I had to do something while I waited for the men to get back from town." She offered it to Mother.

Ruth Kenyon came with a cup of lemonade made of sweetened water with a few drops of lemon essence added. "Mary, you won't believe it but these Indians are leavin' us beggars ourselves. They're not satisfied with bread anymore. They come with pots and buckets to fill. I'm not interested in their trinkets and beads either."

Mother politely listened to the ladies as she sat pondering why the Oregon Territory had to be so far away. Just yesterday she'd heard Sam Emigh ask Nathan and Stephen that if they'd covered three hundred miles, how many of the two thousand miles remained? She'd been busy and couldn't call to mind what he said. However, she remembered thinking at the time, three hundred from two thousand? Only three hundred miles in twenty-eight days. She didn't have time to worry or take note of such things, she had other matters to take care of.

Papa helped Mother up beside him, the children leaned out the back of the wagon for relief from the intense heat inside and to better watch the activity around them.

The two oxen pulled the lumbering wagon, with the horse, the milk cow, and the spare ox tied on behind, into the town of Moline.

Martha and her sisters were unprepared for what they encountered. Martha could understand why Papa and the men would never have been able to describe the sounds and smells. She too was speechless.

Stephen continuously climbed back and forth between the wagon openings to see the town from every vantage.

It excited the girls to hear the sound of a piano. The music reached out to remind them of the little pump organ Grandpa and Grandma Lane had given to Mother but that they'd had to leave behind. Papa promised them a bigger and better one when they reached the Oregon Territory and settled.

Bertha was enraptured by the elegant dresses and big hats covered with flowers, plumes, and voile. She gasped in delight at seeing dainty, gloved hands holding parasols. She discovered, for the most part, everyone was dressed as she and her family.

Mr. Kenyon pulled into a line of wagons waiting to board the paddle wheeler with the rest of the wagon train.

The Burt girls turned their faces and muffled their giggles as unlady-like vocabulary floated up to them. Papa had demanded they wear their bonnets. The wide brims may have interfered with their view but not their hearing.

This was a river town with different classes of people and there was little Mother could do to protect her young daughters from hearing the men's crude remarks.

Papa and the other men had gone for supplies. The girls watched them navigate between moving wagons on their return. The wagons passed so close the girls could have reached out and touched them and feared the men might be knocked down and run over by the big wheels.

Men of every conceivable lifestyle winked, smiled, or grinned at the young ladies as they passed, bringing a blush to the faces of the girls before they could quickly look away in ladylike discernment.

Hawkers and peddlers approached the wagons, selling trinkets, good luck charms, and tonics against evils for the long, rugged journey ahead. A lemonade vender, his little cask strapped across his chest, was an entice-ment for the children as they imagined the taste of the sweet, tart liquid, but Papa thought the water from the barrels sufficient. "It isn't a good idea to drink from cups everyone uses," he said. However, the tepid, tasteless water in the barrels didn't appeal to their thirst like they envisioned the lemonade would.

A deafening whistle blast from the river startled the Burt family. "Our boat's comin' in," Papa shouted as he climbed aboard the wagon.

Another loud blast signaled its farewell to shore as the paddle wheeler below them changed places with the incoming ship.

A cool, refreshing breeze swept in off the water as one by one the wagons moved forward to the boarding ramp in the side of the large ship.

The Burt children's excitement mounted as they watched a paddle wheeler float into its slip. Before them was the biggest boat they'd ever seen. It glistened in the afternoon sun in its white-painted splendor with gleaming, brass-scrolled railings and brass fittings, with a massive, square paddle wheel at the end.

People from the top deck came down to their buggies, wagons, and horses. They waited their turn to leave the ship as cargo and freight were unloaded. Two big commercial wagons were harnessed to so many mules it almost emptied the hold as they hitched up and drove up the incline into town. A United States Mail coach with passengers was returning from ALL POINTS WEST painted on its side. Guns hung from the hips of men mounting up for the ride into town.

When their turn came to board, Papa escorted the family up the gangway around the side of the boat and climbed the steep stairs to the highest deck. There he left Martha and her sisters with instructions to wait until he'd seen to the care of the wagon and team and made sure Mother, who had wished to remain in the wagon, was comfortable.

The children were fascinated with the black men below them, sweating profusely and chanting in singsong rhythm as they loaded large wooden crates, trunks, and cargo aboard. They led reluctant livestock into the gently rocking ship.

For the families, the waiting seemed an eternity before the captain blew his whistle, and at the same time the approaching boat announced its arrival.

Passengers covered their ears at the sharp blasts from the departing ship. Those on the deck waved to those below as the paddle wheeler slowly pulled out into the Mississippi River.

Martha and her sisters were finding it difficult to keep their faces discreetly hidden behind their bonnets and still observe their surroundings. Especially with the three young men in black suits and flat, black-brimmed hats whom the girls decided appeared to be near Martha's age.

The girls tried not to stare as they shared the same railing, but it was impossible not to overhear the young men's conversation.

Neil walked up the stairs to see the young men glance at the girls with interest.

He also witnessed the girls from behind their bonnets shyly observe the men. An uncomfortable tightness swelled in his chest at seeing Martha, her head lowered, peeking from under her bonnet towards the strangers. He arrived just as the one with a bushy beard nodded in her direction.

Neil quickly stepped up beside Martha to take her arm and asked loudly, "Care to walk with me, Miss Burt?"

"Oh, Neil, I'd love to, but Papa told us to stay here until he came back. Do you think he'd mind, Bertha?"

"I don't believe so; you can't go very far," Bertha said as she pretended a preoccupied gaze to a point beyond the men.

Neil steered Martha as the two exchanged nods and smiles with others promenading the deck, back to where the big paddle wheel was churning up the water.

Martha marveled at the power of the big trough paddles pulling up water and spilling it back down into the river. A fine spray off the falling water from the paddles created a mist to wet passengers walking by as the big steam-driven wheel rotated on its axle.

Bertha and Ruthie were glad to see Papa. Each took one of his arms, as they noted other ladies doing, and with unsteady footing they set about to walk as sedately as possible on the moving deck. "The wind off our bow is much stronger than on the aft side," Papa said to reassure them in their awkwardness.

The girls were shown where the history of the boat was kept telling of its building, measurements, tonnage and how many passengers it could carry. They continued down the companionway to bring Mother up with them but found her asleep.

Stephen caught up with them as they returned to the top deck. "Papa, I've been all over, and there's this man they call the Capt'n and he took us down to see where the engine is, and Papa, you should see these big arms movin' 'round to make the ship move," he sputtered with excitement. "And Papa, he showed me how to squirt a special oil on the big arms. Johnny got scared, but not me. That's 'cause I'm gonna be a sea capt'n when I grow up, Papa."

Stephen rudely pushed past Papa and the girls to catch up with his friends.

"Oh no, Ruthie, look; we're over halfway across," Bertha exclaimed as she took her place against the railing.

The young men, who had never moved from the railing, overheard her remark, smiled, and turned to look and see for themselves.

Papa and the three men tipped their hats to each other. "You fellers from Nauvoo?"

"Yes, matter of fact, we are," the bearded one replied. "We just finished university and we're on our way to Utah. You're a Mormon too?"

"No," Papa explained. "But I've heard about your being run out of Illinois. Have you been treated as bad as I've heard tell?"

"Ohhhh yes," the taller of the three answered. "Hard to tell these days who's your friend. The folks in Illinois are afraid of us. They think we're trying to take over the state. Brigham Young, our leader, is sending us to Utah to set up the settlement and get ground broken for crops before we send for the families."

"How long you think it's gonna take ta get yourselves situated?" Papa inquired.

"Two or three years afore we get everyone out here."

"We're meeting up with a wagon train at Council Bluffs in 'bout two or three weeks to finish our journey."

"You men're farmers then, I take it?" Papa asked.

"No, actually, I studied law." The bearded man reached out his hand to Papa. "Name's Adam. Brother Hyram here's a doctor, and Brother Peter teaches school. We're all ordained ministers for the Church of Latter-Day Saints." The men shook hands with Papa as Brother Adam finished telling Papa about themselves.

Bertha and Ruthie, who had never seen Mormons before, were captivated with the conversation between Papa and the three men. To Bertha these men didn't appear any different from other men, except for their clothes.

"It's sure been a bloody struggle for your people," Papa expressed his sympathy.

"Sure has." Brother Hyram sucked in his breath softly. "Sure has. We've shed less blood with the Indians than with our own race." Brother Peter shook his head in agreement just as the paddle wheeler emitted a whistle blast to announce the crossing was about to end.

"We need to get the family together," Papa said. "Now if I can lay my hands on Stephen."

"Good luck, Papa; he's probably already talked the captain into signing him up for the return trip." Martha's comment brought laughter and chuckles from those around her.

Bertha leaned over the railing to look down into the water. *My sister and I don't seem as close as we once were. Martha seems like ... she isn't interested in me anymore.*

Gazing down into the water, Bertha arrived at the conclusion the river was nothing but a muddy old river; it wasn't beautiful at all, neither was this smelly old boat.

She turned back to Papa, introducing the young Mormon men to Neil and Martha *My sister and Neil, I have to admit, do make a handsome couple.* It was at this moment that Bertha understood Martha's preoccupation: it had to do with Neil.

Martha glanced over to see Bertha lift her chin and straighten her shoulders, a faint smile on her lips, as she reached to take Papa's arm. Martha thought she actually saw her sister swish her coarse Lindsey Woolsey skirt as she gracefully and as majestically as any queen took leave of the boat in her well-scuffed, tattered moccasins.

Martha watched Bertha cast a glance over her shoulder as if to casually take note of the family; but Martha knew Bertha, and she knew her sister was looking beyond the family to the three young Mormon men behind her, who incidentally were bound for Council Bluffs, as were the Burt family.

Chapter 18 IOWA

Martha, by firelight, attempted to record the events of the past few days. When she glanced up, the sun had spread a golden splash of color across the morning sky.

She reread her entry of May 10, 1846. *Our six wagons have been joined by twenty wagons since the Mississippi crossing, making the long line seem to stretch on forever. We are broken into three groups, with two droves of cattle between us.*

She paused to wet the pencil lead with her tongue before she continued. *We are now on our way to Council Bluffs.* She reached down to scratch an insect bite on her ankle without breaking her concentration

Mr. Emigh says we can't be sure how many miles we have to travel because the rivers change their boundaries when they overflow in the spring and wash out the roads, but we have about three hundred and twenty-five miles to cross Iowa.

Our wagons safely crossed the Mississippi River. Iowa is beautiful with green, rounded hills and blue rivers. Massive oak trees and wild roses are everywhere, and little yellow birds sing ever so sweetly. The weather has been holding good, only raining at night.

We passed through Muscatine County, with many small towns and farms where we were able to buy milk, eggs, and fresh vegetables.

Late yesterday afternoon we crossed the Iowa River on big barges. The drovers had to swim their cattle across the fast water and wasted little time catching up to us.

Mother still has the misery in her head but is feeling some better. I have been busy seeing to the family's needs.

Papa came to request his first cup of morning coffee. Martha closed the journal and set it aside to fill his cup.

"Let's finish our coffee before we get the family up," he suggested.

"Papa, does Iowa have two names? I hear it called Hawkeye and Iowa."

"The names are Indian names, Martha. Iowa is one of the tribes under Chief Black Hawk, who we refer to as Hawkeye. Chief Black Hawk is probably the greatest chief the Iowa, Sauk, Fox, Kickapoo and Illinois tribes ever had; he even went to war alongside his people during the Black Hawk War back in '33 you've heard me tell about."

Papa was seated down on the ground and stretched his legs out beside the fire. "This territory once all was under Black Hawk's rule. The white man came to claim the land. Actually we bought it from them and divided it into two territories, Illinois and Iowa. The Indians still aren't convinced of our claim to these territories, and the old chief Black Hawk died back 'bout eight years ago. That answer your question? It's gettin' late. While you wake the others, I'm gonna yoke up the oxen."

"Time to get up." Martha nudged her sleeping sisters. "We need to get moving."

"I'm in the middle of a dream; go away, don't bother me," Bertha fussed.

"I just got to sleep," Ruthie complained, squirming deeper under her warm quilt.

Stephen, who always woke refreshed, was ready to greet whatever came his way.

Martha had bread baking and a pot of antelope meat and beans cooking. She decided to use some of the fresh eggs and make a batter-dipped bread, fried and served with sorghum or sweetened, sauced dried apples.

Papa returned, pleased to see everyone assembled around the fire. "I see it's going to be another nice day. Mr. Emigh said it got up into the sixties yesterday. Ah, Martha, you've got our breakfast ready," he said, dusting off his hands. "Did your mother eat something this morning?"

"She says she's feeling much better," Martha replied, handing Papa his plate. "Papa, the cow's cut way back on her milk."

"Yeah, I know. I s'pect she's trying to dry up. She'll be that way till after she calves again, or maybe she'd just tired and worn out like your mother's feelin'. By the way, girls, I 'preciate yur helping yur mother right now. I know she 'preciates it too, and Stephen? Unless you ask one of us, you're not ta give anymore food ta the Indians, and don't ya go botherin' your mother about this either."

"Papa, yesterday I traded this little boy like me some Pilot crackers for a pair of moccasins, and ya know what he did?" Stephen asked, wiggling his way onto Papa's lap. "He ate up my crackers then come back with this really tall, mean-lookin' Indian and he told me I had ta give him back his moccasins. Did I have to do that, Papa, after he ate my crackers?"

"Didn't I tell you not to give him any food?" Bertha reprimanded him. "It's your own doin'."

"Did you give him back the moccasins, Stephen?"

"Yes, Papa, but the man scared me. I sure don't want him mad at me—whush! He's a really big man too. What am I s'pose ta tell 'em then?" he asked, shrugging his shoulders and gesturing with his palms up.

"You tell 'em ta come see me," Papa instructed him.

"They look so pitiful," Martha remarked, collecting the empty plates. "Women and little children, begging in those eyesore clothes they wear, and with such thin, haggard faces."

"Listen ta me, these Sauk are a proud people. They make beautiful clothes and fine jewelry. If they'd learn farmin' our way, they could be successful with all this rich land. It's up ta them; they have ta help themselves if they're ta survive. We can't do it for 'em, and feedin' 'em ain't helpin 'em."

"Martha, anymore coffee? Now I have something important I wanna share with ya'. Last night we wanted ta park together when we stopped, but the droves of cattle formed a barrier and our wagons were unable to link themselves into one formation like we're used ta doin'."

Martha knew it had come about after the Iowa River crossing that the drovers had forced their way and their incessant bawling cattle between the wagons.

"Now we men have devised a plan," Papa explained." Ya see, our trouble is when ya have one road and a bunch of drovers who think nothin' of drivin' their cattle over ya if ya try ta pass 'em, and they'll pull a gun if anyone threatens 'em. It's hard ta reason with such men. We decided ta move out this morning. Mr. Kenyon is on the other side of the herd we need ta get 'round, so he's ta let us know when ta make our move. Don't worry 'bout cleanin' up; just pack up and let's have things ready ta move out."

"I'm so glad, Papa," Bertha exclaimed. "Haven't you noticed how swollen, red, and sore my eyes are? I think it's from all this grit and dirt in the air."

"Every morning my eyes is stuck shut, and when I get them open they feel like there's dirt in 'em," Ruthie complained.

"We need ta get past these cattle. That's why I have the oxen already yoked. I usually do this while you women get the wagon packed. I'm glad your mother's feelin' better. I miss her not bein' out here with us. While you finish packin' up camp, I'm gonna look in on her."

Martha, with hands on her hips, regarded the burning firewood. There wasn't anyway she could save it. Dry wood was becoming dear. There wasn't time to cut and chop it, and wood was burdensome to carry. With so many settlers progressing west, wood, like the grass alongside the roads, was becoming an issue.

Martha glanced over to see that the drovers were relaxed, seated around their campfire eating breakfast. *If only they were aware of the action about to take place.* Just then Mr. Kenyon's sharp whistle signaled it was time to go.

Papa had climbed down to fill Mother's coffee cup. When he heard the whistle, he motioned the children into the wagon. "Here we go!" he yelled, running for his seat.

Five teams followed Mr. Kenyon's lead out of the road, across a field, past the startled drovers, and up over a hill; they even proceeded to span a ditch. The teams seemed to understand what was expected of them and without hesitation they charged forward, pulling the wagons leaping precariously behind them over the rough ground.

Mother, who had been unaware of the plan, was bounced about on her bed inside the lurching wagon. Martha silently hoped she'd packed things away securely in her haste. Bertha was keeping watch between the front and rear openings of the canvas as the wagons gained space between them and the cattle.

The wagons, one after another, pulled into new positions behind surprised folks, who had been ahead of them and knew nothing of their problem.

"No use laying in a sick bed when a body's floundering around like this," Mother stated as she managed to stand up. "What's going on anyway? Would someone like to tell me, or were you planning to leave me behind after I'd been pitched out of the wagon?"

Everyone, talking at once, told her how Papa and the others decided to get around the cattle and drovers this morning.

"They's trying to keep us from gettin' to Oregon, Mother, but Papa showed 'em," Stephen sputtered in delight.

"Mercy, my face—my hair—I must look a sight," Mother said, grabbing her bonnet. "Maybe this will help hide some of my grief. I'm on my way to your papa. He needs a piece of my mind. Driving those oxen like this, indeed! He could have turned this wagon over and killed us all."

"I'm glad to see your feeling better, Mother."

"As I said, Martha, it's time I was up," Mother replied as she tied her bonnet.

Papa had settled back on the seat to relax . *Two big droves of cattle without wagons between them. What a mess. Those drovers're gonna have ta keep the cattle separated. They deserve this.* Pleased with the outcome, he laughed out loud. The move he'd just made had him feeling like a contemptuous fool, but it served them drovers right.

Several hours and a considerable distance from the cattle later, Neil came riding back. "The Kenyon's say to pull off up ahead in that field over yonder. We'll stop for a bite of cold dinner."

The plan was to do as other wagons had been doing as they pulled off to stop, then pull back into line to resume traveling.

With the long line ahead and a cloud of dust embracing him, Papa's overview didn't permit him to perceive the wagon coming towards him with a woman handling a team of four big horses. Somewhere in front of him a wagon had pulled to a stop, forcing the folks behind it to stop, and this in turn allowed the dust to settle.

"My husband's sick inside the wagon," she told them. "Our head man drowned a few days ago trying to swim our stock across the Elkhorn River back there. Watch out, it's a silent, ugly river. I'm not having anymore," she told them. "I'm going back."

The group worried for her. What about the Indians and her small youngsters? They inquired as to where she was headed. Did she want to join them?

"I've had more than my share of trouble and hard knocks," she told them. "I'm bound for Missouri. I've made it this far by myself. I plan to keep goin'."

You've got some pretty ornery drovers up ahead of you, she was told.

Everyone expressed their fears and pity for her. Going back alone? They could only shake their heads as they returned to their wagons.

It was during the dinner stop that the men decided with the weather in their favor they better leave the wagon train and do some hunting.

As he waited for his dinner, Alex Kenyon commented on the scenic beauty around him. "It's a peaceful land ain't it?" he observed. "And quiet, now we're away from them durn blasted cattle."

The men inhaled deeply breaths of dust-free air and watched as a hawk above them screamed at the loss of its prey to a competitor, who had quickly and expertly dived down to grab hold of its bounty with powerful talons, then gracefully lifted up and soared away, avoiding its screaming rival.

"This territory's opposed to statehood, you know?" Sam Emigh remarked. "The citizens don't want to pay their elected officials' salaries from local and state taxation."

David Wilson wondered aloud, "How long can they get away with this kind of politics?"

"Probably within the year—its inevitable. I hear they're working on a state constitution now. Prob'ly it'll be accepted by the end of this year," Sam speculated.

The Burt women hastily put together a dinner and had barely set out the biscuits, cold beans, and meat when Papa came running to the wagon. "Into the wagon!" he yelled. The women stared at him in surprise.

"Look behind ya." He was up onto his seat, reins in hand, before they could move.

The cattle came charging towards them. The head teamster with his drovers were whipping, hollering, urging the crazed animals on. The men were near enough for the Burts to hear their cursing. A dust cloud spread out and around the cattle, making it impossible for the Burts to determine how close the thundering hooves were from them.

The wagons in front of Papa were also hoping to put a distance between themselves and the threatening, bawling cattle.

Papa stood up, snapping the reins over the backs of his oxen to speed them up as he exclaimed to Mother. "Sam's right, we earned this road too hard ta give it back to them."

"Eli, these drovers are acting foolish, putting us in harm's way like this, and you—you men—have you all taken leave of your good senses?" Mother clutched onto the edge of her seat with both hands, praying that her life and those of her children might be spared.

"Hang on, Mary," Papa shouted, urging his oxen to run for their lives as they pulled the vaulting wagon behind them. Through a dust-filled haze, Papa now and again caught a glimpse of the wagons in front of him as they too endeavored to outdistance the cattle.

The girls in the back of the wagon were being bounced about but kept watch on the head teamster through the dust. When they saw him throw up his hands and shrug his shoulders in a show of giving up, they squealed with joy.

"Papa!" they shouted. "They've given up! The head teamster just gave up."

"No, don't stop, Papa, I like this!" Stephen excitedly requested as he scrambled to the front of the wagon. "Is this the Oregon Territory?"

"No, son," Papa laughed, settling back down on his seat. "But I don't believe those cattle and drovers'll bother us anymore. My oxen weren't meant to run and pull this heavy a wagon."

"Now, Eli, if you're through acting ferhoodled, what about our dinner? I'm hungry!" Mother inquired.

"We eat while we're movin',' Mary; we're not stoppin'."

"What do you mean we're not stopping? Now Mr. Burt, if you think—"

"No, ma'am," Papa interrupted her. "We're on our way to the Oregon Territory."

"Well—not all in one day, I would hope tell." Mother wasn't able to be serious with Papa any longer and had to give in to laugher at his remark.

Stephen didn't understand what Mother found amusing but he joined her. For Papa, the day was pleasant with his wife beside him, and the drovers and cattle behind him. He settled back to relax, letting the oxen pick a comfortable pace.

It was late afternoon when Neil rode back to tell them, "The Kenyons suggest we men leave the train and do some hunting before it gets much later. The women are to handle the teams. Mr. Emigh and Mr. Wilson have offered to stay with the wagons should there be any trouble. Mr. Kenyon says we men will find you by the fires later tonight." Having delivered his message, Neil circled around to the back of the Burt wagon, hoping to see Martha.

Martha and her sisters were sitting on the tailgate between the horse and the little milk cow, leisurely swinging their bare feet as they guessed the names of the wildflowers about them, when Neil came riding around the wagon. He slowed to press a hand to his lips, then thrust it out towards the girls without breaking his stride as he continued on around and back down the line of wagons. He didn't rightly know what possessed him to make such a silly gesture but he enjoyed himself. *I believe Martha returned my gesture too,* he thought.

His sentimental act sent her sisters into gales of laughter, but his gesture aroused a sensation in Martha. Neil was a good friend. However, the quickening of her heart told her he was far more than just a good friend.

The six wagons pulled off the road and into a field, allowing the cattle, drovers, and other wagons to continue moving past them.

Left to manage wagons, teams, and youngsters, the sweaty, dirty, thirsty, and tired women looked around them. There didn't appear to be any firewood, water, or shelter. The grass had been gleaned from both sides of the road, leaving little forage for their livestock. After a quick decision, they decided to travel on through the fields in tall prairie grass, up over the hill in front of them in search of adequate camping.

It came as a surprise to Ruth Kenyon to realize this was the first time she and the women had the entire responsibility of the wagons and families to themselves.

Dear Lord, she prayed as she led first in her wagon, *If you please, Lord, would it be possible for the Indians to find something better to do than pick on defenseless women and our young'uns tonight? That is, should the idea occur to them.*

Chapter 19

Sam Emigh and David Wilson had volunteered to stay with the women while the men left to hunt. The two men led the wagons, with the women handling the reins, through waist-high prairie grass in search of shrubs or brush clustered together as a possible indication of water and a campsite.

The wagons traveled some distance and descended into a valley yielding a good-size stream, grazing for the livestock, and wood for campfires.

The men would have assisted the women in parking the wagons, but Mrs. Kenyon insisted, "This is as good a time as any for us women to learn how to maneuver our wagons."

Numerous attempts had to be made with shouts of advice and encouragement until each woman pulled her wagon into the usual circular formation with the wagon's tongue resting on the inside rear wheel of the wagon in front.

Mother led her little cow outside the wagon enclosure to milk her. She was worried Papa might reason the cow wasn't producing enough milk to warrant keeping her, but he'd not hear a word from her. She finished milking and set the milk bucket aside to put Patsy in with the other livestock and discovered the corral was empty.

Shading her eyes she frantically scanned the horizon. "They're gone!" she shouted. "Our livestock's gone."

The others came to watch as their animals sprinted to the far end of a wide, open meadow.

"They're moving so fast," Mother whispered.

"Yes, and how on earth do we stop them?" Ruth's comment mirrored the thoughts of the others.

"Ya'd think they'd be worn out after all thet runnin' they did today." In her exasperation Jenny McGraw could only heave a loud sigh.

"Hrumph," David Wilson grumbled. "They learned how ta run today"

The weary group stood helpless as they watched the livestock run on.

They suddenly noticed the animals pause, then hesitate. The horses and oxen had circled around and reversed their direction. They were headed back towards the campsite. Then ever so faintly was heard the voices of the children, who had been sent to gather firewood.

Sam Emigh instructed the women, "Put down a couple of the wagon tongues and we'll herd them back into the corral."

The girls, to keep abreast of the livestock, struggled with their long skirts through the waist-high prairie grass. Bertha with one arm held her skirt above her knees used her other arm to flag at the animals.

Paul and Karl Kenyon, across the field from lil' Joe and Junior Mc-Graw, yelled for them to help herd the animals from their side back to the waiting women ahead, whom they could see had their skirts fanned out to funnel the livestock into the enclosure.

After the last animal was safe in the corral the exhausted children tumbled down into the grass to catch their breath.

Mr. Wilson discovered one of the wagon tongues had either been knocked down or had fallen, creating an opening that allowed the livestock to escape.

"I'll take Major here with a couple of ropes and let's go retrieve the wood," Mr. Emigh suggested to the children, who picked themselves up off the ground to trail after him.

On the way to collect the wood, Mr. Emigh called attention to some strangely shaped mounds in the fields around them. "I read somewhere these mounds you see are thousands of years old. They're burial tombs erected by the Indians living here long ago."

"Can we see inside them? Do they still bury Indians in them?" The children were inquisitive and full of questions as they observed the strange mounds, out of place against the landscape.

"What would happen if we tried to open and get inside them?" Louie Crawford inquired.

"We wouldn't, Louie. We honor and respect the Indian dead just as we want them to respect our dead. I think they're sealed anyway. You might have a difficult time getting into them."

"Did they bury the people alive?" Paul Kenyon eyed the mounds with fascination.

"I couldn't tell you. I don't know all that much about the Indian customs back then," Mr. Emigh replied.

"What are the mounds made of?" Lizzy questioned.

"Perhaps adobe. Adobe bricks were made back then and they last a long time," Mr. Emigh told her. "Adobe is a mixture of mud, grass, and straw pressed into shapes then dried in the sun. To the south of us, the Indians make and live in adobe houses."

"They sure must hold a lotta dead Indians," Stephen remarked. "Johnny, I don't smell nothin' comin' from 'em, do you?"

The wood was loaded onto Major's back and the group returned to camp. The youngsters amused Sam as he watched them walk backward or take quick glances over their shoulders. *It's as though they are expecting something to rise up out of those mounds at them.* He decided he had some good spine-tingling story material for around the campfire. "Come along, everyone, let's step lively. Major here wants to get back and finish his nap."

Mother helped herself to kindling stored in Papa's utility box under the wagon seat. She happened on his carpenter's plane with its two handles attached on either side of a long, sharp, flat blade. By drawing the blade through the wood, she sliced off a few fragrant wood curls. The pine scent stirred memories of the little stove she'd left behind.

As she waited for the fire to take hold, Mother realized how extremely weary she was, and there was supper yet to prepare and food for tomorrow. When the men returned, the fresh meat would need to be dealt with. She glanced over to see her girls; they too were tuckered out, but the water barrels needed replenishing.

While they filled the barrels, Bertha confided to Martha, "We can turn our dresses into comfortable outfits that will cover our legs. We'll still be decent without these miserable long skirts getting in our way."

"Hmm—I don't know, Bertha. What will Mother say?"

"Let's not tell Mother or Papa. We'll make 'em first and then surprise them."

"I don't quite understand how you intend to make them."

"They'll be like pantaloons, with suspenders; the waist top will come down over the pantaloons. Oh, you're just gonna adore 'em, Martha. But we can't tell a soul; not just yet."

Martha was skeptical. Bertha was always thinking up something strange.

"But Bertha, what will the other women say?" There was something about her sister's plan that was against her ingrained nature of how a decent woman dressed. Martha wasn't sure she was ready for such a change.

She didn't know who made the original preposterous dress rule for women in the first place. It wasn't Eve. The Bible said she'd hid behind some leaves, not a long, cumbersome dress.

"Maybe when they see us, the women will want us to make them outfits too. You don't have to if you don't want to, Martha." Bertha tossed her long hair over her shoulders. "I'm making myself an outfit. I can't stand wearing these clumsy dresses. Besides, aren't you the one always telling me how we women are so—oh, you know what I'm trying to say. Yes, restricted—yes, that's the word."

Mother came up to inquire what the girls were talking about. She detected an impish grin from one, and the other an admission of guilt as color quickly stained her neck and face. She was about to question them further but Stephen interrupted.

"When're we gonna eat, Mother? I'm hungry."

"While I fix your supper, you run and ask Mr. Emigh if he'd care to take supper with us."

"Mr. Emigh's eatin' his supper with the Crawfords and they're already eatin'."

"I'm on my way to put something together for us right now, Son."

"Do you have a headache again, Mother?" Stephen questioned as he took her hand in his and looked up at her with grave concern.

"No, darlin', but let's not suggest it to my head or it might think it has to give me the misery again. I know—how about griddle cakes with the bit of ham I was saving to cook with beans? I'll make a special supper for you."

Supper over, David Wilson and Mother relaxed with their coffee. Martha and Bertha were busy with their projects laid out on the tailgate of the wagon.

Mrs. Kenyon wandered up to share coffee and the campfire. "Can't help but wonder what's keepin' the men. It's getting dark." She settled down on a provisional box and accepted a cup of coffee from Mary Burt.

" I know God created beans for us," she commented, "but I'm beginning to understand better those folks in the good book that complained about that mana fallin' from the sky every day. Can't believe, of all the things I thought important to bring, I brought beans to plant when we get settled."

Mother had to chuckle. "I don't care how you fix them, they taste like beans, don't they, Ruth? Mine were dry tonight, with most of the broth sloshed out of the kettle after being jostled around in the wagon today."

"My, my, your girls—they're busy as a couple of bees tonight," Ruth said as she glanced over to the girls.

"Yes," Mother agreed. "They're being very secretive about something. This journey is difficult for them. Between the way we live and what we have on hand to work with, it can't be much. I'm sure you understand."

"Say, not to talk out of turn," David Wilson inquired, "but do either of you ladies know how to fix jerky? I heard it can be stored for some time."

"Way I do mine is to cut the meat into thin strips and lay 'em over small poles hung on scaffolds a few feet from the fire," Ruth instructed. "We just need to lift our grates higher, Mary, then hang the strips on the grate over the coals."

After the discussion, the three decided to employ the method. The youngsters were sent to collect branches and small limbs to erect the scaffolds.

Martha paused; it was the twilight hour, the last light of day. She needed more light; however, the women had all gathered around the campfire and were sure to ask questions. "I can't see to sew anymore, Bertha."

"The seams are straight sewing, Martha; pretend you're blind."

"Blind people sew, Bertha? I don't believe you." Martha pricked her finger just then and quickly put it to her lips to ease the pain.

"The fellows sure have been gone a long time, seems ta me." Ruth Kenyon batted at annoying mosquitoes. The other women were busy stripping bark from the branches to complete their scaffolds in anticipation of drying jerky.

The youngsters down by the creek suddenly stopped their play. Without being told, they ran for the wagons. At the sound of horses hooves, terror gripped the women at how vulnerable they were. The sound of horses, the darkness, and the indistinct misshapen images in the night intensified their menacing fear.

"Everyone, to the wagons." Mrs. Kenyon fought to keep the anxiety from her voice and not betray her fear. The women scattered to collect guns, pots, pans, anything they could use as a weapon if called on to have one. They waited with hearts racing, breath muted. Even the cicadas, frogs, and birds were hushed.

In the stillness, suddenly Stephen' shout sounded loud. "It's Papa! Papa's back." The men's voices became more distinct as they approached the camp. Their silhouettes emerged into the firelight as each rider with a massive piece of meat tied to his back, and more meat slung across the rumps of their horses, had appeared out of the darkness as grotesque images.

The women instantly busied themselves with food for their hungry men, who were sent to clean up in the creek before coming to settle around the Kenyon's fire, where they were handed plates of beans and bread.

The children helped Mr. Emigh and Mr. Wilson care for the horses before they and the women gathered around the men to hear the story of the hunt.

Neil began by telling them, "We didn't wanna stir up the herd, or we might have been stampeded." He glanced up to see if he had Martha's attention.

"Ah'm tellin' y'all," Brian McGraw interrupted, "we's fraid if'n we startled 'em they'd a-run straight for this here camp." He shoveled a heaping spoonful of beans into his mouth along with a big bite of bread, chewing both at once.

Neil told how "we got this big feller cornered, singled away from the rest of the herd, but it was like he had us figured out and he wasn't gonna let hisself be trapped." He paused to take a bite of beans and make sure Martha was still attentive.

Papa took over the story. "He kept putting his head down, snortin', makin' loud gruntin' noises, then he'd duck away from us as we tried workin' him away from the rest of the herd."

Neil broke in, "We's tryin' ta keep away from the herd. One of those buffalo outweighs my horse easily, and we're tryin' ta keep this big bull singled out, but he just kept dodgin' us, zigzaggin' back and forth."

Martha felt a thrill of excitement at the dexterity the big bull showed in avoiding his captors, as Neil went on to relate the skill the men used to maneuver the animal.

Mr. Kenyon set aside his plate and stood up to imitate the big bull with his head lowered and his hands placed on either side of his ears to resemble buffalo horns. He captured the youngsters' interest as he pawed at the ground with his boot. "He shifted ta face us an' we knowed he's gonna charge." The children's eyes grew wide in wonder at Mr. Kenyon's animated demonstration.

Neil once again took over the story. His voice had dropped to a soft monotone. "We saw him hesitate. We knew he's gettin' ready ta turn on us at any moment, and that's when I raised ma' rifle." Neil raised his arms to show how he took aim. "Ka-blewey, got 'em straight on, right in the middle of that big head."

He paused. "You know, I never noticed before—but their eyes're more on the sides of their head. Well, kind of—anyway, I hit him right there in the middle of his head. He never moved, just stood his ground and stared at me with them mean, beady little eyes o' his, like he never felt a thing."

The children had moved closer to Neil, hypnotized by his account of the action.

"I had ta stop and reload, but Mr. Burt up and let fly with another blast. Thet big bull never moved, never so much as blinked one of them little eyes." Neil's audience was spellbound. "Right then, Mr. Crawford up and blasted away at 'em. That big ol' bull still stared us down. Then he slowly fell ta his knees and dropped. Whump—he's down and over on his side. Now you've never heard anything like the thunder them Bison make when they took off. The ground shook somethin' fearful. Wonder ya didn't hear 'em clear up this way. Off they went over yonder someplace. We had too much work waitin' for us ta care where they went.

"We jumped down. We had ta work fast, slittin' him open and guttin' 'em. We was hoping the Injuns didn't hear us shootin'. We kept lookin' fer 'em and keepin' a watch out for the herd that might decide ta circle back. That herd woulda tromped us ta death if they'd come back."

"Thing that amazed me most," Mr. Crawford explained, " was how the wolves gathered. They came out of nowhere. Kept their distance, pacin' back and forth, waitin' for us ta leave. Their eyes got a strange shine to 'em in the dark, but they stayed at a distance. I could hear 'em whinin'. Guess the fresh kill made 'em anxious."

"My, oh my," Mrs. Crawford commented. "Wonder thou didn't shoot each other or get run over by those wild buffalo. It's gettin' late and we've a lot of meat here. Best we get busy, ladies, and take care of it, wouldn't thee say?"

By the light from lard torches and firelight, the men dug pits and lined them with hot rocks and grass. The Dutch ovens were filled with chunks of meat and beans, and were then lowered into the pits to be covered with more hot rocks and grass before shovels of dirt were piled atop them, leaving them to simmer throughout the night.

Mrs. Kenyon had demanded that each family keep vigil for the four or five hours needed to dry the jerky and ward off hungry predators who might attack for the meat.

Martha, after helping Mother slice their portion of the meat for jerky, at last crawled into bed and pulled her quilt up around her shoulders. It had been a disturbing evening for her. She wasn't sure how the women were going to accept the new outfits. It saddened her to hear the men's excitement at killing the big bison; her emotions for Neil were confusing to her. He was so like Papa with his stories and dreams, but she wondered what role she played in his dreams.

She didn't feel comfortable sharing her feelings with Mother or her sisters. She wished Granny were here; she could talk to Granny. Oh, how she missed the dear, sweet, little old lady and Kohee. Did the little dog miss her? Her best friends were so far away tonight.

Warmed under her quilt Martha relaxed and gave in to sleep.

Chapter 20

Martha awoke to the tantalizing aroma of roasting meat. She joined Mother, and the two worked quietly side by side, turning the strips of buffalo jerky that were slowly drying over racks hung on scaffolds around the fire.

Papa, who had come to refill his coffee cup, paused to watch the two at work. "That old bull musta weighed in over fifteen hundredweight," he commented.

"This last batch of jerky should be done around midmorning." Mother brushed hair back from her brow.

Martha offered to fix breakfast. "Griddle cakes or the stew, Mother?"

"Griddle cakes, dear. I need to fry up the liver with some wild onions. Have you noticed all the wild onions? The fields are full of them." Mother straightened up slowly, pressing both hands into the small of her back, stiffened from bending over the drying racks.

"I took advantage of the fire to make up extra bread and fix a couple of dried apple cobblers. If you two can't wait till breakfast, eat some jerky."

Martha chewed on a strip of tough, dark brown, dried jerky on her way to wash her face in the creek, She decided to wait for the bread to finish baking before waking her sisters. The jerky wasn't helping to settle her queasy stomach. She prayed her parents didn't notice she had on her one and only good dress.

"I think the bread's done, Martha. I'll start breakfast while you wake your sisters and Stephen."

Martha decided to let Stephen sleep while she and her sisters dressed.

Mother looked up to greet the three girls and drew in her breath sharply. Her mouth dropped open as she hastily set down the pan she was holding.

"What—what in tar—nation?" Papa drawled softly.

"Papa, these are our new outfits." Bertha pirouetted to show her tunic top pulled down over a skirt divided into two pant legs.

"Ho, no, you girls go get into some decent clothes," Papa sternly commanded.

"The men—the folks—everyone will be talking about you." Mother, who had gained her composure, paled as she whispered, "You are indeed a pitiful sight."

"You look ridiculous in those disgusting outfits. Now do like I said," Papa snapped with anger.

Bertha drew herself up in quiet dignity and bit down on her lower lip to hold back a sharp retort to Papa's criticism.

"Oh," Mother groaned. "Whatever will the others think of us, Eli? Girls, you can't let anyone see you. We'll be a laughing-stock around here. Oh Eli, what are we going to do?" Mother hid her face in her apron.

Stephen had come to join the family. He rubbed his eyes, stretched, and emitted a yawn before he noticed his sisters. "Oh, you girls look funny. Don't they look funny?" He was about to laugh, but then he saw the frowns etched on his parents' faces.

Bertha stepped up behind Stephen and tweaked the hair on the back of his head.

"Ow!" he yelped. "Bertha, what'd ya do that for?"

"Be quiet, Stephen," Bertha hissed through clenched teeth.

Mother winced to see Ruthie squat down and fill her coffee cup with her knees spread apart. "Ruthie Mae, put your knees together. A lady would never think to expose herself.

You never consulted me, or your mother. This is unacceptable, young ladies."

Bertha resented her parents making her sisters and her appear foolish. She lowered her eyes, and her cheeks burned as she fought against outrage at the way her parents were accepting the outfits.

Ruthie's head lowered; her voice was barely audible as she apologized. "Papa—I'm sorry, I didn't mean to shame you and Mother."

This is so unfair, Martha thought. *We're being treated harshly by stupid rules. Men would never think of wearing long, cumbersome dresses. Yet they demand it of us women.*

"We're a good Christian family. When you see how the others treat us, maybe you'll come to your good senses." Papa's rebuke made them feel even more guilty, and there was no mistaking his disapproval.

Mother hastily exclaimed, "Why, mercy me, I've never found my dresses to be inconvenient. I'm able to move about as much as I want." She was unconsciously twisting her apron. "It isn't acceptable girls—please don't embarrass your papa and me—Eli, we'll be asked to leave the train, won't we?" She worked to smooth out the apron she'd crumpled in her frustration.

Martha wanted to speak out in defense of herself and her sisters, but realized if she said anything she was inviting severe punishment.

It surprised her to hear Bertha plead with Papa. "Papa, let us show you, please? However, if we're going to be a distraction for you and the other men, we'll go change into the only dresses we own."

"Your only dresses?" Mother gasped. "You've only your good dresses left?"

"I guess you three have to find out the hard way how ridiculous ya look. Just remember your mother and I told you, and don't be mistakin' yourselves; we'll all have ta suffer this shame you've brought on us."

Just then the sound of horses drew the attention and silenced the family as three buckskin-clad Indians approached and dismounted by the Burts' campfire.

"Meat smells for long ways. We're hungry," one of them told Papa as they proceeded to help themselves to the jerky. They squatted down before the fire and selected strips of the dried meat; as they finished one, they helped themselves to another. Martha and Bertha became uncomfortable under their bold, appraising stares.

Lizzy Crawford and Ginny McGraw met the Burt girls halfway between the wagons. They exclaimed over the outfits and said they wished they were able to convince their parents to let them do as Martha, Bertha, and Ruthie had done.

"I wouldn't dare, though," Lizzy quickly stated. "My daddy would thrash me within an inch of my life. I'm not as brave as you girls."

"They'd be surprised at first, our folks were, but they'd come to understand." Martha told them.

Papa recognized the Indians and stated, "You're from the Fox tribe?"

"Our chief was Black Hawk," one of them gestured with a sweep of his arm. "This territory belongs to Black Hawk's people."

Papa didn't feel it was appropriate to discuss the land issue with them, so he explained how it was members of the Fox tribe taught him to trap the beaver when he was a young lad. The men listened politely as they continued to help themselves to the jerky.

Papa asked if there were any hostile tribes around the settlers should be aware of, while Mother passed around slices of fresh warm bread.

The oldest appearing of the three, a stern-looking man, answered, "A young Fox Indian is leader for his renegades. He wears a blue stone around his neck. He is outcast from the Fox tribe, he and his men. They steal and kill. This is not the way of the Fox people."

Mrs. Kenyon, on hearing of the outfits, came to inspect them. She was impressed; however, she would never have admitted it in front of the other women. "Tell me," she asked in way of interest, "what holds the pantaloons up."

"A drawstring, Mrs. Kenyon." Bertha exhibited her design. "I cut the skirt from the dress top and folded the top of the skirt over."

"The suspenders are just in case the string comes untied," Martha added.

"Fancy this—don't the divided skirts looks comfortable? You must understand, it isn't that we women wouldn't like to wear something like this; we need to get the men's approval, but maybe—just maybe…." She stepped back with one hand on her hip, and the other cupped her chin as she cocked her head from side to side. "Let me think on this," was all she said.

The families stayed a polite distance from the Indians, but kept a close watch on on the activities around the Burts' campfire.

Sam Emigh requested Nathan help him get ready for the moveout. He was glad Neil wasn't around; he didn't need his son provoking any problems this morning.

Martha felt the need to challenge Mrs. Kenyon's wisdom for an explanation. "Men dress comfortable, Mrs. Kenyon. Why shouldn't we women be allowed to?"

"I'm sure your mother's told you," Mrs. Kenyon explained. "We women have our place and we have no choice but to accept these values. Men enjoy fine things, like a lady dressed in a purty dress. You charmin' young ladies know it brings out the best in the fellers."

Bertha's unspoken thoughts of Ruth Kenyon were *I can't imagine you knowing what a pretty, fragile young thing is, dear lady, no matter how fine was your dress.*

"Then, Mrs. Kenyon," Martha asked, "how do we convince the men our intentions aren't meant to be trying to them? We women don't change inside by what we wear."

Mrs. Kenyon folded her arms over her ample bosom. "My dears, I understand how you feel. However, there are ways we women go about gettin' our freedoms, and it has be done quietly and cleverly, so's not to let the men folk know. You'll learn; it comes with experience, to make them think it was their idea in the first place. I must get back to my wagon now, but I like your spirit."

The sisters looked at each other and shrugged their shoulders. To the ladies retreating back, Martha murmured, "Thank you, Mrs. Kenyon. My sister and I do so value your opinion."

She heard Bertha smirk at the comment.

The Indians, having eaten their fill of jerky, massaged their greasy hands through their hair as they stood up to leave. The tallest of the three spoke up. "The stone the young renegade wears is an honorable gift from his mother's father. He and his men make trouble for those who would travel across the land." The others nodded in agreement.

The shortest of the three, who had remained quiet up until now, gestured to the girls. "Your woman for sale or trade? They have shirts and blankets to carry with them?"

"No parley; women are my daughters," Papa told them as Mother handed them food, which they stowed in skin bags draped over the back of their horses.

"You can make pemmican?" the tall one inquired of Mother.

"We don't know about pemmican," Papa replied.

"Dried jerky made fine with dried berries and buffalo fat. Packed in skin bags to take for many days' travel. My squaw, she knows to teach you," he said. This was the only sign of recognition the men afforded Mother Burt.

The Indians made their way to the creek to water their horses and quench their thirst. The families were uncomfortable under the Indians once-over as they mounted up.

After the Indians departed, the wagon train resumed its normal routine, except for the issue pertaining to the Burt girls and their new clothes.

"No, absolutely not," Tom Crawford explained in a voice Lizzy and her mother understood meant no more was to be said. "There's a reason women wear dresses: you're made different than men. You mind your business and leave those girls to their father. I don't wanta hear another word, you hear me?" Mr. Crawford growled.

Mrs. Crawford's actions confused Lizzy. First off, she didn't understand if her mother was disgusted or pleased with the outfits. First her mother said she did find dresses were indeed difficult to move around in, always getting caught up on something. The hems of the long skirts became ragged after being dragged through the brush and dirt; but then she told Lizzy, "Thou best listen to thy daddy, Elizabeth."

Brian McGraw's ranting was heard throughout the camp. "No decent wimmin Ah knows woulda showed off'n herself like them Burt girls're a-doin'. Your momma an' me brung ya up right. Ya hain't goin' 'round showin' yourself off. No—hit ain't decent."

"What are they afraid of—we've turned into witches or demons?" Bertha muttered.

"I don't like hurting Papa and Mother," Ruthie said. "I love them and I don't like it when they're angry with me."

"We love them too, Ruthie, but we've done nothing bad." Bertha gently pushed hair away from her little sister's sad face.

"They'll survive, Ruthie. You wait and see. You'll be able to outdistance the boys from now on, maybe even the Indians if they chase after you," Martha assured her.

"I think changes like this are hard on older folks like our parents," Martha said in a way of explanation to her sisters. "If you noticed, neither Mr. Emigh or Mr. Wilson laughed nor seemed offended."

"I did notice, Martha," Bertha informed her. "In fact, I thought they looked approving. I'm waiting for Neil to say something, and if he so much as snickers or laughs, I'm apt to slap his silly face. And Ruthie, I think Mother would look nice in an outfit like ours."

After the Indians rode away, the men hastily made their way over to Papa. "They can see we took only meat for our use." Tom Crawford was nervous and defensive.

"When they looked around, they could see we aren't intending to stay," David Wilson quickly added.

"Guess, we's ain't got nothin' here they's wanted 'septin' fer your daughters, eh, Eli?" Brian McGraw's bawdy laughter eased the men's tensions, and though Eli Burt laughed at the jesting, he didn't go about it wholeheartedly.

"They're from the Fox tribe and smelled our meat cookin'," Papa explained. "They warned us to be on the lookout for the Indian with the blue stone.

Martha and Mother overheard Papa tell the men about the Indian with the blue stone and how they should watch out for the rowdy bunch."

"Mother!" Martha whispered. "The Indian, the one with the blue stone?" She'd many times wondered about the young brave and if she'd ever seen him again.

"Yes, I'm surprised too," Mother replied. "I thought when we left Illinois we left him and his kind behind."

"Mother, Papa told me Illinois and Iowa are all a part of Black Hawk's territory."

"Chief Black Hawk, Martha. Show respect, dear. He's as important to the Indians as President Polk is to us."

"They always refer to us as just white people, Mother."

"Martha, settlers, pioneers, immigrants, trailblazers—we're all the same, looking for land. Pilgrims are different only in that they set up holy places."

Ruthie, listening to the conversation taking place between Mother and Martha, spoke up to ask, "If I'm an immigrant, pioneer, and settler, like you say, then when you and Papa die and I bury you in a graveyard, will I be a pilgrim too, Mother? Is a graveyard a holy place?"

"Yes, Ruthie, something like that, dear," Mother replied, putting her arms around the little girl and hugging her close. "You're awfully young, Miss Ruthie, to be so full of such important information, aren't you?"

Bertha held out the legs of her new outfit and twirled in a circle. "Mother, see, the Indians were even willing to buy us in outfits like this."

It surprised the girls when Mother answered, "I'm sure the thought crossed your papa's mind even before he was asked. We just don't have enough quilts to send with you is all."

The wagons moved out to travel as many miles as daylight permitted. To Martha, they were no longer a solitary group using the road. Since crossing the Mississippi, groups traveling ahead and behind them weren't unusual.

The girls felt carefree under the warm, late morning sun with a breeze gently moving through the fields of amber and green prairie grass filled with brightly colored wildflowers. Off to the north of them, tiny black specks moved back and forth across the horizon as buffalo fed.

"Martha?" Ruthie shaded her eyes with her hands. "Do you think those buffalo remember Papa and the men from yesterday?"

"As long as they stay that far away from us, Ruthie, I wouldn't worry," her big sister told her

"Oh—oh! Martha, look!" Ruthie pointed to a large butterfly as it fluttered from flower to flower within reach of them.

The girls broke into gales of laughter when Bertha wondered aloud, "Hmm—now is this a pioneer, a settler, or a trailblazer?"

At first Martha hummed softly to herself, but before long her sisters had picked up the melody and began singing. Even Papa, hand in hand with Mother, joined in as they walked along at the oxen's steady pace

"Such a glorious day," Martha exclaimed.

"And let's hope it stays this way," Bertha agreed.

Martha and Bertha watched as Ruthie dashed out into the meadow where the breeze teased at the legs of her pantaloons and a butterfly flitted just beyond her grasp.

Chapter 21

"This is all I could think to put in the journal." Martha read aloud: "*We've gone through Johnson, Iowa, and Powsheik counties and we're riding in the wagon until the sun warms the chill from the morning and dries the roads. I can't write while we're moving anyway.*"

"Write later, Martha," Bertha suggested, peeking over her sister's shoulder. She understood Martha's dilemma; she didn't like recording in the journal either.

"Martha, did you enter that we barged across the east fork of the English River day before yesterday?" Mother called from her place beside Papa on the wagon seat.

"Martha, how about the three days of rain with all that of thunder and lightning?" Ruthie reminded her. "We never get dried out between those noisy storms. I hate 'em."

"Be sure to say the road has improved after the rains and we're making better time," Mother called back.

"The Indians haven't given us any problems to speak of," Papa added. "I'm impressed with this fertile land and friendly people. Martha, be sure to put down that this area is predominately made up of Mormon settlers. They're hardworking farmers from what I see."

Martha had to agree; the fields were laid out like patchwork quilts in patterns of varying browns and shades of green. She'd recorded earlier that their sod homes were the result of clearing the fields for farming. The uniform-size pieces of sod were cut to construct durable homes with wooden doors, and some even had a window or two.

Mr. Emigh had explained to her how the root system from the grass intertwined and gave strength to the structures. Every year the spring rains set the houses ablaze with flowers imbedded in the sod. Inside, the soil compacted along with the dirt floors to make the homes cozy and safe against the elements, but it also inhibited many insects.

"Make note that we're coming into Council Bluffs," Papa instructed. "It's the place Lewis and Clark gathered all the Indian tribes together to inform them the land was ours through the Louisiana Purchase. I don't believe the town's officially named this; it's just referred to as Council Bluffs, part of Iowa's territory."

"You want me to write all this down?" Her pencil poised, Martha waited for his reply, but Mother interrupted to point out a farm ahead.

"Eli, if you care to stop I could use some fresh eggs, and how does fried chicken for our supper sound?"

Papa turned down the dirt lane to a one-story sod house with its window looking out to the east. The house was surrounded by well-tended gardens and fields. A gentleman who appeared to be Papa's age walked out to meet the Burt family. "Howdy folks, nice day for travel, yah?"

Papa held out his hand. "Name's Eli Burt. My wife here wanted to stop and see if you folks had some eggs and chickens for sale."

"Yah, das ist' meiner Fraus' business. Vhen they stop, she be taken care oft' die peoples. I be Gus Pendergast. I be please ta meet mit ya."

Mr. Pendergast nodded in the direction of the house to Mother. "Mein Frau is back behind das haus."

Mother, going in search of Mrs. Pendergast, couldn't help but notice the little children, who ranged in different sizes and ages, as they peeked out the door. She found Mrs. Pendergast hanging out her wash. A baby played contentedly nearby on a quilt in the warm morning sunshine.

"Mrs. Pendergast?" Mother inquired.

"Yah, guten morgen," came back a friendly, thick, guttural greeting Mother recognized as German or Dutch.

Mrs. Pendergast hastily dried her hands on a big white apron and tucked a wisp of stray hair behind her ear before she extended a rough, reddened hand to Mother.

"Would you be having a few eggs and perhaps a hen or two for sale?" Mother inquired. "Mr. Burt, my husband, felt it was too costly to travel with chickens. They eat too much and we have so little room. I do miss the fresh eggs."

Mrs. Pendergast understood Mother as she pointed to a wooden cart, with wooden wheels on either side and a sturdy handle, tipped up alongside the house.

"Yah." She drew in a deep breath. "Vhen vee come from Illinois mit der cart vee vas under vay to Utah, mit meinem Mr. Pendergast, das vas before den kinders. Und many of our kind come mit us. Some died, some vas killed, und some settled, like us. Und the rest traveled on to Utah. Mein mann liked dis place to lif. Mein mann, makes a goot garten, und now vee help build das village in Newton, down die road."

While Mrs. Pendergast went for baskets to collect eggs, Mother gazed with envy at the little house, the big gardens, and the clean washing blowing in the breeze. She followed Mrs. Pendergast out to the chicken house attached to the sod barn. Nesting boxes aligned both sides of the walls when the women entered the coop and reached into still-warm, straw-lined nests to collect the brown and white eggs.

"Someday, when this journey is over, I hope to have a garden like yours," Mother complimented Mrs. Pendergast. "This journey makes it so difficult to maintain any order in my life. I'll be glad to settle down."

Mother knew Mrs. Pendergast understood the life of a woman traveling on a long journey. She had only to look at the hand cart leaned against the house.

Mrs. Pendergast opened the barn door to collect a burlap bag for the hens, and a litter of furry puppies escaped to scamper about, delighted to be free.

Stephen and Ruthie lost little time in jumping down from the wagon to cuddle the soft, round, wiggling pups. Ruthie sat down on the ground, nestling two of the warm bodies at a time to her face.

"How much do I owe you, Mr. Pendergast?" Papa rummaged in his pocket.

"Mein Frau asks twenty-five pennies for twelve eggs und ten pennies for vun hen. That vill be right mit you Mr. Burt? Oh und ya take some of das goot dry vood? It be hard to find goot dry vood. Here take ten, twelve pieces. Ya got room for ten, twelve pieces, Mr. Burt?"

"That's right nice of you, Mr. Pendergast. Wood is a problem. There isn't time to cut and chop it. I didn't plan on the wood being in such short supply, but then again—it's not surprising with all the wagons coming through. Mrs. Burt and myself are grateful."

The women exchanged embraces as the men shook hands before the Burts boarded their wagon.

On their way once again, Papa shared with Mother how his discussion with Mr. Pendergast about the land. "Mary, he says its fertile; yields are good. They're helping to build a village with a school, church, and business to attract other Mormon families. I'm sorely tempted to stop here."

"Eli, I was impressed too, but we should let the others know of our decision if we decide to stay."

"Papa," Stephen whined, "why can't we have a dog?"

"Stephen, you know the answer. It'd get sick, get ticks, and get lost or killed. This is no journey for a dog."

"But Papa, we'd take care of the dog. You wouldn't have to worry none," Ruthie begged in a wistful voice. "Can't we have a puppy, please, Papa?"

"When we settle you can have any dog you so desire, but we need to settle first."

"You know, Mary, if I stayed I'd never know what was out West. I have to go see for myself." Papa reached for Mother's hand.

"Does this mean you're not going back, Eli?" Mother asked. "Do you know that Mrs. Pendergast told me they moved everything they owned in a little cart with wooden wheels? They pushed it all the way out here from Illinois. I'm more comfortable teaching our youngsters our ways besides, and did you know they don't drink coffee? Mrs. Pendergast says it's not good for you—nor are spirits."

"You're glad we're going on, Mary?" It made Papa feel good that his Mary wanted to continue their journey.

Martha and Bertha had decided to walk beside the wagon. They were complaining how dried out their skin was from the constant exposure to the weather. Bertha stated, "These wrinkles on my forehead and around my eyes are becoming creases." "Deep crevices is more like it," Martha said as she ran her hands over her face.

"My eyes are g'tting' squinty too, from facing into the sun for so many hours," Bertha lamented. "My clothes and hair are so stiff with dust and grime they won't bend."

Martha agreed with her sister. "We must look a sight. You know, Bertha, it isn't going to get any better either. We've still a long ways to go."

"You best do something about you're hands," Bertha warned Martha. "Neil isn't going to like holding your prickly hands. I hear Indian maidens have soft hands from working with the bear and buffalo hides. He might find he likes being touched by their soft hands instead of your pronged claws."

Martha wondered why she always let her sister's comments bother her. It seemed every chance she got, Bertha poked fun of her and Neil. Martha remembered Uncle Joe telling her one time, there wasn't such a thing as pure jesting; there was always some element of truth in it."

"Yes, you're right, Bertha," Martha sighed, "and their bodies and hair smell of rancid grease. I'm not worried. I can't believe Neil would enjoy that either."

The girls watched as Papa ahead of them pulled the wagon to a stop, and they heard him shout, "McGraw, what happened? Need some help?"

The girls came around the wagon in time to witness a disgruntled Mr. McGraw kick at a back wagon wheel.

"How'd that happen?" Papa asked

"Junior an' thet stick he's been a-carrin' wit him. He stuck it 'tween the spokes whilst the wagon was rollin'. Sounded like a rifle crack whin it busted. Thought we's bein' shot at. Durn kid anyway. Ah've half a mind ta—Ah otta'—"

"Mr. McGraw, ya'll watch your language out there, ya hear?" Jenny screeched from inside the wagon.

"Mz McGraw, git yursilf down outta there so's I kin fix this broken spoke. We needs ta git back on the road afore hit gits dark, or was ya plannin' ta settle here?"

"None of the others know about this?" Papa asked, removing his hat to scratch his head as he contemplated Brian McGraw's situation. "We can send my wagon with the women and the youngsters on ahead while we mend your wagon wheel here, or—"

"Think ita be safer ta stick together, Eli. 'Sides," Brian McGraw sputtered, "ya wasn't thinkin' Ah'm a-gonna unload this wagon by ma'silf now, did ya? We's pulled out of line whin one of ma' young'uns done puked up inside. An' whin we started out again is whin Junior done broke the wheel spoke."

Mother climbed down from the wagon. "Here, Mrs. McGraw, let the girls and me give you a hand unloading your wagon,"

"I'm much appreciated ta ya Mz Burt; one of ma' young'uns done puked inside here earlier," Jenny answered. "Musta been somethin' he et. He seems ta be alright now."

"Got an idea, Brian. When we stopped ta get some eggs, the feller gave me some chunks of wood. Soon as the women empty the wagon. Let's put 'em under the axle ta hoist the wagon. Just hope we don't manage ta break your axle."

"You, Junior, git yursilf over ta Mr. Burt's wagon and tote thet wood over here. Ya knows how ta bust a wheel, then ya gotta learn how's ta fix hit. Git yursilf busy now, ya hear me? Miz McGraw?" Brian McGraw roared. "Git this wagon emptied."

By the time the spare wheel was put on, the was wagon loaded, and they had a quick dinner the wagon train was miles ahead of them. Papa and Brian decided if they pushed their oxen, there was a chance they could catch up to the others.

"I feel bad for ma' oxen, but I don't look forward to campin' out here with two wagons," Papa explained to the family. "I know it's done, but for me this would be the night the buffalo or wild horses decide ta stampede or the Indian's attack."

Bertha was forced to run at times to keep pace with the wagon. "I wonder how those Mormons kept dry in the rain," she asked breathlessly. "How could they get everyone under one of those little carts?" She was gasping for breath. "Oh, I can't walk this fast. I hafta slow down, Martha. I don't understand how those folks ate. We keep our Dutch ovens full most of the time. How were they able to make bread?"

Before Martha could answer, Papa yelled for Mr. McGraw to hold up. He explained to no one in particular, "The sun's way over there. I think we best think about a campsite for tonight." Martha knew the men had hoped to catch up with the others or find protection of another group to travel with before night fall.

The men decided to cross up over the hill in front of them before looking for a campsite. As they crested the hill they sighted a group of wagons parked alongside some gigantic oak trees over in a large meadow. These folks also had hoped to unite with a wagon train, they said, as they warmly welcomed the two families into their circle.

Mother hung a kettle of water on the tripod over the fire. She selected a block of the Pendergast's wood, then lifted one of the hens from the sack and positioned its head over the edge of the wood, then deftly swung Papa's hatchet down onto the outstretched neck.

The girls covered their faces from the grisly scene of a headless chicken flopping around in a death dance before coming to rest at Mother's feet. Before it had ceased its movement, she repeated the execution of the other bird.

Martha was sent to bring the kettle of scalding water to dunk the chicken before the girls plucked feathers from the inert bodies.

"Phew, these wet feathers stink," Bertha grumbled as she twisted her mouth to blow flying feathers away from her face.

"Think how good these will taste when Mother fries them up for us," Martha giggled as she watched her sister's futile feather-blowing attempts.

Papa finished asking the blessing and the family settled down to a supper of crisp, golden fried chicken with milk gravy and biscuits when Neil rode up.

Martha quickly lowered her head at the sight of him, but she was unable to still her heart with him standing before her so tall and handsome; his wide, muscular shoulders were so strong appearing. His smile, when she dared to glance up at him, only quickened her beating heart more.

Martha, at Mother's suggestion, fixed him a plate of food. As she held it out to him, he managed to cover her hands with his before he settled down between her and Ruthie. She was no longer hungry, in her excitement of his being near; she picked at at the rest of her supper.

As he ate, Neil explained how the folks worried when neither family showed up. "So I said I'd ride back and see if there was a problem—but fried chicken! I'm glad I came back. Oh, and to see all of you, of course." He and Martha exchanged quick glances. "I tell ya this sure beats them beans and bread Pa's fixin, Mrs. Burt.'"

"We just got back on the road after gettin' these chickens and found Mr. McGraw with a broken spoke," Papa related. He paused to select another piece chicken.

"Junior stuck that walkin' stick of his in the wheel. Ya know the one he's carried all the way out from Chicago with him? Mr. McGraw said it sounded like a rifle shot when the spoke broke. He put an end to Junior's stick: he smashed it inta a million splinters. Man's got a temper. Time we got back on the road, you others were miles ahead. We came across these folks and they invited us to camp here with 'em tonight."

"Papa, Junior told me he brought that stick all the way from Arkansas. Why didn't they come by a closer route?" Bertha questioned. "Wouldn't it have been faster?"

"They came to Chicago first to live," Mother explained. "Mr. McGraw was a smithy not far from where Grandpa and Grandma Lane live."

"It's difficult for me to imagine why people would pack up everything they own, go off, and leave their families to traipse out West. They come from places I didn't know even existed," Martha commented.

"It's for the land, Martha," Neil exclaimed with excitement. "This country's so big nothin's ta keep folks from lookin' for their dreams. Miners're lookin' for gold, trappers for fur, farmers ta farm. Look around ya, Martha; this land goes on forever."

Martha, thrilled by Neil's enthusiasm, thought, *If he asked me to go with him right this moment, I think I'd follow him to the ends of this earth.* But Mother suggested, "Girls, please clean up the supper dishes."

Martha heaved a weary sigh. There were dishes to do, beds to be made up, and chores to prepare them for the move out tomorrow. She was secretly pleased, though, for Neil's decision to stay the night with the family.

Mother looked at the remains of the chicken. She'd hoped to have some left for dinner tomorrow, but she had beans soaking and there was plenty of buffalo jerky.

A festive mood settled over the camp as the folks watched the last brilliant colors sink below the horizon and darkness pushed the day out of sight.

A fiddle sounded first, followed by the melancholy sounds of a harmonica blended with the melodious strains of a lady strumming an auto harp. Mr. McGraw joined with his Jew's harp and Junior blew bass on his jug.

The music had just begun when a man, who was either a trapper or prospector, came leading his donkey into camp. After being invited to spend the night with the families, he rummaged inside the bags he'd removed from his donkey and came out squeezing a well-worn concertina and settled himself down to join with the other musicians.

However, he would disappear from time to time. "Jist been wettin' ma' whistle," he said as he returned. " Somebody around here brought some mighty fine homemade likker." Each time he was in better spirits, and his endeavor was to speed up the tempo of the music until he disappeared again.

No longer strangers, the folks united to sing song after song until someone began "All Through the Night." The darkened curtains of night had by now wrapped around the group with only the winking campfires to light their way to bed.

Neil whispered for Martha to stay with him a bit longer. Folded into the warmth of his arms, she found it comforting to lay her head against his chest and listen to his even breathing. She turned in his arms to face to him as Papa walked up.

"Beautiful night out, isn't it?" Papa said, gazing up to a star-studded sky. Martha pulled abruptly away from Neil but allowed him to hold her hand.

"Mr. Burt, I've been meanin' ta tell ya this all evenin'. Pa an' me met up with two brothers early on today and they told us about there bein' three of 'em before some Injuns came onto 'em an' there was a fight. The only Injun with a rifle killed one brother, so's the other brothers returned fire, killin' two or three of 'em including the one with the rifle. Pa and I got interested in their story 'cause it sounded like it might've been the Injun with your rifle, Mr. Burt. The others Injuns demanded guns and ammunition from the three brothers just like what happened back there at Rock River."

Martha felt a sadness overwhelm her listening to Neil's account. Was it possible the young Indian with the rifle was the same one who gave Papa the blue stone? Could it be that by giving away the stone, his talisman, his lucky piece, he had lost his life?

How would she ever know if it were the same Indian. She would always believe in her heart he meant the blue stone for her. Now she would never know; the stone was gone forever, and now so might be her Indian brave.

She heard Papa softly say. "They just don't learn, do they?"

"Aw, Mr. Burt, they don't have to live this way; they could learn our ways."

"Neil, this is their land. They're scared; they're not takin' care of their responsibility, their born duty to protect the earth's spirits. They're threatened when outsiders like us come to claim and harness what is here for everyone. Killing us is their answer to survival. It's not right, but it's being done in anger at the white man's ways."

"They can't kill us all, Mr. Burt," Neil said softly.

"Right, Neil, and maybe in time they can accept living on reservations, but I've heard 'em complain. The pieces of land given to 'em by the great White Father are the bad pieces of earth nobody wants, and nothing can survive on them."

I grew up with these people, Neil; I've heard them speak of their fears. If he was the one killed, I'm sorry to hear it. And where did his anger get him?"

A silence engulfed the three before Papa turned for the wagon. "Mrs. Burt made up beds for us under the wagon, Neil. Best we get some sleep."

Lying beside her sisters, Martha reflected back to the young Indian. *Someday,* she thought, *I'm going to tell my children and my grandchildren about my Indian brave who tried to carry me away with him on his great horse. I wish I had the blue stone to show them of his devotion to me.*

Chapter 22

Ruthie, Stephen, and Nathan Emigh fidgeted impatiently as Mr. Emigh, at great length, explained the historical importance of the Fourth of July.

The children already knew their wagon train from Chicago had reached Council Bluffs, Iowa, and they were to unite with wagons from all over the United States to travel the Oregon Trail mapped out by the Lewis and Clark expedition back in 1805. This same trail was also known as the Mormon Trail made later by the Mormons, a religious order. The children were also aware of the Mormons traveling out to Utah with them.

Mr. Emigh droned on about a Redemption Bill of 1842, entitling families to free land if they improved it. They would benefit under the Homestead Act by providing a service to the national economy in developing and cultivating wilderness areas into farms, ranches, and towns.

The Emighs and Burts were assembled around the campfire with cups of hot, fragrant coffee as they watched a the bright sunrise, bringing a promise of another torrid, oppressive day.

Martha was used to rising early, but today she and her family were anticipating the Fourth of July celebration with citizens of the small town.

Mr. Emigh continued with his discourse. "Our United States is seventy years old today. We are now in the middle of the United States here in Council Bluffs. We're officially on our way out West and we're called pioneers or settlers. Out of the two thousand miles to our final destination we've traveled seven hundred miles."

Nathan had long ago grown bored. "Pa, there's so much going on," he interrupted his pa.

"Has anyone said anything about a picnic for the occasion?" Papa was leaned back against one of the provisional boxes. He enjoyed Mr. Emigh sharing his wealth of knowledge for the benefit of the youngsters. It was important for them to know these facts, but he understood for the youngsters it was also an exciting day.

"I'm about to serve up some griddle cakes. Stephen, will you ask Mr. Wilson if he's ready for breakfast?" Mother stirred the batter, delicately dipped her finger into it, and tasted it before spooning it out onto the hot griddle.

"He's already eating with the Crawford's mother, and Mrs. Crawford's baking cakes," Martha said. "When we were walking around the wagons earlier, Mother, these ladies were baking some kind of bread draped over the blade of their garden hoe. They didn't put the bread over the fire to bake them but beside it, and when the flat cakes were done they lifted them off the hoe blades and filled them with a stuffing. While they ate, more cakes were set to cook."

"I'm sure we'll be learning many new things with all these families around us coming from so many different places," Mother replied.

Martha and her sisters had to cover their ears as every so often as guns discharged followed by shouting voices in salute to the country's birthday.

Smoke from the campfires along with the aromas of meats, breads, and coffee filled the covered wagon area as food was being prepared in celebration of the holiday.

Stephen with the McGraw boys came to ask, "Papa what's a parade? There's gonna to be a parade, but what's a parade?"

"Do you know what time and where it's going to take place?" Martha asked as she and her sisters waited for flatirons to heat enough to press their good dresses.

"Stephen, we need to go find out more about the parade. Tell you what, I'll go with ya after we eat." Papa didn't realize how hungry he was until the smell of the pancakes reached him.

Mother passed around griddle cakes with warmed molasses and dried apples sauced as she made a mental list of food she had on hand for their picnic.

"Oh, look!" Ruthie exclaimed. "Everyone has flags. Oh, I wish we had one. How come we didn't bring a flag?"

"Martha, have you read some of the banners on the wagons?" Neil pointed to a wagon parked with a sign "Oregon is the Omega."

"Whatever does that mean?" Martha commented as she delicately tested the heated flat iron with a moistened finger.

165

"The end, Martha. It's where the Oregon Trail ends," Mr. Emigh explained.

"How about that one over there? 'Settlers to Settle Indians,'" Neil laughed.

"Oh!" Bertha's excitement was growing by the minute. "Papa, we have to do something," she exclaimed as she flounced up to him. "Can't we paint our wagon or fly a flag? Can't we do something? It's a special occasion! That wagon over there—it just has California in big red letters on the canvas. We could do that." Ideas tumbled through her mind as to what her family might contribute as she tackled her griddle cakes.

Mrs. Kenyon made her way thought the bustling crowd of pioneers. She found the Burt youngsters with their little friends excitedly chattering about the Fourth of July celebration and something called a parade.

"Its a nice morning but its going to be a real scorcher later on. Say, I was just wonderin'—all these wagons and we'll be moving out with them tomorrow, won't we? Whata ya think of the idea of havin' everyone share a picnic with us after the parade? It'd be a good way to get acquainted with each other, wouldn't you say?"

"What time does this parade take place, Mrs. Kenyon?" Sam asked.

"Why, I believe I heard it starts at ten. And you know there's to be a dance tonight after dark? Oh—my goodness—that gunshot sure was close. I hope nobody gets hurt with these folks shooting off their guns like this. I'm near deaf now from these crackers."

"I remember hearing Chinese crackers like these back in New York," Mother said. "They were just as loud and noisy then too. The odors from the gunpowder and sulfur they're made of leave such a nasty smell in the air."

"What are crackers? How are they made? What makes them blow up? What's in 'em?" The children fired off inquisitive questions.

"They're expensive, noisy, and dangerous is all I can remember," Mrs. Kenyon said as David Wilson walked up in time to join the discussion concerning Chinese fireworks. "In my opinion," he stated, "I find they leave a body hackneyed from their blasts."

The families from Chicago intermingled and visited together with other new families with their plans for a combined picnic after the parade. Several wagons pulled into the campgrounds during the day, and the families were invited to join in the festivities.

The women, using limited provisions between them, planned to serve up a feast to include meats roasted, boiled, and grilled along with baked and boiled beans, stews, potato dishes, dried corn dishes combined with lima beans, and hominy with cured pork. Breads included everything from cornmeal hoe cakes stuffed and rolled to contain succulent fillings, to melt-in-your-mouth, raised yeast rolls. The list of dessert was endless: cakes, pies, fruitcakes, gingerbread, cobblers, and buckets of lemonade to slake the thirst.

Martha was intrigued with the foods representing the Deep South to the far northeastern United States; dishes using the basic staples women had with them, though special spices seasoned them from the part of the country in which they originated.

Martha found it exciting to imagine how recipes would be exchanged throughout the long journey. Little-known spices and herbs were traded back and forth for the enjoyment of everyone.

Children taught each other new games. "Pull, Willie, pull," Stephen shouted during a tug-of-war, and, "Red rover, red rover, send a boy right over," as they hurled themselves back and forth trying to break a human arm chain. "Hang on, Johnny," he yelled to Johnny as they cracked the whip.

Ruthie, with her new friends, played at "Button, Button," or "Mother May I?" The girls collected wildflowers and wove colorful crowns for their hair for the dance.

Neil joined the masculine competition of horseracing between the Indians, cavalry, and settlers. He wood chopped, ax tossed, and arm wrestled. He competed in target skills using rifles, crossbows, and regular bows.

There were peddlers with their wares and medicine men peddling their elixirs, and their entertainers preformed along with traveling mimes, and Punch and Judy puppet shows.

Games sent youngsters, no longer strangers, racing for pennies in the straw and fighting for positions in gunny sack races. Mrs. Kenyon delighted the folks in her group by winning the rolling pin toss.

The hot weather came as was predicted. The air filled with dust and the odors of gunpowder, animal urine, and human sweat. The aroma of food heightened everyone's hunger as the day progressed.

A lively marching band, made up of the town citizens, carrying red, white, and blue American flags, was a spectacular sight to behold. Men took off their hats, placing them over their hearts. Little boys mimicked the men and stood ramrod straight to salute the passing flags.

Well-groomed horses, adorned in lavish harnesses with brightly colored pom-poms on their halters, pranced by, pulling decorated buggies carrying town dignitaries, who waved proudly to the cheering crowd of bystanders.

A troop of cavalrymen dressed in impeccable uniforms and shiny black boots, riding spirited horses, passed by the noisy crowd, who clapped in admiration and approval.

The parade ended with members of the Fox, Sauk, Iowa, and Kicka-poo Indians astride lively little ponies riding in honor of their beloved Chief Black Hawk. They were dressed in elaborate, beaded buckskin gar-ments, the chiefs displaying elegant, feathered headpieces. They passed in review by a hushed crowd. Indian squaws with children followed behind the men, with papooses wrapped mummy fashion in strange little baskets attached to beaded headbands around the mothers' foreheads and hanging suspended down the backs of the women.

Papa began clapping and before long the crowd was whistling, cat-erwaulin', and clapping along with him in recognition of the tribes. This was their country also. Speeches were heard from a platform erected in the town center, draped in red, white, and blue bunting. Then came the picnic spread out for all with its abundance.

After eating, the folks sought out places to rest and relax from the heat or to compete in the continuous activities or simply watch the peddlers' entertainment.

The little town of Council Bluffs had turned itself out to celebrate the Fourth of July.

Though the evening remained warm, it didn't lessen the celebratory mood. Guns still sporadically erupted in deafening blasts throughout the evening. Firecrackers popped, snapped, and chattered.

To the west, the sun, a molten, red-hot torch, slid out of sight, giving relief to man and beast who had endured under it through the day.

Folks left to care for jittery animals before they congregated again in the town center. The stage was now filled with musicians. The pioneers were invited to tune up and join the town orchestra for dancing. The dances ranged from formal waltzes and cotillions to Scottish Highland flings and Irish jigs. There was a square-dancing group assembled in the nearby fields along with their musicians playing for clog stomping, polkas, and schottisches.

During a dance with Neil, Martha commented, "Neil, it seems so strange to me; we call ourselves Americans, but we're from all over the world, aren't we? What is a real American? What I mean is—is there a true-blooded American here?"

"Not unless you're thinking of the Indians," Neil offered, swinging Martha about.

"Watch Mother and Papa, Martha," Bertha whispered later to Martha as they watched their parents dancing. "They look so elegant when they dance, don't they?"

"Yes, I wonder how they ever learned so many kinds of dances? Tonight I'm plannin' to dance myself near to death, Bertha, and I can hardly tolerate standing here waiting to be asked again."

A handsome young man, in a well-fitted uniform stepped up to Martha. "Would you care to be my partner for the next dance?" She eagerly waited with him for the music to begin. Her hand laid lightly on his arms, as she'd watch Mother do, he led her out into the crowd with the other couples to take their place for a cotillion.

Neil watched Martha dance. He was painfully aware of her smile, her flushed face, her long black hair pulled atop her head, and of how much he cared for her. He grew impatient waiting for the dance to end. He'd claim her for the next dance before someone else asked her.

When the dance ended, Martha and her partner walked, much too slowly in Neil's opinion, from the dance area. He stepped in front of her and announced, "I'd like to claim you for this next dance, Miss Martha." He reached for her arm so quickly, Martha had little time to properly thank the young soldier for a dance she'd just enjoyed.

In his impulsiveness Neil decided he was going to keep her for himself for the rest of the night if it meant dancing every dance with her, whether he knew the dance or not.

A young man, dressed in buckskins, came to request Martha for a dance, but Neil insisted he'd requested the dance first. Martha would have enjoyed dancing with the young gentleman, but she politely refused him. Neil deftly steered Martha towards the music and dancing.

Martha looked past Neil's shoulder to where the young man was standing. She hoped he'd ask her to dance again. She was enjoying herself. However, she wasn't sure she appreciated this possessiveness Neil was showing, requesting every dance.

"You're very light on you feet," Mr. Wilson told Bertha as he deftly swung her in a turn. She felt herself being held much too close for comfort. When the dance ended, he pulled her tightly against him. She could feel every inch of her body pressed against his. She couldn't honestly say she didn't like the sensation. She was just uncomfortable with the possessive pressure of his body so close.

Glancing quickly around, she hoped to see Papa or Mother. Even Martha would do if she needed an excuse to get away from this man. "Thank you, Mr. Wilson, I enjoyed the dance. I love watching my parents dance. They make it look so graceful."

Bertha walked back to where Neil and Martha were watching Papa and Mother gracefully execute a cotillion.

Bertha removed her hand from Mr. Wilson's arm. Grabbing on to her hand, he lifted it to kiss the tips of her fingers. Bertha gasped with embarrassment. Mr. Wilson bowed low. "Thank you, Miss Burt, for the dance. May I request the next?" "Perhaps later, Mr. Wilson? I promised Papa the next dance." She hoped he'd leave.

If only she could attract Papa's attention. She hadn't a reason not to like Mr. Wilson, but she was uncomfortable with him. Sighting Papa, she stood on tiptoe, held up her arm, and waved to draw his attention.

"Well, maybe after your papa, you'll keep the next dance for me, bella mia?" Mr. Wilson requested in a low, husky voice, disgusting Bertha even more.

"My goodness, Bertha, Mr. Wilson's such a gentleman isn't he?" Martha was unaware of her sister's dilemma with Mr. Wilson.

"Mr. Wilson is making an annoyance of himself," Bertha replied softly through gritted teeth. She was glad to see Papa come to her rescue. "Papa, you promised this next dance with me, remember?" she informed him coquettishly.

Papa, though surprised, exclaimed, "And so I did, Bertha."

"Oh, thank you, Papa. I don't want to dance the next dance with anyone but you."

"Bertha, do I detect some reason for this, young lady? I saw you dancing with Mr. Wilson; he's a good family friend and a fine gentleman. You didn't insult him? You weren't rude were you? We need to be kind to Mr. Wilson; it's a difficult time for him."

"Oh, Papa, I haven't danced with you yet this evening. I thought now would be good time as any." She looked up at him with innocence and wide, blue eyes.

It was difficult for him to refuse this daughter of his. She was not only beautiful but glib of tongue. She was graceful and so very feminine. He wondered if she knew he found it difficult to refuse her wishes. He could understand how it might be for any other man.

Guiding Bertha to the dance area, he saw his wife had been asked by Sam for the next dance, which turned out to be a lively polka, to the enjoyment of Papa and Bertha.

David Wilson, watching Bertha dancing, found himself filled with desire for this beautiful creature. She was so alluring and exciting. He suddenly felt very lonely, watching her. It was becoming unbearable, being alone day after day. The journey was becoming a burden, having the responsibilities all to himself.

I miss my Abigale. It's difficult making a new life, and the children need a mother. Where am I going to find a woman? I'm aware of the feelings Neil has for Martha. Bertha would make me proud. She would take away this loneliness.

He knew many young women married and cared for households at Bertha's age. He'd even find a girl for her like Abby had, but chose to come away without. He shouldn't have listened to her. Maybe his wife would be alive today if he'd insisted she keep the darkie. Indian girls came cheap. He could afford to buy Bertha an Indian girl to help her. *Lord, how I miss my woman.* His insides gnawed in frustration.

Watching Neil and Martha dance, an idea came to David Wilson. He'd add a bit of competition to young Neil's life. *What harm was there? The night's still young. Oh, yes, this miserable night's young, and I don't like being alone, and why should I be?*

He decided to refresh himself with a drink first. *Then I'll come back and ask Martha to dance. I'll show the young lady a good time while I enjoy watching her hot-tempered plowboy's reactions. I'm going to treat Martha like a lady likes to be treated. Whatever comes about, so be it.*

Yes, he'd enjoy showing up Neil's ineptness and inexperience with a women. *I'll teach him how it's done. I'm prepared to handle the consequences too.* He laughed softly as he walked to his wagon for another quick drink to fortify him.

Folks traveling in the trains weren't used to the late hour. However, this was their country's birthday. As long as the musicians, dancing, and whisky lasted, so would they.

The last dance was announced; the torches on stage burned low.

It was well after midnight when everyone departed the town square. Exhausted, they crawled into their wagons for a few hours of rest.

"Papa, shouldn't we sleep outside?" Stephen asked, trying to peek around Mother to Papa as she helped him under his quilt.

"Not tonight, Stephen; too many wagons and people. Off to bed with you," was Papa's reply.

"Thank you for the dances, Neil. I really enjoyed myself. Did you?" Martha asked as they walked slowly arm in arm back to her wagon.

"This is what I thought was going to happen every night when we first joined up for the trip," Neil replied. "You looked 'specially pretty tonight, Martha." He traced the back of her hand with his fingers. "I couldn't help but wonder—you seemed…. You had a good time dancing with—uh—Mr. Wilson, didn't ya?"

"I enjoy myself with you, Neil. You're a very good dancing partner. Thank you, I had a wonderful evening."

"You're a good partner too, Martha. Mr. Wilson—he holds his dancing partners purty close, doesn't he. I just happened to notice, you understand."

"No, Neil, can't you understand? It's you I enjoy being with. Mr. Wilson likes to dance. See you tomorrow. Sweet dreams." She stood on tiptoe to deliver a quick kiss on his lips.

"My dreams will be about you—about us; you know that, don't you, Martha?"

"Oh good. Then I hope we dance all night." She let go of him to climb up into the wagon, her soft laughter floating back to him.

He liked to make her laugh. He'd liked to hear her laugh from the first day he met her. He nearly collided with his pa, leaning against the tailgate of their wagon, observing the night sky.

"Looks like another hot day tomorrow. You have a good time tonight, Son?"

"Yeah, it was right nice. The music sure was good." Neil disappeared into the wagon. His last recollection of his day was of Martha. She sure was making herself a place in his life. Gettin' in his way, but he didn't mind. He drifted off to sleep.

Sam Emigh pondered about his son, *We still have a long ways to go. Let them take their time, those two.* He was certain his son and Martha Burt would come to terms with their relationship before the journey was over.

Give them time, old man, he thought. *You've better things to do than be a matchmaker. That's women's work.* But down deep, he was disturbed. *Wilson was a good man, but he was also a lonely, single, desperate man.*

Sam was aware of what took place between the three of them tonight. He felt Neil was far too inexperienced to understand the situation David Wilson was leading into. He was sure there were a few drinks behind Wilson's actions.

Same knew he had no right to interfere with what he witnessed to-night. He'd just have to hope for the best.

In the darkness, Mr. Emigh thought he could make out David Wilson, but he decided against the idea of going over to talk with him. *That man has to deal with his own problems. I too have to bed down alone at night.*

Chapter 23

Martha awoke, after a spectacular Independence Day celebration the day before, to bright sunlight filtering through the canvas. She lay listening to voices outside and the sounds of breakfast being prepared. There were forty wagons in the train, she'd heard someone say.

She yawned and leisurely stretched. It was nice of Papa to allow her sisters and her to sleep later than usual, but it was becoming warm inside the wagon; she needed to get up.

Papa had poured his first cup of coffee when Alex Kenyon appeared. Papa greeted him, saying he couldn't remember who told him but the only thing weather like this was good for was growin' corn. "It makes travelin' rough; it saps the life out of us and the teams. Ever notice how dry prairie grass tends to hold heat?"

Alex agreed with Eli before he exchanged his information about their wagon master. "The feller was hired by the agency." Alex paused to accept a cup of coffee. "He's traveled out on the Oregon Trail once before, he tells me. He's requestin' we all attend a meetin' this morning. Somethin' 'bout electin' a committee," Mr. Kenyon said as he blew gently on the black, bitter brew before gingerly taking a sip.

Martha and Mother were serving a breakfast of cracked wheat mush, along with buttered bread and preserves, when Papa announced, "There's a meetin' takin' place after breakfast so's we can meet our wagon master. You know, Mary, I'm surprised my insides're empty after all I ate yesterday," Papa confessed, accepting his bowl of mush.

"This meeting—it's for you men? I hope so. I need to stay here and load the wagon. And the beans could use a bit more cooking before we leave," Mother said as she poured milk over Stephen's bowl of mush and handed it to him.

"Actually, I believe, we're all supposta be there, ma'dear," Papa commented. "There's a lot of new folks we need to get acquainted with."

When breakfast was over and Papa had stowed the last provisional box back in the wagon for Mother, he asked, "Are we ready? Let's head over and find a place with the others."

Persistent flies irritated the families as they congregated in an open field cleared of everything edible by the livestock. Heavy wagons had dug deep gouges in the earth, and the stench of animal manure hung in the air, mixed with the aroma of wood smoke and coffee.

As he walked past them, the man's mustache caught the attention of the young ladies, the way it curled out from his upper lip into two fine points across his cheeks.

"Wonder how much time he has to spend on that hair on his lip?" Bertha whispered to Lizzy Crawford and Ginny McGraw, who had come to sit by her.

"Shush, Bertha, he'll hear you." Martha roughly nudged her sister to move over and make a place for Neil to sit with them.

"What did she say?" he asked sitting down tailor fashion.

"I said it's getting crowded here," Bertha remarked caustically.

"Yes, Bertha, so why don't you and your little girlfriends move someplace else?" Martha suggested, wiping perspiration from her forehead on her dress sleeve.

"Neil, you must accept my apology. Girls my little sister's age are disgusting with their infatuation of older men. I think the man looks quite fetching myself."

"Speaking of older men, Martha," Bertha asked loud enough for the benefit of those around her, "did you fret yourself over Mr. Wilson last night?"

"Mr. Wilson did appear to take a fancy to you and not Bertha." Neil pretended to be interested in the activity going on around him. "I sensed your little sister wasn't too fond of him myself, but you, on the other hand...."

Martha would have objected, but just then the tall, slender, mustached man called attention as he blew a sharp whistle and held up his hand for silence. He was dressed in cloth britches stuffed into worn boots. A battered, sweat-stained Stetson hat sat over shoulder-length hair. His demeanor portrayed one of authority; with feet apart and arms folded over his chest, his face expressed impatience at having to wait for everyone's attention.

Beside him were two gentlemen wearing deerskin shirts, pants, and sturdy boots. He introduced himself as Rupert McKinley, wagon master. "And this fellow is Mr. Charlie Reynolds, Indian scout for the United States Militia. He handles our Indian affairs along the way. The Indians love him for his red hair and beard, and that's why he's still alive."

Mr. Reynolds raised his cap to reveal a head of thick red hair. Mr. McKinley waited for the laughter to die down before he continued. "Mr. Buland here has been my assistant since our last successful trip, and Cookie over there," he gestured to a short, barrel-chested, thick-muscled little man, "feeds and cares for my men and me."

"I've been hired by your agency to get you over the Oregon Trail. We'd have been on the road by now had we started on time today, but I need to discuss some ground rules before we move out.

"We start at six every morning from now on," his deep voice broadcast his audience. "I hope to put in as many as twenty miles or more a day by the time we stop for supper. If not, we keep movin'. We travel six days and you rest on the seventh, or we forfeit the seventh day if we need to make up time. If we put in the miles early, we park early; if you fall behind, it's up to you to catch up. I wait for no one.

"Once we cross the Missouri River," he continued, "we'll be coming into some rugged wilderness areas with little water or firewood, and savage Indians. We'll experience sandstorms capable of blowing the tops off your wagons, rain likely to drown ya, and grass fires liable to destroy everything you own. Your teams may die from bad water, no water, heat, and exhaustion. The Indians are unpredictable. And I can't empathsize cleanliness enough. The United States Militia demands it of our troops. Wagon trains before us have suffered pestilence and disease that wiped out entire families from lack of good cleanliness.

"Once across Nebraska Territory," Mr. McKinley told them, "we'll be climbing through some treacherous mountains. But I'm aimin' to have you in Oregon City, the end of the Oregon Trail, by supper time 'round the first of October."

He was answered with a rousing cheer from the crowd.

"I take it ya like this idea."

The crowd applauded with more cheering, caterwaulin', and whistling.

He held up his hand for attention. "You're not gonna be happy about this next, but—sizin' up your wagons, I insist you leave behind your heaviest furniture, table, stoves, chests, and yes, even trunks."

Oh no, not my rocking chair—oh please, no. Mother sent up a silent prayer. She quickly glanced over to see Papa, much to her relief, shake his head at the request.

"If there's a problem deciding what to leave, Mr. Reynolds, Mr. Buland, and I are impartial, and will gladly help you decide. Far too many wagons here need to lighten loads. Above all else, we must conserve our team's strength, and you'll find you can travel faster with lighter wagons.

"I need two men a night as guards. Mr. Reynolds here will record your names. Every man has the obligation of serving night duty.

"I also work with a lead man. When Mr. Reynolds is busy and we're going through Indian territory, I need someone who can speak and understand the Indian dialect or has worked with Indians. I'm told, Mr. Burt—where are you, sir? I've been informed you have such knowledge, so for today I'd appreciate your being my lead until we elect a man for the position. Mr. Burt, if you will, sir?" he requested of Papa.

"Each night after we camp I need to meet with the men briefly. At our first stop, you can decide who you'd like for your lead. I'll go along with who you elect. Any questions?" His gaze slid over the crowd. "If not then let's get ready to move out, folks."

Before Neil could return to his wagon, Martha couldn't help but comment, "Mr. McKinley doesn't paint a very exciting time for us, does he? It's scary to think of what we're expected to brave, or was it his purpose to scare us to death before we started?"

"Why wouldn't he tell the truth? It ain't gonna slow me down. I'm anxious ta get started. I'm lookin' forward ta stakin' out some free land— for us, Martha."

Mother pondered Mr. McKinley's words on the return to her wagon. *We women aren't brave adventurers. We're not fragile weepers either. We'll just have to be indifferent to what we've just heard about the challenges we're to face. I'm determined to make this strenuous journey by depending on my faith. We must, for the sake of our children and husbands. It's a move that will make a better life for us all, but there are limitations. We women are vigorous and energetic in our efforts to see the great move to its finish. Oh dear God,* she pleaded silently, *help us all.*

"Mary, did you hear me?" Papa interrupted. "You daydreaming?" His voice softened. "Dreamin' about the day you'll be settin' up housekeeping, are you?"

"Eli, you have no idea how fearful Mr. McKinley's words have left me." She forced herself to sound cheerful and drowned out her fears.

"I understand when we get down ta the river, we're gonna unload our wagons, then pull off the wheels and cross the river on a barge. Mr. Reynolds just told me the barge isn't all that big and only two wagons can cross at a time. It's gonna be an all-day affair gettin' us all across. If I have ta stay and assist Mr. McKinley; you and the girls will have ta take over the oxen till I can catch up with ya."

The Burts paused to watch Mr. Wilson struggle with a beautiful cherry wood chest. "I never wanted ta haul this out here in the first place and I sure don't need it now."

Papa went to assist and carry the chest to the pile of growing discards.

A melancholy enveloped Martha. "Mrs. Wilson didn't live long enough to see her furniture in her new home. All we have left are the memories of our friend," she whispered to Mother and her sisters. They silently watched as Abby's furniture was placed alongside the other pieces set out in the field.

Women who had struggled to bring a gentler way of life with them watched as cherished furniture pieces were tossed aside and later would be picked over by peddlers, merchants, and the town's citizen, who had pulled up in buggies and wagons, waiting for the pioneers to leave. Even the Indians would take away pieces for their use. The remains would be burned.

Mr. McKinley kept to himself how eventually the men would be trading their tools and implements for vital supplies at trading posts or to farmers along the way. The discards would attest to their need for survival, their skeletal remains of hopes and dreams marking the trail west.

The pioneers turned their heads away from their belongings as they pulled into formation to make their way out of Council Bluffs, Iowa.

Mr. McKinley and Mr. Reynolds rode up beside the Burts' wagon. "Mr. Burt, you ready for the crossing?" Mr. McKinley asked. "Hey there, sonny." He looked up at Stephen, who was proudly sitting on the seat beside Papa. "Ya ready ta swim your oxen across the river? You can swim, can't cha?"

"Mr. McKinley, my sister Bertha says she'd like to feel your mustache," Stephen blurted out. "She wanted to know if it's sticky. I like the way you got it twisted like that."

"Stephen! Mother!" came a shriek from inside the wagon. "Mind your business, Stephen," Bertha wailed. "Mother, I would never say—did you hear him?"

Papa and Mr. McKinley laughed. "Sorry, Laddie, but I spent too much time gettin' it to stay just the way I want it," Mr. McKinley informed Stephen.

Mother consoled Bertha, who by now was in tears. "Mr. KcKinley understands you would never say something like this. Stephen, what ever possessed you to say this about your sister?"

"'Cause I heard her tell Lizzy and Ginny that. 'Sides, I wanted to touch it." Stephen quickly slid over on the seat closer to Papa.

"Oh, Mother, I'm getting out. You go on without me; I'll walk back home. Every time Mr. McKinley sees me all he's going to remember is that I said something about the hair on his lip."

Martha could understand Bertha's embarrassment. "I'm sure Mr. McKinley has much more on his mind than to remember what a silly foolish little boy said."

Mr. McKinley excused himself to ride back down the long line of wagons.

"Keep movin', Mr. Burt," Mr. Reynolds ordered. "I'm waiting here ta make sure Mr. McKinley doesn't need me 'fore I help you unload for the crossing."

His oxen weren't as fast as the teams of horses, and the decent to the river was a steep, downhill grade. Papa decided to allow the oxen to take their time.

Mr. Reynolds, riding alongside Papa's wagon, remarked, "Hear you know the Black Hawk tribes pretty well, Mr. Burt."

"Yeah." Papa was concentrating on the steep descent to the river. "I happened to grow up tradin' with 'em. I understand the Fox and the Sauk, but don't know too much about the Iowa or Kickapoo. Didn't have many of 'em up around Chicago, where I grew up."

"We'll be facing new Indian tribes all along the way. Say, Laddie," he inquired of Stephen, "you know the Indian word for Nebraska, this new territory we're on our way to? Indians named it 'Land of Flat Water.' Bet ya already knew that, didn't ya?"

Mr. Reynolds went on to explain to Papa, "The Black Hawk tribes are pretty peaceful compared to some we'll be meeting. Always liked the Hawk tribes myself; pretty decent bunch of Indians, far as Indians go. Wait till ya see some of the ones we're going to meet up with. They're unpredictable as—" He turned to Papa and noticed Mother sitting beside him. He lifted his hat. "Excuse me, ma'am. Let's just say unpredictable—best way of puttin' it."

"I hear tell few pioneers are settlin' in Nebraska," Papa stated.

"Not many. It's considered Indian Territory still. Once it's a state, our Indian friends'll be forced ta live on reservations if they want to keep their government. Not a whole lot of good land for settlin' either; too sandy and dry. A lotta big changes comin' 'bout for Nebraska. Excuse me, I'll be right back. I need to slow down these folks behind us."

Papa glanced over to Mother. "Seems like a likable chap. Whata ya think?"

Papa, holding the reins in one hand and the brake with the other, climbed down to a barge floating next to a wooden pier. The barge was not much bigger than a wagon in length or width. Both sides of the wooden pier were lined with small boats and canoes. More were tied to willow saplings growing along the edge of the river.

Papa studied the spoked wooden wheel used to maneuver the ferry's large rudder that would navigate the wooden plank barge across the river.

Martha experienced a profound sadness as she gazed out at the massive Missouri River before her. She was getting farther from her home each day. She gazed up to the green plateau above. *What's on the other side of this river?* She didn't have time to ponder the issue. Mr. McKinley rode down to request they unload their wagon as quickly as possible.

"We'll pull off the wheels and tie your wagon bed to the boat, then load your supplies back on," he explained to Papa. "The wind's not bad today or we'd have to take your canvas down. A good wind blowing under the canvas can lift the wagon bed and tip the barge over.

Before the wagon was unloaded, the family crossing with the Burts was introduced. People came to assist unloading the two wagons and before long both families were ready to make the Missouri River crossing.

Jeb Cobb, his wife Amy, and his pa James Cobb were from Missouri. They had arrived late into Council Bluffs yesterday because of an axle tree breaking. Jeb Cobb had worried he would not make it down the steep incline to the barge. He explained, "We come this way 'cause we heard the Mormon side of the river was safer."

The Burt women welcomed young Amy, a weary mother with three small children and a new baby.

"I sure never know'd this was going to be such a hard trip," she exclaimed in her soft twang. "Ma' momma told me it 'tweren't no picnic. Guess she know'd what she's talking about. It ain't been no picnic so far, believe me."

The loaded barge pulled slowly out into the murky water. Those watching gasped as Neil came running and made a flying leap onto the moving deck. "Let me steady the livestock fer ya, Mr. Burt," he said as he caught his balance on slippery, wet boards.

Papa, silently observing the water's depth below him, was glad his brother Ernie had insisted they tar the wagon's seams at the time of its construction. The weight from the wagon was setting the barge dangerously low in the water. The oxen, tied to the side of the barge, appeared to be swimming comfortably along beside them.

The gentleman who was navigating the barge explained to Papa and the Cobbs, "There are Bateaux used to cross the river farther north, but that Mr. McKinley preferred crossing at Council Bluffs rather than travel back down to get back on the Oregon Trail."

Neil held tight to the halters of the horse and cow; his soothing voice calmed them and impressed Martha, who was finding so many things about Neil she appreciated.

The families were quiet during the crossing. They were wrestling with sheer terror. Several times swells caused the barge to rock or list to one side, sending everyone to grab on to the wooden slats that formed side rails.

The youngsters were sitting on the deck or atop the supplies stacked around them, and were made uncomfortable with the water only inches below them.

Martha fought panic at the thought of the barge tipping. Who could save them out here in the middle of the river? What if one of the animals became scared and tried to break away? She forced herself to concentrate on Neil. He was dividing his time between the horses, cows, and oxen to calm them.

The oxen were showing signs of nervousness at the lengthy crossing. They had been bobbing alongside the barge, but suddenly they began loudly blowing water from their distended nostrils and their eyes widened in fear.

"Don't look down, look ahead or up at the sky, don't look down." Mother read the unspoken anxiety in the children's faces.

"We're sitting too near the water, Mother. I don't like this feeling," Bertha exclaimed. "Stephen—sit down! You're rocking the boat. He's going to make us tip over, Mother—make him sit down."

"We're almost there, Bertha." Martha modulated her voice as much as possible against her own fear. "Ruthie, you're alright, aren't you?"

"No, Martha, I can't breathe. I'm too scared. Does it hurt to drown?"

The barge pulled up to a wooden dock extending out into the river. The dock floated so low in the water that any weight sank it even lower. The family was forced to wade through water, sloshing over it before they could make it out onto dry land.

The men quickly untied the wagon beds, pulling them through the water and up onto the riverbank, while the Burt youngsters cared for the livestock. The supplies were then carried through the water and stacked along the river's edge.

The barge, once emptied, departed with Neil, who had hoped for some time alone with Martha. He wasn't successful in getting her attention as she and the others busied themselves getting the wagons reassembled and loaded.

The Burts and Cobbs rushed forward to assist the Kenyon and Crawfords, who arrived next.

Mrs. Kenyon grudgingly complained at having her arms full of supplies and not being able to keep her long skirt from being dragged through the water.

Papa used the coffin board carried under his wagon to hoist the wagon beds onto a set of stair steps and support the wagons while the wheels were attached.

Mr. Kenyon told them, as they fitted on his wagon wheels, "Some of the bigger wagons are tipped over on one side and the wheels place over the axles, then pulled upright using ropes. The wagons, once righted, could balance while the other two wheels were set in place. It took the combined effort from all of us to get them reassembled. A lone feller would never have been able to manage a wagon alone."

Martha watched as the livestock took advantage of the grass growing along the riverbank, with the gentle wake lapping at the shoreline, while she waited for the wagons to be reassembled.

Amy Cobb frantically ran about, rescuing her youngsters. "Oh no, no, Freddie, get away from the water. Benjamin! Freddie, get your brother away from the water," she yelled as the toddler repeatedly made for the river.

After the wagons were loaded, Martha, with the two oldest Cobb boys, began the steep climb to the top of the cliff above them. Soft, dry, powdery, dust covered their feet.

The elderly, bald-headed Mr. James with his wide, toothless grin, cheerfully assisted in the reassembly of the wagons and moving them away from the river's edge to make way for the next two wagon on the approaching barge.

As the wagons were reloaded, the women walked on ahead, ascending the steep incline above the Missouri River. They were about to step onto the red sandy soil of Nebraska and be greeted by a parching heat rising up out of the earth.

"Nebraska's four hundred miles from east to west," Martha remembered Mr. Emigh read aloud to the Burt family from his little book on Nebraska.

Martha, at the top of the cliff, gazed out around her. A hot, brisk wind tugged at her pantaloons. Far below, the river looked cool and inviting with diamond sparkles reflected off the sun-speckled water.

Pivoting, with hands shading her eyes, she gazed out at the land before her. It was desolate and, except for the wind, it appeared sinister and silent. However, there was something strangely beautiful about this Nebraska Territory she was about to journey across.

Chapter 24

Nebraska Territory

Mr. McKinley's two wagons were the last to make it up the steep incline from the Missouri River. It had taken him two days to ferry the forty wagons across. He must now face the hard ride to catch up with Eli Burt, whom he'd delegated to manage the train. He quickly glanced over his shoulder for a last glimpse of Iowa on the far shore and the wide Missouri River below him, before he turned to head west.

Earlier, Papa wondered aloud to Alex Kenyon and Jeb Cook, "Guess we're just suppose ta keep going. I'm headed in the direction of the Platte River. Believe this is the route we're to take."

"Think that's the idea, Eli. McKinley'll catch up sooner or later. We'll just keep the wagons movin'."

"Think they took the whole night crossin' everyone over?" Jeb questioned. His pa behind him snorted nosily but otherwise remained silent.

Papa tossed the remains of his cold coffee on the ground and watched as it was quickly swallowed up by the parched soil. "Best get to movin' then."

The wagons had been traveling for several hours when Papa looked up to see riders approaching.

"Someone's comin', Son." Papa stopped the oxen and ordered the boy into the wagon.

Mr. McKinley rode up beside Papa on his sweat-lathered horse. "Ya recognize 'em?"

They're Indians, but I can't make from what tribe." Eli Burt squinted into a blinding mid-morning sun.

The Indians pulled up a short distance from the men; both parties extended their hands in the traditional Indian greeting.

The Burt women had favored walking to riding in the oppressive heat inside the wagon. On seeing the Indians, they quickly alerted the folks behind them before running for cover.

Martha and her sisters quietly watched from behind the flap cover as curious Indians rode their ponies around several of the wagons. They observed other Indians in the party waiting quietly beside their leaders and the men.

Men carrying their guns made their way cautiously to join the assembled group.

Bertha, from her obscured position behind the flap, whispered, "I'm surprised these Indians didn't come on to us screaming and waving their arms like the others have done."

Mr. McKinley with Mr. Reynolds and Mr. Buland had climbed down from their horses to walk alongside Papa to where the Indians remained on horseback.

"Our Iowa brothers, what brings you here?" Mr. Reynolds inquired.

The chief spokesman for the Indians, in a deep, resonant voice, replied, "Our people bring word that the Sioux are restless. They attacked a group of settlers between Freemont and Fort Klearny. We do not know how many people from either side were killed. We come to warn you there is unrest between the Sioux and his white brother."

"It is good our brothers come to warn us. We crossed the Missouri and have not heard of trouble. Come, we will share food with our brothers of the Iowa tribe."

Mr. Reynolds turned to Papa. "Mr. Burt here trapped and traded the beaver furs with our brothers from Black Hawk's Fox tribe. You will take food and gifts to your honorable chief."

"No food; we take guns and black powder. Mr. Burt, you will give guns to us, like you gave to the young Fox renegades."

"We do not carry extra guns," Mr. McKinley was quick to inform them. "Go back to your chief. Tell him McKinley will bring guns for his protection when I come back this way. Your chief is friend to McKinley. He knows McKinley keeps his word. I am good friend to Iowa tribe."

The Indians hesitated at first, then slowly turned to ride away. The men silently watched after them. Did the Indians understand Mr. McKinley's message and would they accept it? The men returned to their wagons.

I've forty wagons with over two hundred and fifty folks to settle tonight and now the Sioux are restless. Mr. McKinley beckoned to the wagons, extending as far back as the eye could see. "Wagons ho!" he shouted. *All I ask for is a peaceful night tonight.*

He instructed Papa, "Mr. Burt, lead out if you will please, sir." He saluted Papa with a snappy, precise hand gesture, at the same time wheeling his horse about to ride back down the line of wagons with his two assistants beside him.

Stephen, who was seated beside Papa, was very proud and feeling important. Mr. McKinley had called his papa sir and saluted him just like he was a real soldier. "Your job's important, huh, Papa?" But Papa was preoccupied and didn't answer.

The fatigued folks traveled throughout the day under the hot sun. They welcomed the sun, setting in a splash of brilliant gold as it painted itself across the sky, hills, and valleys with a radiance beyond their description. Though weary worn they continued on long after the sun set into the dusk of a blue mauve evening.

After crossing the Missouri, Papa had progressed twenty miles through the most beautiful, green, picturesque land he'd never imagined. He told the family the town they passed through was named, "Omaha. Mr. Reynolds told me the name means 'Strong Wind' in the Sioux dialect. It's an undeveloped little town in the making right now, but Mr. Reynolds informed me it's growing rapidly."

"What kind of people are settling here, Papa?" Martha questioned. She was enjoying the walk under the leafy trees that grew alongside the road and filtered the heat from the hot sun.

"Merchants, providing supplies to minors, trappers, and settlers, along with the Mormons who are sharing the Oregon Trail. It 'pears to me it's gonna grow into a fair-size city someday."

The Burt family was traveling on the Mormon Trail charted by the Mormons coming out of Illinois and Iowa, making their way to Utah. The family looked over at the wagons across the Platte River from them using the original Oregon Trail.

Mr. Emigh had informed the family, "The Mormons are such a peaceful, God- fearing people, the Indians are less likely to attack those of us on this side of the river."

Mr. McKinley rode up beside Papa. "Mr. Burt, pull your wagon off in that big area ahead." He pointed to an area clustered with large oaks. "There's water, grass, and plenty of space. When you pull in, bear to the left and start a circle. We need to make a corral for the livestock for those who need it."

These were welcome words not only for the Burts but also for the others when they heard they were stopping for the night.

Mr. Reynolds directed the parking, one wagon left, another right, until he'd created four large circles.

The exhausted families put personal needs aside until the teams were watered, examined for injuries, and turned into the corrals or allowed to freely graze.

Women hurried to build their campfires outside the wagons. Ruth Kenyon passing by asked the Burt women if they were "plum tuckered out" as she was.

"I'm fixing rice with jerky tonight, with bread and that cake you so kindly gave us, Mrs. Kenyon. I'm too weary to think of much else," Mother said, tying on her apron.

"Mother, if I stir up biscuits, that would leave bread for breakfast, and dinner tomorrow. Mr. McKinley says we're to leave by six, remember? You won't have time to bake bread, will you?" Martha inquired.

The wagon master had requested that folks assemble at his wagon after their suppers. They ate by the light of their campfires before making their way though the moonlight to Mr. McKinley's wagon.

"I surely hope this is a short meeting. I'm stumbling over my feet I'm worn so thin," Neil complained to Martha.

"Everyone feels the same, Neil," Martha agreed. "It's hard work when you're pushed as fast as we're going. We haven't had a good rest since the river crossing. You'll feel better after a night's rest." She slipped her hand into his.

Martha overheard a women next to her say, "Babies and the elderly are bound to suffer the worst hardships during this journey." Martha remembered the day she'd started. There had been so many people that day, people she now knew and had grown to care for. They had all suffered, not just the elderly or babies. She couldn't help but wonder how she would feel about these new families moving with them At the end of the journey would she feel the same about them as well?

Despite their exhaustion, everyone cheerfully gathered around Mr. McKinley. They were developing respect for this man who had crossed them safely over the Missouri River, and could handle Indian affairs and their problems. The men congregated on one side, women and youngsters on the other.

Mr. McKinley held up his hand for quiet. "I'm impressed with the miles we've covered today," he told them. "Hate to report casualties but we did lose cattle and horses during the crossing. These are costly losses, and replacing 'em will be more costly.

"In order to get everyone better acquainted, you'll notice how I had you park your wagons tonight? We should be camping earlier from now on, now that we're together. By starting out at six each morning, you'll appreciate traveling when it's cooler and our women need time for baking and washing when we stop for the night.

"We're grateful to the Iowa Indians for warning us about the Sioux attack. Tomorrow, we'll find out what brought about the attack and report back to you. With this many wagons, we aren't likely to be attacked. Indians like picking on smaller groups.

"Now—tonight we need to select a lead man to help me and to govern grievances among you. Any suggestions?" He looked out into the faces before him.

"Mr. McKinley, sir, we'd like to suggest Mr. Collins here. He's been our guide since comin' outta Georgia." A man declared his nomination for Mr. Collins, a distinguished older gentleman, who stood up to wave at everyone before sitting back down.

Papa stood up. "I'd like to suggest Alex Kenyon." The families from around Chicago all cheered, clapped, and whistled as Mr. Kenyon stood to acknowledge himself. The five families acquainted with the Kenyons realized by electing Mr. Kenyon they were also getting Mrs. Kenyon and her opinions.

From the young man in his group, dressed in black and wearing black hats, came a request for "Reverend Hirum." His three fellow constituents sent up brave cheers.

Martha and Bertha nudged each other when they recognized the young Mormon men from back at the Mississippi River crossing.

Following a short interval of silence, Mr. McKinley requested that if there were no more nominations, "Will the three candidates come forward and let's get one of 'em elected. It's getting late."

After introducing the three men, Mr. McKinley requested, "Mr. Reynolds, hand me the three straws if you will, sir. I'm lining 'em between my finger and thumb so you only see the tips, gentlemen. I've done this before and find it's a fast, fair method."

Mr. McKinley held out his hand for each man to draw a straw. Mr. Collins stepped forward first and hesitated a moment before selecting his straw. Mr. Kenyon ushered Reverend Hirum ahead of him to make the next selection. Reverend Hirum pulled on his bushy beard with one hand, while selecting his straw with the other hand. Mr. Kenyon then stepped forward, plucked the remaining straw from Mr. McKinley's hand, and returned to his place.

"Gentlemen," Mr. McKinley instructed, "please compare your straws. The longest straw wins."

The audience waited in quiet anticipation until Mr. Kenyon stepped forward, holding up his straw to show his triumph.

The crowd commenced whistling and yelling on his behalf. However, Mr. Collins stepped forward in front of Mr. Kenyon, putting out his arm to bar him.

"This ain't no democratic election; this is a fraud of the great American system. We came to elect the person most proven for this position. I challenge Mr.—" He turned. "What did you say your name was now? I challenge Mr. Alex here, if he's qualified enough. I come from a long line of wagon makers. I have at my disposal…," he gestured to the crowd, "… at your disposal, two smithies, a qualified medical doctor, two well-educated men teachers, and the most loyal group of people a man could ask to travel with. Mr. McKinley, I'm challenging you, sir, to find a better qualified man than I am."

"The position didn't carry qualifications, Mr. Collins; the leader was to be someone familiar with the Indians and to work with me. That's why I left it to you folks to make a a selection of someone you knew who could do the job and please you."

Reactions were mixed as groups loudly vocalized their opinions. Discussions became so heated Mr. McKinley was forced to request that Mr. Buland fire off a shot to quiet the crowd.

"This wagon train's my responsibility, so I'm asking Mr. Burt to remain my lead man until I've had time to decide more about this predicament. I also believe in the democratic way of getting things done—so until we have more time to solve the issue, I'd appreciate it, Mr. Burt, if you'd keep the position until tomorrow. It's late and we need our sleep. Will the two men volunteering for night watch stay behind for a few minutes? The rest of you get some sleep."

On the way to their wagons, several people approached Papa to express their appreciation for his handling the position and wondered aloud why he didn't get it, "especially after the peaceful way the Indian episode was handled today," they said.

The folks settled down for a few hours' rest before facing another long day. Their ultimate desire was to accomplish the twenty miles so they could earn a rest for a few days.

Mr. McKinley gave instructions to the two men guarding the camp for the night before he bedded down beside Cookie's banked campfire coals.

"There wasn't time tonight to ask for votes to settle this matter," he explained to his men. "I've an idea Mr. Collins is gonna give me trouble to the end of his time."

"He's headed for Californy, only goin' as far as South Pass. Can't understand how come 'e come this route and didn't stay on the udder side of the river where 'e belongs," Cookie commented.

The camp quieted down. There was an occasional stirring from the corralled livestock The singing of wolves combined with the sound from the wind produced a mournful reverie. The moon created eerie shadows in the lonely, desolate night.

"Injuns! Injuns!" A cry penetrated the silent world of the sleeping campers, awaking folks to helter-skelter confusion.

Papa climbed out from under the wagon and began hurling orders into the darkness. "Men get your guns. Women and children, stay in the wagons."

A cloud passed over the moon, obscuring its light to guide them. The pounding of running feet sounded around Papa as people tried to make their way in the dark.

"Men, line up around the outside of the corral," Papa shouted, trying to maneuver his rifle and powder while he assembled the men into a barricade against unseen intruders.

People, who had climbed out of tents, out from under wagons, and out of bed rolls plowed into each other in the dark. Some managed to find guns and crawl into position around their wagons as they waited and listened for the attackers.

Women and children hid in the dark wagons. Some of the women, who had guns took places besides their men. Everyone waited.

Alex Kenyon came out of a deep sleep and scrambled around to prepare himself for action. However, as time passed, he became mystified when there didn't appear to be any activity. Something wasn't right. *Where's the enemy?* he wondered.

In an other camp, chaos reigned. Folks ran around waiting for orders. Women screamed, paralyzed with fear. Some fainted, others followed their husbands around in the dark, their arms full of children. Children cried and screamed in terror and freight. Men with guns ran around aimlessly.

Mr. Wilson and Mr. Emigh's attempt at organizing their camp was to no avail. Mr. Collin's voice was heard shouting, "What durn fool started this? There ain't no Injuns; they'd have attacked by now. Where's the Injuns?"

The livestock ran wildly around the inside of the corral, banging into the sides of the wagons, stomping on buckets and pans that fell in their way.

Mr. McKinley, with a lighted torch, waved it the back and forth to quiet the crowd. The light from the torch cast his face into a ghoulish shape and ghastly green color as he shouted for attention.

When at last he was able to explain, he said, "You've just been through a fake Indian attack. I now see how you'll react in the event of the real thing. I had the guards set this up for me. You're running around like a field full of naked mice without heads. We're lucky you didn't shoot yourselves or some of us. This tells me what kind of qualified leaders I can depend on. I hope you'll come to realize politics doesn't always get the job done. We'll discuss this tomorrow. Now get back to bed," he growled.

Mr. McKinley could hear Mr. Collins's indignant voice, well above the others, as he returned to his wagon.

Bertha, wiggling herself down into a comfortable place under her quilt, grumbled, "This is what Granny Burt would have called a real she-nanigan."

"Oh Bertha, and can't you hear her saying, 'You shan't be forgettin' this expensive lesson, Ah'm a-thinkin'.'" Martha mimicked Granny's voice.

"Let's pretend we just woke from a bad dream, Bertha, and now everything's alright and we can go back to sleep," Martha suggested, sitting on her quilt, her knees hugged to her chest.

"Martha, it was a bad dream alright, a nightmare. I'm not going to sleep another wink all night," Bertha complained. "You can sleep after this, I ask you?"

"It really scared me too." Ruthie shivered before diving under her quilt.

Out of the darkness came a small voice. "Martha, it's cold up here. Can I come down there with you?"

"Bring your quilt and pillow, Stephen, but only if you protect me from the Indians," Martha told him.

Ruthie came up out of her quilt. "Yes, you have to save us all, Stephen."

"I will. I can do that easy. I'll get my bow 'n' arrows an' I'll shoot 'em with a flamin' tip. They'll run so fast, Martha. You should see Junior, Martha; he can get 'em by the neck like this an' twist their heads off."

"Ow, Stephen, let go my neck. You wanna sleep down here or get back up there in your own bed?" Martha scolded.

He snuggled down beside her, warmed under his quilt and the comfort of someone near. He quickly fell asleep.

As sometimes happens after a stressful event, Papa and Mother commenced to giggle.

"Mr. McKinley has a way with words." Papa wasn't able to contain his convulsive laughter. "Can't you just see fat ol' Mr. Collins running around buck naked?" Papa had to place his pillow over his face to keep from disturbing those in nearby wagons.

"While I was running around out there in the dark, I kept running into people," Mother confessed. "I didn't know who I was knocking down. I thought they might be Indians and I was too scared to help pick 'em up."

"Those Indians might not know much, but they'd know a fine women if they ran into her," Papa whispered, but Papa couldn't whisper softly. "They wouldn't have stopped with you till they got clear away from here. You best believe me. Now come over here where you belong, woman."

"Shhh, Eli—we'll wake the children."

"The children would like to get to sleep first, before you wake us, thank you very much." Bertha whispered so loudly in response to Papa and Mother that the whole family was set off in renewed peals of laughter.

The girls' giggling and murmuring cease. Silence followed, except for a nocturnal chorus from howling wolves, the fluttering of the big canvas overhead, and the stirring of restless livestock. Inside the wagons the families had surrendered to sleep.

For Martha, lying the darkness, the thoughts of her relationship with Neil were becoming unbearably difficult. The proper distance and respect required of them was an increasing struggle with their impetuous youthful nature and their unpredictable future.

Here we are, settled in beds, unable to reach out to each other, unable to share our thoughts, our desire to protect and care for one another. A sense of loneliness invaded her before she gave into sleep.

Chapter 25

Mr. McKinley was crossing the wagons through Nebraska's most desolate land. Without surface water, the hills were barren of trees, bare rocks lay exposed, and grass was sparse, brittle, and baked dry under the hot summer sun.

Martha was finding the walk endless as she and the settlers forged their way across the silent, shifting, red brown, sandy soil, past what Mr. Reynolds referred to as "blow outs" in the hillsides carved by incessant wind and the passage of time.

Papa climbed from under his wagon to face another sweltering day. *We've got to make Court House Rock. This heat's sapping us and I don't have enough water to satisfy my oxen's thirst. I can't even wash my face. I never bargained for such heat.*

Mother started a fire from a meager supply of buffalo chips and watched a cloud of blue smoke roll up from them. *I hope there's enough chips here to cook breakfast. I'm so thankful we stopped Sunday and I could do the wash and bake bread.*

She missed not attending church and prayer services but there hadn't been time. Whenever time permitted, she read a bit of scripture from her Bible, and she enjoyed singing hymns as she worked. She'd noticed many of the other women were forced to do the same.

During breakfast the subject of the deadly river water came up. Papa said a fellow told him, "They saved their ox by forcing melted lard and flour worked into a paste down its gullet. I don't know—seems to me that by the time a fellow'd do all this the poison would've worked itself into the body. I got the feelin' Mr. McKinley didn't place too much faith in this method either."

Martha and Bertha were discussing a little brown bird they'd heard earlier. "It does have the most delightful, melodious song," Martha agreed.

Yes, I heard it too," Papa interrupted. " It sure does have a purty song. The other day, Mr. Buland was with me and we happened to hear one close by. He called it a meadowlark; natives of here. 'Specially in the grasslands. They're not a good-eatin' bird, though."

"You know that fellow with the snake bite?" Papa reminded the family. "Mrs. Kenyon tells me there's nothin' more can be done for him. She thinks he's gonna need his foot cut off."

"Oh no. How, Papa?" Martha gasped. "How do you cut off a man's foot?"

"Get him good and drunk, that's how." Papa poured himself more coffee as Mother handed him a plate of griddle cakes. "It's that or he'll die, Martha."

Breakfast over, the wagons were loaded and headed for Court House Rock on the north side of the West Platte River.

Mr. Emigh had informed them last night that he'd read about the Platte River from the *Nebraska Chronicles*, one of the books he'd brought with him. The Platte River, or "Flat Water" as it's called by the Oto Indians of the region, runs east to west through the territory and branches off in several places along the way.

As the day progressed, the winds howled and the parching sun created an insufferable inferno for the families and animals. The nearby Platte River was covered with deadly foam and soap suds from natural chemicals. It tormented and aggravated both man and beast in their craving and unquenchable thirst for water.

When David Wilson stated to Sam Emigh and Eli, "We can't keep going like this without water. We're gonna lose our teams," he was voicing the worry and concern of everyone in the wagon train.

During dinner, Papa, with one hand clamped over his hat, complained, "I'm eating more dirt than bread." He fought a continual battle to keep his hat, which, if it ever came loose, he'd never be able to reclaim.

Mother served her family from her rapidly dwindling supply of buffalo jerky, along with Pilot crackers and a handful of dried apricots and apples. "They tend to make moisture in a dry mouth." She urged the children to eat them.

How is it possible to get juice from dry fruit?" Ruthie complained, wishing there were some way to quench her persistent thirst. Her ration of water didn't satisfy her need.

Throughout the morning, the Burt's were entertained by people attempting to capture objects the wind sent skimming across the dry earth.

"Mother," Bertha chided, "if we keep putting everything in the wagon, pretty soon there'll be no room for us. The wagon is already full and we're still stuffing more in."

"I can't abide things banging against the outside the wagon is why," Mother explained. "We'll manage, dear." She watched as Ruthie chased after a bucket the wind picked up and skipped across the arid sand. "My head simply can't stand the incessant clamor."

Papa came back from checking the livestock. "Ma oxen're lookin' bad. I gave them a portion of the water, but it's not enough. We've been travelin' the best part of two weeks through this heat and it's scorchin' the life outta us."

"I think, Papa, Mother Nature's got the best of you this time," Bertha said, licking her dry, cracked lips. She tired not to smile. It was torture for her to stretch the skin on her sore, sun-blistered face.

The perpetual wind commenced to blow with more fury than the pioneers had experienced earlier. The teams struggled to pull the wagons through the drifting, sandy soil and against a fierce, blustery wind.

Papa, through blowing grit, saw the man in front of him was stopped. The man's hands were cupped around his mouth, but his words were whipped away in the wind. Papa beckoned to the man, and by pushing themselves against the stiff gale they met halfway between the wagons. "McKinley says to take cover. There's a bad storm comin' at us. He says to pass the word along," the man shouted above the wail of the wind.

After inquiring if the gentleman and his family would be alright, Papa, his hat clamped down over his head, was pushed along in the wind past his wagon to relay the message to Sam, with instructions it be passed along.

It distressed Papa to see his oxen trying to huddle against the powerful wind. His mood was apparent as he climbed into the wagon. "I feel bad for ma' oxen. There's no shelter for 'em, and that blowin' sand smarts when it hits."

"Let's bring them up alongside the wagon away from the wind as much as possible," Mother suggested. "It should buffer them some."

"I don't want ta take a chance with the wind catchin' the wagon just right and tippin' it over on 'em. I can't afford ta lose one."

"Eli, we'd all be killed if the wagon tipped over. For goodness sakes, what a grievous thought. Can't they suffocate from the sand in the air?"

After her parents returned, Martha had to fight against the strong pull of the wind to secure the flap over the canvas opening.

The world of the pioneers was filled with the sobbing, mournful moan from the wind, and at times it raged around them, shrieking and howling. Families in the wagons felt themselves being rocked by the powerful turbulence. Daylight disappeared and they were in total darkness.

Inside the wagons the air was stifling. Fine grit and sand filtered through the pores of the canvases, filling the air with a powdered, choking dust. Those inside felt the wind's fury as objects were hurled against the wagons and canvases.

Papa struggled to pry open the flap and see outside, but the darkness prohibited him from seeing but a few feet in front of him. He could only wait, hope, and pray his oxen would survive.

"Martha?" Ruthie, cuddled close to her sister, whispered, "I'm really scared. What will we do if our oxen die?"

"Animals can live through this, Ruthie." Martha put an arm around her sister to comfort the little girl. "The buffalo have nowhere to go. But they'll cuddle together like us. They'll be alright, Ruthie. We just have to wait out the storm like they do."

A driving gust of wind rocked the wagon violently. Mother sat quietly, gently messaging Stephen's head lying in her lap. Perhaps by rubbing Stephen's head, she could ease the pain in her own.

Inside the dark wagon the heat intensified. Sounds were obliterated by the ferocious wail of the wind outside.

Suddenly Papa felt the wind wane and slow to a low moan. He bolted up to release the flap. It was light out, and the air had cleared as he stared out at the devastating scene before him.

The family gathered around Papa to look out at the wagons with canvases blown off, wagons on their sides or pushed up against each other. Animals were down. They watched people crawl out from their wagons and aimlessly wander around perplexed with their predicaments.

Papa, after finding his livestock were safe, joined Mother and the others who were able to care for the injured, and began the monumental task of righting the wagons and making repairs. The dead livestock would be left for the buzzards and carnivores.

The pioneers working as a community contributed buffalo chips from their hoarded supply to build a communal fire. Mrs. Kenyon demanded a donation of their precious water for coffee and medicinal purposes.

Mr. McKinley and Mr. Buland moved about giving support where they were needed. It surprised them when they heard Mr. Collins commend the women.

"A bad situation," he cajoled them, "'specially when I s'pect ya ladies must feel like rantin', ravin', an' throwin' up yer hands in despair." The two men were unable to hear Mrs. Kenyon's reply, but they watched Mr. Collins back up, stripped of his charming smile, and make a hasty retreat.

Martha, overhearing Mr. Collins, noted that the women did have control of their frayed emotions and indeed were offering comfort to the terrified and hysterical, and sympathy to the bereaved.

She recalled what Mother and Granny said was courage: "The stuff makes us women able to carry on." These had been Granny's exact words.

She wasn't able at the moment to recollect that special word Granny called it—add—adversity—that was it. Granny had said, "Women are capable of incredible feats in the face of adversity." She wasn't sure what it all meant, but that it had to do with giving women courage.

Martha remembered the day they left for this journey, Granny told Mother, "You can do it?" Granny knew what she was talking about. She'd come across an ocean when she was young with her family of small children, and that to Martha took courage.

She was suddenly brought back to her senses by a man's plea for help followed by a woman's piercing scream.

"We's be needin' help here! Lordy! Hit's a-comin—hit's a-comin'!" The woman's cries were more pronounced with the canvas cover gone from the wagon.

"Oh for goodness sakes," Mrs. Kenyon sputtered, "ya can always depend on 'em comin' at the most inopportune time, can't cha?" She handed her wooden spoon to one of the ladies, wiped her hands on her apron, straightened her bonnet, and marched off to assist in the birthing of Jenny McGraw's baby.

In her usual brisk manner, Ruth Kenyon spit out staccato orders to everyone within her reach. "I need the privacy of a birthin' room set up best we can, and have me plenty of boilin' water ready."

A physician from the Collins party stopped by to offer his services and was confronted with what he later referred to as "a cranky old biddy." Ruth Kenyon, hands on her hips, informed him, "Women take care of women's birthin's, only natural and proper."

The doctor hastily ducked away to leave her in charge. "Any problems arise, I'll be glad to take over," he called back over his shoulder as he scurried away.

Had he stayed, he would have heard Mrs. Kenyon mutter in disgust, "There won't be any problems. I know full well what I'm about. I'm a women ain't I?"

The men who witnessed the account between the two were amused, but enjoyed a hearty laugh at Mr. McKinley's opinion of the situation. "Let a woman take charge," he said, "and they can maneuver the entire militia single-handedly. Wonder President Polk hasn't figured this out yet. I'm lucky to keep my position in this wagon train with this many women around. Takin' charge is an instinct born in 'em."

Mr. McKinley determined which wagons were worth repairing and which were to be abandoned. Ripped canvases could be spliced together to make one canvas. Torn canvases still attached could be mended.

He sent the young men to round up the scattered livestock, and the young women and children with burlap sacks to gather buffalo chips.

Thunder rumbled in the distance, and big dark clouds rolled across the sky. The pioneers watched lightning flash and strike out as a storm moved closer. Their fears returned when they realized how helpless and vulnerable they were out here in this vast open space.

The baby was spanked once and yelled in protest as he joined the Mc-Graw family. There was a brief pause of reverence among the settlers upon hearing his lusty howl of life.

Brian McGraw took on as if he'd birthed the child himself, so great was his pride.

The event lightened the mood for the travelers. From somewhere a jug was produced and the men gathered to toast Brian McGraw and his new son, who, he decided, was to be named, "Robert Brian Mc-Graw. We'll be callin' him RB fer the rist of his borned days," Mr. McGraw crowed, before he gulped a swig. Jenny McGraw, on hearing her husband announcement of the baby's name, cooed, "Your ma' Lil Robby, Sonny."

Eli Burt searched out David Wilson, whose wife and baby's death were still a new and painful reality for him. Eli made sure the jug was passed by David a couple of times before he sensed the man relaxed a little.

Mr. McKinley joined the men in commemorating the event. Perhaps the whisky would help soften the sharp edge of remorse he was feeling over the deaths today. He took his responsibility for these people seriously and he'd lost three of them. He was keeping to himself the water problem.

The drink made him feel guilty when the Mormon gentlemen politely refused to imbibe and said they'd offer their prayers instead, but his guilt wasn't long lived, as a glow from the fiery swallow of good homemade whisky mellowed him.

A man was found pinned under the wheels of his wagon and a young mother and daughter were crushed under their overturned wagon. A stunned, stricken husband with three small sons, in stair-step sizes, were faced with traveling on without their wife, mother, and sister.

Graves were hastily dug in the soft sand and the bodies lowered side by side. Reverend Hirum gave a short service for the departed, who were to be left here alone with their dreams in the obscurity of their graves.

Those attending closed the services with a hymn that faded into the evening. Darkness had gently covered the world of the pioneers returning to their wagons, leaving behind them three little wooden crosses to the mercy of nature, the passage of time, the endless shifting sand, and to settlers moving west who would little note them.

The families went about reconstructing their caravan for morning. Mr. McKinley suggested to families they might double up as much as possible, but some of the families knew they had little choice but to settle wherever they could until they were able to replace their wagons and resume the journey, if ever again.

"The wagons must move on," was Mr. McKinley's final proclamation.

Mr. McGraw and the other smithies waited for the buffalo chips, fanned by the wind, to produce enough heat to bend iron. Their anvils rang throughout the evening as they pounded pieces into various shapes needed to repair the wagons.

It was after dark when Mr. Reynolds arrived back in camp to report, "There was bad storm damage ta wagons all along the trail."

"No one knew the apparent reason for the unprovoked, brutal Indian attack in which fifty or more Sioux were involved. They had come up to the wagons appearing friendly, but then something went wrong. Men were killed with their women and children looking on."

He told of a little girl who had survived and was taken in by one of the families. "She was barley alive when I left 'em. Don't appear ta me she's likely ta make it. The Indians carried away several small children and young women. I tell ya', I hated ta leave 'em out there."

Mr. Reynolds said, " I suggested, they come to join up with us. But they felt they wanted to keep going. It's gonna be hard on 'em with so few men. I tell ya, I hated ta leave 'em. They're a pitiful group."

The youngsters crowded around Mr. Reynolds eager to question him how he and Buddy, his horse, were able to survive the storm.

"Storm like this ain't new ta Buddy. Why, I told him ta lay down," Mr. Reynolds replied, "then I rolled up in ma' blanket next ta 'em ta wait it out. If'n anything had come along and hit me I wouldn't be here ta tell about this, now would I ? Outside of being tumbled about several times, we rode 'er out. Old Buddy here buried his nose in ma' blanket ta keep from breathin' in the sand. After it was over I took Buddy fer a drink of water, and you shoulda seen him."

Mr. Reynolds was so amused at his own tale, he had difficulty containing himself as he rambled on. "Ol' Buddy raised his head up and sand was drippin' outta his teeth. It's the most comical thing, I believe, I ever did see."

"Sand? Was it wet sand?" asked Stephen, who was captivated with the story.

"Oh no, Laddie, 'twas dry. That durn wind blew so hard it moved the river and left nothin' but dry sand."

The children dissolved into gales of laughter to visualize such a sight. However, while some thought the tale believable, others like Stephen quietly speculated about it. After all, wasn't the river water poisoned? Stephen liked Mr. Reynolds and didn't pursue the matter further.

Martha, who had joined the women gathered around the fire preparing kettles of stew for the first time, noticed the woman Mrs. Kenyon had handed her spoon to when she was called away for the birthing.

Martha found herself staring at the woman, who stirred the big Dutch ovens, tended the fires, baked cornbread and biscuits, and mothered her children, who were images of her.

She's strange, Martha decided. *No, not strange—she's different.* She tried not to stare; it wasn't polite, but she was intrigued with this dark-skinned lady, who walked about humming in a beautiful, deep, husky voice; whose hair was tied up in a bright scarf; and who didn't walk but gracefully swayed as she moved. Her smile was pleasant and her teeth were whitest Marta had ever seen. When the lady listened to someone, her dark eyes opened wide and the whites were pure white.

200

Martha was fascinated with this woman; she had never encountered a black-skinned person. She imagined the lady to have been a queen from somewhere, she was so beautiful and dignified. It was as though those near her were cast under her carefree spell. Everyone smiled and laughed more.

It amazed her at first how this woman could draw people to her, but on watching her closer, Martha discovered it was done with her captivating smile and soft laughter.

Martha glanced around. "Where's my mother?" She had to find know more about this lady.

Chapter 26

Martha awakened in the early morning darkness to the sound of rain. She snuggled deeper under her warm quilt to revive yesterday's events.

Called to assist in birthing the McGraw baby, Mrs. Kenyon handed her spoon over to a lady, whom Martha watched mesmerize the entire wagon train. At first the woman was reserved around them, but with their engaging smile and polite manners, she and her family were accepted.

They were the Jackson's, a family of nine, with their milk chocolate skin and big brown eyes. They were traveling in a regular covered wagon, with their team of four skinny mules and a sickly husband and father.

Martha learned from overhearing Mr. McKinley tell Mr. Emigh that "the Jacksons won't be welcome in the Oregon Territory. The independent government of the Oregon Territory didn't want to involve themselves with the slavery issue. Slaves are not allowed to own land, even free slaves, and across the Columbia River at Fort Vancouver, the English, under British rule, weren't allowed to sell land to settlers who weren't British subjects.

"There's a black settlement established itself up north of Fort Vancouver," Martha heard Mr. McKinley say. "Seems the Indians have a lot of respect for these people. They're being allowed to clear the land and set up small farms, which are of value to the British. Our Jacksons with their newly signed freedom papers, are headin' for this promised land. I'm seeing 'em only as far's Oregon City."

Martha watched a friendship develop between her little brother, Stephen, and Toby, his new friend.

Stephen asked Toby if he wanted to make blazin' arrows.

"Ya wanna know how ta catch crawdaddies?" Toby asked. "They bites your toes off if'n ya don't catch 'em right. They's got sharp claw pinchers. Ma mammy boils 'em up an' we eats 'em fast as she kin cooks 'em. C'mon, I shows ya how."

Little Toby taught the children to wade into the river in search of crawdaddies camouflaged under the rocks. He would grab them behind the front claws to keep from being pinched by the big pinchers extending from the upper section of their bodies. The Jackson youngsters were skilled at finding and snatching the miniature lobsters before they could attach themselves to their tender toes.

Martha and the other women of strict Puritan heritage quietly and serenely went about their work, but not Mrs. Jackson. She expelled a radiance. Going about her work she lustily sang gospel songs and folk melodies that stirred up an infectious atmosphere. Martha found she and the other ladies were soon humming along with Mrs. Jackson, and even the men were heard whistling the melodies.

It had been Mrs. Jackson who informed them when supper was ready the day Mc Graw's baby was born. Reverend Hirum invoked the blessing before they savored the spicy stew of corn, rice, beans, and meat with piles of hot, flaky biscuits and warm cornbread. She made sure bowls were filled and refilled until the big Dutch ovens were empty.

Mrs. Jackson said she was taking food to the new baby. Martha asked if she might come along to look in on Mrs. McGraw and see the new baby.

"Miz McGraw, ma'am, ya'll need ta make milk fer thet new boy chile," Mrs. Jacks said as she handed a bowl of the stew with a tasty biscuit to Mrs. McGraw.

"Dis gots ta be de most beautiful chile I ever did see." Mrs. Jackson cradled the tiny baby in her arms.

"Ya'll eats up your stew now. He be needin' lots o' good milk, if'n he gonna grow'd ta be a big man, jist like his daddy, ya hear? He be needing good food from his mamma, Miz McGraw, ma'am." She'd handed the new baby for Martha to hold while she neatened Mrs. McGraw's bed.

Martha's reminiscing was disturbed by the sound of raindrops dripping somewhere inside the wagon.

Last night, when the storm began, Mr. McKinley requested everyone to put out buckets to catch the rainwater.

"Put out buckets? What the tarnation for?" Mr. Crawford grumbled. "They'll only fill with sand."

During the night, sheets of rain poured down forming gullies, and gushing water became swift rivulets turning the sand into a quicksand consistency.

This was the scene as Martha opened the flap to peek outside. Mr. McKinley was nearby telling a group of men, "There's little hope in starting out on time this morning. We can't see till it's better light."

She heard Mr. Reynolds complain, "I'm gonna have ta show that Cookie how ta build a fire inside his cook wagon. I'm sure not lookin' forwards ta startin' my day without a hot cup o' coffee."

Oh no, this means Pilot crackers for us. I should be thankful we have them, but they're so hard and tasteless. Martha ducked back behind the flap.

"Martha?" Ruthie whispered. "I need to use the commode."

"Let me pull the curtain." Martha drew the curtain across the inside width of the wagon for privacy and heard Bertha moan, "Oh bother, isn't there a bush somewhere outside we can hide behind? I hate to use the commode in the wagon."

Mother handed out dried apples and apricots along with strips of buffalo jerky and Pilot crackers for their breakfast. "That sandstorm yesterday forced the pores in the canvas to open, and now it's leaking like a sieve, isn't it?" she said with disgust. The family looked up to water droplets forming on the inside of the canvas before they fell.

After a cold breakfast, and under a steady rain, the wagons prepared to move out.

The Burt women watched the teams slip and slide in the liquid earth, searching for secure footing as they hauled the big wagons behind them. Mr. McKinley, Mr. Buland, and Mr. Reynolds directed the wagons that were not mired down to form a train and move on.

After the first wagons moved out, Mr. McKinley yelled to the men, "Let's get these teams doubled up and pull the rest of the wagons out."

It became a tedious, time-consuming job, and took up the better part of the morning. The wagons listed dangerously at times as double-hitched teams struggled to drag the heavy wagons out of deep sticky mud that clung to the wheels.

Sam Emigh and Papa were working side by side. "Eli, I'm going to have to exchange my horses next fort we come to. They're eating more than I anticipated, they can't exist on green grass alone, they need some oats, and they're exhausted. Clydesdales aren't adequate horses for this long a journey. I have to admit, I was warned against buying them. I've noticed lately Major's favoring his right front leg."

As the morning progressed, the water-soaked earth dried under a white hot sun, but the desolate red cliffs did little to liven the disposition of the travelers.

Sam Emigh, using the scarf tied around his neck, wiped his face and swabbed the inside of his hat and his neck. He put the scarf over his head and anchored it with his hat.

"The Platt's quite wide across in places, you notice?" he asked Papa. "What a waste of water; it's so full of alkali."

Mr. McKinley rode up. "We'll stop for a quick dinner at a water hole ahead. It's nasty-tastin' water, but we'll be able to water the stock if the buffalo haven't beaten us to it."

"Papa, why do some of these pools of water, like that one over there, have that crusty white stuff around them?" Ruthie covered her mouth and nose with her hands. "Pew, I can smell the stink from these dead animals around here too."

"I've never seen so many bones lying around in one place." It amazed Martha, the the amount of bleached-white bones surrounding the pools of water.

"I think the pools have an evil look to them," Bertha stated. "Almost like they're warning us not to go near them."

Sam Emigh agreed with her. "They're evil alright; they're wicked. Thirsty buffalo and other animals are driven to them, and once they drink the poisoned water, they die."

The girls caught up to Mother, who they found talkative this morning. "I'm so glad Mrs. McGraw and the baby appear to be doing so well. The baby is a pretty little thing. But what a shame we had to lose one child as another was coming into the world. You know, girls, we women are expected to accept so much suffering. We have little choice but to accept it time after time. We have only so much endurance. If anyone asked, who would like to turn back? I'm sure there would be few women left in this train willing to endure anymore of this difficult journey."

"Mother, there are times I wish we could go back. I don't know about you, but this isn't all the fun I thought it was going to be," Bertha stated.

Martha walked on quietly. *I must believe Oregon is worth this journey. I can't help but wonder at times if my family will be fortunate to make it all the way.*

It became necessary to walk on either side of their restless, thirsty teams to deter them from the alkali river and the poison backwater pools.

Papa noted the scruffy-looking shrubs growing along the riverbank. There wasn't a blade of grass for his oxen, who were showing signs of weakness from the lack of good forage and water.

The girls had been given sacks to pick up buffalo chips as they moved along. "The wind's blowing sand over them, Mother; they're buried and hard to find," they complained.

The travelers first saw the Indians at the crest of a hill, to the left of the wagons. There were between twenty or thirty of them spread out, walking towards the train. They slowly worked their way through the soft soil towards the wagons.

Mr. McKinley and Mr. Reynolds raced down the line of wagons, as rapidly as they could push their horses in the sandy soil. "Don't fire!" they shouted to the nervous settlers.

Papa and Sam Emigh watched the Indians continue in the direction of the wagons without displaying a sign of greeting. Papa walked forward to meet them, holding up his hand to display the universal greeting of peace, just as Mr. McKinley rode up and quickly alighted to extend his hand in greeting.

Mr. Reynolds spoke to them and signed in the Sioux language. They nodded, signed, and pointed towards the last two wagons.

Men arrived with guns; fearful women and children watched.

Mr. Reynolds turned towards Papa and Sam. "They want food. Can you spare them a couple o' sacks o' corn?"

Papa returned with a sack of flour. "This is all I have. Mr. Reynolds; we're short of supplies."

Mr. Reynolds signed for the Indians to take the sack. Four of them stepped forward. One of them, taking his knife, cut into the bag of flour, spilling the contents onto the ground in front of him.

The wind blew the flour over the others, dusting them in white powder, setting off an outburst of laughter from their comrades.

Papa watched as the sack, its contents destroyed, was caught up in the wind and sailed out across the ground.

Several angry Indians, in their dialect, spoke out and gestured to the little milk cow tied to the back of the Burt's wagon.

Martha, standing near the cow, thought they indicated her. Her heart lurched and began beating wildly, her throat constricted, and breathing became difficult. She fought panic welling up inside her as two Indians started towards her.

Oh dear God, they mean me. These savages are coming for me. Isn't Papa going to stop them? Is no one going to help me?

Mr. Reynolds's words flashed to her. *They appeared friendly but turned mean. They killed—they killed.* She willed herself not to move.

Her heart pounded so hard it pushed the blood thundering through her head. She must not give in to the terror, but remain calm.

Everyone's watching, but nobody's going to save me. They're all too afraid. She was paralyzed with fear. *They'll kill my family. I can't save them. I can't run. Where can I hide?* She lowered her eyes. *I refuse to look at them, to look in their faces.*

The two walked past Martha, untying the cow. Every eye watched as they turned back to their group, dragging the balking little animal behind them.

One of the Indians stepped forward. Lifting his tomahawk, he brought it down on the bovine's head. Stunned from the blow, her knees buckled. Folks, opened mouthed, watched horrified as the defenseless cow staggered and jerked violently to keep from falling.

An Indian on either side of her, their knives flashing, cut into her throat. Two others cut away at her hide, peeling it from her still live body.

The little cow tossed her head in protest and pain, guttural cries escaped her severed throat, and ejected blood caught in the wind was broadcast around. She struggled to gain footing, but the Indian once again lifted his war ax and brought it down on her head.

Stunned from the lethal blows and lack of blood, she succumbed to an agonizing death, falling into a pool of her own blood, quickly absorbed into the sand beneath her.

The Indians finished stripping the hide from her twitching body, continued their brutal butchering before the horror-stricken crowd.

Mother had grabbed Ruthie and covered their faces in her long skirt. She was unable to help Bertha, who wailed aloud in protest and dashed forward in a frantic rescue attempt.

Papa reached to seize Bertha with one hand and covered her mouth with the other. She fought him, flailing her arms in his attempt to subdue her. He glanced back at Mother and Ruthie. He'd never felt so helpless.

Martha experienced a floating sensation overtaking her. She was no longer able to control the weakness that drained her as she sank into darkness.

A mournful, angry murmur escaped the crowd watching the savage violence. Women hid their faces and those of their children in their long skirts; some fainted, others retched.

Martha came out of oblivion confused. Her head was in Neil's lap; she heard him talking to her in a soft voice.

Still confused, she sat up, looked past his shoulder, and immediately recalled the deplorable scene. Able to comprehend what had taken place, she burst into tears. She reached blindly for Neil and buried her face against his chest. She sobbed uncontrollably until her terror and fear eased, but her anger at the vicious death of the little cow remained.

Neil assisted her in standing and brushed the sand from her clothes. Still clinging to him, she forced herself to once again glance over at the Indians, who were covered with blood. They were hastily cutting chunks of meat from the remains of the little cow. Some were chewing on the raw, bloody pieces. She fought an urge to vomit.

She glanced over to see Mr. McKinley's facial expression of unspoken concern for her. He quickly turned back to the people who had watched the tragedy. "Let's move on, folks." His voice was stern and he maintained absolute control of his emotions.

Mr. Reynolds and Mr. Buland also encouraged the crowd to move along. The three men were grateful the crowd had remained calm and restrained themselves throughout the ugly ordeal.

Papa enfolded Mother, Ruthie, and Bertha in his arms. Mr. Emigh and Nathan comforted a loudly bawling Stephen, whom they'd quickly turned away from the grisly scene earlier.

Martha's horror returned as again she recalled Mr. Reynolds's words: *They appeared friendly but turned mean. They savagely killed—they killed. These savages hadn't been friendly; they came mean.*

"How can I save them?" she hysterically whispered. "My mother, my sisters, Neil—they'll come back and kill us. Neil! They'll kill my papa." She pulled herself free of him and frantically, wildly searched for a place to hide. Terror overcame her; she became hysterical, filled with fear.

Bertha noted her sister and looked around for help, but everyone appeared busy.

Neil, startled by Martha's reaction, managed with Bertha to get her to one side of the wagon, away from the scene. He pinned her thrashing arms against the wagon. "Bertha, we have to make her listen."

Bertha sought to capture one of Martha's flailing arms. She could feel her sister's uncontrollable trembling. "Martha, don't be afraid," she pleaded. "Please don't be scared," but Martha's sobbing and incoherent babbling didn't lessen.

"Martha, listen to me." Neil's face was inches from hers. "Martha?" He caught her chin roughly in one hand. "Listen to me. They're hungry. They only want food; they don't want us. They won't kill us, Martha. Can you hear me? They won't kill us."

Martha heard and her mind slowly absorbed the details. His arms comforted her, and the steady, rhythmic beat of his heart calmed her.

"Martha, stop this." Bertha was holding tight to Martha's hand. "You're acting plain *ferhoodled.*"

Martha looked from Neil to her sister. "I'm sorry," she managed to whisper. "I lost my composure, didn't I? I'll be alright. I made a complete fool of myself, I'm sure."

"She stepped away from Neil. "I should be brave. Poor Papa and Mother. I'll be fine now." She quickly smoothed out her skirt and patted at her hair.

"Yes, Martha." Bertha hugged her sister. "Mother is feeling bad, and so is Stephen and Ruthie. I'm so glad you're feeling better. Martha, Neil's been with you all the time, did you know this?"

Neil and the girls came around the wagons to see the Indians walking away, toting pieces of their savage, bloody slaughter across their shoulders.

The crowd had returned to their wagons and was discussing the brutal tragedy that had befallen the poor Burt family.

Neil looked ahead to see Stephen and Nathan on the wagon seat. Nathan deftly flipped the reins over the backs of the two big horses. Neil saw his pa pause and wait for him. There was a comfortable silence between the two men as they fell into step beside the moving wagon.

Neil glanced back at the Burts. They appeared weary. He knew it must be difficult for them to put the visions of this ordeal behind them so quickly, but there were still many miles to cover in the remainder of the day.

Bertha with Ruthie for company touched the reins over the backs of the oxen. The big wagon creaked and groaned as it slowly moved forward.

Papa and Mother, ahead of Martha, were in a deep discussion.

This is why they're so brave and strong: they have each other. I hope that Neil and I can be such good friends, Martha sighed. *Right now, I'm plain tuckered out; worn thin, as Neil would say.*

Through the intense heat, the pioneers struggled forward, their eyes squinted against the sun's glare, their lips dried and cracked. Their exposed skin burned and browned as they moved each day from early morning into evening.

They were in search of a place to settle for the night and end this day.

Chapter 27

The Indian episode of yesterday behind them, the pioneers continued on their way to Courthouse Rock in the western section of Nebraska.

Papa disliked the sound of deep rumbling coming from the chests of his oxen. Their lungs were slowly filling with dust, suffocating them to death. The meager ration of water did little to slake their thirst, and they were limping on sore hooves from grinding through the miles of sandy soil day after day. They were dying and there wasn't any way to save them.

Mr. McKinley wasn't comfortable with the wagons formed into small groups spaced so far apart. Hostile Indians could take advantage of a weakness in the chain of wagons.

"Pull this train into a tighter formation," he yelled to his aides. He glanced behind him, and noted a dust cloud moving from the northeast towards the train. It might possibly be a cattle herd and drovers headed for the water hole he'd promised his people. He'd best keep a close watch; it might also be Indians on the move or a buffalo stampede.

Those drovers'll push to make it before us, if they can. They know every water hole from here to Wyoming. Ornery, hardheaded men. He decided to ride ahead and prepare the Kenyon's for the "the watering hole," as he liked to refer to it.

Walking beside their wagon, Ruth Kenyon, taller than her husband, had to tip her head down to converse with him. "Alex, if 'twere me I'd hurry the first five wagons to the water first 'cause Mr. McKinley didn't say how big a place this is. That way, it'd give us a more orderly way of takin' care of everyone."

"I'd think five or six wagons at a time taking turns. We could get our barrels filled while the teams're drinkin'. Were you thinking along these lines too?"

Alex Kenyon, a man of few words around his wife, nodded in agreement. He approved of his wife's ideas, but then didn't he always? He found he got along better with her this way.

A good fill of water for the horses and us. We should be out of this dust hole by tomorrow. The thought encouraged him. Glancing behind him, he calculated the wagons were spread out for some distance. He wondered if it weren't wiser for him to get to the water first, but then again, if he alerted the first five wagons, things, as Ruth had said, would move faster.

"Karl," he called, "ride back there and tell the wagons behind us to hurry it up so's they can get to the water hole first and get out before the rest catch up. Tell only the first five wagons, understand?"

"Ah—Pa, you're gonna let 'em get ta the water first?"

"Karl, ya mind yer Pa. Maybe you and your brother will have time for a nice cool dip before everyone gets to the water," Ruth Kenyon suggested.

Mr. Buland made his way from one group of wagons to another. "Move it along, folks," he coaxed. *Wonder why McKinley won't tell them about the lake ahead. It'd encourage 'em ta move faster.* He couldn't help but feel sympathy for the hot, weary folks. *The water'll bring 'em around.* He clucked his tongue and urged his horse towards the next group lagging behind.

As Mrs. Kenyon suggested, Alex and the five wagons crested the rise and beheld before them Lake McConaughy, an oasis in the desert. The lake was large enough for the entire wagon train to water their teams and fill water barrels at the same time. The air was moist and cool by the clear, blue lake. After drinking their fill, the livestock reached to strip succulent leaves from the shrubs growing along the water's edges, while the settlers took advantage of a quick, refreshing dip in the water. The women wet their feet and soaked cloths to put around their shoulders.

Mr. McKinley kept watch on the dust cloud still moving towards him. *This is a big lake; there's plenty of water for all.* He appreciated that the folks, after watering their stock and filling empty water barrels, were moving out. He didn't look forward to mixing with the drovers and their cattle, which he was sure they were.

Several wagons traveling to California decided to cross over the Platte River to Ogallala and follow the route south. Those crossing would wait on the other side to join a wagon train due in a few days heading that way. At first, everyone was apprehensive about their crossing and the Sioux. However, the Indians using the same crossing were friendly, and the party was optimistic about their decision.

211

To Martha, the travelers and teams refreshed were moving along with renewed energy.

Suddenly, she became aware of a commotion near the front of the train, bringing the wagons in front of her to a standstill. She watched the men around her hurry off towards the disturbance.

A man rode back to relay the message. "A little girl's fallen under the wheels of her wagon and she's bad hurt."

To parents this news was alarming; the youngsters had found they could get off the moving wagons by letting themselves down onto the wagon tongues. Then, climbing between the moving teams, they'd leap onto the ground.

The mother's scream at seeing her child fall had frightened the team of horses. They had panicked and pulled the wagon forward over the child's leg.

Papa and Sam Emigh arrived on horseback as the father, after fighting to bring his his team under control, climbed down to pick up his little daughter with one of her legs dangling awkwardly.

"She caught her dress on my shovel handle, sticking out up there, and fell," the father murmured to the growing crowd as he held the body of the little five-year-old child in his arms.

Mr. Hammond was not a man gifted with speech. A slightly built man, his face registered little expression as he held his daughter and waited in quiet resignation for his wife, a frail, tiny woman, who was hysterically weeping, to get control of herself and tell him what he should do.

After he'd made a quick observation of the situation, Mr. Buland rode for the doctor.

"Don't look ta me like there's much we can do here," someone stated. The folks agreed and decided to return to their wagons. Several patted Mr. Hammond on the shoulder and offered their sympathy as they passed by.

Mr. Hammond, without eye contact, stood mutely holding the limp body of the child, her dark hair cascading over his arm. Her eyes were closed in an ashen face. In quiet submission and acceptance, Mr. Hammond waited for his God to guide and direct him, as he'd been brought up to believe God would.

Wagons pulled out around them, leaving the Hammond family to wait for the doctor.

"What you wanna bet McKinley'll make it to Courthouse Rock tonight?" Sam Emigh suggested to Papa.

"Wish it were Fort Williams. We can't be more than another day's travel from there," was Papa's reply.

The men arrived back to find the Burt family waiting without shade, and the sun beating down without mercy.

The men told of the little girl's falling under the wagon wheels and Mr. Buland's going for the doctor. "Looks ta me as though they'll have ta take her leg off," Papa explained.

"Cut her leg off, Papa?" Stephen squinted against the bright sun to look up at Papa. "But how can she ever walk if they do that?"

"She'll have to use a crutch, that is, if she's lucky enough to live." Papa squatted down to put his arm across the boy's little shoulders. "This is why your mother and I get upset with you for jumping down from the wagon. It happens so fast, Son. Just one wrong step is all it takes."

"Oh my, how sad. A little child crippled for the rest of her life." Martha heard Mother moan and saw Stephen nod his head vigorously in agreement with Papa. But Martha wondered if Papa's warning was enough to slow down her little brother.

The Burt family, as they passed the Hammond wagon, stared at the doctor's black bag open on a clean, white bed sheet spread over the tailgate of the wagon, with strange-looking instruments lying beside the quiet body of the little girl, her bloody leg exposed.

To ease the minds of his family, Papa explained, "The area we're coming to, has some interesting big rock formations. I heard Mr. Reynolds tell about them being unusual, out of place in this otherwise flat land; they're relics from a long time ago and are still standing."

"Everything's strange out here, Papa," Bertha sighed. "I can't get excited about a couple of big old rocks."

"Wait till you see 'em 'fore ya pass judgment, Bertha. If ya look out yonder, they're still a purty far piece ahead, but from here they're pretty impressive, if you ask me. If this is what's left after thousands of years of wearing away, think of how big they were when the earth was new."

Mr. McKinley called a stop for the night just this side of Courthouse Rock. For the pioneers it meant another night without water or firewood

After their meager suppers of biscuits and gravy made of lard and flour browned to make a roux and water added, cooked over dry grass and buffalo chips, the Burt's joined the group assembling in the dusk of the evening for the meeting.

213

Mr. McKinley began by explaining his idea to make up time. "Fort Williams is another two days away and we are in bad need of supplies and water. Tomorrow let's plan to travel through the night.

"The Platte water is still unsafe to drink, so I hope you ration your water supply for a little while longer. No matter what happens tonight we leave on time tomorrow. We'll have time for a good rest once we get to Fort Williams.

"One more suggestion before you turn in. If you can lighten you wagons—I know, I know. I hear ya moanin'. But if ya make it easier on your exhausted teams, it means they'll live longer. See what you can do."

Papa's thoughts were of his exhausted oxen with their deep coughs.

Over in the vicinity of some wagons, men's voices could be heard loudly arguing. Everyone turned towards the hubbub. There was just enough light to see two men about to exchange blows as they yelled at each other.

Stephen, with the other little boys, ran to watch the two.

"What'd ya mean, ye ain't in charge. Ye've no business bad mouthin' us. If Mr. McKinley tells the doctor ta stay back there, it's his business." A husky man and rough-looking blond fellow were standing toe to toe. Muscles bulged in rigid arms hanging by their sides. Their fists were clenched into hard balls. Each dared the other to make a first move.

His cap atop a shock of unruly blond hair, his vest unable to restrain his big chest stuffed into it, the blond man argued, "Good thing fer you I'm not in command. And if'n Mr. Collins had been put in charge, like it shoulda been done in the first place, why ya sorry greenhorn," he sneered. "Ya think yer better than the rest of us, don't cha?"

The blond fellow brought his arm up, swinging a blow squarely for the big burly man's Jaw, but it glanced off his shoulder and knocked him backwards. The big man quickly regained his balance. His body a solid fortress of muscle, he charged. Head lowered, his intent was to use his thick neck and head as a battering ram as he came at his assailant.

The blond fellow, called "Jim Bob" by his friends, was a known troublemaker wherever he went. He was now being cheered on by his whisky-drinking comrades.

He cleverly sidestepped Mr. Jake, who had hurled himself full force, lost his balance in the soft dirt, and sprawled face down. He made a desperate attempt to get up, but not before Jim Bob flung himself over the fallen man, pinning him down, delivering Mr. Jake a blow to his head.

Mr. Jake, unfazed by the blow, grabbed Jim Bob by his vest and tried putting Jim Bob beneath him. But the man, being younger and more agile, was able to block Mr. Jake from accomplishing the strangulation hold he was intending.

Mr. McKinley arrived as Jim Bob extricated himself from his aggressor.

"Men, to your feet." Mr. McKinley pulled the two up off the ground and held them apart as he would have a couple of scuffling boys.

They came apart, breathing laboriously, as they let go one another and were hoisted to their feet. Sweat coursed down their faces. Jim Bob bent over, his hands on his knees, to catch his breath. Mr. Jake towered above him, flexing his fists.

"What's the call for this, gentlemen?" Mr. McKinley demanded.

"You tell this here sodbuster ta keep his mouth shut." Jim Bob squinted his eyes, scowled, and jabbed a finger at Mr. Jake's chest.

Before Mr. McKinley could say a word Mr. Jake bellowed, "This 'ere bloke seems ta think you're showing a bit of favoritism ta some of us, Mr. McKinley." His eyes narrowed. "'e says Mr. Collins woulda 'ad us outta this 'ell 'ole afore now; says 'tis the waiting around fur us green 'orns that's losin' time, and 'e don't like the idea of ya leaving the doctor out there fur them Indians either."

Jim Bob spied his battered cap and sauntered over to retrieved it. He stopped to dust it off on his knee before flipping it back over his unruly head of hair.

"Mr. Jim Bob, sir," Mr. McKinley growled. "You listen to me. I'm wagon master of this train. I manage this train for everyone, you understand me? Not a few but everyone."

Those watching the fracas heard the authority and command in Mr. McKinley's voice. "You don't like how I'm doing, then drop out—move on. We've had a trying day, we're tired, and I've no use for troublemakers. If you men decide to leave the train, you stay clear of us, you hear? And Mr. Jim Bob, sir, you make sure this message gets to Mr. Collins, you hear me, sir?"

Mr. McKinley turned abruptly and walked away, leaving the two men to settle their differences. Looking around, he found it interesting that Mr. Collins was no where in sight.

Everyone watched after Mr. McKinley. They witnessed him hesitate and slowly turn back to face the crowd.

"Mr. Reynolds has been dispatched to bring the Hammons and the doctor in. I never intended for this train to leave until these folks were reunited with us. Now go get some rest. We're travelin' all night tomorrow, remember?"

There were murmurs of approval concerning the Hammons and the doctor from the crowd as they returned to their campsites.

On the way to their wagons, Sam Emigh and Papa fell into a discussion about their situation.

"What bothers me most, Sam, is we can't seem to get in our quota of miles crossin' through this territory. Didn't McKinley say we'd be in Oregon 'bout October? We're never gonna make it. Our teams're worn out. We can't keep pushin' 'em like this without water."

"We need to bring in some meat too," Sam added. "We've not had too much time to hunt, and it's important we keep up our strength. Oh—say Eli, you remember Mr. Goodman? We met him back at the LaSalle settlement. He's right across the river from us. We'll be meetin' up with their wagons at South Pass. The trail splits there, and those traveling on to California turn south. Fellow up ahead told me. I forgot how Mr. Goodman came into the conversation; reason doesn't come to mind but a name I remembered."

Mother found it difficult to trudge back to the wagon with Ruthie. She was so tired. "That was a disgusting fight tonight. I can't believe I've let something so unimportant upset me. I think I'll stay up a bit longer and see what I can do to lighten the wagon. You ready for bed, Miss Ruthie, or you want to help me?"

"Mother, now how can I go to bed if you're working in the wagon? Besides, how are you going to see in the dark?"

Once inside the dark wagon, Mother began rearranging things. She found and handed out the two wooden churns, then she consolidated a provisional box and handed out the empty one.

She decided to throw out some of the quilts she'd brought to trade for supplies. "They feel damp. It's a wonder they aren't sour and smell," she told Ruthie. She wouldn't let herself feel guilty about throwing them away, even through she remembered how family members quilted them for the journey. The oxen were more important to her now.

Papa persuaded Mother to stop working for the night and finish in the daylight. He suggested she keep a few of the quilts and he'd leave behind some of his heavy iron pieces.

"With Mr. McGraw along, I won't be needing them or this." He untied and stacked his plow on the pile.

Martha and Neil stayed behind the crowd. They walked slowly and silently side by side, lost in thought of their tomorrow what didn't include Indians, heat, or misery.

Martha broke the silence. "Neil, there's something about this land. It's so beautiful, but it can be so mean and brutal. Any life seems to come alive at night, have you noticed? Otherwise, it's so quiet except for the wind and these pesky mosquitoes."

"I'm glad your along, Martha." Neil reached for her hand. "I like seeing things the way you do. If you weren't here I'd probably only see the dirt, the hard work, and lose my temper because we don't travel faster. My ma, she always saw nice things the way you do."

Neil appropriately wished the Burt family a good night after depositing Martha at her wagon.

Martha sedately wished him a proper good night but paused to watch after him. *It would have been nice if in our parting tonight we could have been alone,* she thought before climbing into the dark wagon to help Mother arrange the beds.

Perhaps one day, I'll be setting up a bed for Neil and me, and it won't be in any old cramped wagon either. She felt her face flush and was glad for the darkness. She had to chuckle at her imagination.

"Did you say something, dear?" Mother asked.

"No, Mother, I was just sighing. I'm worn thin."

"Yes, isn't this true of us all." Mother reached to pull the flap down over the front of the wagon's opening for the night, just as Martha reached for the other flap. They secured the flaps to close out the world until tomorrow morning.

Chapter 28

WYOMING PART OF NEBRASKA TERRITORY

Martha enjoyed the comfortable temperature and sight of green foliage. She inhaled deeply the fragrance of pines and cedars warmed under the benediction of a morning sun.

She knew the pioneers were in better spirits after their struggle through Nebraska's seemingly endless, red sandy soil, the constant wind, and under a blinding hot sun.

Ruthie, skipping along beside Martha, had pulled off her bonnet in the warm Sunshine. "Courthouse Rock, Chimney Rock—who named these rocks, Martha? How come they don't have Indian names?"

"Ruthie, all these rocks are good for are snakes, scorpions, and those little leapin' lizards," Bertha said with disgust. "Me? I'm pining for the sight of trees, green grass, and plenty of cool water."

Martha glared at her sister. "Bertha, if you're feeling poorly, keep it to yourself. Ruthie and I happen to be in good spirits this morning."

Bertha wasn't able to understand. "Why is everyone so smitten with these red rocks? They're just big lumps of rock out here."

Martha didn't care to share with her sisters that Neil had carved a heart with their initials and date on the side of the spectacular Chimney Rock. He'd even wiped axle grease over the carving to preserve it, as others had done. Trappers, miners, and folks crossing the flat, foreboding country had gone their way after leaving names, dates, and messages recorded on the surface of the soft rock.

To Martha, these magnificent sculptured formations were strong sentinels from ages past, continuously tested by the winds. She was sorry for Bertha, who didn't have an eye for their beauty.

"How do we know which tribes these Indians are from?" Ruthie questioned. "They all look the same to me. I can't tell from looking at their teepees and wigwams either."

"Papa says most of them are friendly; this is all I know." Martha too had wondered how to identify the different tribes. "Ruthie, let's see if I can name some of the Indians. There are the Missouri, Oto, Sioux, and Pawnee. Oh, I didn't do very good. I know there are more."

"I guess we've left the Black Hawk behind us," Bertha said. "There's also the Blackfeet, Cheyenne, Arapaho, and Comanche, Martha. But I'm never going to forget the mean, cruel Sioux, who killed our little cow. I'm never going to forgive them."

"Oh, Martha, here comes your beau, churning up the dust." Bertha couldn't resist teasing her big sister. She shaded her eyes with her hands. "Looky, he's comin' straight to you."

Martha's temper flared at her sister. "Bertha, pull your bonnet on. It's vulgar to stare at him like you're doing, and mind your mouth. Neil and I are simply friends, that's all. Why must you keep referring to him in front of everyone like you do?"

Papa, ahead of the girls, was complaining about the oxen's limping to Stephen. "The lightnin' prob'ly started the prairie fire and left this charred grass sharp as bristles. The oxen already have sore hooves from walking through the hot sand. This stubble's irritatin' 'em worse. We don't have time for 'em ta rest properly, and rest is the only cure I know of for damaged hooves."

"Papa! Neil's back." Stephen was glad for an excuse to get away from Papa.

"Yep, looks like the boy's got himself some game," Papa agreed.

Neil and three companions rode towards the wagons. Four carcasses with hides and antlers removed were hanging over the rumps of their horses, followed by a cloud of blue flies hovering around the riders and fresh meat.

There had been little fresh meat during the Nebraska crossing; buffalo and antelope, in abundance, were feeding in areas away from where the wagon trains followed along the Platte River.

Sam Emigh pulled his wagon out from the train. "Fine, big antelope you got there, son. We best get it cut up and out of sight of our Indian friends."

The folks made little note if they were the Sioux or Pawnee Indians riding by on their fast little ponies, nor that they paused and hesitated before riding off, leaving behind a choking cloud of dust. The adults were busy sidestepping children who darted in and out, and Indians on horseback or afoot who milled around constantly begging for food.

Mr. McKinley called for a dinner stop. He was pleased the folks had been up and on the road early again this morning, and they were making good time. He'd be surprised if they didn't make around twenty miles again today, crossing this flat country.

Mr. Buland rode up beside Mr. McKinley. "I sure hope the folks get their rest day Sunday. They need it. The horses and oxen all've got sore hooves. They been going hard since we left Courthouse Rock two days ago."

"I'd like to see 'em push for a few extra miles myself," Mr. McKinley answered. "We needed to make up time, and don't forget we're not through the mountains."

"I understand, sir," Mr. Buland replied.

Mr. Reynolds, who had joined the two men, added, "Not only are the teams in poor shape, but the men need ta repair wagon wheels; rims're actually fallin' off the dry wheels, and those squealing wheels're gettin' ta me."

"This is a wagon train not a sightseeing expedition," Mr. McKinley informed the two.

The women had congregated around a water hole, waiting their turn to fill their buckets, exchanged a bit of gossip.

"Sure would be nice to wash clothes," one of them remarked.

"I'm lookin' forwards ta ma' man gettin' us some fresh meat," said another.

"I'd feel privileged to accept some fresh meat," Mother said. "I'll exchange meat for bread. I'm hoping to bake this evening."

Returning to the wagon, Mother wondered why Papa hadn't gone hunting. She and Martha were capable of handling the oxen.

Martha agreed with her mother. "We need the meat. Remember the big buffalo Papa and the others brought back from the last hunt? I'm off to fill the coffeepot."

Bertha and Ruthie returned with firewood. "I'm so glad we found some wood. I hated eating my vittles cooked over buffalo patties." Ruthie scowled at the thought.

"At least they didn't touch the food or season it," Bertha laughed. "They don't smell bad. It's just they're—just nasty is all. The worst is picking them up with my bare hands." Bertha shuddered, and the hideous grimace that crossed her face made Mother and Ruthie laugh. "And those dainty little gloves you gave me, Mother. They didn't do any good. I still had to pick them up with my hands."

"Oh dear, these beans are sour. Well—we'll just have to make do until I can soak and cook more." Mother heaved a weary sigh. She recalled the Indian incident a few days ago, when Papa failed to please the Indians with a sack of wheat flour instead of dried corn. Later that day, she'd been grateful to accept some dried corn along with chili peppers from another family. Tonight she'd make a corn dish for their supper.

Families gathered for their noonday meal, while the Indians continued begging for food in exchange for beads and moccasins. They wanted guns and black powder, but the folks insisted they had only enough for themselves. Everyone tried to keep watch on the Indians, who were quick to steal valuable livestock and little children for trade to other tribes.

It wasn't the food the Burt family complained about but the annoying mosquitoes and flies irritating them as they ate their sour beans, and biscuits with strips of buffalo jerky. Their constant diet of dried apples, apricots, and jerky was monotonous. However, a cloudless blue sky with a whisper of breeze made their dinner relaxing and enjoyable.

"My friend and me, we counted graves and I counted eighteen," Stephen boasted, his mouth full of biscuit.

"Now, Stephen—who taught you to count that high?" Bertha questioned.

"Wall, I din 'xactly; it was Pauly told me. That's how I know," Stephen replied. "An' that don't 'clude tha Hammond girl either. Pauly says she don't count; girls don't count." Stephen continued chewing and talking at the same time.

"Stephen, for goodness sakes, don't talk with your mouth full," Mother said, wiping his face with her apron. "And she doesn't count—not don't—say doesn't. She's your age, Son."

Stephen pulled away from her and quickly stuffed the rest of the biscuit in his mouth.

"I hear tell Mr. Hammon's ailin'," Papa commented, finishing his coffee. "Folks around 'em are helping the family, much as they can."

"Eil, I'm sure the poor man's dying of a broken heart. He probably blames himself for the child falling under their wagon. I know I'd feel the same. More coffee, dear?"

Before Papa could answer, Mrs. Kenyon, her face flushed, gasping for breath, hastened up. "Say, you folks didn't see ma' Pauly, did ya ?" she asked. "I've yelled ma' self blind callin' for him. No one seems to've seen him. Stephen, when did you last see him, child?"

"When we was talking 'bout grave markers, Mrs. Kenyon, and them Injun's come, so's I run back to the wagon. I din't see Pauly after that."

"What Indians you talking about, Stephen?" Papa prodded him.

"You know, the ones on horseback? They rode up real fast and then left?"

"Not the ones begging for meat?" Mother inquired.

"No—you 'member, Mother, the ones made all that dust?" Stephen was growing impatient trying to explain himself. Suddenly his eyes grew wide; he looked from Papa to Mrs. Kenyon. "You think they mighta took Pauly, Mrs. Kenyon? Papa!" Stephen cried, upsetting his plate of beans and flinging himself into Papa's arms.

"You gotta do somthin' Papa. Them Injuns got Pauly, an' he's my bestest friend." Stephen's voice quivered at first, before he opened his mouth and wailed loudly. "Them Injuns, they took Pauly away, Papa."

"Settle down, Stephen. Pauly's bound to be around here somewhere," Papa said to quiet the boy. "The children—Mr. McKinley, you've asked them all. Mrs. Kenyon?" He questioned.

Mother took Stephen from Papa. The girls froze as fear clutched their hearts like a cold hand. *Little Pauly taken by Indians?*

Mrs. Kenyon was fighting persistent doubts that surfaced to dominate her suspicions that her little boy had been kidnapped by the Indians.

"I best get back. It's not like him not to answer. He's always underfoot. I wonder why he doesn't come when I call him?" Her voice had faded to a whisper. Her head lowered; her shoulders drooped. The Burts weren't able to distinguish if it was a sob or a sigh as she turned to walk away.

"Mrs. Kenyon, wait." Papa went for his horse. "I'll take you back to your wagon."

In order to mount the horse, Mrs. Kenyon climbed up on the wagon wheel. It was her intention to let herself down gracefully and ride proper sidesaddle behind Papa. The spirited horse, however, was not expecting the sudden weight, and lurched. Mrs. Kenyon grabbed onto Papa. She wrapped her arms tightly around his waist and clung onto him in hopes of not sliding off, but she could feel him being pulled off with her.

Papa grabbed onto the horse's mane and clutched it in his struggle to pull himself up onto the saddle and control the galloping animals at the same time. Mrs. Kenyon could only hold on for dear life as she perched precariously over the back end of the racing horse, jouncing them along.

Folks were keeping their feelings to themselves. They couldn't help but question the chances of ever finding a little boy out here in the wilderness. There were savage Indians everywhere. And after they moved on, what then? How would they ever know what became of the little Kenyon boy? It could very well be one of their own.

Mr. McKinley was talking with a group of men, when he caught sight Eli Burt with Mrs. Kenyon and turned towards them.

"Mrs. Kenyon, these men have asked around, but no one seems to have seen your boy," he said, helping her down. He admired her composure. He'd just told the men, "Ruth Kenyon might be a tough old bird on the outside, but I've seen her compassion. This isn't an easy life for her or any of our womenfolk, for that matter."

One of the men admitted, "We expect our women to carry on no matter what befalls 'em. It amazes me how they've been stronger and braver than I ever expected."

Mrs. Kenyon quickly recaptured herself after the harrowing ride with Mr. Burt. It embarrassed her to think of how she must have appeared. *Whumpin' up and down on the rump of Mr. Burt's crazed horse.* But she had little time to wonder what the folks might have thought.

Mr. McKinley escorted Mrs. Kenyon to her wagon. "It pains me to tell you and your wife," he looked for Alex to Ruth Kenyon, "but we have to move out. The wagons must keep moving while there's daylight."

Alex Kenyon admired his wife at this moment. *She'll not let it show, I know her. She's got her feelings down inside. She's been through a lot in her life—her family murdered when she was just a young'un. Her Father, being a military man, raised her to be strong. She's got him to thank for this. I can't imagine what's she going through just now with the boy's disappearance.*

Before him their noonday meal lay spread out untouched. "Come on, Ruth, we need ta git movin'. Here, let me give you a hand stowin' these vittles away." His mind raced with thoughts of leaving his son out here somewhere alone. *If I ever get my hands on the dirty, heathen savages so much as lay their cursed hands on my boy, I'll kill 'em. I swear—I'll kill 'em.*

Alex wasn't able to face his eldest son, Karl; he'd already seen the look on the boy's face and it was asking too much to face his wife. Incapable of speech, he jerked off his hat, twisted it savagely before clutching it to his chest, and turned away from his family. A painful tightness gripped at his gut.

I'm no help to 'em, he thought. *I'm no damn help to my family; I'm no damn help to my little boy, my son. I don't know which way to go looking for him. This misery inside me—hurts bad—I've never in my life felt so worthless. I've no strength left.*

Alex Kenyon inhaled a quivering breath before turning back to face his wife and son. He forced himself to display a courage that wasn't in him.

Neil came upon Martha sobbing, her head leaned against a wagon wheel. He took her in his arms to console her.

"Oh, Neil, we're going to move on. Papa says there nothing we can do for the little fellow," she hiccuped through her sobs. "He must be so scared. I'm so sorry for the Kenyons. I can't bare the thought of going on and leaving him out here alone." She covered her face with her hands, unable to stop the tears.

Neil drew her hands from her face. "Martha, listen to me. You have to look at this another way. He might be scared but he's alive. They won't kill him. He's old enough to know his name. He can escape, that is, if he was stolen in the first place. There's a chance he'll get to another wagon train or someone will see he's a white child. He'll find his family. Somehow, I believe, he'll show up. You haven't given up hope, have you?" He hoped his speech of confidence on Martha's behalf would boost his own as well.

Neil glanced up to see the wagons were preparing to pull out. "The meat—it hasn't been taken care of. Martha, you've got to help me—the meat!" Grabbing her hand, he pulled her along with him. "Wait, Pa. We'll help you. I'm not giving any to these ignorant savages. I got it for us. Let 'em get their own."

"Son, best to make friends with them. They might be willing to trade meat for information about the Kenyon boy. Ask them and if they don't speak English, then give it to anyone who offers any information."

"But Pa, I'd hoped ta give meat ta the Burts and some ta the others. Besides, what if they lie just ta git some meat?"

"Neil, hand me my saw. I'm going to cut up these legs for them. We can't use all this meat, and it won't keep in this heat, either."

"Martha, take this to your Mother." Mr. Emigh handed her a portion. "Neil, give these shanks to the Indians. When you talk about the lad, describe him. How tall he is, color of hair, and how old he is."

"Mother will be pleased. Thank you, Mr. Emigh, Neil; thank you for sharing. I heard Mother say she was baking bread tonight. I know she intends some for your family."

"Fair trade, Martha. But I'd enjoy it more if your mother would make some of that delicious stew of hers in exchange." Sam Emigh glanced up to note Martha's red, swollen eyes.

He admired her. She was much too young to have endured the hardships she'd been through these last few months. He shared her misery about the little Kenyon boy, but there was nothing he could do or say that would help her.

Martha paused to witness Neil's encounter with the Indians. She watched his gestures as he described little Pauly and how they shrugged their shoulders and shook their heads negatively. It disgusted her how they grabbed the meat from Neil.

She hurried to her wagon so he wouldn't see her cry again. *I hate this miserable journey. I hate these mean Indians. Why can't our men be satisfied with what they had? How many of us will be fortunate to finish this journey?* Tears filled her eyes, spilling down her face and onto the meat.

The caravan moved out. Neil and his companions decided to take their guns and ride out in search of the Kenyon boy. They'd meet up with the wagons later. Those watching the young men ride way wished them well and Godspeed in their brave endeavor.

Martha fell into step beside Mother after Neil rode away. *Why do I fear so for him?* She wanted him to go, to bring back little Pauly. She wanted them safely home.

The afternoon dragged on for the weary folks with raw, worn nerves that were like festering wounds with their fears and anger. Drained of energy, they were irritable with one another. The unpredictability of this vast, uncivilized, untamed land was casting a gloom over them.

Mr. McKinley sensed the attitudes of the travelers. He'd hoped to cheer them by sending word they were less than fifty miles from Fort Williams and approaching Scott's Bluff.

"Named after a trapper beloved by his Indians friends, who, when they found his remains at the site, buried him on the spot, then named the place after him," said Sam Emigh.

He enjoyed interesting historical information and sharing it with anyone who'd listen. Even if they weren't interested, he educated them. Today it was Nathan and his friends.

Papa fretted about the steep hills he was coming into. It would be a struggle for the oxen with their sore hooves and persistent deep coughs. However, he had little choice but to nurse them along. He hoped they'd make it to Fort Williams. He'd have to trade them off. Even then, would the replacements be in sound health like the ones he'd started with?

Martha tried to shake off her downed spirit. She'd been grouchy with Bertha earlier, then little Pauly's being kidnapped by the Indians had upset her, as did the little Hammond girl's passing after having to have her leg removed. Now Papa was upset about the oxen. She heaved a drawn-out sigh. *I'm too flagged to care what happens next.*

"Martha, don't you sound weary?" Mother commented, taking Martha's hand in hers.

"It's such a long ways, Mother. We've passed plenty of good land and water for Papa to settle. There's always going to be Indians. What does he want? Why does he keep going anyway?"

"He shared with me that if he doesn't go all the way to Oregon, he'll never know what he missed. When I married up with him, I promised to go with him wherever he went. You'll understand when your turn comes, Martha. He needs us."

"Mother, it's selfish of him to take us away from our family, our friends, and everything we've ever known. Look around us, Mother; these people, they're dying, being kidnapped—killed."

"My darling daughter, you've heard the marriage vows. A woman leaves her family and takes up her husband's way. You obey him, Martha. We'll have a home again; a bigger one, with bedrooms and a parlor with an organ. Your Grandfather Lane was the same as Papa is when I grew up. You've heard Papa talk about how it's going to be."

"You must love Papa a lot to give up so many nice things, Mother."

"It's God's plan, Martha. I have the respect of your papa, and I have you children. I'm doing something I could never dream of doing alone. It's the divine plan for us women here on earth.

"This journey serves to test us women on our sustenance of courage, Martha. Our responsibilities are to our husbands' happiness, having our babies, and creating homes. No matter where we're asked to go. There is no greater joy for us women than this, my dear. My cup is full and I wish for yours to be soon."

"Not me, Mother. I don't care to keep house with a pesky bunch of young'uns hanging on *my* skirt," Bertha stated emphatically. "I'm going to learn how to dress proper and be a fine lady that will make other women turn pea green with envy.

"Bertha!" Mother had to laugh. "It's not nice to make others envious of us. That's pride! And besides, pride isn't ladylike."

At first resentment welled up in Martha at seeing Mrs. Jackson coming towards them. She'd invade the camaraderie Mother and her sisters were sharing. But then again, this women brought laughter and cheer.

With a change of heart, Martha lifted her arm in greeting to Mrs. Jackson.

Chapter 29

Wyoming Part of Nebraska Territory

During the evening hours a light rain started to fall and continued throughout the night, much to the dread of the pioneers. But by morning, the storm had passed, and the day burst with breathtaking beauty under the warmth of a bright sun. The roads were pleasant for traveling and, without any mishaps, the wagons pulled into Fort Williams in the late afternoon, the last week of August.

Martha knew how much the layover meant to everyone. They had been on the road for four months now, and the men needed time to repair wagons, exchange livestock, and replenish their supplies. The women would have time to wash and cook before they were to begin their climb into the rugged mountains ahead

At the evening meeting, Mr. McKinley explained the importance of a meeting he'd initiated between several large Indian tribes and the pioneers.

He'd had success with the gathering the last time he'd been through and felt it had established a peaceful existence between the pioneers crossing through Indian territory and the British, who insisted this part of the country was their rightful procession, even though the Louisiana Purchase defined it as otherwise.

He would provide the supplies for the feast, but asked the women to prepare the food and the men to be representatives with him at the council.

"Earlier," he told the folks, "I sent Mr. Reynolds ahead to the fort with a message to be sent out for a gathering of the tribes here at the fort."

The next morning, Martha heard few complaints from her brother and sisters over their breakfast that consisted of stale biscuits covered with the usual water gravy; they were excited about visiting the busy fort with all its activity.

Mother agreed to leave her domestic duties and accompany the family. She was a bit nervous, leaving her wagon with the curious Indians who were poking around the camp.

"They're so nosey, it upsets me," Martha commented. "They take anything they see, even if they don't know what it's used for or how to use it."

"Their noise bothers me too. When they get together they make such a racket I wonder— if in a hundred years from now will they still be so uncivilized?"

"Martha, are you *ferhoodled?* A hundred years from now?" Bertha commenced to giggle at the notion. "Don't fret. I don't believe you'll still be with us, dear sister."

"Yeah, Martha," Ruthie scoffed," who cares about a hundred years from now. That's a long ways off. Are Indians American citizens?"

"I don't think they are, Ruthie. I can't help but wonder how this wilderness will look in a hundred years. Will the Indians always be content with us wandering across their land?" Martha asked, looking from one sister to the other. "There's many others like us coming and they'll be looking for land to settle on, you know."

On their way walking to the fort, they passed weather-beaten, wooden shacks, some with curtains at the windows; others were bleak, bare, and stared vacantly at the passersby.

Visible behind the shacks were fair-sized, well-tended vegetable gardens with colorful flower beds that reminded Martha of the gardens they'd left behind.

On the outside of the fort, the Indians had spread out blankets to display moccasins, blankets, herbs, and jewelry, along with buffalo pemmican, jerky, and hides for barter, trade, or sale.

Around behind the fort were pens constructed of peeled pine poles stacked atop each other to hold livestock for sale or trade. A blacksmith shop was already busy doing business at the other end of the livery stable.

The Burt family entered the fort with its wide, wraparound porch. Homemade, rough-hewn, straight-back chairs with rawhide seats, set against the walls of the fort, were being occupied at the moment by gentry, lounging around, smoking and conversing with each other as they observed the comings and goings of everyone using the fort.

Martha's interest was caught in listening to the various dialects. The French and English she could identify, and she decided the majority of the

229

men were trappers, miners, and mountain men. The Indians spoke to each other in their languages or used broken English. However, she was becoming more aware of the British accent than she'd noticed before.

The fort was constructed of upright pine poles with spiked tops. Inside, the open sky looked down on an earthen square where two rusty cannons faced at attention in the center of the court, each pointed in the opposite direction towards the two wooden gates.

Sam Emigh informed the Burts that this was a trapper fort, not to be confused with the military kind. Martha and Bertha had been surprised when they first were introduced to the forts to find that most of them were supply establishments for the trappers, miners, mountain men, and Indians but were becoming a necessary stopover for pioneers moving west as well.

A high ledge ran the perimeter of the interior, with holes in the tops of the logs for firearms to be inserted during an Indian attack or when the French or English, who from time to time during a drunken skirmish, declared they'd "come to take their country back."

"Those inside closed the big wooden doors to all outside sources for a couple of days," or so said Mr. Emigh, relating his knowledge of the forts, "or until the parties have had time to cool off. Deprived of their favorite beverages, they were only too glad to apologize for their bad manners, promise to be peaceful, and resume trading again."

The girls on entering the fort viewed the assorted small business that were adjacent to each other along the inside walls.

The largest was the mercantile in combination with a popular establishment known as the "saloon." A wall separated the two, and two swinging wooden doors led into a cave-like darkness that was forbidden to proper ladies and where the clientele of the establishment couldn't be seen once they went behind the doors. The tinkling of a piano, the scrape of chairs on the plank floor, the clink of glasses, and soft voices were all that came from the depths of the interior. Nor were ladies allowed to take part in the never-ceasing card games, where it wasn't unusual for a man to lose his entire "stake or wad" in a single card game. A loud disagreement could be heard from time to time behind the doors.

"Oh, Martha, this is so exciting." Ruthie gripped her sister's hand. "I hope they have lots of pretty things. I love to look at the jewelry best of all."

Entering the compound, the girls were assaulted with the fragrance of coffee, the stench from animals furs, wood smoke, body odors, and the stale smell of tobacco from the saloon. The air hummed with the sound of activity as people moved about.

The girls beside Mother heard her exclaim as she paused to survey the interior of the market, "My goodness, this is it? This is all there is in the way of of supplies? Why, these things are mainly for men and they're going to cost dearly, I'm sure."

The Burt women were disappointed with the meager selection of a few dusty bolts of material, some hair brushes, combs, and a few boxes of face powder to represent the merchandise for feminine appeal.

The women quickly learned the limited supply of merchandise had to do with the expense of overland cartage from the cities in the east. Supplies from the neighboring British carried high tariffs.

Papa had taken Stephen and the Wilson boys with him to the stockyard to look over the oxen. When he found two fairly sound oxen, he sent the boys to bring his two worn-out beasts in hopes he could use them in the trade. While waiting, he took his time inspecting the hooves, and placed his ear to their big chests, listening for smooth breathing that indicated clean lungs.

Papa, who bartered with the proprietor of the stockyard, wasn't pleased with the outcome. Leading the new oxen away, he told the boys. "I don't have much choice. I've too little money, and these new oxen are about as worn out as the ones I traded. They've just had time to rest up is all."

The boys weren't aware that in replacing his faithful, thin, worn-out oxen, who had traveled for so long with him, Papa suffered a few moments of anguish at having to leave them behind, but he needed strong oxen for this journey and he couldn't allow sentiment to get in his way.

Mother waited for Papa to come and pay for their purchases of two hundred-pound sacks of flour, and a sack of dried corn. She selected a dozen fresh eggs, then decided on some honeycomb over fresh butter as a treat to go with biscuits and bread, and it wouldn't spoil like the butter.

She picked out some wilted carrots, beets, potatoes, and cabbage along with some dry onions. To these she added some buffalo jerky, and a sack of coffee beans. To her pile of supplies Papa added two sacks of grain and filled several cloth bags with assorted dried beans from the barrels displaying the different varieties.

The Burt girls found little they desired, and knew the price of what was offered had to be more than Papa could afford. They watched Papa pay the exorbitant total of thirty-six dollars.

Papa suggested they pick out taffy stick treats colored to match the flavors. The girls each picked a different color with the idea of exchanging nibbles between them.

Papa and Mr. Emigh loaded the supplies on the Emigh wagon. Sam said he didn't like the looks of the horses in the stockyard. "Hope I have enough money to keep buying grain for the boys. Maybe there'll be some good pastures along the way to help fill them up." He put the tailgate down so they could enjoy the warm sunshine on their legs as they dangled them over the edge of the wagon and chewed on their taffy sticks.

The hunters returned with prairie hens and rabbits. Mother was glad to trade vegetables for two hens. It pleased her to be able to offer her family a delicious stew with vegetables and dumplings in a savory gravy.

The girls helped Mother wash clothes and give the wagon what Mother referred to as a "lick and a promise" cleaning. Papa made it difficult for them to do a thorough cleaning by insisting it was more important he remove the wheels from the wagon to soak them in the river and tighten up the rims.

Martha, her sisters, and Lizzy Crawford walked out to the edge of the camp to pick berries. They were entertained by the fast, tiny chipmunks darting about in constant chatter. There were tiny, gray-bodied birds with a white stripe on their little black heads, who flitted close to the girls but were not brave enough to take the berries they offered.

They watched bandy-legged Mr. Crawford come sauntering out to the berry patch. He warned them about the rattlers he'd just heard about "apt to be hidin' in these warm rocks." This was enough to send them scurrying back to the safety of their wagons but with enough wild blueberries for a pie and cobbler.

Stephen, in the company of the little boys, had whittled willow saplings ends to sharp points, but had little success in impaling the fast-swimming, big trout as they darted away from the spears thrust at them..

As the afternoon passed, Indian families began to assemble with their teepees or wigwams, portable homes toted on travois pulled behind their horses. As they arrived they were directed around to the other side of the fort away from the wagon campers.

After supper, the pioneers broke out their fiddles, autoharps, jaws harps, harmonicas, guitars, and jugs for bass. The evening was filled with music, dancing, and singing, while over on the Indian side, the sound came from the drums with their pulsating beat and the rhythmic chant of the Indians.

Neil asked Martha to join him in a square dance, and they discovered Mother and Papa had also joined the group.

After several dances, the first dancers had to rest and another group took their place on the hard-packed earth.

Mr. Emigh switched dances with first the Burt women before he swung several of the other ladies through the fast-paced dances. Unable to catch his breath, he apologized for being winded. "I can't keep pace with this fast music and dances anymore." His admission amused the Burt women, who had seen to it he was kept busy as an eligible dance partner.

After several hours the tired musicians, women, and children excused themselves for the night, but the men decided to visit the saloon and card room before they turned in.

The girls snickered when they heard Mother caution Papa, "You're allowed to win, but to pay out good money to play cards and lose?" She considered this to be gambling, an evil act, to her way of thinking.

Papa gave her a quick hug and promised he'd win every time just for her as he hurried off to catch up with the other men.

The girls had begun a round of storytelling between them about a frog and the moon, but before they were able to get the frog, with the help from Mother Nature, to leap far enough off his cloud and onto the moon they had fallen fast asleep.

Mother sat by the last glowing embers of the fire before she climbed into the wagon and under her quilt. Before drifting off to sleep, she heard her family turning restlessly in their sleep. She wondered how much sleep any of them would get with the noisy Indians who were still in their festive mood across the way.

Chapter 30

Far into the night the Indians chanted and danced to the beat of their wooden, rawhide-covered drums beside fires that reached with long fingers of flickering flames to cast light into a dark, shadowed world.

Papa was up before dawn to assist in digging pits and erect the spits. Two trees were felled and snaked in by teams of horses. The green wood was then cut into appropriate sizes and placed in the trenches to smolder slowly under the roasting game.

David Wilson expressed his amazement at the many tribes coming from such distances to attend on such short notice. "I thought it would be more quiet with their camping so far from us. I don't know about you but they kept me awake half the night. There must be more of them than us."

The hunting party Mr. McKinley had sent out returned to find Cookie bustling between the logs burning down to hot coals, and directing the whole carcasses of deer and antelope to be skewered onto long poles then placed over the spit and manually rotated by the men.

The wood smoke and tantalizing aroma of roasting meat whetted appetites long before it was declared ready for serving at Cookie's discretion.

Breakfast over, the women prepared bean and corn dishes along with a variety of breads and the cornbread Mr. McKinley had requested.

Bertha, after braving the icy river water to wash her hair, brushed it out in the warm morning sunshine. She begged Ruthie to share her hair ribbons. "I'm going to wear my hair in a coronet like Mother's. I'll tie it up with ribbons and maybe your ribbons will help me attract a rich, handsome gentleman; I promise to buy you lots of new ribbons if it does." Both girls laughed in merriment at Bertha's suggestion.

"I'm sure the Indians will find you pretty, Bertha," Ruthie giggled, handing her sister ribbons so she could pick her choice from the colors.

At Mr. McKinley's direction the feast took place as intended. The Indian chiefs were seated on an inside circle with men representing the wagon train. Young Indian males formed an outer circle around their chiefs as Mr. McKinley had told the pioneers. "The Indians do this as protection for their chiefs should there be any trouble."

The Indian chief representing each tribe was attired in elegant, fine robes or ceremonial, soft buckskin outfits with beautiful beaded designs. Fringe hung from the sleeves, shoulders, and hems of the garments. Each chief wore an elaborate, eagle-feathered headpiece, some so long they nearly touched the ground.

Mr. McKinley and his delegates sat among the chiefs. The meeting began with an exchange of gifts. Each chief presented Mr. McKinley with a gift from his tribe. Mr. McKinley, in turn, offered sacks of dried corn and silver pieces from the great White Father, President James Knox Polk of the United States.

After the gift exchange, the men settled down to business, the important issue being to tactfully gain the Indians' permission to cross the land, known to the settlers as the Nebraska Territory of the Louisiana Purchase.

Bertha grumbled, while she stirred a kettle of corn and bean stew requested by Mr. McKinley, "I can't believe we have to do all this work and cooking and we don't get to eat together," she protested. "The Indians men don't like women, or they think we'll start trouble?"

Martha thought it strange the young Indian men are the only ones allowed to touch the food. "After all, we women handled it first in preparing and cooking it."

Mother's concern was for getting the pots over to and laid out on the buffalo hides after the business ceremony was ended.

Papa whispered to Sam Emigh, when the meeting was over, "I can't see's we asked for anything different than we've been doing all along. We're not settling, we aren't killin' any more animals than're necessary, and I don't know anyone with the time ta take over their rivers and streams and put a hoax on 'em, if that's what their afraid of."

Papa scratched his head. "I don't understand why they're opposed to makin' the river crossin' easier if our government builds the bridges. That's what my elder brother does for the government back home. And when, let me ask you, do we have time to trap for furs?" Papa concluded.

"Its politics, Eli—it's just Mr. McKinley's way of getting along with them."

At the beginning of the meeting, one of the chiefs had been elected by the Indians to oversee the feast. Their young men hurried forward to serve the council members first before the women and children were allowed to come forward and fill their bowls. The honored chief waited patiently until everyone was served before he held aloft his bowl to signify the beginning to the feast.

Many of the Indians, not part of the council, had become noisy and drunk from the whisky they'd been able to obtain from their white brothers. They rode their fast ponies though the camps, stirring up the dust and shrieking to the discomfort of the pioneers.

The pioneer women washed clothes and cleaned their wagons or visited back and forth with each other.

They discussed the coming season. It was August. The harvesting season back home had begun. Food preservation was of the utmost importance for the long winter months ahead. Without the harvest, they questioned where the winter food supply was coming from.

The young ladies entertained themselves with parlor games, sewing, or they took turns reading aloud to one another.

The pioneer children had been forbidden to visit the Indian camp. They appeared shy at first around the Indian children playing in the fields around them, but before long they were running, screaming, and laughing together underfoot of the pioneer woman.

Martha commented to her friends, "Isn't it strange there doesn't seem to be a language barrier with these youngsters? They don't have time for an interpreter. It amazes me how quickly they learn to understand each other."

"They get along too, have you noticed?" one of the other girls added.

The Jackson family, with their dark skins, were an attraction to the Indians, who openly stared at the family.

"It's disgusting how the Indians ogle the Jacksons," Lizzy Crawford spoke up.

"Do you realize we're really safe with them around?" Martha remarked. "The Indians appear to fear them, or maybe it's out of respect, but you notice they pay little attention to us."

The girls watched the Indians, who would walk past then circle around and slowly retrace their steps by the Jackson's wagon. Their heads were lowered but not enough to keep them from viewing the black-skinned people. Many of the Indian children would quietly covered their grins with one hand then timidly wave with the other to the Jackson children.

"The food smells so good," Martha groaned. "Maybe there will be some left."

"When they leaves," Ginny McGraw stated loudly, "they be takin' it with them too; 'member, Mr. McKinley done tolt us!"

Mrs. McGraw, overhearing the remark, stated, "The food is Mr. McKinley's; he bought it with moneys given to 'im by President Polk. He kin do with hit whatever he pleases."

In his serving the meat, Cookie made sure that the McKinley council members were given ample portions. He knew the vast amount would go with the Indians. It was difficult for him to understand why it was improper for the pioneer women and children to share in the feast. Some of the Indians' ways didn't make sense to him and were difficult to accept. *They sure are a strange people.*

After eating, the Indian women and children, from the various tribes, entertained the Indian and council with dances and chanting.

By late afternoon the Indians had packed up their teepees, along with their generous gifts of food and gifts from the great White Father back in Washington, and took their leave of Fort Williams and the Indian council gathering.

Mother and Martha had a pot of fresh coffee to serve Papa, Mr. Emigh, and Mr. Wilson when they returned with their opinions of the gathering.

The meeting had been a success, the men felt. The wagon train should face little resistance from their Indian friends, who had given them permission to pass peacefully through Indians' land. The men thought Mr. McKinley's plan of entertaining the Indians a wise one.

Martha pondered the men's words: *This land belonged to the Indian. They have fears of losing their hunting territories. Why couldn't they realize they would be so much better off if they'd adopt the pioneers' way of living?* On the other hand, she wondered how she'd feel giving up her way of life to learn about theirs, as they were being forced to do.

These people are strangers to us. How do we know they will keep their word? Indian nations and the chiefs of Indians might decide to go along with the white man, but what about small tribes and bands of Indians, and what if the Indian tribes found it was no longer beneficial for them to give permission to the settlers?

She wasn't about to speak her mind. It would have been out of place for her to do so and would only make Papa angry with her. Besides, they had probably already taken this into consideration at the gathering.

She looked around for Neil. She understood his interest in the respon-sibilities of the wagon train. She guessed he must be with Mr. McKinley. But then, she reasoned, the women certainly have their share of responsi-bilities, and there were some ideas she'd like to share with him.

For instance, wouldn't it make for better peace between the two peo-ples if the women were to intermingle? *We have a great deal to share, with our children and all.* She chuckled at her idea. It would never come about. Women are safer staying in their place. Hadn't Mother reminded her of this time and time again.

Slowly the families drifted to their campfires. There was supper yet to prepare, and preparations were made to be on their way in the early morning.

To the west, Martha shaded her eyes with her hands; the lofty, snow-capped mountains were outlined in a blinding, golden sun, taking its time, to slowly slid behind them.

Chapter 31

A group of independent wagons rolled into the fort, which had quieted down after a day of noisy festivities, and parked across the field from the McKinley wagon train.

Little five-year-old Paul, after the wagons were parked, happened to glance over to the wagons across the way and recognized them immediately.

"Thet's my wagon over there, Mr. Goodman. Thet's ma' pa and ma's wagon. Thet's them." Paul jumped down and grabbed onto one of Mr. Goodman's hands, pointing to the wagons.

Mr. Goodman, with the boy in hand, started across the field. Those overhearing the boy were curious and followed.

At the same time Mr. Goodman and Paul were headed for the McKinley wagons, three Mormon men were headed for the fort.

Reverend Hirum Adams abruptly stopped. "That's the Kenyon boy, isn't it?" The three turned and raced back for the Kenyon's wagon.

"Excuse me, what did you say?" Mrs. Kenyon appeared from inside her wagon, hastily wiping her hands on her apron.

Reverend Adams, uncharacteristic of his usual dignified composure, breathlessly explained, "Your boy—we just saw your boy, Mrs. Kenyon! He's coming this way with a gentleman. It's your boy, Mrs. Kenyon, I'm sure of it."

"What'd ya say?" Mr. Kenyon came from around the wagon. "What'd ya say?" Without waiting for an answer, or his wife, Alex took off running. He passed the three Mormon men and ran out through a field of corn separating the two wagon trains.

The news stunned Ruth Kenyon. From the time of his disappearance she'd had difficulty resigning herself to the fact of never again seeing her little son alive. It had been torture for her to accept his being kidnapped. It was unbelievable to hear he was alive, he was here, and he was on his way to her.

239

Though the news left her lightheaded, she climbed down from her wagon and flew in pursuit of her child. "Look out." She pushed her way through the crowd. "Pauly, ma' baby," she cried. "Pauly! Outta ma' way, please. Oh, dear God, ma' lil' Pauly's alive."

Ruth Kenyon wasn't able to cover ground fast enough; her breath came out in great sobs. She had gathered her long skirt up to her knees, and tears blinded her. "Pauly, oh—ma' baby," she sobbed loudly.

The two groups met among the rows of corn. The McKinley folks could only exclaim in their excitement at seeing little Paul, "It's unbeliev-able; it's a miracle."

Ruth Kenyon with tears flowing down her cheeks grabbed her little son; she smothered him in her ample bosom, enfolding him in her arms that had been empty far too long. "Ma' baby, oh, ma' baby," she crooned as she rocked him.

Mr. Kenyon wrapped his arms around them both, and Karl managed to slip in between the three to hug his little brother.

Women wiped at their eyes or covered their faces with aprons to weep quietly. The most stalwart of men brushed hands across their eyes at the compassionate sight of the Kenyon family.

People gathered around Papa, who was pressing Mr. Goodman for details of little Paul's capture.

"Some Indians, Shoshone, I believe, come up to us requesting food and guns. Whin I seen tha' lil' boy, I didn't know 'em, of course, but I seen he was a white youngster. I waited till I found out what them In-dians wanted fer 'em and I handed over ma' gun ta them in exchange. After they left, I asked the lad where he's from. He's a right smart litter feller. Said he was with the McKinley train, and even know'd whur his folks was headed fer.

"We're cuttin' off at South Pass, but I's sure someone'd a-know'd of 'em an' we'd be meetin' up along the way. Glad we come across each other. Musta been in the good Lord's plans." Mr. Goodman took off his hat and smoothed his hair over his head as he related his story.

"You gave up your gun, Mr. Goodman? You're a brave man," Papa exclaimed.

"Yep, I give 'em ma' gun and powder. Figured I got me the best of the deal." Mr. Goodman nervously reached up to rub the back of his neck. Being a modest man, he wasn't at ease explaining himself before so many faces.

"We gotta look out fer each other, way I figures it."

240

Those around him were moved; before them stood a humble man who was not only a gentleman but also a hero to have saved a little child.

"Mr. Goodman, I can't thank ya enough, sir! I plan ta make good, whatever ya folks're out. I heard ya bartered your gun away. I'm pleased ta replace it, Mr. Goodman."

Alex Kenyon shook Mr. Goodman's hand so vigorously, Papa was forced to intervene. "Leave the man his arm, Alex." Papa's words set off a flood of laughter. Those from both trains, in their exuberance over the miraculous turn of events, found themselves laughing much louder and longer than was intended.

"What can I say, Mr. Goodman? I'm indebted ta ya forever for saving ma' son's life. I'm indebted ta ya, sir, ma' wife and I." Alex Kenyon paused and quickly cleared his throat. Those listening caught the way his voice quivered and broke with emotion.

Mr. McKinley rode up, climbed down from his horse, and without a word squatted down and gently gathered little Paul into his arms. The little boy's response was to wrap his arms tightly around the big man's neck.

After a few moments Mr. McKinley stood up. He tousled the boy's hair affectionately. Paul, not used to the attention, turned and grabbed on to his mother's long skirt and proceeded to wrap himself in the folds.

Those observing the scene could never have said of Ruthie Kenyon that she was beautiful, but they witnessed a transfiguration that made her appear soft and feminine as she gazed down with love at her child.

The McKinley party invited the Goodman folks to share their supper, but the Goodman women insisted they contribute to the occasion.

Though not all may have accepted the saying of a blessing before the meal, every head bowed in reverence before plates were heaped high with an abundance of food.

The provisional boxes were laden with bean dishes: pots of dried stewed corn and rice; big Dutch ovens of hot biscuits and cornbread, some with meat gravy; and the desserts, though few were served, along with fresh-brewed coffee, provided a satisfying meal.

Martha and Bertha were proud of their fresh, juicy berry cobblers, with their fragrant aroma. The girls also noted how quickly they were devoured.

Martha was grateful for little Pauly's return, and for the acquaintance of new friends.

I've so many blessings. I never would have them if it wasn't for this journey, this long journey I find myself sometimes hating with a passion.

Papa, sitting with Mr. Goodman, commented, "Those were some mighty fine fish you gave us back at the La Salle settlement. You got a special way of lurin' 'em?"

Mr. Goodman had just rejected Alex Kenyon's offer of a horse. "I'm worried about havin' enough feed fer the team I got. Don't need another mouth ta feed, but I surely thank ye anyways." He did accept a gun and powder. "I'm needin' a gun fer protectin' ma' family. Much obliged ta ya, Mr. Kenyon."

Martha and Neil arrived in time to hear Mr. Goodman tell Papa, "Well—myself, I find fish bite best fer me whin the moon ain't full. Moonlight helps 'em see ta feed."

The couple left the men to join those tuned up and playing a bit of music before they retired for the night. The two moved on to where the women congregated around a campfire, swapping ideas and suggestions for making the expensive coffee and flour hold out for the remainder of the journey.

They listened to Mrs. Kenyon recount the story of her little son's return and the ordeal the boy had endured. And though she repeated the story several times, everyone was polite and listened attentively.

Martha pulled Neil way with her. "Neil, remember the day Pauley disappeared, and you were sure he was going to come back? I've come to depend on your judgment so much." She gently traced an imaginary line down the front of his shirt. "I'd just thought you'd like to know."

It wasn't that Neil didn't enjoy Martha's company, but he'd heard a hunting party was being organized. In his excitement to get back with the men, he found himself pretending interest in the things that entertained her.

"We're gonna have time to talk, you and me, around our home fire on cold winter nights." He placed a quick kiss on her upturned lips. "Right now, though, ma' darlin', I'd kind of like to find out what's being planned about a hunt tomorrow. I hate to leave you, but you can understand, can't you?"

In the moonlight with her upturned face to him, she was so beautiful he was tempted to stay with her, but there was a growing impatience within him to join the fellows.

"Go." She playfully pushed him away. "I see this isn't the proper time to discuss our future especially with hunting on your mind."

He felt a rush of exhilaration to hear her say she understood his desire. He'd heard something about plans to leave early in the morning before the train moved out for the day.

Martha, with a sigh at her submission, turned towards her wagon. On the way she glanced up at the moon, a large, round, shining orb above her.

Granny, you told me you and I would be looking up at same moon at night. I wish with all my heart and soul you were here. Then I could tell you of all that has taken place since I left you so long ago.

She wondered how long it would take for news from the home she'd left to reach her. *We've come such a long ways, Granny. This country is so big, larger than I had ever Imagined, and we've still such a long ways to go.*

Chapter 32

The morning after the Indian gathering, the sun rose bright and warm, in an expanse of endless blue sky.

Martha, sensitive to the ways of nature, knew the hours just before dawn, when the game came to water in the early morning, were the best hours to hunt.

With the men gone, she knew it was the responsibility of the women to take leave of Fort Williams, to follow along the well-traveled, deeply rutted dirt road between meadows of lush prairie grass that headed west.

She and the others had just began their day's journey when Papa and Mr. Kenyon arrived. Mother pulled the wagon to a stop and expressed her delight at seeing the good-sized deer each man had brought back. After the excitement, Martha discovered that Neil wasn't with the men. She asked Papa about him and was informed that the men had spread out to hunt and he hadn't seen Neil after that.

Lizzy Crawford and Ginny McGraw, accompanied by a group of friends, came to walk with the Burt sisters. Martha thought Ginny appeared nervous as she chattered and laughed too often and too loudly. She wondered what ailed the girl.

Suddenly a flurry of activity attracted the girls' attention. "What's going on?" Lizzy asked as they watched Mrs. Burt come from behind the wagon, dragging a protesting Mrs. Jackson behind her, and make their way down the line of wagons.

"No, Miz Burt, I cain't let you do this. I only thought, maybe, if'n 'twere alright with your Mr.—Miz Burt, no, please, ma'am. I don't mean no disrespect to no one. If'n we's could travel 'hind ya folks. Please! Miz Burt. I cain't have ya involvin' yoself with troubles 'cause o' us'n."

Mrs. Jackson fought to pull her hand free of Mary Burt, whose tight grip on her wrist was forcing her along. Realizing she was no match for the woman, Mrs. Jackson gave in to submission.

Mr. McKinley, glancing behind him, saw the two women coming his way. He pulled his horse to a stop and waited. He hated getting involved in women's troubles. They weren't fair fighters; they handled their problems by getting hysterical when they were angered.

"Mornin', ladies." He tipped his hat to them. Mary Burt, her faced flushed and her breathing labored, without returning the greeting poured out her complaint.

"Mr. McKinley, my friend here, Mrs. Jackson, has just been ordered to move out of her place in line. She's been informed," Mary gasped for breath, "that she's no right to travel there, but she's to go to the end of the train. She's her freedom papers, you know. But she and her family are still considered slaves, according to Mr. Collins.

"Mr. McKinley, if she's no right to travel with us, and Mr. Collins has taken it upon himself to decide who can travel in this train and who can't, then will we women need to leave because we're women? We've no rights either, sir."

The gathering crowd made Mr. McKinley nervous, and the wagons had come to a complete stop, which angered him more. *Where were the husbands of these women? Why did it seem Collins looked for ways to agitate him?* He drew in a slow, deep breath to gain control before he replied.

"Mrs. Burt, Mrs. Jackson, I'm your wagon master and I've not authorized Mr. Collins or anyone else to make such a judgment. I thought I made myself clear the last time this troublemaking issue came up, but let me explain it again. I do not tolerate troublemakers in my train. Does there seem to be a problem understanding this?"

He glared out at the crowd before he continued. "Ladies, if I'm to oust Mr. Collins and his party, they'll find themselves out here alone in this wilderness, with little assistance. However, should I chose to be lenient with them," he looked directly at the members of the Collins party, "they may remain but they will abide by my rules as wagon master. If they don't like my rules, let them leave of their own free will."

One of the ladies, shading her eyes with both hands, a sullen scowl on her face, challenged, "Do I hear you saying, Mr. McKinley, sir, that we's done somethin' wrong? You don't 'pear ta me ta be fair by not hearin' us out."

245

"Mrs. Baldwin, I don't tolerate bias-minded, one-sided folks. We travel peacefully together." Mr. McKinley's eyes were mere slits in his darkened face.

"Mr. McKinley, you need to understand, sir, we from the South aren't used to our darkies being outspoken." The soft drawl came from a bystander. "We've been taught they aren't really ever free; them being so backward and all, they don't know the first thing about carin' for themselves proper, sir."

"Mrs. Winfields's right, Mr. McKinley," Mrs. Baldwin hastily agreed. "They look to us ta watch o'er 'em, sir. Why, we treat 'em like our lil' children. We wouldn't think of lettin' no harm come to 'em, sir."

"Ladies, as far as I can see, the Jacksons can hold their own. They haven't depended on you for anything. I've noticed they try to get along with everyone.

"Let me tell you ladies something. I'd hoped to put a few miles behind us today, and here we sit. Can't you understand we need to keep moving? You look to me to get you to your destinations on time, but you're holding us back. We're gonna get caught in the mountains in bad weather if we don't keep moving."

"Mr. McKinley, Mr. Burt and myself are glad to have the Jacksons travel with us. We know you have far more important issues to deal with than petty quarrels. We've no problem with the Jacksons joining us."

Martha listened to her mother and wondered if she was aware of the hostility she was creating for herself among the Collins women.

Watching the interaction between the women was upsetting to Martha. *There should be peace with us women. Our strength is in each other. I'm proud of my mother, but we women must get along. I remember Granny saying when women unite, no one has any business gettin' between them and their powers.*

Mother turned her back to the women and loudly instructed, "Mrs. Jackson, please wait in your wagon until my family comes by." She walked away from the crowd, her head held high.

Mr. Reynolds, beside Mr. McKinley, turned in the opposite direction. Mr. Reynolds emitted a noisy, "Whew, ya got ta admit, this is sure better than last year's group that got themselves riled up. We lost two of 'em in that knife fight, if ya recall."

"These folks aren't tired enough. They need to get good and tired, then they won't have time to bicker among themselves. The Jacksons are in for some tough times, and they're gonna have to learn to live with 'em if they hope to survive. They're not gonna be accepted by everyone. Wait till they get to Oregon." Mr. McKinley hesitated. "Mr. Reynolds, I need you to push for as late as we can keep 'em movin' today." Mr. McKinley flicked the reins on his horse's neck and trotted on.

Mr. Reynolds watched after him. *When are these people gonna learn to stop provokin' the man. He gets ornery every time somethin' like this annoys him. They're just gonna have ta learn the hard way, I guess.*

"Yep," he said aloud, "they don't agitate the man and he don't fight back, and we don't lose any of 'em this way."

How foolish it'd appear, ridin' inta Oregon with everybody kilt or done in fer. He reasoned, *Tween sickness and Indians, we're lucky to show up with as many as we do.*

Durn it anyhows—I was lookin' forward to some fresh meat but Cookie needs time ta cook, and from the looks of things we ain't gonna get any tonight. Wish there's some way I could persuade the boss ta change his mind. Maybe, if'n I suggested steaks fer supper. He chuckled at his idea as he signaled the folks to quicken their pace.

Mrs. Jackson waited for the Burt wagon, with the intention of pulling in behind them, but Papa motioned her to get in between his and Mr. Wilson's wagon.

Papa's sympathy was with Mr. McKinley. He knew Mary and she could be like a dog worrying after a rat when she had a cause to settle. He was proud of her nevertheless.

The Burt girls, with their friends, were moving on together, when suddenly Ginny erupted with information she could no longer contain.

She had visited with Mrs. Kenyon during the time little Paul was thought to have been kidnapped. She explained how kind the lady had been to her and how she'd even been encouraged to come and keep Mrs. Kenyon company anytime.

"Yesterday," Ginny excitedly stuttered, "I was visitin' whin Mr. Wilson come by ta see how little Pauly's doin' now he's back, and I heared 'em tell Mrs. Kenyon about his lady friend.

"Whin I tolt my momma, she says it ain't nice to mention the lady's name 'cause o' what she's done. It ain't decent fer proper ladies to discuss."

Ginny proudly announced. "Mr. Wilson said they's gonna have ta git married. He says ta Mrs. Kenyon, 'Kin ya help me do things up quiet and soon's possible?' Thet's 'xactly how he said it. Cross ma' heart an' hope ta die." She quickly signed a cross over her heart as she swore the oath.

"Ma' mommy near ta died whin I tolt her what he'd said. She says it ain't proper so soon after his lil' wife's passin', and him havin' to bury his new baby an' all. She says, 'It's disgustin', him gallivantin' 'bout with some lady already.'

"Ma' mommy says it ain't proper. At least that's what ma' momma says 'bout it." Ginny's story angered Martha. *The girl's puffed up like a milkweed pod ready to burst. If I were to tell her this in front of the others, they'd laugh at her and her feelings would be hurt. But this is gossip and it's mean.*

"Mr. Wilson is a handsome man, one has to admit," Bertha replied.

"This woman—but he has three children—I wonder if she knows?" someone asked.

"Oh, she knows. I heared him say she know'd. I seen her and she's purty," Ginny boasted importantly. "'Tis jist she talks kinda funny-soundin' is all."

"You mean she drawls?" Lizzy asked. "You ever heard yourself, Ginny?" The girls snickered and giggled at her remark.

Martha slowed down to walk by herself. She wished she hadn't heard this about Mr. Wilson. He was a lonely man and his children needed a mother. She was sure he would never have said anything to Mrs. Kenyon if he'd been aware Ginny was eavesdropping. The very idea of her telling everyone. This was not only impolite but inconsiderate. Why, then, is Ginny so anxious to announce this to everyone?

She recalled the Fourth of July celebration and Mr. Wilson. The evening had been an embarrassment for her, but however amorous he'd been, he'd treated her with respect since.

She wished Neil would return. What was keeping him?

Mr. McKinley kept to his word and pushed the wagons until dusk. The exhausted travelers and teams had slowed to a crawl. The day had been long, and they would soon be making their way in the dark.

When at last they were ordered to set up camp in their usual circles, the settlers grumbled and complained about the late hour and the chores they had yet to do.

Mr. McKinley decided to meet with the men while the women prepared suppers.

Papa took Stephen and Nathan with him. Nathan scanned the horizon for his big brother, walking backwards most of the way to Mr. McKinley's campfire.

Martha, while she prepared coffee, also watched for Neil. She worried he'd be caught in the coming storm, as thunder rumbled in the dark sky and flashes of lightning crackled, and stabbed at the earth much too close for her comfort.

Papa and the boys returned sooner than was expected. Martha decided the aroma of cooking food must have whetted their appetites.

Mother had made a corn dish cooked with wild onion and chilies. She roasted fresh strips of venison, and with batter-beaten biscuits fed her hungry family in the flickering light from the campfire.

While the family ate, she set bread to rising. She looked out at the dark sky and hoped there would be time to finish baking before the storm arrived.

Martha continued to watch and worry about Neil during supper.

Stephen, Homer, and Johnny had a running dialog between them about their newest discovery. The prairie dogs.

"There's thousands of 'em," Homer exclaimed. "I liked to hear 'em whistle."

"How can they all live together in one big room under the ground?" Stephen wondered aloud.

"When we passed 'em I seen 'em all run down one hole and come up another'un. Up and down like this." Stephen mimicked them by pulling himself into a sitting position, then laying back down. He tried his best to whistle in imitation of their shrill squeals, but it was difficult for him with his two lower teeth missing.

"Maybe there are a lot of them and they just changed positions, but it seemed like they're the same dogs." Homer with his myopic sight squinted at the boys. "The first ones run down when we pass and a batch of new ones run out another hole, I betcha."

Papa and Mother, too weary to become involved, paid little attention to the boys' incessant prattle.

Bertha and Ruthie were glad when supper was finally cleared away and they could climb into their beds.

Martha continued to keep watch for Neil throughout the evening.

The pioneers, one by one, climbed into their tents and into or under wagons as a heavy rain commenced pouring down so hard it extinguished campfires. The settlers found there was little protection to be had under the canvases damaged during the severe Nebraska sandstorm.

As quickly as it came, the rain passed, leaving many with damp bedding, but the exhausted families had given into sleep despite their conditions.

Martha was disturbed by Neil's absence and slept fitfully.

Suddenly gunshots and the sound of running feet were heard in the dark.

The Burt women woke to hear Papa grumbling, "This always has ta happen just when I get ta sleep." He grabbed his rifle and ordered the women to stay in the wagon as he took off in search of men's voices he could hear in the dark night.

The women and children huddled in their wagons were overcome with terror.

Mother whispered loudly for Stephen, who had climbed out of the wagon with Papa. "Stephen, can you hear me? Get back up here in the wagon with us."

In the darkness, Mother could neither see nor hear the boy and became alarmed. "Stephen, you answer me right now," she demanded.

"I'm here, Mother," came his disgusted reply. "I'm listenin'—I can't see nothin'. I'm listenin for Papa—think I better go find him—I'll be right back."

Martha, sensing Mother's anxiety, coaxed Stephen, "Come wait with us, Stephen. I'm sure Papa expects you to protect us women from whatever's out there."

"Martha, you'll be alright," he assured her. "I wanna go see what's takin' Papa so long."

"Oh Stephen, it can't be much." Bertha, awakened so abruptly, was cranky. "I don't hear any gunshots or yelling going on. It was probably just some Indian trying to steal a horse."

To the waiting women, the drawn-out suspense in the silent, dark night did little to ease their fears, even when they heard explosive men's laughter.

On his return, Papa related, "Mr. Cobb said he remembered he forgot to take the bridle off his horse. He thought he could sneak upon his horse, but it spooked as he grabbed the reins and was draggin' him around in the dark. The night watch thought he was an Indian stealing the horses, so they fired their guns ta scare him off.

"Mr. Cobb was terrified one of us would shoot 'im," Papa laughed. "Here he was, half naked, being dragged by his own horse. He told us it was useless to yell; he wouldn'ta been heard by the fellows shootin' at him. Said he prayed, but what pained him most was not knowin' which was gonna happen ta 'im first, being stepped on by his horse or being shot, and he didn't want you ladies findin' him in his underwear.

"Mr. McKinley told Mr. Cobb he was a lucky fellow ta still be alive. The night men were only doin' their duty. And if Mr. Cobb had been shot it woulda been his own fault."

"I'm sure Mr. McKinley was pretty upset," Mother agreed. "Mr. Cobb should have alerted the guards first and not upset the entire wagon train."

Somehow, Martha didn't think Mother found the event as amusing as Papa did.

"First the gunshots to wake us up, then Stephen scares us by not answering Mother. It's night—aren't we suppose to sleep at night?" A grouchy Bertha pulled her quilt up over her head and disappeared from sight.

"Yes," Papa suggested. "Let's all crawl back into bed and finish out the night. Stephen and me's gonna catch a few winks afore daylight, aren't we, Son? I'm finding our womenfolk without their sleep aren't very pleasant, don't you, Stephen?"

Martha kept her fears for Neil buried in her heart. This country around her was so big and wild it frightened her. There was nothing anyone could do or say to ease her fears. She'd just have to hope her prayers would be answered and he'd return safely.

"Martha?" Mother whispered in the darkness. "Don't fret, dear; he's probably back and was so tired he went right to bed."

"I don't know. I didn't see him out there, Mary."

At Papa's remark, Martha had to fight tears. She hoped Mother was right. Maybe he'd come back to camp late and gone straight to bed. But the gunshots—wouldn't he have heard them?

She had to hope that he had slept through the excitement and she'd see him come tomorrow.

Chapter 33

Papa's voice awakened Martha in the predawn. "Martha, wake up. Your Mother's not feeling well; her headache's still with her. Can you make us some breakfast?"

"Yes, Martha, please." Mother's voice sounded tired and weak. "Would you take over for me? This headache just has to wear itself out."

Martha wondered if the family would ever become resigned to Mother's frequent sick headaches. She reluctantly pulled herself out from under her warm quilt, yawned, and stretched.

They had traveled from Fort Williams to Independence Rock. Martha's imagination hadn't prepared her for the magnificent beauty of the solitary, gigantic, gray granite rock, setting majestically in the field. On closer inspection, there were names inscribed over its entire surface.

Martha had remarked to her friends, "Do folks plan to return and search out their names and dates?" She wondered if travelers coming upon the big rock recognized any of the names of those who had come before them.

She reached into the sack for coffee beans to roast for morning coffee. "I wonder if this coffee is expected to last till we get to Fort Hall," she commented to Bertha, who'd been awakened to help her.

"There's only a sack and a half of flour too," Bertha confirmed.

The Emighs along with the Wilsons were gathered around the Burts' fire to share breakfast. Martha, seeing the faces, knew she would have her hands full taking care of everyone and getting out of camp on time.

"Thank you, Martha," Mr. Emigh said, taking a bowl of mush from her. "You feeling alright, Eli?" he asked, his face expressing concern. "You look a bit peaked this morning."

"Can't put my finger on it, Sam. Probably from the other night; got chilled out there huntin'." Papa accepted a bowl of mush, but set it aside. "I'll feel better once I get ta movin'."

Sam Emigh noted Eli was pale and beads of perspiration stood out on his forehead. "You sure don't look good, Eli. Let me know if I can be of help."

"You sure you're alright, Eli?" David Wilson reaffirmed Sam's observation.

"Thanks, fellows, 'preciate your concern." Papa pulled himself to his feet to see the men off, but a weakness in his legs caused him to shuffle, which he hoped the men didn't notice.

After the men left, Papa turned to Martha. "Help me, Martha." The hand he held out to her was trembling uncontrollably. "Hate to admit I'm feeling so poorly; got ma'self a raging headache, and ma' guts feel like the devil's stirrin' up ma' innards. Think you and Bertha can manage ta get us movin'? Let me rest a bit. I'll be good as new. I just need a little rest is all. Feels like I'm burning up. Ah—no, fetch me a rag. Ma' nose is startin' ta bleed again."

Martha helped Papa into bed, covering his shaking body with a quilt. Coming down from the wagon, Bertha was waiting. "Papa's ailin' isn't he, Martha?" she whispered. "We best get ready to move out. Everyone's leaving, Papa's ailing—Mother's got a headache. What are we going to do?"

Martha suggested, "If you'll drive the oxen, Bertha, I'll walk with Ruthie and the boys until you need a rest."

Mother came out to walk in the strong sunshine with Bertha. "I'm worried about your papa. He's burning up with fever. Think I'll give him a dose of laudanum. We've moved things around so many times, I'm not sure where I put it, and besides my head's too sore to think."

"I saw you put it in one of the little pockets in the canvas." Bertha was having difficulty with the oxen. It seemed that no amount of urging would move the sluggish beasts any faster. It bothered her that the other wagons were putting such a distance between them.

"Neil?" Sam Emigh called to his son. "Ride back and see if everything's alright with the Burts. I'm worried; they're so far behind."

"Probably takin' their time, Pa," Neil replied as Mr. McKinley rode up.

"Mornin', Sam." Mr. McKinley nodded his head in greeting. "You folks doin' alright here?"

"Yes, sir, we're doing fine, just fine, thank you. Is there a problem?" Sam questioned.

Mr. McKinley pulled up close to Sam's wagon. "I think we may have either a cholera or typhoid outbreak in the train. Got three wagons so far with folks all showin' the same kind of ailments. You say everyone's fine here, though? Let me know if there's a change, won't cha'?" Mr. McKinley saluted, reined his horse about, and headed for the Burts.

Neil decided to ride along with Mr. McKinley to where they found a frustrated Bertha, trying to hurry the oxen along.

"Mornin' there, Miss Burt, how's everything with the family?" Mr. McKinley inquired. Mother, inside the wagon, was busy administering laudanum to Papa and was unaware of the riders outside.

"My papa's feeling poorly this morning," Bertha told him.

Mr. McKinley, not wanting to alarm her until he was sure of the sickness, suggested, "I'm sendin' the doctor back to look in on your papa." He turned abruptly to ride away as Mother appeared at the canvas opening. "Good morning, Mr. McKinley," she called cheerfully.

"Mrs. Burt." He nodded in acknowledgement. "Miss Bertha here just told me your husband's ailing. I'm taking the liberty of sending the doctor over to look in on him." Before Mother had time to question him, he tipped his hat and rode away.

"My, what's his hurry?" Mother watched him ride off. "What did you say to him?"

"I told him Papa was ailing—Mother, would you tell Martha I'd like a break please?"

Mr. McKinley's worst fears were happening. In a matter of hours the train would be separating. However, should there be a cholera or typhoid outbreak, what then? He couldn't send the wagons on. No other train would want to travel with them. *What of the Indians? If they were to get wind of sickness in the train, they'd blame the white folks for the bringing the ailment; and if they come down sick, then we'll have more trouble on our hands.* Mr. McKinley was so engrossed in thought, he was oblivious to the wide-open Great Plains they were crossing.

It grew increasingly warm as the wagons rolled along. Out in the fields, running alongside the wagons, the youngsters were sailing buffalo chips through the air to each other. Their game captured Mr. McKinley's attention. It amused him how the dry chips sailed through the air. Some disintegrated in midair and others flew apart in the hands of the catcher.

He momentarily pulled his horse to a standstill and evaluated the skill needed to catch one intact and return it. This meant the women would be back to picking up the chips by hand for fuel.

Mr. McKinley recalled his knowledge of epidemics. They came from bad water, improper sanitation, and living conditions, but what could be done differently? These folks were forced to put up with the poor conditions; they had no choice. He'd learned from a past epidemic on his train that one out of ten would die before nightfall, if it were cholera. And he was helpless to save them.

If they were lucky enough to survive it, the sickness lasted from twelve hours to three days, but few survived.

Mr. Kenyon rode by to ask about Papa and to tell Mrs. Burt, "A decision has been made to stay the night this side of South Pass. Mr. McKinley says we're to stop for the day. We'll start out again early tomorrow mornin'."

After the doctor confirmed the deadly cholera, Mr. McKinley began the gruesome task of separating the healthy from the stricken family members.

Mother refused to leave Papa's side. Sam Emigh took over the care of Stephen. The Burt girls were not allowed back inside the wagon. Mother handed out their bedding. They'd have to bed down under the wagon tonight.

Mrs. Kenyon insisted, "Alex, tell everyone you see to drink plenty of water laced with lemon essence and sugar; it helps flush out our innards and helps fight fever."

An early dinner for most consisted of bread made into a stiff flour-and-water dough, rolled into balls, patted into flat patties, and fried on hot skillets. The flat bread for the Burt girls ranged from blackened outsides with doughy centers to a crisp cracker consistency, depending on the heat from the buffalo chips and thickness of the dough.

Many used the hoecake method of drying them before the fire over hoe blades. Martha and Bertha hadn't mastered this technique.

After dinner, Mr. Collins, with his people not afflicted, weren't taking any more chances with the sickness. They decided to depart the train along with several other pioneers who requested to travel south with them.

Using crude maps he'd brought with him, Mr. Collins planned to follow a route south. "Those left behind can catch up later, or go on to South Pass and make their way south from there," Mr. Collins informed them. "There'll be plenty of wagon trains headed south; you can hitch up with any one of 'em."

Mother firmly insisted she'd take her chances and stay with Papa. The girls were busy with not only their own chores but they also had to assume Papa's. After watering the oxen, and afraid they'd wander away, the girls took turns tethering them in different places to feed their fill of the plentiful prairie grass. Wagon wheels were greased, buckets of water were carried for family use, bedding was arranged under the wagon for the night, and a continuous fire was fed from the collected buffalo chips.

A big Dutch oven was simmering over the fire, with dried corn, unsoaked beans, and onions the girls were able to find added to the last of the venison.

The Burt youngsters, forbidden to enter the wagon, stayed within calling distance of Mother. They watched as bodies wrapped in quilts and blankets were carried and lowered into pits that had been dug for this purpose. The family members followed in quiet, stunned silence to grieve for the loss of loved ones.

Martha watched the few who attended the graveside services, but she knew that out of fear most everyone stayed to themselves. Little wooden crosses were beginning to accumulate around the open pits where the bodies were laid to rest.

"All clothing on the sick is to be burned. Scald cups and dishes of the sick before using them again," Mr. McKinley ordered.

Martha couldn't bring herself to attend a service; she couldn't bring herself to think of Papa being one of the victims. It would never happen to one as strong as her papa. Papa with his hopes and dreams. It couldn't happen to him. She'd keep herself busy, then she wouldn't have time to think or let herself become distraught. Her mother, little brother, and sisters depended on her. She'd keep her composure and be brave for them.

Neil stopped to see Martha, and asked after Mr. Burt. Martha was grateful for his company, even though they had been politely avoiding each other. She had voiced her anger at not being sought out when he returned from the hunt, and he'd informed her she had no right to question his whereabouts, at least not yet.

Mrs. Kenyon stopped by to see how the family was doing. Many others, standing at a distance, inquired as to how the family was managing.

Mother came down to eat a bite; she had little to report of changes in Papa's condition. Martha wondered how her parents could stand the heat under the big canvas. There wasn't any shade or much of a breeze anywhere on this wide-open plain, and the insects were eating them alive.

When Mother found time to climb down for a breath of fresh air, Martha questioned her about his delirium. Mother thought it might be from the laudanum. She said his fever was of concern to her; the cool compresses were warmed as soon as she applied them to his forehead and neck.

From inside the wagon Martha could hear Papa cough, choke, and retch on what Mother told her was "a milky phlegm he continues to bring up."

An exquisite blending of colors painted an evening sky as the sun slid down behind the white-peaked, purple-footed mountains. Martha paused to savor the panorama spread out before her as she kept a prayerful vigil for Papa.

Mr. Emigh came by. "Ah put the youngsters down," he said, "but not before I ended up telling them not one but two stories."

"That first story you spun, Pa," Neil remarked disgustedly, "was so wild it would've kept 'em awake all night. Scared 'em stiff, so he had ta think up another ta quiet 'em down."

Martha suggested perhaps Bertha and Ruthie, who were fighting to keep their eyes open and stifle their yawns, should lay down. "I'll take turns with you, Bertha; that way there'll be one of us awake to answer Mother's needs. I'm sure Papa's fever will break soon and he'll be alright."

Bertha was glad to accept Martha's suggestion. She and Ruthie quickly crawled under the wagon and beneath their quilts.

The twilight faded into darkness. Martha was grateful for the disembodied voices that came to her out of the night. She learned the McGraws had lost their new baby, Robert, and Ginny. She was grateful she couldn't be seen with her tears of grief. The Cobb's lost their youngest child; Mrs. Cobb, who was in the family way again, feared for her life along with those of her other youngsters.

Martha had difficulty swallowing a lump formed in her throat at the thought of so many loved ones who would be left out here in the wilderness, alone, never to be seen again.

Mr. McKinley going from wagon to wagon took a quiet census. "Tomorrow we must move on," he informed the weary folks, who were filled with despair over the deadly, uncontrollable disease. His telling them, "We no longer have a doctor; he left with the group headed for California," did little to lift spirits.

Martha could understand Mr. Wilson's avoiding them. He'd already suffered his share of death with the loss of his wife and new baby, and if his little ones became sick he'd be at a loss to know how to care for them.

Mr. Emigh and Neil were with Martha, when mother stumbled down from the wagon. They noted the droop of her shoulders and the way she staggered. Slowly they stood up as she approached.

"It's over," she whispered in a strangled voice. "He tried, he fought so bravely, but—the fever simply burned him out—Eli—my earthly companion—is gone."

Putting a hand to her forehead, Mother swayed and would have fallen had not Mr. Emigh caught her. The instant fear of everyone was that she'd taken down with the deadly sickness, from the man she'd so devotedly tended these last few hours. However, regaining her composure, she apologized for her anxiety and fears, and at the weight of the sudden grief said, "This is more than I bargained for."

To Martha, Mother's words weren't true. She felt as if she were floating aloft and suddenly she'd been dropped. She was hit with such a jolt it took her breath away, and an indescribably painful sensation surged through her, a sensation different from the Indian attack pain. Then she'd been scared. This was a different pain from a bad dream, a cruel dream.

Anguish suffocated her. She hadn't the strength to cry out or wail in protest against the element called death that had seized her papa.

Her mind flooded with fearful thoughts of what was going to happen to them. How could they possibly go on? How could they carry on without Papa? He couldn't leave them here. What kind of a God would allow this to happen to her?

Granny told her once long ago, time healed everything. Granny told Martha she'd witnessed this as a true fact. But to Martha, Granny was wrong.

She heard Mother tell Sam Emigh, "It'd be best to wait until daylight to tell Stephen and Mr. McKinley." She listened to Mother say she hoped her request for a graveside service before the wagons moved out would be appropriate. She watched Mother, how calm she appeared and in control of herself, methodically planning to move on. Martha felt as if her body was dead and she were overhearing the conversation.

Neil accompanied Martha to wake the girls. Bertha and Ruthie climbed out from their beds. Their eyes widened in shock and disbelief, looking first at Mother then Martha. Tears streamed down their faces as they comprehended what Mother was telling them. Neither was able cry out or give voice to her grief.

For many, it was a long, drawn-out night, but for the Burts there was little time to waste. They must prepare for tomorrow and the move on.

Mr. Emigh brought a torch for Mother, who insisted she prepare her husband for a decent burial, and the insides of the wagon needed to be scoured, while she was at it.

Martha stumbled through the motions of making coffee for everyone.

Mother came down from the wagon to insist, "You men, go get some sleep before the night's over. Tomorrow promises to be a busy day." She tossed an armload of Papa's clothes on the fire.

Martha along with the others watched the fire blazed up and devour the last clothing Papa had worn.

"His clothes, they're being consumed just like the fever that took his life," Mother whimpered, watching the flames grab onto his clothing. She broke down to weep.

Martha wrapped her arms tightly around her mother's heaving shoulders. Mr. Emigh and Neil appropriately excused themselves to respectfully leave the women to their grief.

Mr. Emigh informed Bertha, "We're just across the way if you need us."

Martha held on to Mother. She desperately tried to be brave for Mother, but it was impossible to hold back the tears any longer. The two women wept in each other's arms; for Papa, his hopes, and his dreams; for his life so quickly snatched away. They were forced to go on without him. They must carry out his plan for him. He was no longer here for them to depended on, rely on. Each in her heart knew a different love for him that they would never let die.

On the way to their wagon, the men heard the lamenting, mournful songs from one coyote to another. Both glanced up as a falling star moved swiftly across the night sky, then fell from sight.

"Ever notice how many stars seem to fall this time of year?" Sam Emigh paused, gazing up into the moonless night sky.

Neil knew his pa was having difficulty accepting Mr. Burt's death. His pa and Eli Burt were good friends. Neil remembered his pa had acted like this one other time, when he came to tell Neil his wife, Neil's mother, had died.

"I kinda like the Indians' way of thinkin', Pa," Neil said. "They say a fallin' star flashes by when a spirit's done for here on earth. Kind of like this idea myself. Believe, come to think of it—it was … it was Mr. Burt told me this."

"I believe you're right, Son." Sam Emigh drew in a quick, ragged breath. "I felt him; he was standing here beside us just before that star fell." Sam Emigh's voice broke.

Chapter 34

"Martha wasn't sure if it was the daylight or the multitude of song birds that had awakened her. She must have dozed off for a little while, she decided, as she selected buffalo chips to feed the fire.

She watched people crawl out from tents and wagons. Fires began to flicker, followed by a fragrant aroma of coffee. Her dark, disastrous night was over. She heard Mother scrub at the insides of the wagon. *She's doing this to stay away from her grief,* Martha thought as she glanced over at her sisters, who were wrapped in quilts, and stared silently into the fire.

Martha drew a slow, deep breath. There were chores needed to be done. It had always been Papa who woke the family. She didn't have time to fall into a pit of gloom. The oxen must be cared for.

"Bertha," she instructed her sister, "if you and Ruthie will start breakfast I'll take care of the oxen. I think the best thing for us to do is keep busy."

"Yes," Bertha mumbled, "but shouldn't we find out from Mother what she wants us to do?"

Ruthie lifted her head, which had been resting on her knees, and looked from one sister to the other. "Hadn't we best ask Mother what she wants us to do?" Any other time Ruthie's repeated remark would have been humorous, but this morning her sisters merely sighed. Exhausted from a night with little sleep, they were slow to begin the day without Papa there to instruct them.

Mr. Emigh and Mr. McKinley approached the Burts' campfire. "Mornin', ladies. I'd like a word with your mother, please," Mr. McKinley requested.

Martha returned with Mother to see Mr. Buland and Mr. Reynolds had joined them and offered their condolences.

Mother smoothed her disheveled hair and adjusted her soiled apron as she followed Martha to the fireside. "Good morning, gentlemen." She was glad to see the girls had offered the men coffee.

Martha noticed the dark shadows under Mother's eyes. Her face was pale; her shoulders drooped with weariness. She displayed little of her usual vibrancy. *Overnight my mother's changed—overnight!* The sight upset Martha.

"Mrs. Burt, we need to move on," Mr. McKinley informed her. "It's a difficult time for you, we understand, and we're here to do anything we can to assist you."

"I appreciate your concern, Mr. McKinley, gentlemen." Mother's hands were clasped tightly together under her apron. "I have one desire—request—if I may. I'd like my children to see their papa buried decently. I've prepare his body for burial."

Her voice caught; she paused and slowly drew in a breath. She was about to continue, but just then Stephen had come over from the Emigh wagon, where he'd spent the night. She saw the look of confusion cloud his face as he looked from one person to another gathered around the campfire.

Mother was suddenly drained. Stephen needed to be told of Papa's death. She must prepare for the move out. Everything demand her immediate attention. Her responsibilities became burdensome and difficult beyond imagination.

"I don't see why your wishes can't be carried out, Mrs. Burt." Mr. McKinley had liked Eli Burt; he'd been a help to him. It was just that he didn't want to convey to the others, who had lost family members, that they could request individual burials. There wasn't time. "We have to make up the time lost as it is. Mrs. Burt has the benefit of an early morning in her favor."

"Thank you, gentlemen," Mother voiced in a whisper. "It pleases me—" she paused, "... for us—that you'd allow us the time. Also, Mr. McKinley, I hope you still consider us a part of your train, sir. I realize, when we started, my husband—our plans were to...." Mother rushed on but her voice faltered. "I fully intend to see my children carry out their papa's wishes. I'd like to make the rest of the journey to the best of my ability, and with the youngsters' help, of course. I'll try to make as little demand on you as possible, Mr. McKinley, if you will see fit for us to go on with you."

Mr. McKinley silently pondered his situation. *They all want to go on, these lonely, frail women. I need strong men to make this journey. It's difficult enough for a man, but a lone women? On the other hand, what choice do I have? I don't trust the Indians. If I were to leave 'em alone out here, they'd never make the journey back to their homes alive. Sometimes, like now, I wonder why I didn't stay with the militia, fightin' the Mexicans down south. Cant be more difficult than what I'm faced with.*

The men too questioned if this small, brave woman, who pleaded to be allowed to finish the long journey, could make it, with rugged mountains to cross, her oxen worn out, the rough river crossings difficult beyond imagination, the shortage of supplies, and the possibility of her wagons breaking down, not to mention illness, the Indians, and the questionable weather conditions.

None voiced his opinion aloud but stood in silent admiration of Mrs. Burt. It would mean more protection, they reasoned, for her family if she continued on.

"We'll do our best for you, Mrs. Burt." Mr. McKinley turned to the men. "Let's plan to pull out right after the service." To Mother he said, "You and your family are welcome to travel with the train, Mrs. Burt. We're here to assist you when problems arise."

Martha watched him tip his hat to Mother, nod to her sisters and her, before he turned away with the others.

"Stephen." Mother held out her arms to the little boy. "Stephen...." She groped for words. "God called Papa up to heaven last night. He was terribly sick and I couldn't make him better. My darling, we have to move on and leave Papa's body here to rest. His soul isn't in his body; it's gone up to live in heaven. Do you understand?"

Mother cleared her throat, but the lump in it wouldn't go away. *Dear Lord, I'm not prepared for this, Eli; how ever will I have the courage to endure this alone? Oh Lord, I'm afraid—so afraid. Please guide me.*

Stephen took her face between his little hands. "Mother—Mother?" He demanded her attention.

"Son, we have to get ready to go on." Her voice broke. "We must make Papa's dream come true. You have to be the man of our family now."

Stephen looked from one sister to another, his big, blue eyes wide in a Solemn, small face. "Did Papa know he was gonnna die and leave us?" He confronted Mother.

A scowl darkened his face. "How come you didn't come to get me so I could say good-bye? 'Sides I don't wanna be a big man yet; that was Papa's job."

Tears blurred Martha's vision. "Stephen, none of us said good-bye to Papa. He didn't know—we didn't know he was going to leave us. He didn't want to go this way either. We'll say good-bye to him this morning before we leave."

"Can I see him? I wanna see ma' papa," Stephen wailed loudly.

"Stephen, we'll say good-bye to Papa," Mother told him. "We'll say it together. None of you children were allowed with him but me, remember? He was sick and I didn't want you to get his sickness."

"I don't care. I wanna be with ma' papa." Stephen's face crumpled.

Mother enfolded the boy in her arms and began to sob. Unable to hold back any longer, tears streamed down Mother's face and those of the girls. Martha wondered if the tears would ever end.

Stephen suddenly stopped crying and wrapped his arms around Mother's neck. "Mother, don't cry no more. I'm gonna take real good care of ya."

"Mother," Bertha wiped tears from her face with her fingertips, "we're not ready. Look at us. The men will be coming back and we'll not be ready."

Ruthie brushed tears from her wet eyes. "Why does Bertha always have to be so cranky with us?"

"Ruthie, you have neither washed your face nor combed your hair. You look awful, a frightful mess," Bertha exasperatedly explained.

Martha was thankful for Bertha just now. She might be vain and hard to get along with at times, but when the family needed brought back to their senses, she did it best.

"Stephen and I will get out some dried apricots and apples and Pilot crackers for breakfast," Mother said. "Martha, you care for the oxen. Bertha, you get your and Ruthie's hair combed." To her family, Mother sounded off like a major general ordering them around, but it gave pause to their burdened hearts.

With as much grace and dignity as time afforded, the Burt family laid Papa to rest.

Sam Emigh, for all his statistics and knowledge, wasn't aware this day would be noted along with the thousands of deaths caused by disease during the twenty-year period of migration out West by wagon trains.

Sam Emigh struggled in an unsteady voice to say the right words over the quilt-bound body of his good friend Eli Burt who'd been lowered into the grave.

Neil supported Mrs. Burt on one arm, and the other he gave Martha. Ruthie, her bonnet pulled down over her tear-stained face, clung to Mother. Stephen stood over the open grave as far as possible to view Papa's body, while Bertha hung onto his shirt tail for fear he'd fall.

263

Lizzy Crawford stepped forward and handed Mrs. Burt a hastily picked bouquet of wildflowers after Mr. Emigh finished his eulogy. Before the men picked up shovels to cover Papa with earth, Mother handed each child a flower to leave with him.

One after another, the Burt children stepped forward and dropped their flower down to be with their father. From behind them came the melody of a well-loved hymn. Voices joined in song with Ruth Kenyon and finished it together.

Mr. Crawford came forward to mark Mr. Burt's grave with the symbolic little wooden cross; on it he'd burned the epitaph for those later coming upon it to read.

Eil Stephen Burt
1810-1846
Beloved husband of Mary Lane
and his children
Martha, Bertha, Ruth Ann, Stephen
keepers of his dream

After the ceremony, Mother turned to face those gathered with her. She thanked them for their support of her and the children as their beloved Father was laid to rest. She quickly, before her stamina failed, announced, "Mr. McKinley wants us to move out as soon as possible. We've a long day ahead of us."

At Mr. Emigh's suggestion the Burts pulled in front of him and behind the Jacksons.

Martha guided the oxen, and with her family watched until Papa's grave with the little cross could no longer be seen.

Papa, you're a long ways from your homeland in Illinois and far from the land of your dreams, Martha thought as she forced herself to swallow around the perpetual lump lodged in her throat.

Martha came to the realization that her family wasn't the only grief-stricken family. Mr. McGraw's loud voice was still. The family grieved over the loss of Ginny and baby Robert, both gone. She hadn't known the new baby well, but she would miss Ginny. Ginny had spirit. How could this have happened to one so full of life?

Martha overheard Mrs. Kenyon tell Mother, "Me and Isabelle Purdy had to practically hog-tie that pitiful Mrs. Cobb when they buried her little boys."

Martha watched wagons throughout the day drop out of line at various times, and she knew it was to leave behind their dead. She was heartsick. There would be so few who made it to the Oregon Territory. They would have been better off never to have left their homes.

What makes them come out here? she wondered. *What brings them out here when they know the chances they must take with their lives?*

Some time later, Mr. Buland rode back to report the heat up to 100 degrees. The mosquitoes were so bad the children grew cranky and became fevered from the many bites. The teams were irritable, nervous, and difficult to handle with the persistent insects that plagued them.

Martha wondered how the others could suffer through the nauseous stench that lingered in the heat of the day, with fly blown carcasses of horses and oxen lying beside the trail where they had fallen.

Mr. McKinley had the choice of two routes on the other side of the Great Divide. So many members of his train had departed the night before for California, he decided to take the northern route to the Green River. It would mean two and a half days less travel, a distance of forty miles to the Rocky Mountain, South Pass cutoff. There the wagons would split for the southern routes, the Mormon settlement, and the Pacific Northwest.

With lack of sleep, in a heat that taxed their strength, and with excruciating loneliness for Papa, the Burts stumbled along.

Martha, as she methodically guided the oxen, decided, *There has never been a day in my life as difficult as today—never. And I hope and pray there will never be another.*

Chapter 35

Martha awakened to daylight. With her sisters still asleep beside her, she let herself reminisce about the journey since Papa's death.

The day after leaving Independence Rock, Mr. McKinley had informed the wagon train, "We'll travel north to the Green River, then cut back to follow the Sweet Water River. It passes through a natural chasm too deep and narrow for us to get the wagons across, so we'll plan to cross over at South Pass."

The pioneers were surprised, after following the Sweet Water River and making their way past Devil's Gate known as the Gap, to a wide-open valley that stretched out before them for twenty or more miles. They had been prepared to begin the climb through the foothills into the Rocky Mountains.

A campsite had been selected for the night, and suppers were finished before folks assembled for the routine meeting with Mr. McKinley.

It amused Martha when Mr. Emigh said, "This is the only pass in the entire Rocky Mountain chain and it just happens to be in our way."

"You're correct, Mr. Emigh," Mr. McKinley agreed. "Tomorrow morning, we part company. Those for California and the Mormon settlements head south from here. Those of us going to the Oregon settlement will continue west."

Mr. Emigh interrupted, "Are we to understand that we're officially in Oregon Territory?"

"Here at South Pass is where we cross over what's called the Continental Divide, isn't it?" someone else asked.

"Yes, you're both right," Mr. McKinley said. "You youngsters might take note: any rivers you see from now on will be flowing west towards the Pacific Ocean."

There were few gathered around Mr. McKinley, Martha noticed. This could only mean there were still many suffering the dreaded cholera and who chose to remain to themselves, or had Mr. McKinley requested they not mingle with the rest of the folks? *How long is this plague going to endure? How many more lives will it claim?*

Last night, she remembered how excited and enthusiastic everyone was about the move out this morning.

Martha heard Mother outside. *When does she sleep?* She'd awakened during the night to hear Mother's muffled sobs in the darkness. Mother didn't know she'd heard her. Martha felt inadequate; she didn't know how best to comfort her.

It's like Papa's with us every day and our heartache is agony. We miss him so. Martha decided to wake her sister and get up. Her thoughts of Papa were too painful to lay here and think about him.

Martha had come to dislike mush ever since Mother threw the grinder away to lighten the wagon load. Whole wheat kernels weren't tasty like the cracked wheat. She wished there was enough flour for biscuits this morning. It would be nice to have fresh milk too, but few cows were still giving milk.

Mr. Emigh was at the fireside, awaiting breakfast, when Martha and her sisters came down from the wagon. They heard him tell Mother, "He'd heard oxen didn't take to the mountains. Climbing over rocks wears down their hooves. It's one reason I didn't get oxen. They're not as surefooted as my mules."

"Mules?" Neil arrived at the fireside the same time as the girls, and heard his father. "We ain't got mules, Pa. Whata ya talkin' about?" He took the bowl of mush Mrs. Burt handed him, thanked her, and winked at Martha.

"I'm joshin'," Mr. Emigh laughed. "These horses aren't adequate like the big boys were. Wish I could have afforded to keep feeding the big fellows."

Mr. Emigh, the first to finish breakfast, stood up to shake the coffee dregs from his cup. "Look at the height of those mountain! Can't help but wonder how we're ever going to make it over the peaks."

He handed the empty cup to Martha. "Well, guess we best get moving, boys. Much obliged for the breakfast, Mrs. Burt." He nodded to Mother as he and his boys departed.

Martha sensed Mother was unusually quiet this morning, and she appeared to move more slowly. Martha felt compelled to question her.

"Just a headache, dear." Mother heaved a weary sigh. "If I rest a bit, I'll feel better. I'll wait until we pull out, though, before I lay down."

Martha recalled Papa saying the exact words his last morning. She refused to let her fear build. Mother was known for her headaches, wasn't she?

Martha walked alongside the oxen. Her thoughts turned to what she'd heard said about the young fur trapper responsible for finding this pass people now referred to as South Pass, a gateway through the Rocky Mountains built with a fort as a way station for those traveling the Oregon Trail.

"Robert Stuart built the crude fort," Mr. Emigh had said, "according to Mr. McKinley, after he discovered the pass."

The wagons had been traveling for some time in the warm morning sun. Big, fluffy clouds moved leisurely across the sky, shading the earth here and there as they passed over.

The ground suddenly vibrated, which was followed by the sound of thunder. The pioneers quickly observed a herd of buffalo filling the entire valley to the north of them, and they were heading straight for the wagons.

The earth's rumbling grew to a deafening roar, reverberating off the mountains and into the valley below as the massive bodies propelled themselves towards the pioneers.

Mr. McKinley instinctively knew what was happening and thought he had enough time to warn the spread-out, long line of wagons to fortify themselves as best they could against the advancing bison.

He cupped his hands and yelled, "Stampede!" but doubted he was heard above the noise.

The livestock's keen senses warned them of the danger. Frightened horses tried to break free. Oxen threw back their heads and bawled in protest. The teams became agitated in their confines as the wild herd of a thousand or more buffalo in no time were upon them.

Earlier Mr. McKinley had sent his assistants on ahead to do some business, leaving him alone to manage the wagon train.

It became impossible for those handling the teams to control them. Those who could struggled to turn their wagons in the same direction as the oncoming buffalo.

The maneuver might mean less damage to the teams; it would split the path of the buffalos and help keep the wagon from being overturned.

Mr. McKinley realized he wouldn't be able to ride down the length of the train. He had to find shelter, and quickly. He raced for Cookie's wagon just in time keep from being trampled.

In moments, it seemed to the settlers, the forceful, big bodies plunged through the line of wagons, hitting them on all sides. The bison wavered neither left nor right. The sound of screaming horses and bawling oxen was muted in the surge of pounding hooves.

Grunts and deep breathing billowed from the buffalo as the frenzied beasts pushed side by side, one after another, never slowing their pace as they charged ahead.

Women and children screamed, and cried in terror, as they felt their wagons being lifted and moved along in the relentless wave and thrusts of bodies with big hairy heads and mean, beady little black eyes that glared at them. The great bison shoved everything out of their path as they plummeted though the wagons, leaving everything in the valley demolished behind them.

Martha realized she had little time to respond. Once in the wagon seat, she grabbed for the reins attached to the oxbows and pulled them up short to hold the oxbows tight and maneuvered the oxen's heads in the same direction as the oncoming herd. She held the leather reins so taut they cut into her hands and her arms ached from the exertion. She hadn't time to be aware of the grave danger she or the oxen were in.

Mother, Bertha, and Ruthie watched Mr. Stern, ahead of them, pull his team to a stop and jump down to call his children. He misjudged the speed at which the buffalo were traveling. It stunned the Burt women to watch his wagon, as if it were weightless, picked up and overturned, pinning him and his wife beneath it.

The panicked horses dragged the overturned wagon behind them into the midst of the buffalos until the wagon tongue plowed itself into the earth and stopped them. At the sudden stop, the two head horses stumbled and, unable to pull themselves up, were forced under the weight of the bison, who passed over them with razor-sharp hooves.

Mrs. Jackson, with all her strength, managed to hold her team, but felt the big wheels wrenched from her wagon as the buffalo pressed against its sides. She stood up, struggling to keep her balance and hold on to her mules. Her sick husband was of little use to her, and there wasn't time to comfort her children. Her mules continued to run with the bison, her wagon bed wedged tightly between the bodies of the big animals.

As the last of the buffalo raced past, Mrs. Jackson found herself on the seat of her wagon; the wagon bed with the hoops still attached lay flat on the ground. Gasping for breath, and unable to stop her uncontrollable trembling, she covered her head with both arms, opened her mouth, and rendered an ear-splitting wail.

As the dust settled, damaged wagons could be seen scattered about. Women sobbed and cried. Moans came from the injured. The teams that were still alive stood exhausted in their webs of tangled harnesses.

The big ruts gouged out by buffalo hooves and a stillness in the air. that followed were all that attested to the buffalo stampede having passed through.

Families slowly drifted out of their wagons. Those with wrecked wagons walked around quietly to survey the damage. Families frantically searched for missing family members. Some of the children had managed to climb into the nearest wagons. Others found refuge and protection by burrowing under bedding inside their wagons.

Mr. McKinley began the painful task of accounting for everyone. One by one the families, wagons, teams, and damage had to be evaluated.

Folks at the front of the wagon train line had been frightened, but they hadn't been in the direct path of the stampede. Mr. McKinley, with the men who were able to assist him, estimated the middle wagons in the train had been hit the hardest, leaving fifteen to twenty badly damaged wagons.

There were five deaths for which graves needed to be dug as quickly as possible. The Sterns' mangled bodies were discovered half a mile away off the road.

Their deaths orphaned three frightened little children. Two small children remained unaccounted for. They had been last seen out in a far field; in all likelihood they never made it to a wagon in time.

Mr. Dixon's head was retrieved. It was decided he had been knocked from his horse into the path of the buffalo.

Julia Dixon, his wife with six young children, on seeing her husband's head, started a scene that impacted the emotion of every woman in the train. Until now, Julia had control of herself, as was expected; but when the realization set in of how alone she was, she wasn't able to deal rationally with her emotions or the circumstances surrounding her.

"I wanna go home, I wanna go back, I've lost everything," she moaned, her pain so acute she was doubled over in anguish. "Oh, Mr. Dixon, how could you leave me out here with nothing?" she wailed. She stood up and with clenched fist raised towards the sky, she cried, "Oh God, where are you? God help me. I can't bare this alone. I can't do this." Her eldest boy, a strapping young man, reached to gently take her in his arms.

"I just wanna go back to my people," she sobbed against his chest. "I just wanna go home." Her son could do little to comfort her.

After watching Julie Dixon's demonstration, sympathy for her mounted until it had ignited the women into a mutinous mob. The female populists of the wagon train rebelled against their husbands.

They grabbed for whatever was at hand, or with clenched fists they raised their arms in unison. "We wanna go back," became their chant.

"We've had enough, let's go back, we've had enough, let's go back."

They hurled accusations against their deplorable, intolerable conditions, the loss of lives, the lack of provisions, the wrecked wagons. They refused to move one step further.

Their conduct left the men speechless, seeing this undignified, unladylike behavior from their mothers, wives, and daughters. Listening to them, the men were unsure what these crazed women might think to do next.

One man dared step forward, with the intent to bring shame and to humble the women in his family. "Get yourselves back to the wagon," he ordered them. "My pa woulda beat ma' ma within an inch of her life for pullin' a stunt like this."

His wife and daughters stood their ground. "You dare lift a hand ta me and your daughters?" his wife snarled. "I've given all Ah'm a-gonna give ta this little adventure of yours. Your daughters and I're thinkin' o' leavin' whilst we're still alive."

Another woman protested loudly, "I refuse to watch my children be slaughtered for a fool man's benefit. Ya'll go on by yourself, ya men."

Alex Kenyon watched unbelieving at his Ruth, before him a rifle in her hand, protested, "We've lost nearly everything we own. What's left, Mr. Kenyon? I nearly lost ma' boy. I'm not for goin' on either. You best settle down right here."

Alex, in his heart, knew her demands were valid, but right now unrealistic. In her present state of mind he'd never be able to argue convincingly; he'd have to leave that for someone else to do.

The men formed a group on one side of the road, with the women on the opposite side. The women continued to hurl accusations at the bewildered men.

"Husband, thy promises mean little to me anymore. What do I have to look forward to? Day by day, I'm losing everything I hold dear. Thou treat me no better than a hired hand," Mrs. Crawford yelled across the road, a heavy skillet raised up in both hands as she threatened Mr. Crawford.

"Ah, Elsa, please don't get mean on me now," Mr. Crawford pleaded. "Let me explain. This move out West is for you and our children."

Mr. McKinley had never experienced such behavior as these ladies were demonstrating.

He had to take control of the situation before these women lost all their common sense and killed somebody. *I'm going to open my mouth and you, oh Lord, best guide my words, or there's apt to be an ugly massacre right before Your eyes.* His sympathy lay with these angry women, but he had to get control of them somehow.

Mr. McKinley, unsure of what to expect, bravely walked into the middle of the road and held his hands up for attention. "Quiet—quiet!" his shout sounded with authority. Abruptly the women stopped their clamor.

"Ladies, put down your weapons. Please, don't shoot your men in front of your young'uns."

Clubs, guns, and pans were slowly lowered and dropped.

Mr. McKinley waited for everyone's attention, but just then the preacher, who happened along, interrupted, "Allow me to pray with these poor ladies, and for they're shameful, sinful ways, sir."

Mr. McKinley was unable to silence the preacher before he could start his sermon. "You wimmin, you're an abomination in the eyes of your husbands and your innocent little children. You have overstepped your bounds. You've forgotten your place. You need to repent your sinful ways. Let me pray with you for forgiveness, my sisters, and ask for salvation for your souls, in the name of our Lord, Jesus Christ."

Mr. McKinley groaned. He reached for the preacher's shoulder and applied a bit of pressure as he firmly and politely said through clenched teeth, "We don't have time for this preacher, sir. If you'll kindly step aside and allow me—thank you for your concern for these ladies' souls. You'll find them grateful, I'm sure. Prob'ly even give ya some hot supper tonight."

The scrawny preacher stumbled back, tripping over his too-long legs. His head bobbed up and down on his skinny, long neck as he rubbed his shoulder and tried recapture the attention of the crowd. He wasn't through saving souls. He'd liked to make a few more helpful comments. However, Mr. McKinley had gained back the attention of the crowd, and the elbows of the men thrust the preacher behind them.

"Ladies, this catastrophe wasn't planned by your husbands. The air, sun, clouds, a fly—who knows how it started. We can't make this journey without working together. We're over halfway to the goal you've been sacrificing for, working for, and dreaming of." He hesitated, allowing both sides to digest his words.

272

"Let's not waste time with talk about turning back. Those of you who find yourselves alone, you must know we'll take care of your and your children.

"My plan right now is to get a group of men to help repair the wagons. Another group will bring in some meat from bison crippled during the stampede. Don't forget to offer the Indians meat. Remember, there's ta be no slaughter but to the crippled animals.

"We need our dead buried. We'll conduct proper graveside services as soon as the graves're dug and the ladies have prepared the bodies for burial.

"Ladies? Care for these frightened youngsters. I need you to nurse the injured and fix supper for us."

"Mr. McKinley, what about those Indians riding back and forth out there? Bet they set those buffalo off. Think they'll be a problem if we take the meat?"

"We're mindin' our own business and we're allowed meat for our use, Mr. Baldwin. We have nothing to fear," Mr. McKinley assured him.

After dismissing the folks to get about their chores Mr. McKinley overheard a woman pass by him say, "I know'd them Injuns spooked them buffalo ta stampede 'n' try ta kill us. Mr. McKinley hain't pullin' no wool over my eyes."

On the way to his horse, Mr. McKinley couldn't help but hear excerpts of conversations. "Anythin' kin spook a bison, they got no brains." "When we take sides like we's doin,' we's only exposin' our weakness to the Injuns." "Ta think I growed up thinkin' women was weak."

Mr. McKinley mounted up to go in search of Mrs. Jackson, relieved that tranquility had been restored.

"Mrs. Jackson, you're gonna need some assistance here," he stated, after noting the condition of her wagon. "I'll see it gets fixed right away—would you be so kind as ta indulge me? We need food prepared. Will you accommodate us with your cookin'? I know Mrs. Kenyon'll help you. Say, you know about some kind of herbs growin' around here that'll make us feel good? Like the Indians eat ta make 'em happy, or do they smoke 'em? Throw a few handful in the stew if ya come across any, will ya? Maybe help cheer these folks up a bit, ya think?" He winked at her.

When he heard her hearty laugh, he knew things were going to be alright. He had to admit he felt in better spirits himself as he rode away.

Mr. McKinley was listening to Mr. Kenyon's advice regarding the repair of the Jackson wagon, just as Mr. Buland and Mr. Reynolds appeared.

"Whooey, 'pears like a bad wind storm done hit," Mr. Reynolds said. "Don't believe I've ever seen so many ruined wagons at one time."

"Somethin' spooked the teams?" Mr. Buland asked.

With a look of disgust, Mr. McKinley responded, "Just a herd of senseless buffalo decided to move today and we happened ta be in their way."

"Looks like we got our work cut out for us, Mr. Buland. Say, hold up here—just a minute fellers. 'Member ma' not gettin' ma' steak supper the other night?" Mr. Reynolds reminded them.

"Yeah?"

"Well—I'm havin' me a steak tonight if I gotta fix it ma'self. Let's go get ourselves some buffalo meat so's Cookie can take care o' this steak ma' belly's been itching for. After a stampede, there's always a dim-witted critter 'er two manages ta get itself crippled up."

Mr. McGraw's white-hot fire forged iron parts needed to repair as many wagons as possible. His anvil rang out into the late afternoon and night. He put to use every board, scrap of leather, and piece of iron on hand.

Martha watched the Mormons roll up their sleeves and create two wheel carts. "This model of conveyance," she heard them tell Mr. McKinley, "is called a 'wind cart.' It's been said to travel faster in the wind; however, they are lighter and aren't weighed down with the heavy loads like the four-wheeled wagons are. This small version can be pulled with one horse. We can make covers for the carts from torn canvas covers."

Martha could see Mr. McKinley was impressed, but heard him question if they were sturdy enough to make it through the mountains.

Mrs. Jackson and Mrs. Kenyon saw to it the women contributed vegetables and legumes to the big pots of stew with fresh buffalo meat. Pans of cornbread and biscuits baked alongside the pots of stew, and the fragrance of coffee filled the air, stirring up appetites.

The injured were cared for and the children comforted before the women, working side by side, helped each other straighten the insides of the wagons for the night.

A burial service was conducted before supper by the preacher, Mr. Smith. Comfort and support was administered to the bereaved as they watched loved ones laid to rest and the ever-present little wooden crosses set in place.

A quiet crowd slowly returned to supper. The preacher quietly departed the train. He decided he'd be about God's business elsewhere. He hoped the Indians would be more receptive.

"My mother certainly surprised me," Lizzy Crawford said on her way back to camp with the other girls. "I'm proud of her, and she is right when she says we women have given up so much to make this journey."

"Yes, one has to admire and respect them," another young woman agreed.

"But, did you notice?" someone else commented. "They did what they tell us is not ladylike to do?" Her comment was followed with laughter.

Bertha commented, "My heart goes out to the ones who will finish this journey alone, like my mother; she is a brave one."

"We can't know their fears and how difficult and lonely it will be for them. But we can help if we work together. We have strength and the courage it takes."

The silent group agreed with Martha. They'd just witnessed their mothers demonstrate this.

"After their little tantrum today," Martha continued, "our mothers joined together, did you notice? They put aside their fears, anxieties, and look what they were able to accomplish. I think it's important we women understand, whatever adversity we face we can overcome it and adapt; we have what it takes.

"Give us a set of wheels and something to pull them and we'll move on and finish this journey."

Martha's speech came as a surprise to Bertha. Her sister's words sounded so grown-up all of a sudden.

I'm beginning to sound like Granny, Martha thought. *If you'd been here, Granny, I'd like to think you'd have approved of us women today.*

Chapter 36

Martha was humbled at the sight of the turbulent river pouring over and cascading down in spectacular falls. Mr. Emigh, standing beside her, shared her sensation. "They must be a quarter of a mile high," he wistfully commented.

The night before, she and Neil, beside the campfire, had gazed into a moonlit sky and at rocks straight up and down with overhangs. "I'd guess them ta be a height of two hundred feet or more above us," Neil surmised. "I never knew a world like this existed."

The valley was indescribably beautiful and peaceful, with sweet grass for the animals and cold, clear water from Deer Creek nearby. Martha was grateful for the serenity after the buffalo stampede

Mr. Emigh had been most informative the night before about Fort Bridger, their next destination. The forts were a big disappointment to Martha; they weren't military forts but trappers' way stations.

She found herself enjoying all there was to learn about this new country she was passing through. The scenery changed from day to day. Friendly Indian women and children came out from their camps and waved to them. She didn't understand the mountain men and trappers with their prejudices against the Indians; yet they found it necessary to take Indian women to live with them, and always the irritating mosquitoes, no matter where they went.

Martha walked beside the oxen. They were leaving the valley and slowly beginning their ascent into the steep mountains ahead. It always surprised her that after they'd climbed a while they'd come into another valley or large meadow. Some were covered in dry prairie grass and others had rock floors covered with little forage. When there was little for the livestock to eat, the folks had to dig into their coveted grain that was fast dwindling.

Mr. McKinley called for a cold dinner break in the area ahead called the "Little Sandy." "Has plenty of grass and water," he said.

Stephen came to announce, "Mr. Reynolds told me I'm supposed to call these Indians 'round us 'diggers.'"

"Mr. Reynolds is going to get you scalped if you call Indians bad names, Stephen," Bertha cautioned him.

When Mr. McKinley came riding back to look in on the Burts, Stephen confronted him about calling the Indians "diggers."

"It's a nickname for the crop-growing Indians coming from the California Territory to the Pacific Northwest. It was given to 'em by the trappers of long ago."

The wagons had come down off a plateau and were headed into another valley. Mother's back and shoulders ached, the girls were tired, and they hadn't had appetites at dinner. They were hours away from setting up camp for the night.

Ruthie came running back to the wagon. "Mother—look! Look out there. Doesn't that look like smoke?"

She had no more called attention to the dark, billowing smoke rolling swiftly towards them than frantic voices were heard shouting, "Prairie fire!"

The Burt women, in terror, watched the black cloud moving in their direction.

Mr. McKinley, hands on his hips, felt he'd been dealt more than his fair share of problems lately, though there hadn't been any new cholera cases in the past few days and the troublemakers were headed south and out of his hair. There also hadn't been any skirmishes with the Indians and the women had settled down. *Just when I thought things might roll along smoothly*—he sucked in a noisy breath—*along comes a prairie fire.*

"You know what has to be done," he shouted to Mr. Reynolds and Mr. Buland. "Get the wagons into a circle and get folks diggin' trenches. It's our only salvations." His words were whipped away in a hot wind.

"Mother, I'm scared." Ruthie tugged at her mother's skirt. Martha and Bertha were mesmerized by the fire sweeping towards them.

Stephen, Homer, and Johnny arrived breathless. "Mother, the fire— it's gonna get us. I wish Papa were here," Stephen whimpered.

"Circle the wagons," Mr. McKinley shouted as he raced down the line of wagons that had pulled to a standstill. "Hurry it up, folks, we don't have time to lose."

277

Mr. Emigh hurried to help Mary Burt, who was attempting to maneuver her wagon into formation. "Push those oxen if you have to," he ordered. "Make them move."

Mother desperately flicked the reins over the backs of the oxen as she'd watched Papa do. Anger welled up inside her; she was doing the best she could and she was well aware everyone was impatient with her.

Once the oxen smelled the smoke, they lifted their drooping heads and panicked. It took all her strength to keep them from heading across a field, with its protruding rock formations that could break a wheel or tip over her wagon.

A brisk wind fanned the fire, moving it closer to the wagons. To Martha, it came at them in the storybook form of an enormous, ferocious dragon, belching smoke, a roaring inferno with tongues of hot flames that greedily flicked out to ignite the prairie grass and sagebrush. It devoured everything within its path. Its hot breath spewed out live sparks, cinders, and hot ash.

Mr. McKinley's two aides and Cookie began digging a trench around the perimeter of the wagons. "Grab your shovels and dig out as far from the wagons as possible," the men instructed the pioneers above the noise of the exploding sagebrush. Men and women frantically began digging a boundary between them and the oncoming fire.

The livestock inside the wagon enclosures nervously ran around the circumferences of their pens, searching for a way out. Several screaming horses, after they attempted to hurl themselves over the wagon tongue barriers, had to be blindfolded.

Live sparks carried in the wind became a concern. There wasn't enough water to wet down the big canvases. Everything that could be done, the pioneers had done to protect themselves and their teams against the rapidly leaping fire about to envelope them.

The children watched groups of Indians with their teepees and possessions loaded on travois dragged behind harnessed horses. The excited voices of the women and children carried in the wind as they ran beside their horses moving in the direction of large outcrop of rocks and the mountains beyond.

Martha caught sight of the frightened herds of antelope and deer, and packs of coyotes, racing towards the hills and mountains, away from the path of the fire as the Indians were doing.

"Women and children under the wagons," Mr. McKinley shouted. He and his horse braved the heat and hot ash to make sure he was heard.

The smoke shrouded the world with a choking darkness. Mother was unable to see her wagon. Her clothes, wet with perspiration, clung to her back. The digging had bruised and blistered her hands. Her dry throat hurt and her eyes burned. Flying sparks had scorched her clothing and bonnet. She suddenly felt lightheaded and feebly called out for Martha. She wondered if her voice was strong enough to be heard above the noise of the fire.

The little boys were having difficulty breathing, and visibility was near impossible. "Put something over your faces!" Martha yelled to them. She and Bertha were stuffing quilts around the underside of the wagon to lessen the smoke getting to them when she heard Mother's faint cry.

"I'm coming, Mother!" She crawled out from under the wagon, lifted her arms in an attempt to ward off hot cinders, but the thick, black smoke concealed Mother from her view.

Mr. McKinley hoped the trenches, though not deep, were deep enough to slow the fire. His plan was for the fire to detour out around the wagons.

"We'll just have to hope and pray," he commented aloud to himself as he used the handkerchief from around his neck to mop his face and neck.

Martha strained to see in the darkness, her eyes burning and her sight blurred. She was afraid if she wandered far from the wagon, she'd lose her way in the dense smoke. The noise from the fire and wind were too intense for her to be heard if she tried to call Mother.

Neil had stumbled onto Mrs. Burt, who was overcome by the smoke and was choking. He came up from behind, grabbed hold of her, and forced her face into his shirt front. It allowed her to catch her breath. The handkerchief he'd tied around his mouth and nose did little to filter out the fumes. Together, they struggled towards the Burt wagon.

With Mother safely in Martha's care, Neil hurried to grab a burlap bag from his wagon and joined the men at the fire line. Working side by side with gunny sacks, they beat at flames that reached up and attempted to leap over the trench.

Women and children, huddled under their wagons, could feel the intense heat even before it threatened the camp.

Hot sparks and cinders rained down to ignite some of the big canvases, sending the victims to beat at the flame or to use what water they had in a futile attempt to save them. Everyone felt at the mercy of this ruthless fire demon. If their livestock were killed, how could they possibly go on? Their wagons were a necessity to their lives.

Like the live monster Martha imagined it to be, the fire consumed the fields, moved around the wagons, and continued on its way to lay waste to the entire valley.

The Burt family remained quiet, listening to the raging fire. Mother sensed their lives were in a delicate balance. She needed to impress upon her children their strength and courage through faith. She wasn't sure she could be heard, so she bowed her head and folded her hands in prayer. She felt the bodies of her children draw close to her and instinctively knew they were praying also.

Mother massaged her temples to ease a throbbing headache when she detected rumbling. She hesitated; she wasn't sure what she'd see outside as she raised a quilt edge. Her throat was sore from having inhaled smoke, and her voice come out in a croak. "I'm not positive, but I think I heard thunder."

The pioneers had protected themselves with bedding and mattresses they hung under wagon edges, but they weren't able to see that the fire had moved on, nor did they hear the thunder or see the flashes of lightning.

As it had become accustomed to doing every afternoon, it began to rain; a cloud burst poured down so fast and with such force it smothered and suffocated the prairie fire that had left shrubs and bushes smoldering behind it.

The change from fiery heat was welcomed, and though warm steam or smoke could still be seen rising off hot cinders and ashes, the rain cooled the earth as it passed over, leaving it refreshing and pleasant for the first time in hours.

Men, women, and children opened arms wide to absorb the moisture. They lifted faces in gratitude, letting the rain soak into their parched skins, their clothing, and run off their heads until they were thoroughly drenched. The children danced around each other, their shrill laughter and screams of joy a testimony to their survival of the fire.

Martha, on her way back to the wagon, discovered one of the oxen lying in the mud. She fought an urge to cry in protest for the poor beast. She could see it wasn't alive. It had succumbed to smoke and the intense heat. It simply hadn't the strength to survive.

Neil came from behind his wagon to see Martha down in the mud beside the ox. Mother, at the same time, saw the ox. She covered her face with her hands, unable to bring herself to look at it, knowing instinctively what had transpired. *Without my oxen, how am I going to survive?* she wondered.

Through tears of rage Martha managed to say, "What a pitiful way for poor Red to die, here in the mud, after all he did for us."

"We've got to move on." Mother had gained her composure enough to reply. "I'm going to let the other one go too. I've no choice."

A surprised look crossed Neil's face. "But then ya'll only have two oxen if ya do that, Mrs. Burt. Wouldn't it be better ta keep it?"

"Yes, I understand your reasoning, but I can't afford to feed the ones I have. Turn it loose will you, please, unless someone else wants it."

Those who had gathered were in agreement with Mrs. Burt's wise and courageous decision. To drag along a weakened animal wasn't a suitable idea, especially when there was so little food. However, she might have brought it along to sell or trade when they came to the fort, that is, if she had enough food to keep feeding it.

"Mother, you can't—he'll starve to death," Bertha argued. "We can't turn Rex loose out here. Wild animals will kill him. You just can't leave him."

"Bertha, gather up the quilts and get in the wagon." Mother sounded stern as she thrust the extra oxbow in the wagon. "I haven't time to argue. I need to yoke up."

"It seems a shame we have to leave all this meat," Mrs. Kenyon stated. "It's just gonna lay out here an' rot."

Martha gasped at the anger in Mother's voice. "Please, help yourself, Mrs. Kenyon. I've no stomach for this just now." Her back was to Mrs. Kenyon as she massaged and fondled the heads of her two remaining oxen. Martha overheard Mother mutter something but it wasn't loud enough for her to hear.

The Burt girls watched the attention Mother gave the oxen. "What do you suppose she's saying to them?" Bertha whispered.

"You know Mother, Bertha. When she's through charming them— they'll run up the side of the mountain ahead of everyone, or they're apt to pick up the wagon and carry it on their backs, if she tells them to."

Neil released the ox and set it free. Those gathered watched it meander off across the blackened, muddy valley. When they turned back for Mother's reaction, her back was still turned. She busied herself adjusting the oxbow.

"Yeah, seems a durn shame ta leave hit go lake thet," Mr. McGraw grumbled. "But what's a body ta do?" He shook his head, shrugged his shoulders, and scratched at his shaggy beard before he turned away. "I's got plenty a problems of ma' own," he mumbled.

Martha disliked the acrid stench coming off the blackened fields. Here and there, she could still see wisps of smoke coming from burned sagebrush roots.

Mr. McKinley's eyes were red rimmed and bloodshot in a black soot-streaked face as he sat staring out at the fields. "Cookie, looks like we've been marooned on an island. Look at us, sittin' here in the middle of this field. We got that ditch dug just in time."

Cookie watched him rein his horse around, turn, and yell behind him. "Wagons out—we've got ground to cover while there's still daylight."

"I's hopin', boss, ya'd be tempted fur a roasted rattler fer your supper, but your in sich a durn fool hurry I ain't had time ta find ya one. Ye'll be gettin' sourd beans and biscuits instead," Cookie said, disgruntled. He moved the horses and his chuck wagon out along the rock-strewn trail, just as the sun appeared.

Under the warmth of the sun, with the creak of wagons, the constant clanking, jingling, and clinking of harnesses and hardware, the pioneers moved out onto the blackened, muddy road.

Martha noticed how cinders clung to muddy boots, trouser legs, and skirt hems as the weary settlers moved forward to finish another day of their journey.

Chapter 37

Mr. Emigh was following the Burts in case a problem arose, but he was becoming impatient with their wagon lagging behind the others.

Perhaps, he decided, the oxen hadn't been yoked properly. However, on closer observance he realized the animals were in such poor condition they weren't likely to make the journey much farther.

He chose not to inform Mary Burt of this, but then again, perhaps she already knew and was hoping they would last till Fort Hall and she could trade or sell them for a new team. But Fort Hall was still a good two days away.

Martha, walking beside the sluggish oxen, had tried her best to coax them to quicken their pace. She felt the sudden cool change in the temperature and knew from the darkened sky the rain was on time. Some time ago, Mr. Buland had prepared them to expect the daily afternoon storms for the next several hundred miles.

The storm announced itself with a few raindrops at first, but commenced to fall fast and hard within minutes. Martha had experienced a rain so heavy it had filled the wagons with several inches of ankle-deep water for them to wade though.

"The rain's refreshing to our spirits, isn't it?" Martha remarked to Mother. It plastered down their hair and molded sodden clothes to their bodies. It also turned the road into sticky, thick mud, which the wagon wheels dug into, leaving deep ruts.

The rain had slacked off just as Mr. McKinley came riding up to tell them, "The Raft River crossing's just ahead. You need to empty your wagon and remove the wheels in order for the canoes to ferry it across. The fee changes with the owner's mood. Mr. Reynolds is discussing the toll with him right now."

On approaching the river, Martha saw there were several independent wagons lined up to cross. Young Indians boys and men were loading the five or six very long, brightly colored dugout canoes with a wagon and its contents distributed between them.

Mother unyoked the oxen and requested Bertha and Ruthie take them to feed on what little grass there was, while she, Martha, and Stephen unloaded the wagon so the wheels could be removed and their possessions made ready for the canoes.

Martha observed Mr. Reynolds talking with a man she believed must be the owner of the canoes. He was a powerful-looking, florid-faced man with large, muscular arms and a swollen chest stuffed into a deer hide-fringed shirt. She watched Mr. Reynolds shake hands with the man before he turned away, his face darkened in a scowl.

When Mother heard it would cost eight dollars to cross the wagon and a dollar per animal, she nearly shrieked in horror. She too had watched Mr. Reynolds discuss the fee with the owner and come away disgusted. She'd have to pay the exorbitant fare from her already meager cash supply.

"Oh dear, Papa would be unhappy with me swimming the oxen, but what am I expected to do?" Mother said, more to herself than to the girls.

The Emighs came to help Mother when her time came to load the canoes. "What else can I do, Mr. Emigh? I'm not used to handling money, and I'm worried to say Mr. Burt didn't leave us too well off."

Sam didn't share with Mrs. Burt, but he hoped the oxen would be strong enough to make the crossing.

It was an awkward climb into the canoe for Martha. She put out her hand to the nearest Indian for support and saw the young man she guessed to be her age hesitate before he held out his arm to her. At boisterous laughter from his friends, she glanced up to see she'd embarrassed him.

During the crossing, she felt him watching her. It wasn't a look of contempt or insolence but rather a curious stare.

She averted her face, but when she did glance over at him, he appeared shy, and quickly look away. *He's like all Indians*, she decided. His aloofness and superior manner didn't impress her.

He, on the other hand, thought the white mother was kind, like his mother, but the pale-faced daughters weren't beautiful like his spirited brown-skinned sisters, with their black hair and flashing dark eyes.

White people fascinated him; their faces were open. Not like his people, who kept their feelings hidden and kept in control of their facial expressions.

At the end of the rough crossing, Martha waited for the Indians to stack the family's belonging on the riverbank. Before he and his friends pushed off to cross back over the river, she saw the Indian's head lowered as he glanced in her direction.

A silent communication was passed between them. In mere seconds they conveyed a spark of interest in each other, but seconds later they were transported back to their cultures.

After the wheels had been replaced, Martha busied herself with arranging the inside of the wagon. She wondered what there was about Indian men that kept them from smiling. She wondered at the barriers they put up between themselves and the white man, but shrugged it off as just part of their nature.

Mr. Reynolds warned them there'd be no water, and they needed to fill their barrels before leaving the river. Mother frowned at the brown water but realized she had little choice.

On their way again, Martha found she was trudging through soil of a soft, sandy dirt combination, and for miles the land was covered with bluish, green gray sagebrush.

The sagebrush produced an offensive odor to some, but to Martha it had a fragrance. She discovered it was a strong, tough bush; it was difficult to break off the dry branches and impossible to pull up by its roots.

Several hours later, Mr. McKinley called a halt for the night to set up camps. The only shade trees around were dwarfed and scraggly. After they had settled, Ruthie and Bertha went in search of firewood only to find their armloads of wood burned fast and hot and didn't leave enough coals to cook with.

They had just started to go in search of more firewood when Mr. Reynolds happened by and warned them to watch for the "timber rattlers," a highly venomous snake native to the region.

"It'll make a holler', rattlin' with its tail when ya venture into its territory and before it strikes ya. I seen men die instantly from its bite through a heavy boot," he said. "Once it bites inta ya, it can't take its fangs back out an' keeps a-pumpin' poison inta ya."

The men, after settling for the night, decided there was still time to ride out for a hunt. Without forage and water nearby, they knew in order to find any game they would have to ride some distance from camp.

They had been gone but a short time when the sound of galloping horses alerted the campers to the approach of riders. Neil materialized out of the dusk, towing an extra horse with a man's body across its back.

Mr. McKinley and Mr. Buland quickly moved out to meet him. The men conversed at the edge of the camps before leading the horse and Mr. Wilson's body back with them.

Neil explained to the curious folks gathered, "Mr. Wilson was a skilled horseman, and when he spied this big antelope he gave chase, but his horse stumbled and fell, throwin' him head first onta the ground. He musta broke his neck. His horse broke its leg and we had ta put it down. One of the fellers lent me his horse ta bring Mr. Wilson back and I come soon's I could."

The men gently lifted the lifeless body of Mr. Wilson from the horse and carried him to his wagon. Neil needed to return the borrowed horse to its owner, so left immediately.

A profound silence followed the tragic news. Those who had traveled with David Wilson and had been with him during his wife's burial along with that of his stillborn son were in a stupor. For the woman who carried his child, the tragedy made an incomprehensible impact.

The members of the wagon train were too polite to question the relationship between David Wilson and his lady. He had moved his wagon behind her parents' soon after they met, and after Papa's death the Burts had seen little of him.

Martha remembered Ginny McGraw's overhearing Mr. Wilson explain his dilemma to Mrs. Kenyon and how excited she had been to share it with her friends. Now, however, Ginny was gone and she'd never know the outcome of the romance, and because she liked Mr. Wilson, Martha hoped for the best for a young woman she didn't know. The situation was something she knew polite society didn't discuss aloud. Families kept things of this sort to themselves.

The startling news of Mr. Wilson's tragedy was difficult for Mother Burt. The Wilson youngsters, mere babies, were orphaned. They had been underfoot since the beginning of the journey. If David was married, he had neither attempted to take baby Pearl from the Crawford family nor requested his boys stay with him more than to sleep at night.

Her question was who should tell the boys about their tragically devastating circumstances?

As it turned out, Mr. McKinley took Homer and Johnny aside along with a few members of the wagon train who knew them intimately and explained to them, "Your Mother is much too distraught to comfort you right now and you might be better off staying with Mrs. Burt for a while."

Martha heard Mother insist, "Homer, Johnny, and Stephen are the best of friends and I'd like nothing more than to have the boys together."

Mr. McKinley approved of the situation and said he would speak to the boys' mother, referring to Mr. Wilson's new wife, as soon as possible and get back to Mrs. Burt with her decision about the family's welfare.

The hunters returned to camp soon after, with little results to show from the hunt. They were able to get a few rabbits and game birds but lost their desire after the fatal accident.

Neil gave his catch of three rabbits and a prairie hen to Mrs. Burt. He was at at loss for words. He knew she had just lost her husband, and now a good friend.

He knew Martha was worried about her mother. She'd told him her mother hadn't been the same since the father's death, and how the burden of making the journey was difficult for her, no matter how much the girls tried to help. Now the little boys were without a family, and she'd added to her burden by taking them.

Neil highly approved of the decision made concerning the Wilson boys. *I loved my mother very much, and after I lost her, I'd have liked to have had a mother like Mrs. Burt, should I have been blessed with one.*

Homer couldn't bring himself do anything but sit by the fire. He was alone now. He remembered feeling alone when his momma died, but he'd had his dad; now he had no one. What was to become of him and Johnny? He didn't even know his baby sister anymore. The hurt inside of him was real bad, like he'd had before when he realized he'd never see his mother again. The hurt was so bad he didn't want to do anything but lay down and sleep and maybe the hurt would go away.

Johnny clung onto Mrs. Burt. He was scared. He'd never been alone before. What if something happened to Mrs. Burt? He wished he hadn't loved his momma. He loved his daddy, and now he was gone. Johnny was lonesome, angry, and he was afraid of being alone. Stephen and the other boys encouraged him to come play with them, but Johnny hid his pale little face in Mrs. Burt's skirts and stumbled along beside her.

Ruthie was watching Mother and Martha at a distance prepare the rabbits for supper. Mother reached up to brush hair out of her eyes and saw Ruthie shudder with distaste at the soft, lifeless bodies and big, liquid, staring eyes.

287

She flopped a rabbit down on the tailgate, and with hands on her hips glared at her youngest daughter.

"Its time you learned to prepare food for our welfare, young lady. I've let you get away far too long without fixing the kill. Now's the time you learn. Come over here right now and help me skin and clean these rabbits; you'll not recognize them once they've been cooked. Get yourself over here right now," Mother sternly ordered. "Martha, give her your rabbits to finish."

"Oh Mother, I can't! I don't care if they're cooked. I still see them as bunnies. I don't wanna touch them," Ruthie whimpered.

The look Mother gave Ruthie was one Martha had never witnessed before. Martha noted the change in Mother's attitude since Papa's passing. She could be so demanding and harsh at times, and it seemed to be getting worse. This was so unlike her patient, gentle Mother.

Mother grabbed the half-skinned rabbit from Martha and nearly flung it at little Ruthie.

"Mother, I'm gonna be sick," Ruthie gagged.

Martha quickly walked away, taking Johnny with her, leaving Mother to contend with Ruthie. They found Bertha filling a bucket from the one water barrel left after the buffalo stampede. It held all the water there was for them and the oxen.

Mrs. Kenyon walked up as Bertha was about to drink a cupped handful of water.

"Oh no, stop!" Mrs. Kenyon shouted. "Don't drink that water. You have to boil every drop of water you use. Your Mother surely knows this."

Mother, hearing the warning, stopped gutting the rabbit and whirled around with a bloody knife poised in midair. "For goodness sakes, Ruth Kenyon, must you scream at us? You liked to scared me near to death. I could have slipped and cut myself. No one told me to boil the water. You knew this? Why wasn't I told?"

"Well, I never—I'm sure I don't know why you weren't told, but it does seem everyone would have figured out the water just might be—be tainted."

Mrs. Kenyon, not used to being spoken to so harshly, placed her hands on her hips and faced Mary Burt. "And will you kindly lower that threatenin' bloody knife your pointin' at me? I was only thinkin' of your girl, after all—I'm sorry if I frightened you. I only meant—" Mrs. Kenyon paused, then spun around, pulled herself up to her dignified height, and walked in strides so long her dress molded to her legs in her propulsion away from Mary Burt.

Martha looked over to see Mother, her face splattered with rabbit blood, the bloody knife still in her hand. "I can't believe I treated Mrs. Kenyon as I just did," Mother whispered.

Martha was sure Mother would have liked to bury her face in her apron out of shame had not her hands been covered with blood.

Ruthie, viewing the scene, thought, *Serves Mother right for forcing me to handle this brutally butchered, innocent little bunny.*

Bertha had to cover her mouth to keep from laughing out loud at the drama played between the two women: Mother's startled, blood-streaked face when Mrs. Kenyon yelled, and Mrs. Kenyon's face when Mother flipped around with the bloody knife pointed at her. Bertha had to flee to the other side of the wagon to keep her laugher to herself.

Martha's thought, as she watched Mrs. Kenyon stride off, *I can't believe—I've ever seen my mother treat anyone like she just did. Oh Papa, why aren't you with us here? Why can't things be like they used to be. Poor, poor Mother, how miserable her life is anymore She's lost you Papa, her companion, her soul-mate. I can't imagine life from now on without Neil. How is it possible to make your dreams come true without a mate?*

"Oh, Martha." Mother's voice had softened. "I'm so ashamed of what I just did to Mrs. Kenyon. She only meant good for us. I lost my head; I acted completely *ferhoodled.*"

Martha drew in a deep breath. "Mother, we've just lost Papa. Mr. Wilson's death is difficult for us all. You may have lost control but not your courage, and right now all this going on around you is asking a lot of your courage."

Unmindful of Mother's bloody hands, Martha reached to enfold her mother into her arms, and as she did, she felt Mother's shoulders relax and she gave away to great, heaving sobs.

Later, lying under her quilt, Martha recalled her day. It had proved to be a long one, with the slow-plodding, near-dead oxen. Mother was taking Mr. Wilson's death so hard and she'd taken on his orphaned children. The little episode between Mother and Mrs. Kenyon. Ruthie going to bed without supper because she couldn't bring herself to eat rabbit.

She and Neil had so little time for each other today with all the confusion. She'd meant to tell Neil about her encounter with the Indian. She had actually observed Neil wipe his eyes during the graveside service for Mr. Wilson.

It surprised Martha that the face of Mr. Wilson's widow remained impassive as she stood with her parents through the burial. Martha was glad the lady and Mr. Wilson had married quietly; it made things seem right that they were united for the sake of the expected baby. Mrs. Kenyon, when she told them this, said she didn't carry a grudge and even accepted Mother's begging for forgiveness for being so rude to her. It pleased Martha to see them hug each other.

Martha wished Ginny were alive and she could share the word with her of Mr. Wilson's secret marriage.

Martha was worried about Mother. What a frustrating day—time—life it was for her. It was as though, for Martha, she'd lost both Papa and Mother.

The dark, moonless night was cold; she pulled her quilt up over her and snuggled down to a warm sleep.

Chapter 38

Idaho Part of Nebraksa Territory

"It's the last week of August 1846," Mr. had Emigh had informed the Burts at breakfast. "We've completed another three hundred and sixty miles according to Mr. McKinley."

Martha had glanced around and wondered why none of the others bothered to ask how many miles remained of the journey. She guessed everyone was too weary to care. She knew she was. She would always remember hot, dry Nebraska and the majestic, snow-peaked Grand Teton Mountains, which were behind her now.

Mr. Emigh continued to explain about the next three hundred or more miles. "We'll be traveling through big, beautiful valleys and past the Sawtooth mountain range to the northeast of us."

At supper that night Martha had savored her first taste of salmon. The settlers traded clothing to a friendly band of migrating Shoshone Indians for the big fish, then divided them among themselves.

Cookie had demonstrated the removal of the shiny fish scales and preparation of the fresh-caught salmon from the "Mad River," which the Indians called the Snake River. The fish was to become a staple for the pioneers from now on.

He explained how the fish was prized among the Native Indians through the Midwest and western United States. The dried fish was a precious commodity in exchange for dried buffalo meat and pemmican.

Martha watched him grill the fish over the open fire, with a light sprinkle of salt the only seasoning necessary. Cookie said he'd serve his fish with "a mess of ma' pan-fried spuds." The pioneers had few potatoes among them.

Tantalizing aromas drifted throughout the camp from meat stews made from rabbits, game, and prairie hens brought in daily. The beans, moistened from rain and wet wagons during the river crossings, were sprouting in their sacks. They were still used, cooked plain or in combination with spices and rice. Biscuits and cornbread were still plentiful.

Fresh, sweet berries or wild plums picked along the way were made into juicy cobblers, and there remained dried apples to make pies offered along with tea or coffee. Coffee was priceless and brewed with other vehicles such as roasted wheat, chicory, and other herbs. The pioneers were outraged at the staggering price of coffee beans that forced them to change from their favored beverage to British tea.

Mother was unable to replenish her list of supplies at Fort Hall's trading post because of the expense. She and many of the other pioneers who found themselves in financial straits were having to make adaptations to their diets. But their faith remained strong, and as long as the land around them was providing them with an abundance of wild fruits and game, they were motivated with a burning desire to move on and finish the journey as quickly as possible, and hoped their teams would last.

"'Cause o' them damn British, I'm havin' ta swaller this hogwash-tastin' tea," grumbled a man. "Better'n nothin'," his missus reminded him.

Mr. McKinley explained to the pioneers that they had entered into what the British stubbornly considered their territory, but President Polk was negotiating with England, for the land within the legal realm of the Louisiana Purchase and which was in reality part of the United States. President Polk had requested of the pioneers that they keep peace with the British until the boundary lines could be established. There was a growing unrest among the Pioneers moving west, however; they wanted the land promised to them, and it included land the British were holding.

Mr. McKinley also informed them that because they weren't British subjects, from now on they'd hear themselves referred to as "emigrants." The British call the Oregon Trail the "Emigrant Trail."

"I'm so glad we stopped early tonight." Martha joined a group of young folks assembled around a fire of their own. Martha, passing them, noted the adults were in a discussion concerning tomorrow's crossing at a place called "Three Island."

Bertha was sitting next to a new friend, Juan Diego Fernandez. They'd met during the stop at Fort Hall. Juan was on his way out West to book passage on a sailing ship to Mexico. Cookie had befriended him, calling him "amigo"; however, to everyone else he was simply called Mr. Fernandez.

"Señorita Bertha." His voice was husky and melodic. "So which side of the river do your people plan to settle on when you have finished the journey?" Juan asked her, his Spanish heritage inherent in his dark hair, eyes, and handsome features, including a pert mustache he thought added polish to his appearance.

He had just described to Bertha how he'd traveled north from the Mexican Territory the United States insisted they laid claim to, and was seeking land to raise horses. His dream was to breed the short, stocky, Spanish-Mexican horse with the larger North American breeds. He hoped to produce a versatile, appealing work- and pleasure horse. He and Alex Kenyon had become fast friends, and shared information on the subject of equestrian husbandry.

Martha glanced over to Mother sitting with the adults. She was worried about her, though she appeared pleasant enough; her clothes hung on her far-too-slender frame. Martha still awakened to hear Mother's sobs in the darkness, but as yet she didn't know what to do to comfort her loneliness. She missed Papa too. They all did.

She recalled a night previously when she and Bertha had confronted Mother about their stopping to settle and then travel on later. Mother had been outraged at the idea.

"You want to give up? You don't care enough for Papa to see his dream come true?" She wouldn't hear of it. They had only managed to upset Mother and make her cry.

Along with the guilt Martha now carried about the scene, there was Mr. Emigh. She and Bertha had expressed their feelings about Mr. Emigh ever taking Papa's place; and Stephen, young as he was, displayed signs of disrespect he'd not shown before, like sassing Mother, and the girls hadn't appreciated Mr. Emigh's intervening. There was no forgiveness, as Martha saw it, for making Mother miserable.

She leaned her head against Neil's shoulder. She'd come to depend on him, yet she begrudged Mother and Mr. Emigh, and there was Mr. Buland too, who made himself known, dropping by like he did with silly excuses. "Just makin' sure you're comfortable, Mrs. Burt."

Here she was, enjoying Neil's companionship, and poor Mother was alone.

"Fort Hall had been the dream of Mr. Wyeth back in 1832," Mr. Buland was telling them. "Nathaniel Wyeth planned on getting rich by using the trappers and Indians to push a path west to the Columbia River. He'd set up businesses from New England and as far west as the island of Hawaii, with him as the base.

293

"Nothing went right for Mr. Wyeth," said Mr. Buland. "He proudly put up the Stars and Stripes in this uncivilized country above his American trading post, but it wasn't long after that a Hudson Bay Company spokesman paid him a visit. His business was on British Territory. And about that time a Captain Grant, in charge of the Hudson Bay camp, notified the pioneers going west, 'You're emigrants, not British subjects, and it's impractical to travel further west if you've no desire to become British.'

"He dissuaded pioneers from traveling out to Oregon for a few years, and it was enough to hurt Mr. Wyeth's business venture, so he gave up."

Martha shuddered in the chill of the evening.

"Martha, you warm enough?" Neil asked.

"There's a real chill to the evenings now," she replied, snuggling closer.

Mr. Buland excused himself to meander over to the adult group, when he heard Mrs. Kenyon say, "I never trusted them Indians in the first place. They'll shake your hand with one hand and steal ya blind with the other."

Martha heard Mrs. Kenyon say this too. "Paul?" she yelled. "Oh, there you are. Don't be playin' in the bushes after dark."

Martha spoke up. "I remember the night at Fort Hall. We were so tired from laboring to make up time."

Neil nudged her. "What brought this to mind?"

She sighed before offering him a smile. "It just turned out to be a good night."

"I had a good time too that night," Lizzy Crawford commented in a soft voice. "It was so festive, wasn't it? The insides of that fort were so big. Imagine, a fort and no soldiers."

"It was big," Ruthie added. "I hadn't seen my mother so happy in a long time. She got so excited seeing fresh vegetables." She paused. "Did we have plum trees back home, Martha?"

"Yes, we did, Ruthie, along with apricot and apple trees. Granddaddy Burt planted them years ago."

"In Mexico, we have many sweet melons. You would like them," Juan said. "Much like here, we grow many kinds of vegetables and many kinds of peppers also."

"You make Mexico sound so enchanting, Juan," Bertha purred.

"Sí, Señorita; in Mexico we use herbs to eat, drink, and for medicine," said Juan.

Seeking to keep his attention, Bertha requested, "Oh Juan, you simply have to teach me how to use herbs."

"You seem so far away tonight," Neil whispered to Martha.

"I'm just thinking about all the mountains we've crossed, and I can't even remember all the rivers either. Neil, is it any wonder we're so weary? So tired of walking? I'm getting anxious for Oregon. It's nearly September; we're almost there."

"Know what I think is strange?" Lizzy asked. "Snow in the mountains. I couldn't believe there would be snow anywhere in summer. It's almost the first of September and the snow has lasted through the whole hot summer."

Nathan spoke up. "I hope we never have to cross through a place like that Devil's Hole. It's my idea of what Hades must be like. It was scary, so hot, and has all those strange formations. Besides, I thought volcanoes were mountains, but this flat, black land sure isn't any mountain. It's ugly, covered with those strange black mounds of rock. Nothing green; just miles of rocky black land, and a few skinny spiders. It's got to be evil."

"Nat, I think it came up from inside the earth, as liquid stuff, and spread itself over the flat land," was Matt Dillion's theory.

"Ya mean it puked." Nat laughed at his own description. "And that black stuff's what come up."

"Oh Nat," the girls squealed, feigning disgust with giggles.

"That Soda Springs seemed strange to me," Louie Crawford said. "All that stinkin' hot water. Everything strange seems to come from inside the earth. What if it decided to turn wrong side out? Maybe that's what the earth is gonna do: turn itself wrong side out one of these days."

Mother accompanied by Mrs. Kenyon stopped by to tell Martha they were on their way to look in on Mrs. McGraw. Mother asked, "Will you make sure Stephen and the Wilson boys get to bed for me? They should be in bed right now."

"Mrs. McGraw's still ailin' or just upset?" Lizzy had overheard the two women.

"She has that strange ailment she had since she was first scared by Indians."

"But that was some time ago," Lizzy said.

"I think it's because of Ginny and the baby, don't you, Mother?" Bertha suggested.

A brief silence was followed by a noise nearby that attracted everyone's attention.

"What on earth was that?" Mrs. Kenyon wondered aloud.

"Hush!" Juan held up his hand.

In the firelight, everyone saw the expression on Juan's face change to anger at the sound of horses running, their hoof beats fading away in the darkness.

"Aye, carumba! Mia horse!" Juan dropped his guitar, leaped to his feet, and ran in the direction of the horses.

The men at the campfire across the way jumped up to follow him, while the women waited by the firesides and kept a close watch on the darkness surrounding them.

At first they heard the voices of the men, then the voice of Mr. Kenyon, followed by the sound of scuffling, some cursing, and more scuffling.

Mrs. Crawford found the way to her wagon and carried back a lard torch she lit from a campfire; as she held up the lighted torch, the men stepped into the light of the campfires, pushing a young Indian man ahead of them.

Behind the men, Juan's angry voice demanded, "Thees est a stealin', theivin' bandito. He no good. I take care of him."

His arms pinned behind his back, the Indian stood proudly erect, his copper-skinned torso glistened in the firelight. His long, dark hair was held in place by a yellow and red headband and he was wearing only a loincloth and moccasins.

Martha gasped at the sight of him. She stepped back and covered her mouth to muffle her scream. In the firelight he appeared to be her young brave with the blue stone, which brought memories that instantly flooded her mind.

It can't be—it can't possibly be him. My Indian's gone. He didn't came for me like he promised Papa, and Papa sold the blue stone. I believe the story of the two brothers who were forced to kill him. "The only Indian with a gun," they'd said. Papa's gun. It had to have been Papa's gun. She wasn't prepared to reopen a painful past. *They're both gone now—they're both gone.*

Those looking on questioned what there was about the young Indian that startled Martha, and they wondered what had upset her.

Bertha was quick to sense Martha's fear. "Martha, you're frightened? What's the matter?" She took her sister's arm. "You're pale as a ghost. It's seeing the Indian, isn't it?

After her initial shock, Martha was able to regain control of herself. The Indian wasn't even ware he'd upset her. He scowled and tried to work his arms free of Mr. Reynolds's tight grip clamped around his wrists.

296

Everyone had circled around the two but were unable to understand the words spoken. However, they did notice Mr. Reynolds didn't loosen his grip on the Indian.

Before anyone was aware of Juan's intentions, he unsheathed a knife from his boot and charged the Indian. Mr. McKinley quickly stepped between the two, ordering, "Mr. Fernandez, put the knife down."

Mr. Reynolds, seeing Juan, quickly maneuvered the Kootenai Indian out of his path.

Juan's jaw was clenched, his eyes mere slits as he slowly inched his way forward; his body taut, he feigned a few dance steps in his move to lunge at the Indian.

"Put the knife down, Juan," Mr. McKinley again stated loudly. He sensed the young Spaniard's intension by his measured movements. Juan was out to kill the Indian.

Mr. McKinley remained calm, his voice steady. "Juan, the knife—drop it." The crowd stepped back; all eyes were riveted on Juan. They held their breath.

Mr. McKinley knew better than to hold out his hand to ward off Juan, with a knife in his grasp, so he stepped forward, putting his whole body as an obstacle in Juan's path, and hoped the man didn't charge.

In a low, guttural growl, Juan snarled, "Snake die for stealin' horse."

Mr. Emigh, aware of Juan's intentions, also spoke up. "Juan, he didn't take your horse. Who has your horse? Do you know who took your horse?"

Still enraged, Juan threw his knife to the ground and leaped for the Indian, but Mr. McGraw and Mr. Emigh had anticipated such a move and grabbed for him just as he reached for the Indian's throat.

There was no mistaking the anger in Mr. McKinley's voice this time. "Mr. Fernandez, you stand back. It's my authority to question this man and find out where he's from. If your horse is gone, we'll go tomorrow and get it back but we'll wait for daylight. Do you understand? Does your horse carry a mark or brand?

"Mr. Reynolds, see to it this man is tied up and watched, if you please, sir."

Juan, his head lowered in submission, held his hands up in surrender.

Bertha hoped no one could read her excitement. Her body tingled with a sensation she she couldn't explain. Juan stirred her soul. She had never witnessed a man so beautiful. It had thrilled her to watch him go from a gentleman one moment to a powerful, charged savage the next. He exhibited and radiated such a forceful strength. She was certain she'd never be the same person she had been before meeting him.

Her sensation of him was so great it was something beyond any feeling she'd ever imagined. She was positive of her love for him. Suddenly aware of a stillness surrounding her, she quickly glanced around to make sure others hadn't found her out and read her thoughts.

Everyone, satisfied with Mr. McKinley's technique of handling Juan and the Indian, turned to their wagons to prepare for the night.

Martha watched her sister pause. *She's hoping he'll look over her way.* When he didn't, she felt pity for Bertha, who reluctantly turned towards her wagon.

Martha had bedded the little boys down and was waiting for Mother, when she heard giggles and whispers coming from them. She heard Stephen's loud whisper to the others, "Should I tell her?"

"I heard you, Stephen. Tell me what?" Martha demanded.

"Shh, no, Stephen, don't tell," Johnny hissed.

"Too late. I heard you. You better tell me, Stephen—boys—I'm telling Mother."

"Yeah, you best tell us, Stephen, or I'm putting a slimy snake in your bed," Ruthie threatened.

Stephen, resigned, drew in a noisy breath. "'Member when them Injuns come with the fish today? Well, they had this lil' puppy and he didn't have a home anymore they said. So's we took 'em, but you can't tell Ma, Martha. She won't let us keep him. I just know it," Stephen pleaded.

"Stephen!" Martha exclaimed. "What did you just call our Mother? And where is this puppy?"

"Homer and Johnny call their mother Ma, an' she lets 'em. How come I can't call mine that?"

"You know very well, Papa would never have permitted you to speak of Mother like that," Bertha scolded.

"But Papa's not here anymore," Stephen argued.

"You will call our mother by her rightful name, and you will tell her about the dog," Martha stated emphatically.

"Oh—alright, but we're taking good care of it, Martha. You didn't even know we had it afore I told ya. Wish I'd never told ya now," Stephen grumbled.

"If it's got critters," Ruthie piped up, "you're gonna be sorry."

"Oh Ruth Ann, stop badgering the boys. Besides, I'd like to see you pick up a snake," Bertha said disgustedly.

After she'd settled the family down, Martha found herself in a quandary. Should she tell Mother about the puppy? She was bound to find out for herself, wasn't she?

She was far too weary to care, and after the tedious hours of walking in the heat, her weary body craved sleep. She dozed off only to be awakened when she heard Mother enter the darkened wagon.

"Martha, I'm so sorry to be late," Mother whispered. "Mrs. McGraw isn't doing well. Mrs. Kenyon and I were able to get her up and out to walk a bit in the fresh air, but she isn't of this world, let me tell you. She didn't talk, just stumbled along. It's so pitiful. Oh dear me, it's been a long day." Mother fumbled around in the dark to find her way into bed with her quilt.

Martha decided to let the subject of the puppy wait.

She couldn't resist asking, "Mother, are we going to swim our oxen and float our wagon across the Snake River tomorrow?"

"I hear the river's swift. I think we'll go around. We can meet up with the others later. The three islands are laid out like stepping-stones, and we'd have to swim between them." Mother yawned and pulled her quilt up around her shoulders. "Yes, I think I'll go around," Martha heard her mumble.

"But Mother, don't we have to cross the river eventually?" Martha asked.

"I suppose so," said Mother. "Maybe there's a bridge somewhere. I didn't think to ask Mr. McKinley."

"Shouldn't we know these things before we start out tomorrow?"

"You listen to me, Martha." Mother sat abruptly. "Our lives are different. I have to make choices I know little about, and I don't even know how to ask the right questions." Her voice sounded harsh and defensive. "This is the way we've been left by your papa's death, and let me tell you, if we're going to make this journey, this is the way we—I have to do it. I take each day as it comes, and no, I don't have all the answers."

After Mother lay back down, Martha felt alone in the dark night. Mother hadn't been like this when Papa was alive.

If only there were someone to talk with, Martha thought. *If only Granny were here. Will there ever come a time when we don't ache with pain from the loss of Papa? What will we do if Mother gets an ailment or something happens to her? I'd never go back. I can't now; we're almost there and I'd want to make Papa's dream come true for Stephen and my sisters.*

Martha drifted off to sleep nagged by a persistent small voice. *You're almost there. You've made it this far. It's not much farther. You can do it.*

Chapter 39

Martha was awakened to birdsongs filling the cool early morning. She sensed Mother was awake and enjoying a few precious moments before the start to her day.

"Guess we best get up," Mother murmured. "Make a fire, take care of the oxen, grease the wheels, get the wagon ready, and breakfast over before Mr. McKinley says it's time to move out."

Martha groaned and stretched out full length, pulling on muscles from the tips of her callused toes to the ends of her roughened fingers. "Wake up, lil' sisters, we've work to do." She nudged sleeping Bertha and Ruthie.

A soft whining coming from where the boys were still sleeping attracted Mother's attention. "What is that?" she asked.

"Stephen's puppy." Ruthie sat upright. "He doesn't want you to know about it."

"A what? A puppy? A dog? Stephen," Mother cried. "Stephen, you get up and take that dog right back where you got it. I've not enough food as it is."

"I can't, Mother." Stephen's voice was groggy with sleep. "I got it from some Injuns an' I don't know their names. Ruthie, how come ya got such a big mouth?"

The puppy resisted Homer and Johnny's efforts to quiet it and continued to whine as it restlessly scampered about the boys' quilts.

"Get up this minute, Stephen, and take that dog outside before it messes. Don't you think I have enough to do without a dog to look after?"

It upset the girls for Mother to be irritated this early in her day. Martha was sorry now she hadn't warned Mother about the puppy last night.

Martha climbed down from the wagon in the first pink tinge of daylight to see Mr. Reynolds, Neil, and Juan Fernandez riding off across a field, with the Indian perched behind Mr. Reynolds.

"I hope Juan gets his horse back," Bertha said softly to Mother and her sisters, who had come down from the wagon to see the men riding off.

"We don't have all day to stand here." Mother abruptly turned away. "Martha, you get a fire going. Bertha, help me feed the oxen and yoke them. Stephen, you boys do something with that dog before we leave this morning."

Martha and Ruthie had pancakes ready with tea steeping, when Mr. Emigh, Nat, Mother, and Bertha arrived. The little boys and the puppy were impatiently waiting beside the smoky campfire for their breakfast.

"Going to be another scorcher today." Mr. Emigh lifted his hat to smooth down his hair.

"Mr. Emigh, is it really safe to venture out into that river? I heard it said last night how dangerous the crossing was." Mother wasn't able to hide her anxiety. "What happens if we get into trouble in the middle of the river?"

"We take care of each other," he told her.

"I'll take my chances on the overland route," Mother said wistfully. "I'd like to think there is another option besides the river."

The two families had just finished eating when Mr. McKinley rode by to assure them. "Mrs. Burt, we're going to help you cross the river. The islands are there to use if we need them. There's plenty of us to help you."

"Would it be possible for me to take the overland route and meet you some place further along the way?"

Martha could see Mother was worried and having difficulty mastering her fears.

"You couldn't possibly cross in that volcanic shale ahead. First of all you'd cut your wagon wheels to pieces and your oxen's feet would come out bloody stumps from walkin' through that lava rock. I've heard that Indians lay in wait for emigrants too; they do it out of spite to the white man. Just when an emigrant discovers the trouble he's in tryin' ta cross by land, the Indians close in and bushwhack 'em."

Mr. McKinley touched the brim of his hat and headed his horse away before Mother could respond.

"I'm certain, if I go slow enough, I can make it overland," Mother muttered.

The wagons worked their way slowly over rocks and rough road for a distance of five miles, by Mr. Buland's calculations, before the Three Island crossing was sighted.

It was a frightful experience to those standing above the cliffs to look down the straight drop-off to big boulders below.

The river's edge for miles was nothing but huge rocks, and those in the water had the river rapidly tearing over them. In the middle of the river were three, large islands so massive that scraggly looking green brush was growing up through the thin layer of soil that covered the surface.

To the wagon train just arriving, it appeared that folks on the islands must have spent the night bedded down under the brush for protection. It didn't look like there was any way to fasten down the wagons or set up tents on the rocky surface.

Mr. McKinley called for the wagons, one at a time, to be chained or roped then lowered down the steep bluff. The horses, mules, and oxen were led some distance along the edge of the bluff to a gap wide enough to allow them to crisscross back and forth down the side of the cliff to the river. Neither the opening in the cliff nor the narrow path were wide enough to accommodate a wagon.

Teams were quickly hitched to the wagons again and then urged out into the swift water of the Snake River.

Mr. McKinley had Mr. Kenyon lead off with another family behind him. When his horses floundered, Mr. Kenyon would urge them cautiously forward until they had made their way around the first and largest of the three rock islands. The wagon following the Kenyons also rounded the three islands and pulled out unscathed on the other side.

With each wagon's crossing, those on the bluff above held their breath as the teams and wagons fought their way through the turbulent river to safety before the next two wagons with nervous families and teams entered the water.

Martha and Bertha watched, paralyzed with terror, as a wagon suddenly capsized in the fast current. The horses became tangled in their harnesses and were tumbled about in the water.

People from above on the cliffs ran for the gap and made their way down the path to the river. Men on the river's edge rode their horses out into the water and maneuvered the wagon to the first island, with the family struggling to hang on.

Once on the island, everyone pitched in to right the wagon and rescue the team. Two men, who had ridden out bareback, untangled the harnesses and calmed the horses before the wagon was again plunged into the water to finish the crossing.

The wagon ahead of the capsized wagon had difficulties of its own with its hesitant team, but it moved on past the second island, out around the third, and finished the crossing safely, to everyone's relief

"I wonder how many have drowned making the crossing?" Martha sputtered in exasperation. "I see why Mother thought the overland route was safer. That whole family could have drowned."

"Mr. McKinley says it's the only place to cross in this canyon," Bertha stated. "I wish Neil or Juan were here to help us."

"Be sensible, Bertha. Indians are never in a hurry when it comes to a parley. The men could be a way all day." Mother was behind the McGraw wagon. They were ready to wade out and begin the river crossing, the safest way to get back on the Oregon Trail.

Mother refused to allow anyone to handle her oxen. She instructed her family to sit down in the back of the wagon. "If the wagon capsizes you can get out."

A gentleman assisting tested the tailgate to make sure it was latched. He could see by their expressions the three young ladies were speechless with fright, but the three little fellers were livid with excitement. He couldn't help but wonder if the mother had as much sense as the good Lord gave a goose. To insist she, an inexperienced woman, was capable of handling the oxen; it was all an able-bodied man could do to keep a nervous team going.

Maybe his being a man alone was why the women in this train appeared to be a different breed of woman than he was accustomed to. *Women are getting too independent for their own good. Comes from educating 'em,* he decided.

"Don't look down at the water," he cautioned the youngsters. "I'm watching you from here. You're gonna be alright. If I see ya need help, I'll come a runnin'."

The man's comment amused Stephen but it did little for the girls.

"He'll come runnin'—through the water?" Stephen parroted to Homer and Johnny, who found the idea hilarious.

The order was given for the wagons to move forward. The boys grew quiet as they bumped and swayed, rolling over unseen river rocks beneath them, and they sensed the power and force with which the water curled around their wagon.

"Oh, I wish Neil and Juan were here to help us." Bertha grabbed onto the tailgate. Martha remembered another crossing. She had been scared then, but she could scarcely breathe now. She wished she was up front with Mother. Why wouldn't Mother let one of the men handle the oxen? She remembered it had been Mother, not Papa, who had maneuvered them safely across the river that day.

Buoyed by making the first rock island, Mother made the second and followed Mr. McGraw's wagon out around and past the third island.

She coaxed the oxen along. If they slipped on the big rocks beneath the water, she allowed them time to secure their footing. She watched them struggle, their heads just above the water at times, to pull the big wagon and family across the wide, swift river.

The "Mad River," the Indians call it. How appropriate, Mother thought.

This crossing, Mother was sure, was something the oxen would never have attempted by themselves. She knew they must feel as she did to pull out of the river with the wagon dripping water. She'd see to it they were fed an extra portion of grain if the grass wasn't plentiful when they camped tonight.

The roar of the river and their view obscured by the two wagons back of them, the Burts and McGraws weren't aware of a catastrophe behind them.

Well out into the river, one of Mr. Long's horses panicked and began thrashing about in the fast water. Mr. Long quickly handed the reins to his wife and made the grave mistake of jumping into the river to try to calm his horses.

His longtime friend and traveling companion, Mr. Peterson, seeing Mr. Long in distress jumped into give his friend a hand.

The two men were unable to contend with the frightened team and became caught up in the rapid current. Before the eyes of their horrified families, friends, and those who made a futile attempt to save them, the two were quickly swept away downriver.

A hushed crowd stared helpless after the bobbing heads and flailing arms of the two being swiftly carried away and disappearing from sight.

Mr. McKinley ordered Mr. Buland and Mr. Reynolds to immediately swim their horses out and assist the hysterical women and frightened youngsters as quickly as possible to finish the crossing.

For those who observed the tragedy, there was hope that further downriver someone would see the two men and rescue them. However, there was little chance they would make it out alive if they were hurled against big rocks in the river, or caught between narrow crevices in the big boulders and trapped under water. Though it was not said aloud, the chances of their surviving in this spirited river was doubtful.

"It happened so fast, boss, we didn't have time to save 'em," Mr. Reynolds said in quiet defense.

"Wasn't anything anyone could do. The men got themselves caught up in the swift current, and the river's depth is unpredictable. If they've a mind to jump in, like they did without waiting for help, we can only do the best we can. We couldn't make this river crossing if everyone did as they've a mind to. Now, let's get the rest of these folks across. It's not gonna be easy after what's just happened."

Mr. McKinley dreaded moving the remaining wagons. The men were nervous, the women and children frightened. It was going to take more time than he could afford to calm and encourage everyone, but it had to be done.

Ralph McKinley felt the weight of his responsibility to these people depending on him. He'd promised to see them to the finish, but the odds seemed stacked against him. Like now. Two good men were gone because of their poor judgment. Two women were left alone with their youngsters. What were their chances out here in this uncivilized wilderness of making a life for themselves and their families? He couldn't allow himself to get caught up in sentiment and compassion. He had work to do.

"Looks like I'm gonna be takin' a wagon train of widder wimmin to Oregon City, way things're workin' for me," he grumbled to Mr. Reynolds and Mr. Buland.

"If that's so, boss, then this is bound ta be a purdy special train," Mr. Reynolds chuckled. "Word'll get back ta them gents in Oregon and they'll be waitin' for this train with a brass band ta welcome us." However, he and Mr. Buland sensed their boss wasn't to be joshed with at the moment.

"All thet boss feller needs is a good wife. She'd have him in better spirits in no time," Cookie suggested to the two men before urging his horses into the river.

After the crossing, the wagons worked their way over and around the rocks alongside the river.

Mr. Buland came riding down the line of wagons to tell everyone they were to stop for a dinner break under some trees up ahead.

He turned to leave, then turned back. "Mrs. Burt, did you know the rim on your left rear wheel is about to come off? Keep an eye on it. If it slips off, you're gonna need ta stop and exchange the wheel."

Mother thanked him for his observation. "Just what I need: another problem added to my load of burdens." She sighed a resigned sigh but grumbled loud enough that her family heard.

"I see a lot of the people backing their wagons into the river to soak their wheels at night, Mother," Martha suggested. "If we stop by the river overnight, we could do that too, couldn't we?"

"It takes quite a bit of maneuvering to back a wagon into the water, Martha," Mother snapped, "but I guess I need to learn how to do this too."

Mother handed Martha the reins to guide the oxen to where the others had stopped. Martha had to park in the sun to take advantage of what little grass there was for forage. With the boys' help she took the oxen to water while Mother and her sisters fixed dinner.

"Is there anyplace out West without mosquitoes?" Frustrated, Ruthie scratched furiously at her arms and face.

Stephen and the Wilson boys were ravenous with hunger. They watchedMother scrape mold from the wheel of cheese before she cut into what was left from her purchase at Fort Hall.

"This ain't near as big a cheese as ma' grandfather Lane give us when we started our journey," Stephen explained to the boys, dividing up the piece he'd snitched.

Thick slices of cheese were put between cold biscuits. With the Three Island crossing behind them, the Burts, Wilson boys, and Emighs settled down to relax and eat.

During dinner, Mr. Emigh described in detail to Mother the disaster involving the Long and Peterson families.

Martha, listening to the account, wondered, *If it were in favor of their consideration, would these women on this train have made this journey? I don't believe any of these women were ever asked. I may be considered a woman, but I'm too young for my opinion to be of any value.*

Martha noticed Mother ate little after hearing the details of the accident. She didn't know what to say or do for Mother, who was acting so different since Papa's death. *Doesn't she understand we miss Papa too?* Martha wondered.

The Burts heard riders coming. They shaded their eyes with their hands as Juan Fernandez rode into view.

Bertha, when she recognized him, jumped up and waved to him. However, when he didn't acknowledge her, she quickly sat down. She had no intention of giving the appearance she'd been overly anxious and make a spectacle of herself.

"The sun's in their faces, Bertha," Martha said, noting her sister's disappointment. "They probably can't make out our wagon."

As the riders rode near, Neil stopped, but Juan continued on.

"Whew! I'm glad this is over," Neil exclaimed. "I'm starved! I stopped by, and Pa's upset over the death of two men. He told me the families aren't near as capable as you, Mrs. Burt. How ya doing?" He climbed down from his horse.

"I see Mr. Fernandez's got his horse back, Neil. He must be pleased. The meeting with the Indians went well then?" Mother pulled on her bonnet to shade her eyes. "How about some dinner? Cheese with a biscuit do? Martha will be glad to fix you a bite. I'm sorry I have so little to offer."

Bertha thought she would burst if she didn't hear what had transpired between Juan, the Indians, and Mr. Reynolds. She made herself wait patiently for Neil to get around to telling them.

Why didn't Juan acknowledge me? Bertha wondered. *He ignored me completely.* Lost in thought, she heard little of the conversation between Neil, Martha, and Mother.

Neil took a big bite of biscuit and cheese, chewed it thoroughly, and swallowed before answering. "It was scary at first, riding into the Indian's camp. They all came out ta meet us—surrounded us is more like it. Their chief, Old Horn, surprised me. He ain't old atall." He paused to finish off the biscuit, followed it with a drink of water, and cleared his mouth before he continued.

"He and Mr. Reynolds seemed glad ta see each other. I didn't understand a word they said, but anyway, a lot of finger pointing went on. Then an Indian about Mr. Reynold's size was brung over. Seems he was the one who took Juan's horse. For a while there, I thought Juan was gonna fight him, but Mr. Reynolds stepped in and took charge. The Indians did some more talkin' and Juan got his horse back. I saw Mr. Reynolds give Chief Old Horn some tobacca and metals of some kind before we left.

"My pa, was he the one told you about the mishap at Three Islands, Mrs. Burt?

"Yes, Neil, and if I'd had a choice, I'd never have crossed that river." Mother sighed. "I'd rather stay on land any time, even if it takes a little longer to travel, but Mr. McKinley argued against it; said the shale or lava rocks were too sharp to walk on or pull a wagon through."

Bertha came to stand beside Martha and silently pointed to the two new girls, whose families had joined the wagon train at Fort Hall, with two big wagons and teams. The two young ladies, Martha and Bertha's age, were femininely dressed, carrying dainty parasols, and both were flirting coquettishly with Juan.

"Martha, look at him swagger. He's probably boasting about last night."

"I didn't see him do anything to boast about. You've taken a liking to him, haven't you? I'm sorry for you, Bertha. We women, who consider ourselves ladies, don't have time to waste with a dandy like him."

"You can say that because you have a beau, Martha, but look at me. I'm just going to be an old spinster lady."

Martha watched her sister angrily wipe tears from her eyes.

"Come, girls, give me a hand and let's gather things together so we'll be ready when Mr. McKinley calls us to move out."

Mr. Reynolds rode by. "Mrs. Burt, we're coming to a toll bridge down the road, owned by the Hudson Bay Company, and they'll be chargin' three dollars ta cross. There's Indians everywhere around ta help us, though." He rode on to the next wagon.

"Wonder what we'd do if we didn't have the three dollars?" Neil inquired. "For some of us, with the cost of things, who has much money left?"

"I certainly have to watch what pennies I have," Mother agreed. "But I'm not about to ford another river today either."

"Martha, in about three more days we'll be at Fort Boise. I wonder if this is just another old fort without soldiers." Bertha was doing her best to sound jovial and not let the others see how disappointed she was about Juan's ignoring her.

"What's special about Fort Boise, Bertha? You say just three more days. How?" Neil started to say, just as Stephen with Johnny and Homer came running up.

"Wanna know what Mr. Reynolds told us? He says the rattlers out here're longer than a horse, from eatin' sagebrush." Stephen gasped for breath. "If we can catch one of 'em alive, the Injuns'll trade us a horse for it. If we catch three of 'em, we'll have our very own horses. Wouldn't that be a good idea, Mother?" he sputtered.

"What did you do with the puppy, Stephen?" Ruthie asked.

"Mr. Emigh's taking care of 'im for us," said Homer, squinting up at Mother. "He'll help us get it growed up, and he said then maybe Mother Burt would let us keep it."

"Yeah, but guess who gets to feed and clean up after him?" Neil laughed.

"Who?" three little boys asked in unison.

"Nathan, and I told him to keep it on his side of the wagon too," Neil told them. "I don't want it messin' on my side."

"I best get the oxen yoked," Martha stated. "We've got to keep moving if we're ever gonna get ta Oregon." She surprised herself at what she'd just said. *Papa used to say the exact words.*

"Martha, I know it's difficult for your mother with your papa gone." Neil helped Martha place the bow over the oxen. "I wonder, though; Mrs. Long and Mrs. Peterson—how're they gonna make it by themselves? Your mother, she seems ta be doing alright by herself—is she? By the way, how're the new oxen workin' out for ya'?"

"I'll never understand what those Indians were doing with oxen, Neil."

"Probably to eat. They ain't particular is why Pa was able to trade your others off like he did. They was stolen, I'll bet cha. They eat horses too, you know."

"You ask how my mother is doing. What choice do we have Neil?" Martha asked. She was glad he couldn't read her thoughts.

Papa got us into this and then left us. What are we women supposed to do? Neil thinks like a man: we're weak, incapable of enduring, not built to stand up under the responsibility. But what choices do we have?

Instead she said, "Neil, with you and your father looking after us, we're doing fine. Without you? I wouldn't dare to think."

She could see Neil was pleased with her response. Now if she could just say something to make poor Bertha happy, and persuade Mother to smile.

Chapter 40

"This evening's rather pleasant after these last three days of sweltering heat." Mrs. Kenyon plunked herself down on the end of the provision box Bertha and Lizzy were sharing. "I'm so thankful to stop and rest a bit."

"Les Bois." Bertha pronounced the words slowly. "I heard Mr. Buland tell Mother that Bois meant woods in French. I wish I could say it like he does."

"These pine trees are what keep it halfway cool around here," Mrs. Kenyon stated. "Them and this breeze comin' in off this river we keep having to cross."

The men, congregated around their own fire, were in discussion over the boundary issue between United States and Great Britain.

"We bought this land fair and square from France," Mr. Crawford said. "That's what the Lewis and Clark expedition was all about, wasn't it? Puttin' down on paper the boundaries and recordin' 'em?"

"That's why I voted for President Polk. It was one of his promises to get the boundary lines settled before we got out here ta set up our farms and towns. We're here. Where's our promised land?" grumbled Alex Kenyon.

"Ever notice any land we lay claim to in this country, we have to fight for?" Mr. Emigh stated. "It's a wonder there's any of us left after we've had to fight off the Indians, the French, the British, and right now we're fighting with the Mexicans. We've always had disagreements with the British. It's difficult enough getting settled without having to take time out to fight a war first. At least this is my opinion."

"Let me tell ya something, fellows," Mr. McKinley replied. "There's not going to ta be any bloodshed if President Polk has his way. He has faith that the boundary issue between Great Britain and the United States can be settled in a peaceful agreement."

310

"My suggestion for you is ta settle in the Oregon Territory until the boundary is settled. If ya lease land from the British, they'll tax ya for it. You can't own the land; you're not British subjects. You may have ta make up your minds, when the final decision is made: do ya wanna be an American or British citizen?"

"So your telling us land promised ta me and my wife by the United States government isn't there if we move north of the Columbia River? News travels slow out here, and what with the Mexican war down South, it might be a long time afore we find out how this boundary issue is settled," Mr. Crawford stated.

"Wasn't nothin' said like this whin we's tolt 'bout land out West," Mr. McGraw challenged.

"I think President Polk thought it would be settled by now, Mr. McGraw," said Mr. Buland. "By the time we get there, it might well be. There's ships arriving up the Columbia every few weeks, both British and American. They'll bring word soon's the the boundaries're established. President Polk might even show up ta tell us himself."

Mrs. Crawford needed to satisfy her curiosity concerning Mary Burt. "Do tell us, Mrs. Burt, how thee manage with all thy own work to keep up with other things? I know thy family is a help to thee, but I'd think it must be difficult for thy widows alone."

"Mrs. Crawford, I appreciate your concern. Didn't we women take care of the Wilson and McGraw families when Abigale and Jenny were so ill? Mr. Buland and Mr. McGraw changed my wheel just this very evening after the rim came off the other one. I find I was doing the work all along, but sharing did make it a bit easier. I'm sure you others in my position agree."

"My, seeing the differences between the DeLong sisters and your girls, you're fortunate to have good daughters willing to pitch in and help," Mrs. Kenyon agreed. "I seen them two DeLong sisters walkin' about leisure-like this afternoon with Mr. Fernandez. I don't think it's proper myself. Mountain men are rough talkin', and the way them Indians ogle white women, I'd worry 'bout a daughter a mine. I don't know about you, ladies, but I'm findin' the DeLongs aren't the folksy kind."

"Yes," Julie Dixon agreed, "they're different, aren't they?"

Martha was angered at what Mother said. When Papa was *here* it had been difficult; but now that he wasn't, Mother's demands were hard for her and her sisters to deal with at times.

I'm old enough to have a husband, children, and a home of my own, but I'm not allowed to make many decisions, and nothing we girls do seems to suit Mother.

"Martha?" Neil beckoned to her. "Would you mind if I didn't join you tonight? I'd kinda like ta join the men. This boundary dispute has me troubled. Would you mind, my dearest?"

"I sensed you've been upset about something all evening." She squeezed his hand to convey her understanding. "You'll share what you learn later with me, won't you?"

After Neil had gone, Martha found a place to sit down on the ground apart from the women. Lizzy, Bertha, and a few of the other young women came to join her.

"I'd like to be free like the DeLong girls," said Martha. "I resent our mother's opinions of us who are 'good girls.' I can very well understand why Juan Fernandez likes being seen with the DeLong sisters."

"The DeLong girls have far too much freedom. They could easily be kidnapped, my father says," said a young woman who had come to join the girls. "He says the Indians would treat them no better than dogs. If a woman is defiled by a white man, she is an outcast from proper society forever."

"Yes, and I'm told," Lizzy spoke up, "that people will forever say the woman provoked the incident, or else why did it happen? We all know this; that's why it's wise we stay within the protection of our families."

"Fort Boise is just a dried mud-wall Fort Hall, isn't it?" Bertha said, appraising the fort. It was her subtle way of changing the subject from Juan and the Delong sisters.

"It's just another trappers' trading post, only this one belongs to the Hudson Bay Company and I've noticed more Indians around. Mother said the prices are out of reason."

"I hear," Lizzy leaned forward in a conspiratorially low voice, "that Mrs. Long and Mrs. Peterson are planning to leave the wagon train. They've decided to stay here at Fort Boise until they can make it to the mission in Walla Walla. They were heard asking Mr.— oh, what's his name? You know, the store clerk—for a sketch of the route."

Bertha gasped, "They aren't thinking about traveling by themselves? Are they *ferhoodled*?" The girls broke into laughter at Bertha's astonished exclamation.

"What's so funny over there?" Mrs. Kenyon asked, straining to see through the haze of smoke off the fire. When the girls didn't offer an explanation, Ruthie came to sit with her sisters.

"Know what I wish?" Ruthie said dreamily. "I'd like some warm, salted popcorn. I wish we had some now."

"Ruthie, Mother doesn't have extra money to buy popcorn. I'd like some myself," Bertha agreed with her sister.

"Popcorn? What is popcorn?" inquired one of two sisters coming to join the group.

"It's a special kind of corn the Indians grow. Some grow in colors. Like blue, red, yellow. When the corn kernels get hot they explode, and turn wrong side out into big, fluffy white pieces," Bertha explained. "With a bit of salt sprinkled over it, as Ruthie says, it's wonderful, warm, and crunchy."

"I've never tasted popping corn," expressed another surprised young woman. "I should like to know about making popping corn."

"How come your mother never comes to talk around the campfire?" Ruthie questioned her.

"Ruth Ann!" Martha gasped at her little sister's forwardness.

"No, she is right to ask, Martha. Ruthie, my mother and grandmother do not speak good English. This is why we don't come among you. My father would be angry with us if we are busybodies, he says."

Bertha tossed back her long black braid in an act of defiance and lifted one eyebrow. "I like to get acquainted with everyone traveling to Oregon with me, but I guess that makes me a busybody then, doesn't it?

"Oh Bertha, I meant no harm. I didn't mean to say your way is wrong. My father is head of our household and my sisters and I have been brought up to think differently. I like to sleep in my bed and have food to eat. He would cast me out if I did not show respect for our ways or traditions.

"If something happened to our father, my mother, grandmother, my sisters, and me, we would be forced to walk to Oregon. Your mother is better able to care for you than the women in my family. Please tell me, Ruthie, would your mother let us ride with you if something happened to my father?"

"You couldn't ride," Ruthie sighed. "You'd have to walk just like us."

"I wish I could accept the rules made for women as you do," Martha replied, her knees drawn up with her chin rested on them. "I don't know why I feel so hindered by traditions. For me, we women are expected to live by rules if we are to be respected, and rules—traditions, they are made by men and not for women's conveniences. Why don't women ever question them, I wonder?"

"I agree with you, Martha," Lizzy endorsed her. "We are expected to obey silly rules. What rules do men have? They are free to come and go as they will, but then if something happens to them, women are expected to forgo the rules and fill the man's place or find ourselves a man that will take care of us and a family."

The girls were quietly meditating over what had been said, when a sound rose out of the darkness like the emigrants had never heard during the journey.

A roar of such tremendous magnitude and so profound that it created a feeling of vulnerability and fear within each man, woman, and child they had never experienced before.

Mr. McKinley immediately recognized the sound. Through cupped hands he yelled, "Run, run for the fort!"

"My gun, Mr. McKinley?" Neil hesitated on his way up the steep incline from the river to the fort. "I need my rifle." The men around him heard Neil and paused for Mr. McKinley's advice.

"Get to the fort. Guns are useless against this beast. Get the women and children to the fort," Mr. McKinley ordered.

Mr. Kenyon feared for his livestock; anything this ferocious sounding could do a lot of damage, and his livestock were his most precious possession. He needed his rifle. He hoped Ruth and his boys were headed for the fort. He reversed his direction to retrieve his gun.

Mr. Crawford had heard a rumbling bellow like this before. He remembered it coming from the woods one fall night when he lived back in Pennsylvania, but that had been long ago. However, he still recalled the devastation it left behind. Like Mr. Kenyon, he'd feel safer with his rifle.

He hoped his missus and the youngsters would be safely to the fort by now. Away from the firelight, it was difficult for him to focus in the dark. His fear so overwhelmed him that his breathing became difficult.

The hideous roar sounded closer this time. It sent shivers through those hearing it. The animals confined inside the wagon enclosures became anxious and restless.

Mr. McGraw turned back for his wagon. His Jenny was inside. Had she heard the noise? There was no telling what she'd do in her condition.

He pushed his big body into a sprint, but his breathing became labored, coming in short gasps, and his heart beat so loudly it impaired his hearing.

He reasoned that surely an animal able to produce so much noise couldn't sneak up behind him; he'd be apt to hear it. He couldn't leave Jenny alone. He wondered if he'd be able to make it back to the fort with her; maybe he'd best stay in the wagon. The canvas was in ruins and not much protection, but he couldn't leave Jenny alone.

Mrs. Kenyon arrived at the fort gates first and threw them open. By the light from torches kept burning through the night for travelers, she was able to identify most of the faces passing by her but didn't see her Alex.

Sam Emigh saw Nathan but not Neil. He heard Mr. McKinley tell the boy not to go back for his gun. Did Neil decide to return for it anyway? He looked for Martha, but Neil wasn't with her. Was he out there by himself?

Ruth Kenyon and Sam Emigh ushered the last people in and pulled the gates closed after them, just as a mighty thud hit against the mud walls, shaking the compound enough to vibrate the ground beneath. A ferocious roar coming from outside the walls sent everyone into a silent pandemonium, seeking a place to hide.

The men living within the fort made their way with their guns to one end where stairs led to a walkway above. They were heard muttering loud enough for those near them to hear as they ran past.

"Durn grizzly, Ah'ma' gonna give it ta him this time," one of them exclaimed.

"We's gotta git ta gether and hit him all ut one time," said another.

"This pepper shootin' ain't doin' no good," their companion agreed. "He just keeps a-comin' back."

"You young'uns—get back away from thet wall. Thet monster's liable ta reach over 'n' snatch one a ya up. He ain't got patience ta chew. He'll swaller ya alive. Now git outta ma' way," a withered little old man with yellow-stained whiskers yelled at the children.

The youngsters took refuge under a set of stairs at the other end of the fort, while the women silently huddled together in the center on the hard-packed earthen floor.

The four men scrambled up the stairs to the upper deck running the perimeter of the fort.

One of the men on his way to join the other men carried a long-barreled rifle. He stopped long enough to inquire of the women, "Are y'all here? I mean—none of your kinsmen are out in the wagons er elsewheres, are they?"

315

The women looked around to discover family members were indeed missing. It took absolute control for them not to panic or become hysterical.

Junior McGraw approached the women with his little brothers, Willie and Lil' Joe. Tears had wet the boys faces; combined with runny noses and grimy little fists that had rubbed their eyes, they had created raccoon faces.

"Pa, he's out there," eight-year-old Junior said in an unsteady voice. "And Ma's in the wagon by herself."

The women hearing Junior realized these three little boys might very well be counted with the Stern and Wilson orphans after this was over.

Mother Burt quickly stepped forward. "Your pa knows what he's doing, boys. He's likely got your momma tucked safely away." She knelt down and, using their shirt tails, she gently wiped their faces one by one." You fellows need to find Stephen. He's with Homer and Johnny; you fellows stay together so we can find you later."

The little boys nodded their heads. Reluctantly, they turned to search for Stephen.

Mother stood up and abruptly bumped into Mrs. Jackson. "Dat fool man o' mine ain't got no sense" Mrs. Jackson moaned. "Won't move eben whin I done tolt him what Mr. McKinley say. Miz Burt, ma' hands was full wit the young'uns. Oh, ah shore do hopes dat man o' mine knowed what he be doin', an' how upsettin' dis be fer me."

"Mrs. Jackson, there's a bear outside our walls and I rather suspect he's not going to venture far off." Mary Burt worked to keep her voice calm. "The way these gentlemen are talking, he's been making a nuisance of himself around here for some time.

"Neil Emigh and Brian McGraw are both out there, and so are little Ilyllia's mother and grandmother. I don't believe we have to fret." Mother held onto Mrs. Jackson's hand to comfort her friend and hoped she was right in telling Mrs. Jackson there was nothing to worry about.

While the men on the platform above worked on a plan, the grizzly rubbed himself vigorously against the thick mud walls, producing thuds and bumps that vibrated the trading post structure. His scratching created a loud racket along with his noisy sniffing and grunting.

The women and children listened to the fracas going on outside as they waited for the men to come to a decision about the bear before it broke down a wall and attacked them.

"Mickey, bring a torch up here," ordered a man from the ledge above. "We got us an idear."

Mickey, the young man who had talked with the women earlier, grabbed a torch from one of the wall sconces. Holding it high, he ran the stairs two at a time to join the men.

"Now," the whiskered old man said loudly enough for the women to hear, "if'n 'em emmogrunts'll wait and not git gun happy, whin thet grizzly sees the light an' rears his head, we's all gonna fire at once an' try ta hit him 'tween the eyes. It ain't a-gonna work if'n we don't pump 'nough muskets into thet thick skull of his. Thet's why he's always gettin' away. We ain't been hittin' him with 'nough force."

Mickey was a short man and he had to reach up to hold the torch over the outside edge of the wall. Immediately, he was met with a defiant roar and a powerful paw with long sharp claws that made a swipe for the torch. "Joseph, Mary, and Jesus, thet monster bear's standin' up on his hindquarters and his massive head's just below us," Mickey hollered.

Gasps from the frightened women lifted up to the riflemen as sharp cracks and barks from rifles pounded lead into the mighty skull,.

The giant grizzly backed down off his back legs. A big paw wiped at his muzzle. He lifted his head and howled in frenzied protest, the cry echoing throughout the valley. The men watched him thrash about in circles as he struggled with pain and for his life.

Those below waited for the men on the walkway above to give them an account of what was happening; as they listened, the big beast delivered a deafening, enraged, murderous roar followed by a wailing howl posed almost as a question. Then the big body was heard to hit the earth. A loud, drawn-out groan followed and the night was still.

When it was declared safe, the gates were opened and people came out to observe the biggest grizzly any of them, they had to agree, would probably ever see.

The coarse, shaggy, brown body smelled offensive, and the massive head with long, yellowed incisors was of unbelievable size. The great claws appeared to be foot long.

Bets were waged as to its size and weight. Mr. Emigh told the children, "This you see before you has to be the great-granddaddy of the grizzlies."

"It musta come down from way back up in the hills for some reason," was the yellow-whiskered gentleman's opinion. "Sure is a big'un, ain't he? Look, his head ain't even damaged after all thet lead we pumped inta it." He turned away, shaking his head.

The four big horses were fidgety and nervous as they dragged the big body a distance away from the fort for carnivores to gnaw on.

"The hide's of poor quality; it's of little value. Hair's scraggly and sparse in places; unusual for this time of year. He must be old as Methuselah," a trapper remarked.

The crowd watched the horses strain in their harnesses to tow the big body behind them.

Back in the wagon, the Burts were preparing for bed. Bertha pulled the quilt over her shoulders. "What happened to Neil, Martha? Did he get scared and go hide in his wagon?"

"No, Bertha, he's with Mr. McGraw, and they're looking for Mrs. McGraw."

"What?" Mother bolted upright. "Mrs. McGraw—she's gone? Why didn't you tell me?"

Martha heard voices and saw the lights from torches illuminate her canvas.

Mother hastily groped for and pulled on her shoes. "You children stay here. It's too dark out there for you to be running around. Do you hear me?"

The children lay quiet, listening to voices in the night exclaim, "We looked down by the riverside in both directions, Mr. McKinley; she's not there."

"We've circled all around the fort; she's not there either," someone else said.

"Call everyone in," Mr. McKinley ordered. "It's too dark out here to do anything tonight. We'll start early tomorrow and comb every inch of the area around here, but we need daylight ta do the job."

Lying in the dark, Martha could hear voices still calling for Mrs. Mc-Graw. She was no longer sleepy, as thoughts churned though her mind. *Here we are, little more than a month's travel away from the new land Papa came out here to acquire. We started with five families and wagons as an extended family. So few of us are left, and I suppose even fewer will finish this journey.*

She remembered Granny once told her, "Nature picks the fittest to survive." *But Papa had been a strong man, one of the fittest, more so than Mrs. McGraw—she'd been sickly from the beginning of the journey.*

Martha allowed herself to consider, *What if I depend on Neil and something happens to him? Then I'd be like Mother without Papa. I don't think I could be brave like Mother, but what else could I do but go on?*

Martha wasn't able to hear clearly what the women on the other side of the canvas were saying in their soft, low voices, but after a while the voices lulled her to sleep.

Chapter 41

At the break of day, Mr. McKinley assembled a search party for Jenny McGraw, who'd wandered away from the wagon train the night before.

Jenny McGraw, during times of great stress in her life, suffered a strange malady in which she became oblivious to the world around her, and in this state of mind, she had simply wandered away without leaving a clue.

Ruth Kenyon prepared a pancake breakfast, with strong black coffee for the hungry folks, as they returned after combing the woods and along several miles of riverbank. The search failed to turn up any evidence of Jenny McGraw's whereabouts.

As the sun rose higher, Mr. McKinley had forfeited as much the time he could afford. He announced, "The wagons must move on."

"We'll inform those at the fort and get word to the Indians." Mr. McKinley consoled Brian McGraw. "Someone's bound ta see her."

Everyone sympathized with Mr. McGraw's anguish. His features were haggard and his plate of food sat untouched.

He'd been stoic when his daughter Virginia and baby Robert were taken by cholera a few months back, but he'd always been able to care for his Jenny.

"Her strange sickness came about," he told everyone, "from her being treated badly by savages whin she's a lil' bitty young'un. She'd been sickly ever since, but she'd always git better after a while."

Martha, bent over the campfire, turning pancakes, took a moment to stand up and stretch. She gazed at the trees and shrubs around her and was surprised to note how fast the leaves had transformed to fall colors. She felt the decided nip in the morning air, and the sun didn't seem to remove the chill from the mornings until around noon.

After breakfast, Martha requested, "Ruthie, and you too, boys, help me scrub up these kettles." But the boys ran off to see the bear, leaving her and Ruthie to wash the dishes.

Bertha returned with the clean slop jar. "The bear's still there." She pointed to where the horses had deposited the body the night before. "After the sun warms the body later on today, I'll bet its going to smell real bad."

The dishes finished, the wagon packed, they were ready to move out. Martha had to call the boys twice, they and other children were so intrigued with nudging and probing at big bear's carcass with sticks.

Men and women had pitched in to ready the McGraw family for the day, against Mr. McGraw's pleading to wait a little longer for his wife's return.

Tears streamed down his face and dripped into his beard. "I brung ma' family out here ta make their lives better," his voice quavered. "An' look what Ah done ta them. Ma' boys ain't got no ma. I ain't got no wife. What'm Ah gonna do? I cain't go on like this—what fer?" He wiped his tear-stained face and nose on his sleeve.

Sam Emigh walked Brian McGraw to his waiting oxen, put the reins in his hand, and gently turned him in the direction of the wagons ahead of him. Sam, without a word, patted his friend on the shoulder before returning to his own wagon.

Mr. McGraw stumbled along in line with the other wagons but was blinded by his inconsolable grief.

Mother heaved a weary sigh, urging the oxen out. She'd have liked to spend another day finishing her chores and baking more bread. She had been able to cook a pot of beans and sauce up the last of the dried apples. The sack of flour had cost twenty dollars and she hoped that God, in his infinite wisdom, knew about the little grain left in the sack to last the oxen. Forage hadn't been as plentiful as she would have liked.

Every rib on the oxen shows, and so do the ones on my boys, but all I can do is pray we get to our destination soon. She didn't allow herself think beyond one day at a time.

She had no idea if she could obtain a portion of land without Eli. She'd discuss her proxy rights as a widow with Mr. McKinley later, or perhaps Ruth Kenyon could help.

Several hours into the day, Charley Reynolds brought word that Mr. McKinley thought they could make fifteen miles today, even with the late start.

This morning Martha and Bertha had put on moccasins. They looked down at their feet buried in deep, soft dust.

"Oh, Martha—my feet. I hate this! Didn't I say I didn't want to make this trip?" Bertha wailed. "Why didn't I stay back with Granny?"

Mother overheard Bertha's grievance, "You straighten up, young lady. You don't have it any worse than the rest of us. If this is all you can say, then keep it to yourself. We don't need to hear your whining."

"Mother?" Stephen interrupted. "Can the fellows 'n' me have some bread? I'm hungry; me and the boys, we need somesin' ta eat."

"Stephen, stop your fretting," Mother snapped through clenched teeth. "If you're hungry, there's cold pancakes in the provisional box."

"But Mother," Martha said, "the pancakes—aren't they for our dinner? I thought we were going to have—"

Mother exploded in anger. "Martha, I don't need you to tell me what to do. I'll find something for us to eat; that's what I'm suppose to do, isn't it? That and Papa's work."

"Yes, Mother," Martha answered meekly. Tears stung her eyes. Why did she always manage to upset Mother?

"Yeah, look what Papa did to us?" Bertha had no more said the words than Mother's hand struck a resounding crack across her face.

Stunned, Bertha reached to cover her cheek, fast staining with color, leaving a white imprint of Mother's hand. Bertha fought to control her rage. She wouldn't give Mother the satisfaction of seeing her cry. She'd never been hit in the face like this. Clamping her teeth down hard on her lower lip she managed to keep her composure.

The Burt children were stunned and stood in shocked silence after witnessing Mother's attack on Bertha.

For Mother, instant guilt flooded her, leaving a feeling of remorse. She'd lost herself; she was taking her low spirits out on her children. Rapidly she blinked away tears and turned towards the oxen, urging them on. A heavy silence developed between her and the children walking beside her. The band tightened across her forehead; the bright sunshine hurt her eyes. The headache was fast developing.

The children followed quietly along. They blamed their conduct on contributing to Mother's burdens. Each knew what not to do, but not what they should be doing.

They trudged along, wading through the deep dust and against a strong, warm wind whipping around dirt and dust. The girls pulled on their bonnets, their eyes squinted against the blowing grit.

Martha watched Mr. Buland ride up, climb down, and walk beside Mother. The girls heard him say, "We'll be seeing Miz McGraw afore nightfall."

"Oh?" Mother was surprised. "What gives you this notion?"

"Any Indian kidnaps that lady, the first time he hears her squallin', he'll bring her back in haste, trust me."

"Why, Mr. Buland, Mrs. McGraw is a loyal friend and a good mother. What a thing to say." Mother was appalled. "She may have spoken forcefully at times to keep her children in line, but squallin'? Is this what folks are saying about her?"

"You ever notice," Bertha whispered, "when Mr. Buland pays Mother a visit, Mr. Emigh invites himself over? Watch this."

"It's only natural, Bertha. Mr. Emigh is friendly with everyone and he does take all his meals with us. He's part of the family."

"Afternoon, Mr. Buland," Sam Emigh greeted the gentleman. "This wind's starting to kick up some." He grabbed his hat, setting it securely down over his ears.

"I've seen 'em out here where you couldn't see the wagon in front of ya from the fog of dust," Mr. Buland replied. "We may end up havin' ta rope the wagons together to keep 'em from getting lost. Dust storms like this'un are common around this dry area."

"I was surprised with Fort Boise," Mr. Emigh commented. "There were only three buildings, a couple of shacks, the Hudson Bay officials, a few Frenchmen. There were more Indians and half-breeds than inhabitants. I thought the Hudson Bay Company fort it would be more impressive, for some reason."

"Oh my, where's that terrible odor coming from?" Mother clamped a hand over her nose.

"Dead cattle," Mr. Buland informed her. "They bring herds of cattle through, not realizing there's no food or water for 'em, an' they die like flies. We'll have this foul odor with us till the Malheur River. Mr. McKinley always likes to camp at a place called Vale; means "Evil Hour" or something akin ta that. It's named by a Hudson Bay Company feller."

"Believe I heard about this place. A Mr. Ogden lost his year's collection of furs here, and isn't this where the Meeks party followed the unfortunate cutoff last year? I overheard something about these events back at Fort Boise," Mr. Emigh stated.

"Someone's coming," Martha exclaimed, shading her eyes with both hands. "Wonder who's in such a hurry in this wind?"

Everyone paused to wait for the rider.

"Martha! Look—it's one of the DeLong sisters. I can tell by that fancy dress she's wearing. Who's with her?" Bertha tried to focus through the dust-filled air.

Mr. Buland walked out to meet the riders. "Whoa there, what's this?" he shouted

The young man jumped down from his horse to assist Miss DeLong down. "Her folks took off without her."

"I was sitting down by the river; it was so beautiful, and I didn't hear the wagon train leave," she explained to Mr. Buland.

"Your folks don't know you're not with them?" Mr. Buland asked in surprise.

"Oh no, sir—my daddy would never have gone off and left me. This nice gentleman came to my rescue. He found me, beside myself with fright. I do declare I believe I was near hysterical." She tilted her head and offered a smile.

Slowly she straightened her bonnet and smoothed her rumpled dress. "Oh dear, I must look a sight." Her words were directed to the young man. "Can someone take me to my daddy? He's going to be so upset when he discovers he went off without me."

She paused before giving her attention to the Burt girls. "Dear me, you can't possible know how devastating an ordeal this has been for me. Oh goodness me, wherever are my manners? I'm Lucy DeLong. You're the little farm girls Mr. Fernandez speaks of, aren't you? My pleasure to meet you." Lucy stepped forward, expending a soft, dainty little hand.

The Burt girls stood mute; neither chose to acknowledge the outstretched hand.

"Girls—Martha, Bertha, where are your manners, ladies?" Mother stammered. "Miss DeLong has just shared a very trying time for her, and you ignore her?"

Mr. Emigh quickly spoke up. "I think the girls are stunned that Miss DeLong is still alive, when any other lady would have been kidnapped by savage Indians and never seen again."

"Oh—my yes, the thought did cross my mind too, sir. How frivolous of me to take such a chance. My poor darlin' parents, they'd blame themselves forever had something tragic happened to me. I beg to take leave of you dear friends and find my parents."

She faced her rescuer. "Would you be so kind as to escort me to my parents, sir?" She lifted a hand for him to assist her up to ride sidesaddle behind him. She managed, in gathering up a handful of billowing skirt, to expose a silk-stockinged leg for his benefit. Everyone watched as Miss De-Long took note of his expression, gazing down on her well-shaped limb. They watched her look of silent satisfaction displayed before she looked over to them. "So nice meeting you, ladies." She delivered her sweetest smile. "I do so look forward to seeing you again soon."

She rode off, fluttering her fingers to the Burt girls. "I'd like to think the Indians wouldn't find much use for her," Bertha stated softly, watching Miss Delong depart.

"Bertha Elizabeth Burt, I can't believe anything that unkind just came out of your mouth. Why, shame on you." Mother's voice was stern.

"Why, Mother? Whatever were you expectin' outta us lil' ole farmer girls," Martha gushed.

"I best get back to see what Mr. McKinley's plans are for me." Mr. Buland hastily touched his hat towards the women, mounted up, and rode off.

Sam Emigh tuned to the Burt girls. "In my opinion, that young lady has a lot to learn about life. Her parents don't appear to have to missed our Miss Lucky Lucy; maybe they'll be disappointed when she shows up."

"Why, Sam Emigh, you're as bad as the girls. Her parents will be appalled when they realize she was left behind. She appears to be a sweet, cultured young lady to me. Why, can you imagine how frightened she must have been to discover she'd been left behind? I have never forgiven myself for leaving my Stephen behind when we first started this journey. Oh what guilt I've suffered."

"I'll bet we've still a few miles to go before we rest. Maybe we should start moving," Sam Emigh suggested. "I'm glad you filled your water barrel, ladies. There's no water between here and the Malheur River. You heard Mr. Buland."

"I don't like being this far behind everyone," Martha complained, just as Stephen came running with the Wilson boys shadowing him. I'm hungry. Are we going to stop? Mother, we haven't even had our dinner yet."

"Why don't you climb into the wagon and rest a bit?" Mother suggested. "I imagine Mr. McKinley will call for a stop soon."

As the afternoon progressed, Martha felt a definite chill in the wind and it spent her to walk against it.

"How are we going to live when we get to Oregon City, Mother?" Bertha asked, looking up to her mother. "We don't know how to do anything and we don't have any money left."

"In this undeveloped territory, there's a need for schools and teachers," Mother informed her. "Mr. Emigh is a teacher, and maybe working together we can start a boarding school for young ladies, with your help, of course."

"You mean for young ladies like the DeLong sisters?" Ruthie questioned.

"Yes, they would be considered," Mother replied.

"They can't do anything without their slaves, Mother," Ruthie stated. "Will they get to bring their slaves to school?"

"Your papa told me that in Oregon Territory they frown on slavery. The residents don't have it and they don't want it brought in. I'm not sure what will happen in the DeLong situation. Maybe they'll be accepted across the way at Fort Vancouver by Mr. McLoughlin, who is head of the Hudson Bay Company.

"Ruthie, climb into the wagon and peek at the boys. It's awfully quiet in there," Mother requested.

Ruthie climbed down from the moving wagon to tell Mother, "They're all three sound asleep."

"Oh dear, and they haven't had any dinner," Mother replied. "But then neither have we."

"Mother, what is to become of Homer and Johnny," Martha asked.

"They'll stay with us, Martha. We are the only family they have. When Mr. Wilson was killed, I asked Emily Wilson if I might keep the family Bible for the boys. I entered Mr. Wilson's name and death date beside Abby Wilson's. I've put it away for them till later. They'll need it to search for their relatives, but until then, they'll live with us. I rather imagine the new Mrs. Wilson has her hands full with the baby coming. She seems most glad that I have the boys, and she didn't object to my requesting the Bible."

It was nearly dusk when the dusty wind settled down in an arid, bare land with little to brighten or lift the spirits of the travelers.

The Burt family caught sight of a horse moving towards them, its hoof beats muted in a stirred-up cloud of powdered dust.

"Mr. McKinley says the river's ahead and we'll be pulling into camp for the night. There'll be plenty of firewood and water," Mr. Reynolds called out, wheeling about his horse to ride back down the line of wagons.

"Oh, I thought this day was never going to end." Bertha had crossed her arms over her breasts to keep warm. "I'm freezing."

"I'll be glad if there's some protection alongside the trees or bushes. After I use what water is needed for cooking and coffee, girls, please, make sure the barrel is filled before we bed down tonight. I'm so grateful to Mr. Emigh for getting us some coffee beans. They were far too expensive for my pocketbook."

The wagons camped beside willows growing along the riverbank. The tired, hungry children were impatient with the women, who had to grope around in the dark and come up with whatever they had on hand.

Martha had recently heard a rumor that many of the parents were going without supper in order to provide food for their youngsters.

Mrs. Kenyon trudged over to visit the Burts before calling it a night. "This has surely been a long day, hasn't it? I don't like travelin' this late at night. It's enjoyable when Mr. McKinley decides to stop before sunset. Heard about the DeLong girl. Like I said earlier, those young ladies have too much freedom. If the parents were upset about what happened, I didn't heard a word. Don't suppose there is more to it than we know about, do you?" Her suspicions were aroused.

"You mean like Lucy might have been running away?" Bertha asked

"Anyone ever tell you, you have big ears, missy?" Mrs. Kenyon asked.

"Well, alls I can say is I thinks it's mighty strange the young lady comes riding back and no one seemed upset with her being gone in the first place."

"How did you hear about her, Mrs. Kenyon?" Martha asked. "Mr. Buland told Mr. Kenyon and me how she'd come riding up to the wagon train, as brazen as could be, and that when he questioned the family, her parents acted as if nothing out of the ordinary happened. Don't seem natural to me somehow."

"I'm sure the family was very upset about the incident and was keeping it to themselves. They seem a very private family to me," Mother was quick to comment.

"Now Mary Burt, I don't understand, with as many black folks as they have doing their work and carin' for 'em, how they can have very much privacy, but this is only my opinion," Mrs. Kenyon huffed.

"Thanks goodness I don't have to lose sleep over more responsibility than I already have. I'm too weary and imagine you must be too." Mother politely stifled a yawn.

"Yes, I need to amble back. Just thought I'd stop by and see how you were." Ruth Kenyon stood up, easing the stiffness out of here knees before leaving.

"Thank you for coming by, Mrs. Kenyon. I hope you get a good night's rest." The girls watched as the two women embraced before parting. Regardless of their differences, the girls knew the two women were fond of each other.

"We've 'round sixty miles to go, Mr. Kenyon tells me, before the Blue Mountain crossing," Mrs. Kenyon called out, her voice echoing in the clear, cold, moonlit night.

Martha paused to gaze up at the moon. "The same moon looking down on you will be looking down on me," Granny had said. *I miss you, Granny,* she whispered.

Martha hadn't seen Neil all day, and Mr. Emigh hadn't said anything about him at supper that night. She hadn't seen Mr. Fernandez either, now that she thought about it.

Chapter 42

Oregon Territory

"Martha, today is September 14, and all we've recorded in the journal for the past two weeks are the river crossings. Mother wrote about the Snake, Lewis, Malheur, and you put down here about Birch Creek and Burnt River, and I get to write we haven't been near any water for the last few days.

"Last time we filled the barrel was at Farewell Crossing," Bertha said. "I can't believe all those people being brave enough to raft down that wild Snake River. It may be a faster way to Oregon City, but I'd rather walk, thank you very much." She turned back to leafing through the journal. "You didn't put anything down about Emily's wedding?"

Martha was engrossed in the splendor of fall colors amid the gnarled, twisted little myrtle and juniper trees that covered the rounded mountains the wagons climbed through. The deep ravine they were now following was spectacular, with red, gold, and russet of fall-colored foliage.

"I like the man she married, though," was Martha's answer to Bertha. "He'll take good care of her. I didn't know how to spell charivari, so I didn't write anything about their wedding."

"I thought it was fun," Ruthie exclaimed, walking beside Martha. "Mother said they'd be surprised but I was right up next to their wagon, beating on my pan, and I heard 'em talking. They weren't asleep like Mrs. Kenyon said they'd be. I don't even think they were surprised."

"I remember charivari's back home," Martha reflected.

"What do you remember?" A masculine voice surprised the girls. They turned to see Neil behind them, leading a shaggy horse. "Who had a charivari?" he asked.

The Burt girls surrounded him, excitedly talking all at once.

"Whoa, one at a time." He held up a hand.

Bertha asked. "Neil, did you cross many rivers? We could have been there by now if we'd had a boat. We've crossed five rivers while you've been gone. Martha's been really grouchy without you here. Just ask Ruthie and me."

Stephen and the Wilson boys came racing up to them. "Mr. Reynolds just showed us some fresh bear scat," Stephen said. "Oh Neil, you're back."

"You got two horses, Neil?" Homer's attention was drawn to the horse.

"It ain't from a grizzly bear either," Johnny attention still on what they'd just discovered. "It's from a lil' black bear."

Mother came around the wagon to greet Neil and overheard the boys. "Bears? They're this close to the wagons? Then you boys don't leave my sight."

"Martha." Neil handed the reins to her. "This filly—I got her—she's for you."

"For me? A horse for me?" Martha threw her arms around the horse's neck. Her anger at Neil for not telling her he was leaving faded in her delight of the horse.

"Neil, how thoughtful you are, but—" Mother hesitated. "But I'm not sure I've enough grain to feed it. What a pretty little thing. Her markings are exquisite. The dark ears, tail, and mane against the light tan body."

"She's a buckskin. I'll help with her care, Mrs. Burt. She's a sound little horse. Juan helped me pick her out. I wanted to bring Martha something special. She needs groomed; and, by the way, she's broke to ride."

"Mother, can I keep her, please?" Martha laid her head on the filly's shoulder. "Please, Mother? She's to be called Ruby; it's my favorite gemstone."

"If Neil's willing to help with her care, I suppose," Mother sighed.

Giddy with excitement, Martha was about to throw her arms around Neil's neck, but pivoted instead and hugged Mother.

"I know where there's a curry comb." Bertha and Ruthie ran for the box under the wagon bench.

"I get to use it first." Ruthie ahead of Bertha rummaged through the toolbox.

"You get a horse all of your own, Martha? I'd sure like a pony," Stephen wistfully complained. "Homer and Johnny would like one too; then we wouldn't have to walk all the time. Our legs get so tired. Walk, walk, walk, that's all we ever do."

"Maybe we should look inta gettin' you boys horses," Neil offered.

"We need 'em, Neil; we get tired of walking all the time," Johnny Wilson stated. The horse jerked her head up and down in response to his rubbing her soft muzzle.

"I see everyone is getting ahead of us again today," Mother grumbled, but her remark had little effect on the family, giving their attention to the new horse.

"Care to walk ahead to my wagon?" Neil asked Martha.

"Would you mind, Mother?" Martha asked, looking to Mother for approval as she handed the pony's hackamore bridle reins off to her sisters.

"It looks to me like you've already made up your mind." Martha was taken back by Mother's remark but noticed a faint smile across her face.

She felt the anger she'd nursed over Neil's thoughtlessness at leaving her so suddenly without an explanation had subsided. She shyly looked up at him. "I missed you."

"I missed you too," he said, looking down at this woman he'd found so difficult to get along with only a few months ago.

At the time, when he and Juan had decided to ride ahead and investigate the land, it had seemed right, but now a nagging guilt made him feel he needed to explain his abrupt departure to her.

"Yes, you've been gone a long time." She too decided he owed her an explanation, and she didn't intend to make it easy for him to explain it away.

He reached for her hand. "I know. I had to get away, Martha. I had to see the country and determine the lay of the land. I had to get an idea of where best to settle, and the train is too slow. I can't explain it, but Juan felt as I did. We needed to see more. I don't know what to say to make you understand.

"On the other side of these mountains is a place called the Willamette Valley, Martha. It's spread out between a range of mountain covered with evergreen forests. The earth is rich, fertile, and there's an abundance of water. Oh Martha, it's purtier than I imagine the garden of Eden was. You'll see, and right now it's all golden and flamin' in fall colors. I lack the words to describe it plain enough for you to see.

"You see, Martha," he continued, "I've plans for you and me. I want to marry, settle down, and have a family. Pa and I talked about putting in an orchard."

Martha was caught by the excitement in his voice and could imagine the beautiful valley he described. She could visualize the orchard laid out in neat, tidy rows of fruit-bearing trees put there by Neil and herself, their roots dug deep into the fertile soil.

"Neil, this all sounds grand, but I can't—I can't leave Mother. She's a poor widow woman Now; she's no longer entitled to a land grant. Besides I would never consider marriage before…." She paused. "I've—well—you see, I always thought when my soul mate came along, he'd court me proper like. You are suggesting marriage?" She could feel her face warm from her remark. *There, I've said it,* she thought.

"You think I didn't want to take you in my arms the minute I came back and saw you? And you, Martha—you hugged the horse but not me, and then I noticed you hugged your mother but not me, and I gave you the horse."

"Oh Neil, I wouldn't have dared," Martha gasped. "Not in front of everyone."

"Why, will your momma run me off with a buggy whip? I'll take ma' chances. I'm sure of how I feel for you. I don't make plans but you're on my mind. I dream of you by my side. Tell me you feel the same, Martha."

An intense silence followed. She knew he was waiting for her answer.

"Is this a proposal then? You're asking me to marry you, Neil? I wish I could, but as I said, I have a widowed mother, two sisters, and three brothers. You'd have to make room for us all, Neil. I can't leave them, and I'm sure you don't reckon to marry my family."

"You've got it wrong, Martha. I'm going to marry you, and your family will be taken care of. Your mother, sisters, and brother."

"Brothers, Neil? Mother says we're keeping the Wilson boys until they're ready to find their relatives, and they have a sister also. Little Pearl, remember?"

"You know, Pa said something about himself and your mother too. Something about a school? But I didn't pay him, no never you mind, because Pa's dream he shared with me was to come West and grow apples."

"Yes, I heard about the school too. You don't suppose they…? Mother did tell us of such a plan, when Bertha asked her what was going to happen to us once we got to Oregon City."

"Pa needs a wife. That would mean double his amount of land, and if I have a wife I can get double the amount too. Martha, do you have any idea how much land that would be? We'll farm next to each other, Pa and me. Oh Martha, what orchards we'd have."

She felt herself picked up and whirled around. "I'm the happiest man alive." He swung her with such force, she had to put her arms around his neck and hang on.

"Just a minute, Neil Emigh." Martha made herself appear serious, and in a stern voice demanded, "Put me down this instant and tell me. Your feelings, they are because I am useful to help you gain more land, or it's me you care about?"

The Burt family watched the two. "Oh no, he's gonna be kissin' her next," Stephen predicted to Johnny and Homer. The boys gave into a fit of giggles.

"Ugh, k-k-kissin' a girl!" Homer squeaked. Johnny covered his face at the idea.

"Mother! Look at Martha—look at her!" Bertha gasped.

"Ladies, your sister knows what's proper. It's time she was married and settled."

"I'm really gonna charivari them good," Ruthie laughed with delight.

"Neil, everyone is going to talk, and they'll say things about me like they do about Lucy DeLong."

"I'm not gonna put you down till you kiss me." Neil held her tightly against him. "I don't care who sees us. It's you I care for, Miss Burt, soon ta be ma' Mrs. Emigh."

Martha felt herself melt with his warm lips pressed against hers. A sensation built within her that she couldn't explain. He slowly set her back on her feet, and she reluctantly withdrew from his embrace and quickly reached to pull her bonnet on to hide her flushed face.

"Will this kiss count towards my courtin' you?" he inquired.

"Oh, whatever is my mother going to say? Everyone's going to think I'm a brazen hussy, and it's all your fault, Neil Emigh." However, unable to conceal her happiness, she wasn't convincing.

"This means we're officially courtin', doesn't it?" he asked. "Your mother won't be angry with us, Martha, I guarantee it; not when I tell her I'm taking the spinster lady off her hands. Why, she'll be happy ta have ya gettin' hitched." He chuckled then quickly ducked away before Martha could deliver a playful blow to him.

"Neil, oh, how dare you," she whispered. But a wonderful sensation had taken hold of her. Martha didn't feel bold at all, only full of an indescribable, elated joy.

"Neil, I have to ask you something; be serious. The other day, I—that is, Bertha and I think—Lucy DeLong might have been trying to run away from the wagon train. The incident took place while you were gone. Do you think it had anything to do with Mr. Fernandez?"

"Martha, ma' love, this was one of the reasons I took off with Juan. Lucy thinks she's quite smitten with him, when he told her he was promised to another and was on his way ta fetch his bride-ta'-be and bring his family north. Lucy promised ta do a lot of things that night. He told me she acted like—what's your family's way of sayin' it? 'Furhoodled?' He has a problem with wimmin'; they all like him too much.

"I'm sorry I didn't take time to say good-bye, Martha. I promise I'll never treat you bad again." He appeared so serious Martha had to laugh.

They were returning to her wagon when she stopped abruptly. "Wait a minute! It takes four years for apple trees to grow. How will we live until then?" Martha didn't want him to feel she was questioning his plans and maybe being too forward; after all, they weren't married yet, but didn't she have the right to know what she was getting herself into?

"I've got it planned out, Martha. I'm gonna get you some chickens and you'll raise chickens, and with the eggs and chickens, we'll supply merchants till the apples get ripe."

With hands on her hips she turned to face him. "Why, all you need is a hired hand. You'd marry me, thinking to get yourself a free hired hand?"

"Martha, I never meant——you don't like the idea? I've made you unhappy. Oh no, don't be angry,. I just thought—I'd build us a house while you tend the—we tend the chickens, and the trees grow. Martha, I don't even have a home for you."

She pretended to concentrate on a Queen Anne's lace bush growing beside her. She plucked a blossom, twirling it between her thumb and finger, and inhaled its pungent odor before she looked up at him. It was difficult to hide her feelings. "Neil, I want to be whatever will keep you in love with me. I love you too, and who knows? Maybe we'll do good at raisin' chickens, eggs, spuds, and apple trees."

"Martha, the reason I know this will work for us is you've the wisdom ta see that workin' beside me, we can do it. We'll make ourselves a great home. Juan and I agree, it's gonna take hard work to make our dreams succeed; and, by the way, we neither of us could see Miss De Long doin' much more than sittin' in a chair with a fancy lil' teacup. Besides, woman, I've loved you for a long time. It makes me feel good inside to be tellin' you this. You ready? Let's go tell your ma and my pa?"

Hand in hand, they made their way to share their plans, but as they came face to face with their families, word had passed quickly and before them were their extended family members gathered also.

333

Later that evening, Martha discovered, as she thought back, she'd ignored her sixth sense that had alerted her when she first saw Neil that very first day of her journey. She was about to marry a man with the vivid blue eyes, same as Papa's, and who came to her rescue and saved the pan of hot, roasted coffee beans. If this were true and a part of the good Lord's plan for her destiny, she was blessed indeed.

Everyone who came to congratulate them had already suspected a wedding would take place, they said. They have even gone so far as to assume they would be part of the coming event. Martha was surprised but also pleased.

Suddenly Martha was horrified to realize, *I've nothing decent to wear for my wedding. Where's Bertha? She'll have some ideas. No, I'm not doing anything till I've finished this journey.* "

Neil received affectionate pats on the back and listened politely to the men's advice. If he'd had any doubts in mind about his coming marriage, the thoughts were put to rest by the fellowship of the men around him, who shared of their hopes and dreams of new land, and the responsibilities they, as men, assumed for their families.

He had difficulty referring to his elders on a first-name basis; however, the male policy was that when he expressed his desire to take on the responsibility of a wife and family, he was accepted as their equal.

"Martha, tell us, how does love feel? How did you know he was the right one? How soon will the wedding be?" Her sisters and the other young women were inquisitive and full of questions as they chatted before the campfire until bedtime.

Ruth Kenyon expressed, "I'm not sure how ta describe ma' feelin' seein' our youngsters gettin' married. David Wilson kept his and Miss Emily's marriage quiet, but it was a necessary wedding, if you follow what I mean. I highly approve of this new husband of hers, under the circumstances."

Elsa Crawford softly voiced, "It's good for us, Ruth. We need to see something good come about from this difficult journey we've so nearly finished. It takes courage for our young women to carry on with life as we live it. And our Martha? She's got the courage it takes. I admire thy daughter. Thou hast been a good mother, Mary."

Mrs. Jackson, who had traveled a long ways with these women, and had had her share of worries, agreed with the others. "With ma' ailin' husband, the young'uns does give a lift ta da weary day afta day of keepin' up our courage. Ta seed a young'un with so much faith gives dis ol' woman hope. You be holdin' grandbabies afore long, Miz Burt. Jist seems like whin ya think ya done got your own babies raised an' struggled ta keep 'em alive. Why ma' own baby girl's old 'nough now, she be startin' her woman's way soon, an' next she be marryin' and den comes ta babies." Mrs. Jackson heaved a profound sigh. "Lordy, 'pears ta me like we women ain't nebber gonna gets no rist on dis ol' earth."

"Juan—Neil, tell us about your sight-seein'? What did you learn, besides the Injuns and the British own this country, or so they think?" Mr. Kenyon chuckled.

"Mr. Kenyon—Alex—sorry, sir. Juan and I learned, we're not gonna get past the Dalles, and overland with wagons. There's steep cliffs and some big falls spread out a good mile down the Columbia River gorge, so we'll have ta go by river ta Oregon City."

"Sí, we need rafts we build ourselves, or rent from Señor Juan McLaughlin one of his bateaux. The wagons we leave behind; the bateaux does not take on wagons or cattle. There is no other way; big boats cannot make it up the river because of big rocks and the falls. To rent the bateaux costs eighty dollars American money."

Mr. Reynolds, whittling on a stick he'd picked up off the ground, spoke up. "The emigrants traveling down the Columbia River Gorge will come out at Fort Vancouver, on the right of the river. It's a British trading post, ya understand; takes in furs and unloads ships coming in from the ocean. Oregon City's just across the way.

"Head of the fort is John McLaughlin, and his boys're told under strict orders ta discourage Americans from settling, but the 'Great White-Headed Eagle,' as the natives call him, I've found ta be a Christian man who goes out of his way ta extend help ta all the penniless, starvin' emigrants he can." Mr. Reynolds held up the stick animal he was in the process of carving to eyeball his work.

"We heard from some other settlers about Jesse Applegate, tryin' ta enlist the United States government in helpin' him open a trail across the inland mountains inta Oregon City by comin' in from the south," Neil explained. "I'm plannin' ta settle in the Willamette Valley. So the shortest way is by water. The Applegate route's too harsh and dangerous. A team would have little chance of makin' it through, 'pears like ta me."

"We were also warned by an Indian tribe, callin' themselves the Klamatha, who incidentally have been known ta raid and cripple passing wagons when they're usin' the inland route." Neil's long legs were stretched out in front of him. He rotated the grass stem he was belaboring to the other corner of his mouth. Relaxed, he was enjoying himself with his acceptance by these men.

"Folks told Juan and me a few wagons have been rescued by the army militia and irregulars riding ta keep watch over the trail, but they can't save 'em all."

"For this reason," Mr. McKinley said, "we take rafts. You can make your own or, as the fellows here say, rent a raft or a bateaux, either way. The inland crossing is too dangerous by foot. Ma' men and I will help ya take the river route from the Dalles; those of you wanting ta go inland are on your own."

"Mr. McKinley, you suggested we go by river at the Dalles, but what if we wanna cross the river, say, ta the Whitman mission? I'm kinda interested in the lay of the land across the river. I realize it's British-held land, but the plateau looks like horse country ta me," Alex expressed. "I'm willin' ta take my chances with the British."

"Sí. Señor Kenyon and myself, we think it better range land for horses. But this is within British territory, you say, Mr. McKinley?"

"Yes, fellows, but try and lease the land from the British, until the boundary lines have been established. I'm pretty sure we'll be hearin' news concerning the boundaries at any time. We, Buland, Reynolds and me, haven't seen near the British troops we saw last year, so they must be pulling back. I know for a fact President Polk has held firm ta the notion that they must back up to the 49th Parallel, and he's willing ta fight if he must."

"Last thing I heard," Mr. Buland spoke up, "it was being referred to as the 'Fifty-four Forty or Fight' in Washington, and it ain't none of it changed far as I know."

"For you thinkin' 'bout takin' the Applegate Trail, there's a toll when you start at Laurel Hill and there's only about 150 miles of finished trail," Mr. Reynolds explained. "There's places where it's so steep downhill, I've been told, folks have ta wind ropes around stumps or drag hundred-foot trees ta slow their wagons down the inclines, and tie wagons to trees or build scaffolds to haul 'em up steep grades.

"This stretch has proclaimed itself the worst trail in the whole of the Oregon Territory. Seems robbery ta me thet you'd pay toll then not make it out alive. Should collect prize money at Barlow's Point fer being able to endure through thet uncivilized crossin', way I see it."

"So what you're sayin'," Mr. Crawford repeated, "is that, this is a way of goin' around that big snow-capped mountain ahead usin' an unfinished trail?"

"That's about it," Mr. Reynolds told him. "Someday it'll be a fast way ta Oregon City, but she's nothin' but a rugged, rough trail right now. For me, I'm glad McKinley here insists on usin' the Columbia ta git us ta Oregon City."

"Señor McKinley, around us the natives, they are much friendlier than the ones from the south, sí?" Juan questioned.

"Oh yes, Juan, the Cayuse, and Nez Perce're friendly buggers, and they'll work hard for a day's pay too. Don't forget they're experts on fishing," Mr. McKinley said.

"Guess I best get some sleep." Mr. McKinley picked himself up off the ground. "The rest of us will probably get a good night's sleep, but our young gentleman here, with love thoughts on his mind." He thumped Neil on the shoulder. "Let me tell ya, Neil, marriage is a good contract when ya got the right woman beside ya, and your Martha's a fine lady in my estimation. She comes from a good family; conducts herself properly. She's a hard little worker. She'll make you proud, Son. I believe I speak for all of us."

"Thanks, Mr. McKinley. My pa had a lot to do with it. He taught me how ta pick out the best qualities in dogs, horses, and wimmin." Neil enjoyed hearing the men's chuckles and guffaws.

"I hope you're not intendin' ta repeat ta her what you said here. Especially in the order ya gave 'em." The men laughed even more uproariously at Mr. McKinley's remark.

"When do I start cookin' fur the weddin' feast?" Cookie wanted to know. "Neil, you best take good care of thet little lady, else ya got Cookie here ta contend with. If'n I's younger, I'd give ya a run fer yur money fur thet lil' gal."

"You know wimmin, Cookie. Next part is up to my bride. I did the askin' ta get her. We ain't got time ta get hitched right yet, but I'll let you know." Neil tipped a saucy salute to the men as he departed the group.

Mr. McKinley turned to Sam Emigh. "Fine man, your son."

Sam beamed with pride. "Thanks, McKinley. I believe they'll make a good match."

After the others were bedded down, Martha waited for Neil. "I'm glad you came by to say good night." Their tender kisses only served to make their parting more difficult. Pulling away, Martha asked, "The women were full of questions and advice. What did you men discuss?"

"How lucky I was ta have such a purdy woman willin' ta marry up with me." Neil held her close, reluctant to let her go.

After the two had parted, Martha stood alone in the moonlight. She inhaled deeply the cold fall night air perfumed with the fragrance of dry earth mixed with sagebrush.

Granny, if you're looking up at the moon tonight, and you, Papa, are you watching over us? Do I have your blessing? Oh, and Papa? Neil is almost as perfect as you. Would—I wonder—could you see your way to give Mother your blessing, if she were to marry again, Papa? My life would be so full if only the two of you—Papa and Granny—you could be here with me. I love you and I miss you so much.

She turned to the wagon and her bed; another busy day of the journey had been completed.

Chapter 43

The evening before, Mr. McKinley had warned the folks of the dangers they would face tomorrow, navigating through the Blue Mountains. "The trail's so narrow at times you'll wonder if there's room for your wagon. Water seeping through the rocks can make the trail slippery; thick brush and fallen logs create problems. Sometimes big boulders will block our path and need to be moved. It's a slow, cumbersome ordeal."

The families followed the trail through pines, firs, and cedars growing with a variety of other evergreens, their roots dug deep into the forest floor, their thick trunks choked together, with their tops lifted into the sky.

The immigrants discovered trees covered the saddles of the mountain range in every direction as far as the eye could see, except here and there where patches of bare mountain rock lay exposed.

Martha drew in a breath of fragrance. "Mmm, the smell from these trees."

"I can't walk and look up at the same time," Bertha protested.

"My neck's tired from looking up through these treetops for the sky," Ruthie said.

"I can tell you this: I could use a torch. These trees filter out so much light," Mother commented. "Then when we come out into the sunlight, the glare is blinding. I've noticed a heavy mist hangs over the trees but lifts as soon as the sun comes through. I wonder if it's like this all year round or just this time of the year?"

"It's like the trees have smoke rising off them in the morning sun," said Martha.

"Watch out, Ruthie," Neil cautioned her as he approached. "Walking backwards like that, you're apt to fall over a log or rock behind you, and it's a long haul to the bottom of this mountain."

"These trees are so big. How do they get like this?" Homer Wilson squinted upwards into the massive limbs and branches of the mighty evergreens.

"Homer, ma' pa says some of 'em was here before Jesus was on earth," Neil replied.

"How can you tell?" Stephen was so inquisitive he didn't see a protruding rock in his way and stumbled over it.

Nathan, beside his big brother, explained, "Pa told me when you cut down a tree, there's rings around the inside to tell how much it grows in a year. I wanna know why it's called timber. Mr. McKinley says we'll be climbing above the timberline."

"This trail is just as Mr. McKinley said. Nothin' but jagged rock and fine gravel. It's a wonder we don't slip and end up down one o' these gulches below," Mr. Kenyon grumbled, urging his horses up a mountainside.

Ruth Kenyon discovered, "This mud Mr. McKinley talked about is simply a thin coat of dirt over the top of these rocks. If we ever start to slide, there's nothing going ta keep us from plunging right off this mountain. For my part, I don't dare look over the side. If I were ta see the remains of a wagon down there I'd be terrified to death."

"That's a wall of solid rock ahead of us. Do we go under it or climb over the top?" Bertha had to fight her way through a thicket of brush and brambles to walk alongside the wagon.

Martha watched the wagons ahead disappear as they descended a steep bluff, to crisscross back and forth down the mountainside until they reached the lowland covered with dry grass and whortleberry, better known as wild blueberry bushes, amid swarms of mosquitoes.

"I'd wager we just made a good three-thousand-foot drop," Mr. Emigh calculated, gazing up to the top of the cliff. "In this gravel, it's a wonder we haven't suffered any fatalities. That stream over there is swift and likely full of quicksand, so that means the wagons are going to mire down."

"Oh my goodness. Lord have mercy," Mrs. Crawford mumbled, as the horses slid and struggled to pull the big wagon through the soft silt that clung to the wagon's wheels.

During the morning, the teams strained to pull the wagons up the steep grades, then backed in their breechings on descent into deep ravines.

Martha was exhausted from the steep climb in the thin atmosphere. At the top of each ascent she noticed she wasn't the only one to rest momentarily and catch her breath.

From her position atop the mountain, Martha observed the thick woods round her deepen from hues of grayed greens to black, dense forest. How easy it would be to become lost in the endless trees. How did trappers and mountain men know to find their way through these thick forests?

"I thought we were following the Oregon Trail," Martha said. "Are we lost or is Mr. McKinley and his party making a new trail? This isn't a trail we're scrambling through."

"We're in the mountains, Martha." Bertha too, was winded. "Look, there's snow ahead of us on those mountaintops. My breath comes out looking like smoke."

"The higher up we go the colder it gets," Mother agreed. "This morning there was a scum of ice on the water bucket. It was so cold last night I could have used an extra quilt."

Stephen, pausing to rest, inquired, "What if I climbed one of these big trees? Do you think it would take me very long?"

"Wow! Ya could see the whole world," Johnny exclaimed.

Mother, breathless from the climb, looked up. "It would take all day to climb one of them. What if you get stuck up there? We don't have time to stop and bring you down."

Her bedraggled oxen, their heads lowered, were exhausted. Mother worried they could finish the journey. The youngsters were tired, but she didn't dare allow them to ride. The oxen were struggling with the weight of the wagon as it was.

"We should be coming to a place to rest soon," she said, as much for her own benefit as to encourage her family to keep moving.

No sooner had she spoken than Mr. McKinley shouted to the procession of wagons coming towards him, "Pull off when you get to the clearing ahead."

He watched the wagons pass him. They were moving slowly but there hadn't been any major misfortunes, so maybe it was better this way. From the looks of the gray sky ahead, he worried about an early, unexpected snowstorm at this elevation.

"It's taken us five hours to get this far," Martha overheard Mr. Reynolds say. Bertha and Ruthie raced back to the wagon. "Mother, we were in the tall grass, behind those bushes over there," Ruthie exclaimed, "and some Indian men were spying on us. When they saw us looking at them they disappeared."

"I'm not picking any more berries for our dinner," Bertha announced.

341

"Girls, this trail is used by trappers, Indians, settlers, and whoever else needs to travel. You need to be careful and not wander away from the wagons. Stay together, whatever you do," Mother warned them.

"Got us some berries to go with our dinner," Mr. Emigh said, coming up to the wagon. "Indian women over yonder are picking whortleberries. The Indian who gave me this hatful of berries, is Nez Percé. Said he and some other men were keeping watch over their young women; they're easily kidnapped."

"Those must be the Indians we saw," Ruthie whispered to Bertha.

"I suggest you stay close to the wagons; there's no way of telling a good from a bad Indian," Mr. Emigh cautioned the girls.

Mother wished she had more to offer for dinner than cold pancakes, but her food supplies were nearly gone. Had she time to build a fire, she'd have made a lard, flour, and water gravy for the pancakes. Her lard supply was low too, as she had to use it for the wagon wheels. She remembered how adamant Eli was about keeping the axles greased.

During the rest break, Mr. Reynolds and Mr. Buland traveled ahead of the wagons to scout the area. At the top of a ravine, they noted they would have to attempt a good sixty-foot climb to the ledge where they were standing. It was clustered with big, precariously perched boulders carried down by winter snow avalanches or washed down during the spring thaw.

Mr. Reynolds advanced to the nearest rock. "It isn't safe for the wagons ta be windin' up this mountain." He gave a hefty push to a big boulder beside him and sent it careening down the mountain side, taking debris with it on its rapid, thunderous crash into the valley below.

"One boulder dislodged like that could move this whole mountainside and bury anyone tryin' ta make the climb," Mr. Buland said. "It's surprising you didn't start an avalanche just now."

"We'll have to travel some twelve to fifteen miles over these mountains in front of us and I wonder there's a trail's wide enough for the wagons," Mr. Buland posed doubtfully.

The men decided getting the wagons down into the rocky chasms below was near impossible for the teams, and any river below would be too swift to navigate.

"And probably the river will be full of quicksand anyway, "Mr. Buland ventured.

While the two were debating the situation, a lone Indian rode up, got down from his pony, and came to squat down beside them. Their exchange of greeting was a silent nod to each other.

Mr. Reynolds broke the silence. "Which way did you come through the mountains?" He recognized by the colors in his headband the young man was Nez Percé.

"You come too far. Pass is between this peak and that mountain." The young, buckskin-dressed Indian stood up to point. The men followed to where he indicated a small gap between the mountains they had just descended.

"Have to backtrack. How did we miss it? We'll lose time but I don't see any other way of makin' it through." Mr. Buland groaned at the thought of the time wasted by having to retrace their steps and cross the mountain again.

After sharing their biscuits with the Indian, who explained, as he mounted up to ride off, he was headed for Fort Boise, the men worked their way down the mountain to give an account of their misfortune to Mr. McKinley.

They explained how the Indian pointed out the gap in the mountain to the southwest they had somehow missed. "There's nothing we can do but retrace our steps."

"My greatest fear is that one of those unpredictable rocks above is gonna plunge down this ravine. It would mean sure death to anyone in the way," Mr. McKinley worried.

The men agreed, but how else would the wagons be able to move out without disturbing the ground and perhaps unsettle the big boulders giving them reason to roll?

"Let's use the rear wagon as the first wagon," Mr. McKinley instructed.

Word was passed down the line for the folks to turn their wagons and follow the wagon in front of them out of the canyon.

Several hours later, after winding their way through the gap, the wagons, with Sam Emigh in the lead, descended into a grassy meadow surrounded with timber on every side and thick whortleberry bushes full of fruit, and with an ice-cold creek rippling through the area.

Wagon wheel ruts, horse and foot prints satisfied Mr. McKinley that they were on the a trail being used by others. The trail they'd come from had been so narrow in spots he was grateful they hadn't met with any opposition along the way.

A distance grew between each wagon, created by the fatigued, lagging pioneers, the high altitude, and the steep climbs, but once they caught sight of the valley spread out below them, their spirits lifted and their steps quickened.

"Looks like the garden of Eden," Ruth Kenyon whispered, "after what we've come through today."

Soon the aroma of fresh coffee blended with wood fires as camps were set up.

Mr. Kenyon, Neil, Juan, and Mr. Reynolds had barely departed for some hunting, when the sharp crack of rifles echoed from the mountains around the camp.

The men were met by excited women and children when they returned with several large mule deer carcasses between them.

Stephen and his friends were playing with the little dog they'd accepted from some Indians a few weeks earlier. The boys would swoop down on the little pup, who bravely charged back at them, licking their faces, when they rolled around in the dry grass. Every once in a while it sat back on its haunches and emitted a ferocious immature growl, sending the boys into gales of laughter.

While the men were busy dividing up the meat, the camp was visited by two Indians on horseback. It was with apprehension that the men greeted their visitors. Down between these mountains, the pioneers knew they were easy targets for invading Indians.

"From the Cayuse tribe," the men introduced themselves. Taking fresh salmon from packs on the back of their horses, they offered a donation to the evening meal.

"Might as well make it a combined meal." Mrs. Kenyon, made her way to each of the twenty wagons to inform the women.

Mother spared enough flour and sugar for Martha to make wild blueberry cobblers. "Make the batter thin," she instructed the girls.

Mrs. Jackson asked for some flour from Mother to add with her cornmeal and made pans of sweet, golden cornbread.

The Indians showed the women how to plank salmon and cook it beside the campfires. Fresh venison strips were laid on racks to roast. The big valley soon filled with tempting odors, sending appetites raging as impatient folks waited for supper.

"Our bread isn't rising properly and the beans aren't done," the women complained.

Cookie explained how in the high altitude, water boils faster and sal-eratus, a combination of cream a tartar and soda, doesn't work properly, but everyone was too hungry to grumble for long.

After eating their fill, the Indians mounted up to head east while there was still enough light to travel.

"Mr. Emigh, would you please see this bread goes with them?" Mother handed him a cloth filled with meat and the unleavened, heavy bread.

The Indians accepted the food from Mr. Emigh, who insisted, "Gifts in return for the fine salmon." Stowing the food in their packs, the two natives lifted their hands in farewell as they rode across the meadow into the mauve and dark purple mountains in the dusk of the evening.

The pioneers were treated to the sight of moose and herds of deer coming into the meadow to graze along side the livestock.

It was a temptation not to kill fresh meat. Mr. McKinley pointed out. "It will only spoil, we don't have time to take care of it properly."

" I feel refreshed now I've eaten." Martha told Neil.

"Do you think you and I might encourage Mr. McGraw to play a little music before bedtime?"

Mr. McGraw was still in mourning for his Jenny. But at the young folks request, though his heart wasn't in it, and he'd nothing better to do, he decided to play for them.

"I'se member how ma' Jenny like ta dance," he said softly. "Thet's how I met up with her. She come ta this dance and she's the purtiest one thar."

Martha caught him as he wiped a big hand across his eyes and hur-riedly turn away for his wagon.

After canvassing around in the disorder of his wagon he appeared with his jaws harp. Junior, too, had to search for his jug. Before long the two of them were sitting on the tail gate of their wagon filling the evening air with melodious music.

Two men from the Delong wagon came to join them. One with a fiddle and the other a banjo. The black man lively strummed his banjo his accompanying antics uplifted those who came to listen.

The folks, who weren't to weary danced, others settled back to listen, clap their hands, and sing.

The DeLong Sisters, Lucy and Desiree, included themselves in the dances and between them monopolized Juan Fernandez. Miss Lucy Delong, as was her haughty way, made it obvious to treat him as cooly as possible.

Martha, watching Mother dance with Mr. Emigh and thoughts of papa suddenly flooded her Mind. A lump swelled in her throat, her eyes filled as memories flashed back to when she'd last watched papa hold mother in his arms. She swallowed quickly to rid herself of the sensation. Would memories of him always be so painful? Mother was so changed, too.

Neil glanced down to see a tear roll down Martha's cheek. " What's the matter?" He whispered. "What's upset you like this?"

" Neil, it's memories of papa and mother. They--" She turned away and made for the sanctuary of her wagon.

Neil caught up to her and took her in his arms.

She didn't refuse or resist him, even when he gently lifted her chin. "Dearest, I know how it hurts. It still hurts when I think about my ma. Let me help you When these sad times come. Please Martha."

He wiped the tears from her cheek with a finger before he lightly kissed her. His kiss was offensive at first, invading the refuge of her soul, but slowly its gentle tenderness reached deep within to ease her pain and fill her with a soothing peace.

Bertha's grumbling by the fireside attracted their attention. "I hate mosquitoes. Isn't there any place on earth without bugs? She glanced up as Neil and Martha approached. " I'm tired of slapping mosquitoes. The smoke tends to keep them away but it burns my eyes.

Martha---what's the matter? Are you crying?"

"Oh, no, Bertha, it's the smoke. It burns my eyes too, but you know what I hate worse than mosquitoes? It's mountain climbing. I'm sick and tired of going up and down and back and forth. Sometimes, I'm of the notion we're creating a trail as we go.

"I know," Bertha confided. " I didn't want to scare Mother, but a coupld of times the wagon wheels were hanging off the edge of the cliff it was so narrow and what if someone were coming up the other side?"

"Have you noticed?" Bertha said, her voice was almost a whisper. "How Lucy Delong's treating Mr. Fernandez. She's being mean and nasty." Bertha itched at her face and arms. "I'm being eaten alive," she squealed. Then in her soft voice. " I'm sorry, but did you notice, she won't let him dance with anyone else?"

In the firelight, Martha detected her sister's impish grin.

Mother pulled abruptly away from Sam Emigh. "Oh, Sam, my goodness, the boys. I completely forgot my little boys." She hastened off towards her wagon.

Neil and Martha glanced up as Mother neared the campfire. " Martha?" she gasped. "The boys--- have either of you seen the boys?"

Mr. Emigh followed in close persuit and heard Ruthie, from inside the wagon. " Mother, we're in here, we went to bed."

Mother's audible sigh of relief was shared by those around her.

"We all need a good night's rest, don't you agree, Neil?" Mr. Emigh winked at his son and beckoned with a nod of his head.

"Oh, yeah, coming." Neil stammered, giving Martha a quick squeeze before he joined his pa.

Mother climbed into the dark wagon without even saying goodnight and discovered the boys, along with a furry little body. "Mercy, what's this." She mumbled.

"The boys asked Nathan if they could sleep with 'Snaggle-tooth.' Tonight." Ruthie yawned.

"What?" Mother voiced loudly.

Homer, who was now awake told her. "Nat said we could have 'Snaggle –tooth' for tonight. We waited to Ask you, but you didn't come back so's we decided to on to bed with him."

Her boys were safe and thought we didn't appreciate the idea of them sleeping with what she considered a dirty, flea ridden pup, there was little she could do about it this late.

Mother came down from the wagon. "I don't know about you girls, but I'm worn far too thin to do anything more than sleep.

"Mother?" Bertha, not yet ready for bed, asked. " I wish we women had pretty dresses like the DeLongs. I hate the way I look and dress. Why can't we be the beautiful ones. I wish I was."

Mother was quick to assure her. " You don't need fine clothes to make you beautiful, Bertha. You've been blessed with beautiful thick dark hair, lovely features and a sweet smile."

She reached to pull Bertha to her. "You've a strong spirits. You're responsible with out the help of salves or servants. My darling daughter, we're going to face a lot more people like them, when we get to Oregon City. We've not much left and we're going to meet women who are already settled and have had more time to accumulate nice things. Your family is blessed to have you. You give sustenance to our courage, my darling. Your day will come. You mark my words. Your papa was always so proud of his girls."

Nothing more was said. The three women with their hearts aching for papa quietly prepared for bed.

347

Martha, before giving into sleep, allowed herself to think back over how demanding and exhausting the day had been for everyone, for the livestock. The climb through the mountains was far from finished.

The chill in the early morning and night air told her that The winds of autumn were blowing. She loved the colorful foliage that crunched underfoot, but it was almost October.

She recalled the morning after the fourth of July, when Mr. McKinley said he'd try to have them in Oregon City the first of September.

Chapter 44

Mother handed Sam Emigh a cup of morning coffee As the Kenyon's Alex, Ruth, and their sons made their way to the smoky, wet wood campfire. Mr. Kenyon stood over the weak flames and vigorously rubbed his hands together to warm them.

" Sit down and share a cup of coffee with us."Mother invited. "I wouldn't have coffee if it weren't for Mr. Emigh, I simply can't afford it. What a miserable, dreary morning. I haven't been warm since that chilling rain yesterday."

"It'd be a waste a' my time complainin' about these awful last few weeks. Let fancy picture for herself the struggle we had gettin' through the mountains. Wonder we didn't lose anyone." Mrs. Kenyon held the warm cup to her chilled cheek. Martha hovered near the fireside. She felt isolated in the cold, foreboding, dense fog that surrounded and shut her in. *At least the rank stench of drying fish is diminished in the thick fog*, she thought, pulling her shawl close around her.

"I'm sorry to be leavin' the train." Martha's attention was drawn to Ruthie Kenyon. "I'm gonna miss everyone. I'll be living out of the wagon till ma' house's built, and the weather's gettin' unpredictable already. Ma' boys need ta be in school. Maybe I'm gonna have to school 'em myself."

Martha wrapped herself cocoon style in her shawl but could still feel the chill and dampness in the uncomfortable mist of the cold October morning.

"We, Mr. Emigh, and my family," Mother explained, "have decided to hire a raft to complete our journey. It's cheaper traveling if we combine our possessions, and far less expensive than hiring a bateaux."

Sam Emigh and Alex Kenyon, with cups of coffee in hand, excused themselves to make their way down to the busy river, where skiffs, canoes, flatboats, rafts, and bateaux were being utilized to convey the wagons and families downriver to points of their destinations.

"Surprises me," Sam Emigh said. "There aren't ferryboats on either side of the Celilo Rapids. The need to haul supplies is bound to increase with the amount of folks coming out West. I've been led to believe Hudson Bay Company stocks the forts from here to Fort Hall by overland and navigating quite a few rivers. It would seem worth their while to dredge a channel through the Snake and Columbia rivers for boats to carry cartage."

"Never be done, Sam. Hudson Bay likes to think of 'emselves as a tradin' post, and besides with the boundary issue, they're not apt to do anything."

"Mornin' there, Tom," Alex greeted Mr. Crawford. "Ya got yer name on one of these boats? You and Sam shoulda built your own rafts, like those fellers over there." Alex nodded towards a new raft made from freshly cut poles flattened on the top side, skinned, and laced together with ropes.

"Mornin'," Tom Crawford grumbled, his shoulders hunched against the chill. "Wonder how many days we'll be holed up here till we start downriver? I'm startin' ta take on the stink of dead fish." He lifted his head, looking around. "Think the fog's startin ta lift some."

"From the looks of these wagons, not many took the overland route from Laurel Hill. I know the trail's too rough for me," Sam Emigh admitted. "I can't help but note how many wagons are being abandoned by folks unable to pay the cost of transporting 'em.

"Juan and Neil went downriver with another family earlier this morning." Sam shook the dregs of coffee from his cup. "The fellows are probably in Oregon City by now, and Juan's boarded a ship headed south."

"I miss McGraw." Alex stated. "It worries me about him taking the overland route. Said he liked the idea of the adventure now it's just him and the boys. Said he'd be seein' us if we ever made it to Oregon City."

Sam and Tom chuckled at Alex Kenyon's remark.

"I hope Brian makes it alright. He's likely ta be six months on that trail, and with winter comin'," replied Alex, "Juan said he'd see me come spring."

"I don't know about you fellows, but I'm lucky to rub two coins together," Tom Crawford said. The men were quiet as they peered through the fog to where they heard water slosh onto the banks of the steel grey river.

"I wanted to start a business, but everything's so expensive. I may have to find work for a year or so, and put money aside," Tom sighed. "I've gotta house the family through the winter. Been debating if I should sell the team and keep a horse. It'll be expensive if I have ta board it."

Elsa Crawford, carrying a pan of biscuits, appeared out of the mist along with Lizzy. "I don't have much flour, so these biscuits are mighty thin. I did put a bit of sweetener and spice in 'em. Lizzy doesn't care for 'em, but with some coffee they're fine."

"The men just walked off somewhere," Ruth Kenyon told her. "I can't make 'em out in this fog. Can't make up my mind if this is a fine drizzle or mist. Maybe it'll burn off like it tends ta do and the sun'll come out."

"I'm surprised to see thou art still here, Miz Kenyon. Thou ladies know Miz Jackson decided to take the overland route, same's Mr. McGraw."

"You know, Elsa, I thought the lady had some common sense." Ruth helped herself to coffee before she selected a biscuit. "Mmm, delicious buns. As I was saying, without a strong man, I wonder if she'll make it with that passel of young'uns and that sickly husband of hers. She's foolish is what she is," Ruth said, her mouth full of biscuit.

"She's out of money. At least she has a fairly decent team of mules and faith in the Lord," Mother offered in defense of Mrs. Jackson. "Martha's upset with me for using the little horse Neil gave her to team up with my remaining ox. No one told me laurel leaves were poisonous. What a miserable death for my poor ox. I don't know about you ladies, but I'm out of nearly all my supplies. I thought I had enough dried apricots and apples to last me forever."

"Know exactly what thou means," Elsa admitted to her own plight.

Dreamily Mary Burt explained how when she started this journey, the wagon was loaded to the breaking point. She had a good man, a sturdy yoke of oxen, a bit of money. Today, she found herself no better than the starving Indians she'd seen along the way.

"Mr. Burt didn't leave us too well off. I'm not sure I'm entitled to any land, and like you, ladies, I've discarded nearly all the housekeeping essentials I brought with me."

"Mary Burt, don't be frettin' and feelin' sorry for yourself. Put your girls to work sewing ta help with your expenses when ya get settled. Martha's to be married. You'll be living with them, I'd suspect. You've got your hands full with the extra mouths to feed." "Say—I was wonderin', if somethin' happens ta you, or you Elsa, who's gonna take the Wilson young'uns? Elsa, you've done a good job with that lil' Pearl. I shoulda took her. I'd like havin' a girl around."

Wistfully, Mary divulged, "I wanted a nice wedding for Martha, but I don't think they want to wait that long. Neil can get more land if he's married. I've been pondering the idea that if the DeLongs have to free their slaves, maybe I could work for Mrs. DeLong; she's not used to doing her own work."

"Mary, hear me out: don't be foolish. I—well—others of us have watched you and Sam. You think on it. I suggest you get married quickly. Love is for youth. You'll be provided for, and Sam gets more land by taking you on. A decent woman can't make it on her own out here alone, Mary. It's a man's world, ma' darlin', no matter what we women may think."

"Why, Ruth Kenyon, speak for thyself. Mary's done fine by herself so far. Our Mary's a fine, strong, Christian woman. Leave her be, Ruth; let her decide for herself. No one bothered to ask her opinion when Mr. Burt was took, now did they?"

"It's good sense, Elsa. We've come a long ways, and we did it with hard work, not hangin' on to some foolish, impractical notions."

"What ever art thou talkin' about, Ruth Kenyon? Impractical notions? I'm not aware of anyone being impractical about anything." Elsa was indignant.

"Excuse me, Mother, we'd like to walk down by the river?" Martha interrupted the conversation between Mrs. Kenyon and Mrs. Crawford.

"You young ladies ain't had your fill of walkin'?" Ruth Kenyon inquired.

"It gives us something to do, Mrs. Kenyon, we're so confined in the wagon," Bertha answered. "And Mother hasn't found any sewing for me to do."

"In this fog, I'd rather you girls stayed close by," Mother requested.

"Lizzy, if you see thy father, tell him I'd like to know what he wants to do next. That man's so fidgety when he's not busy. I've need water to wash and wood for the fire for cookin', but he'd soon as drink pure lye first; that's woman's work, he says. Our Louie's a son of his father I'm sorry to admit."

"All I've left to show for the journey are a few sacks of seeds to plant," Mother said. "Oh—best I stop this grumbling, and count my blessings. We've our health and I've my children." Mary Burt sat quietly staring into the fire. *It's this cold, miserably wet weather that's lowered my spirit*, she thought, putting another stick of wood on the fire.

"It's been a journey, hasn't it?" Ruth Kenyon agreed. "I hope I don't have to get another wagon ready to move out ever again in my lifetime. I know what you're saying, Mary. My boys could use a bit more meat on their bones, but they're healthy. I've nothing much left to set up housekeeping with either."

"The crossing through the Rocky Mountains was easier than what we've had coming through these Blue Mountains," Elsa Crawford said as she dreamily gazed into the fire. "I hope I never, ever have to climb another mountain with a wagon."

The women looked up to see the men approaching the fire with a stranger. "Mr. Knight just crossed the river from Fort Walla Walla." Mr. Emigh offered the rugged little man a cup of coffee. "Mr. Knight tells us the 54th Parallel was peacefully ratified between Congress, President Polk, and Great Britian well over a month ago. Britain argued for the 54th Parallel, but settled diplomatically on the 49th and are on the move north. There's some island they get to keep in the bargain. He says the fellows in Oregon City were glad the offer was accepted without bloodshed."

"Oh no, Mr. Emigh, I beg to differ with you, sir. The whole of the Oregon Territory is angered that President Polk settled for the 49th and didn't go further. You see, sir, let me tell you about Mr. McLaughlin. He's head of Fort Vancouver and the British Territory, you know, and is the greatest man I'll ever live to see.

"You see, there's peace between us and the Indians because of him, and he's helped a lot of emigrants financially. He's granted favors, more than he'll ever see returned. He's done a lot to further the development of the Northwest Territory and now he's lost his position. We American citizens feel President Polk reneged on his pledge to us to settle above the 49th, do ya catch what I mean? Our slogan was "Fifty-four Forty or Fight."

Mr. Knight lowered his voice. "I'm sorry ta see McLaughlin go." His face with red lips barely visible through a mass of unkempt whiskers puckered as he gently blew on his hot coffee, before cautiously taking a sip, then wiping his mouth on a grimy shirtsleeve.

"Mr. Knight shared a bit of interesting information with me." Sam quickly changed the subject. "When Lewis and Clark wintered over with the Clackamas Indians, an issue came up for a vote, and both the black slave of Mr. Lewis, named York, and a Shoshone woman called Sacajawea, acting as an Indian scout, signed their names on the document. Seems Lewis and Clark claimed all citizens of United States had a right to vote. If these facts were known it sure would have upset some law-abiding folks where we're from."

"Interesting, though, the Clackamas Indians weren't invited to vote. Can you imagine changing the Constitution or Bill of Rights? I'm not opposed to having women and black folks vote," Mr. Emigh added. "It just has never come up as an issue is all."

"You've said a mouthful with that remark, Mr. Emigh." Mrs. Kenyon looked him straight in the face. "I venture to say, before this group of women, you've made yourself a hornet's nest. Seems to me any woman ends up alone and comes this far should have the same right to a parcel of land and right to vote as any man."

The three men and Mr. Knight were grateful to see several men approaching the campfire.

"Mr. Kenyon? We're here to help you take your wagon apart and get you loaded, sir."

Everyone gathered to see the Kenyons off. The big barge was made ready, with the disassembled wagons, along with the teams, and the two families sharing the crossing.

Mrs. Kenyon pulled Martha aside. "Probably won't make it to your weddin' but I want to give you a lil' something, Martha. You need something old, and this broach was my mother's. I want you to have it for your weddin' day." Ruth Kenyon took Martha's hand and placed a beautifully crafted cameo broach in it.

"Mrs. Kenyon, are you sure?" Martha gazed down at the exquisite piece of jewelry. "You brought it all the way out here. It was your mother's. I'm so honored. I'll wear it with pride. I can't think of words enough to thank you for your gift." Martha reached to embrace her. "I'll never forget you, Mrs. Kenyon." The two pulled apart, with moist eyes.

Men, women, and children pressed close, wishing a safe journey to those departing. Indians hovered about, waiting impatiently to get the big barge underway.

As the Kenyons climbed aboard, Alex promised to "see ya'll in Oregon City come spring, when we come for supplies."

For those who remained on shore, there were a few tears, and emotions were subdued. The folks were weary and anxious to get settled themselves before winter set in.

The Burt girls, in their hearts, had found Mrs. Kenyon a gruff old lady, but they'd developed an amazing attachment to her during these past six months.

Martha and Bertha were standing apart from the crowd when a heated discussion between a French-speaking man and a young Indian caught their attention.

The girls were appalled when the large, fierce-looking, dark-haired man quickly jerked a knife concealed in his long buckskin leggings, and in disbelief they watched him shove it into the ribs of the Indian.

It happened so quickly, the girls could only watch in stunned horror. The enraged man savagely shoved the startled Indian away from him and pulled back a blood-covered knife.

A surprised expression crossed the face of the young Indian. The girls watched his eyes grow enormous before he slid to his knees and collapsed onto the ground. A pool of frothy blood slowly poured from the fatal wound and formed around his body. The young Indian men standing nearby quickly and quietly grabbed the inert body of their friend and hurriedly dragged him away.

Martha was used to seeing arguments between the white men and the Indians, but she'd never witnessed anything this brutal. She watched the folks around her, going on unconcerned about their business.

She turned, running for the wagon as she fought to suppress a feeling of nausea. Bertha followed her sister and pressed her face against the wagon wheel to quiet her trembling. She was unable to help her sister as Martha vomited.

Mr. McKinley had also witnessed the scene, and followed the girls. "You'll be alright," he comforted ashen-faced Martha, who had pulled the hem of her skirt up to wipe her face. She hated the foul, sour taste in her mouth, but she was too weak to move.

Bertha, with tears streaming down her face, whispered, "It was hideous—ugly. I don't care if he was an Indian, he shouldn't have had to die the way he did."

"Ladies, hear me out. The West is untamed and barbaric. You've already seen and heard a lot of uncivilized things. It's the nature of life out here; it's not delicate."

He paused to search for the right words. "I'm sorry you had to see this, but I wanna tell you something very important. It's you women, good Christian women, who are going to change all this. You're going to demand dignity and culture. You're about to harness this untamed wilderness with your gentle ways.

"It's not easy for you to understand after what you've just seen. It's going to take a lot of patience and courage to tame barbaric deeds. But it's going to get better as time moves on. I'm encouraged that brave women like yourselves will endure this wilderness and someday make this a decent place to live."

He hadn't meant to get carried away with his fatherly advice. He nervously fingered his moustache before he politely excused himself and hurried off in the direction of the river.

The girls clutched onto each other to soothe their frayed emotions. The sisters, hand in hand, walked back to view the mist lifting above the river and the big barge that was carrying the Kenyons to their new land, where they would build on a legal section of land within the Oregon Territory, the land bought through the Louisiana Purchase, now officially part of the United States.

"When is it going to be our turn to leave?" Bertha murmured, watching the barge distance itself from them as it slid across the Columbia River.

"Soon," Martha gently reminded her sister. "Mr. McKinley says we just have to have patience and courage. Everything takes time out here in the West."

Chapter 45

By mid-morning the sun had penetrated the dense, wet fog. Martha's spirits were lifted to perceive the river below change from steel gray to shades of blue green with diamond, sparkling sunlight dancing atop it. The warm sun burnished the red gold of autumn leaves and enhanced the green foliage, but the rank odor of drying fish was a continual assault to her nostrils.

The repetitious diet irritated the already cranky Stephen. "Oh no—not beans and fish again. Don't we got no other food to eat 'sides beans and fish, Mother?" he whined. "You use ta make cobblers. Wish we had some cobbler, don't you, Johnny?" he inquired of his staunch ally.

It's true, Mother thought, *the meals do consist of nothing but dry bread, boiled beans, and fish. They are monotonous, but what choice have I?*

Mother invited Mr. Knight, who had come to the fireside with Mr. Emigh, to take dinner with them. "It's simple fare," she apologized. "I wish there were more to offer, but it's filling."

The families enjoyed Mr. Knight, a pleasant, congenial little gentleman, and he enjoyed himself as he shared his knowledge of the country. "You take the Snake River," he said, "so named because, like a snake, it's wound itself from the east with the intention to join the might Columbia River and make itself more powerful.

However, the Snake River allowed itself to be swallowed up by the mighty Columbia River," he went on to explain, "and at the Wallula Junction, west of Fort Walla Walla, you see, the Snake had come from so far and had worn itself so thin, the mighty Columbia, being bigger and stronger, hadn't had to come from such a long distance, and took away all the Snake's power and the poor Snake no longer flows any further west.

"I've traveled from beginning to end of the Columbia and seen it all," he boasted. "How the river continues on through the territory to Fort Astoria, where it'll end by pouring itself into the Pacific Ocean."

Mr. Knight sympathized with Mrs. Burt, doing the best she could with such a pitiful supply of food left. He knew it was common knowledge any pioneers making it this far were down and out.

To Mr. Knight's way of thinking, after listening to Stephen, best kind of youngster was a sleepin' one. Only kind he could abide. The young master was too outspoken for his liking.

And what of myself? he asked. Here he was accepting their meager fare, and he'd come empty-handed. He'd plan to see Mrs. Burt had some flour before the day was over. There had to be some for sale or trade, but few pioneers would have any he knew.

"Let me tell you 'bout the falls east of here." Mr. Knight hoped to divert the family's attention from the tasteless meal.

"They're 'bout a good day's travel from here. The Indians come from the four corners of the earth to collect their supply of salmon, from Wyam Falls, they call 'em. Means 'Echo of Falling Water.' To us folks, they're Celilo Falls, or 'Thundering Falls.' Anyway—from far back, at the beginning of time, the Indians tell me, they've come to fish these falls."

"Will they let us fish there too?" Homer interrupted, squinting up at Mr. Knight. "Would they let me and us fellers catch any fish?"

"Hush, Homer. Listen politely to Mr. Knight. Eat your dinner," Mother softly reproved him.

Mr. Knight never paused. "The heavy, big rocks making up the falls were once a rock bridge over the river—so the story goes. The Indians shared with me that their ancestors tell of some greedy spirit sisters, who became angry at Coyote, their spirit dog, for feeding their salmon to the starving Indian people, whom the sisters took a dislike for, and in a fit of anger they busted the bridge to keep the salmon from getting upriver. So the salmon are forced, to this day, so the Indian legend goes, to climb up over the fallen rocks when they return home to spawn, they're duty in life.

"The falls are at different heights. Some twenty to twenty-five feet high. Now, the river has no other way to get its big body of water through but to push it though a narrow gap with steep cliffs on either side, so the salmon struggle by swimming against the rapid river, and up over the rocks, to get upstream from whence they came."

Mr. Knight was pleased with himself, capturing the family's rapt attention.

"Only the bravest, strongest, Indian men could build wooden scaffolds out over the top of those dangerous falls," he told them. "And even to this day they stand out on those scaffolds, with long rawhide strips tied to their wrists and a spear on the other end, to spear the salmon trying to leap up over the falls. Once a salmon is caught, it's hauled in by means of the rawhide strips tied to an Indian's wrist.

"You have no idea how death defying it is, standing out over that turbulent water. Why—if they fall, there's no savin 'em in that white, swirling water. It'd suck 'em up and dash their brains out and they're gone. It amazes me how some of them sit out on those old rickety scaffolds and using long poles with sharp spears attached and stab the fish as they try to make it over the falls. The salmon are big; they weigh somewhere 'round forty pounds, you know."

Mr. Knight paused to take a few bites of beans, a hunk of fish, and a bite of dry bread he'd soaked in the bean broth. He wiped his whiskered mouth across a well-worn grimy shirt sleeve, before resuming his story.

"Mr. Knight, how come they have to spawn?" Stephen inquired. "If I's a salmon, I wouldn't want to jump over some falls just to go die."

"Good discussion for later, Stephen." Mr. Emigh made quick eye contact with Mary Burt, who displayed a smile of grateful relief. This delicate subject she knew little about.

Mr. Knight, undisturbed, continued on. "Indian tribes all come to fish, smoke, and dry 'em for their spring and winter food supply. They take turns, one tribe after another, so's all the tribes get a turn. While they're together, they trade smoked buffalo jerky, dried berries, blankets, beads, moccasins, skins, and horses among themselves. Kinda reminds me of the harvest festivals taking place back home this time of year.

"I wish you youngsters had time to see the falls. Someday, when you come back this way, I'll take you to see them," Mr. Knight said. "It's a sight to behold. Been going on for thousands of years. Imagine it'll go on forever."

Later, when they were alone, Mr. Emigh took the liberty to explain the spawning ritual to Mary Burt. "A female deposits her eggs in shallow pools under river rocks, and a male follows and covers the eggs with milt, it's called, to fertilize them," Sam said as he leaned back against a wagon wheel, gazing out at several osprey skimming close to the river in search of food.

"I'm surprised to learn there were so many different species of salmon," he said. "The chinook is the king of salmon, the sockeye or blueback also have red flesh, but the cohos, I'm told, have silver markings and a pink flesh.

"Their life cycle fascinates me. From birth, they swim downriver to spend three or four years in the ocean, before returning to spawn and die in the place they originated."

There followed a brief silence between them. "I hope I haven't offended you, Mary. I thought the information might be helpful—should Stephen question you."

Mary's face was hidden in her bonnet. "Thank you for educating me, Sam. You explained it very nicely. I realize I'm in for a difficult time—with Eli gone. There's so much about life Stephen needs a man to discuss with him. I hope I'm capable when these times come. I'm finding it's difficult without relatives around."

Sam watched as Mary, intently studied her fingers, confessed her inadequacy in dealing with delicate matters. He would have liked nothing better than to take her in his arms and tell her he was here to help her and share her life. *She's not ready yet,* he thought. *She needs time to get her life in order before I ask anything of her.*

To ease the tension, he quickly changed the subject. "Wouldn't surprise me if we didn't leave the Dalles this afternoon. There's still enough daylight hours for the three hours to Oregon City." He pushed himself away from the wagon wheel. "Think I'll mosey down to the river; maybe I can help finish a raft."

Martha made her way towards the river with a water bucket. Leaning down to fill the bucket, she heard a discussion between two men nearby. "Them settlers don't wanna build their own rafts but don't mind jawin' 'bout how much time it takes to build one." One of the men sounded exasperated. "I'm gonna give up buildin' ta hire myself out an' steer rafts downriver from now on."

"I'd like to build a boat big enough to haul foreigners and their wagons, all at one time," said his friend. "'Cept a keel would drag bottom real easy like when pullin' inta shore. Figure if'n I had a boat I'd be so rich afore tha year's out, I'd be gittin' get myself to San Francisco and buy up the town," he gwaffed.

Martha couldn't help but wonder why such an idea hadn't already been considered, a boat like how the Mississippi River boats were made. The wagon trains were losing time waiting to be transported downriver, and how long would this weather last? There must be a better way than all the work and time it took to build the rafts.

These men don't understand us, calling us foreigners, and that we have little money to afford passage downriver. He won't be getting rich fast off our kind. Martha stood up with her bucket. *Back in Illinois, I could look for miles around and the scenery changed little, but here it changes every few feet.* She stood in awe of the world before her. *I wish Papa were here to share this with me.*

Martha watched as a man came up to join the two men. Setting the bucket down, she pretended to busy herself, picking small white pebbles out of the water.

The men appeared to know each other and dressed in the same worn, stained, and greasy outfits. Even at her distance from them, Martha was offended by the reek of stale body odor. She quickly pulled on her bonnet to hide her face as she shyly peeked out to approve of their strong, young bodies.

The new man was eager to tell the others of his luck. "Got myself a dividend," he referred to it.

"I was haulin' this wealthy family, with their darkies, downriver," he said, "and halfway there, up above us on the cliff was a good dozen or more Injuns on ponies, lookin'down at us. I quickly pointed out to the gent that I was friends with 'em, and there was probably a good hundred of them, these being only the scouts that showed themselves.

"The feller got real nervous, out here on the river, nowhere to hide his wife and a couple of sweet lil' fluffs. One of 'em kept trying to catch my eye."

Martha immediately recognized his description of the DeLong family. She continued her search for white rocks as she listened.

"I told the gent, if I gave the Injuns a lil' gift, like some money, they'd leave us alone. Then I said, 'Wonder if ya know Injuns think the black folks possess bad spirits.' You shoulda seen his wife. That little lady flipped around, reached up under her skirt, an' snatched up this lil' bag of money, handin' it to her husband, who nearly tore my shirt off stuffin' it down ma' neck.

"'I'll see the Injuns get this, sir,'" I told him. 'But it ought to be worth somethin' to ya for myself to make all this transaction and such.' The man never blinked an eye—he sweated a lot, though—reached into his coat and handed me some bills for my services. While he's watching, I turned and waved to the Injuns up on the cliff, and they waved back like they always do. I wanted it to appear like I was sending 'em a message. I swear ta you, I saw a look of pure relief on the old man's face—even waved at 'em himself."

"Where was the family headed?" one of the men asked.

"I dropped them off at Fort Vancouver. They couldn't get into Oregon City with them slaves, you know. McLaughlin'll take care of 'em. That old fool's nothin' but a pushover fer them kind of folks. Seen him do it time after time."

The two chuckled at first then, when they realized what their friend had done, burst into uproarious laughter, slapping their thighs at the same time and pounding their friend on the back.

Martha hurried back to tell Mother and her sisters what she'd witnessed. Coming up she heard Mrs. Crawford excitedly telling them, "Mr. Crawford's decided to buy us a raft after all. We're not staying around to build one. We'll be leavin' first thing in the morning."

"Mother, I have something to tell you." Martha pushed her way in to share her story. However, much to her disappointment, her story wasn't received by Mother with much amusement as the men had.

The sun's warmth gave purpose to Martha's day. It would have been perfect, had she known how Neil was doing. He'd left her only this morning when Mr. Emigh sent him ahead to Oregon City in search of lodging for the two families.

"Are you Mrs. Emigh?" a young man coming up to Mother inquired, followed by three bare-chested Indians.

"No, sir. Mr. Emigh should be around here, though. He was just here." Mother shaded her eyes with her hands. "Oh dear, where is he?"

Martha glanced over to see the three Indians staring at her. Their expressions bore insolent leers as they stood with arms crossed over their chests, feet wide apart, brazenly staring her down. Martha was thankful to see Mr. Emigh appear and divert they're attention.

The Burt women heard the man explain, "We've a short, pine pole raft ready, if you're interested. The fellow we built it for found it too short for his use, but she's ready to float, if you're at all interested, and I'll let ya have her cheap. I'll even throw in the use of a dugout for your women folk."

Mr. Emigh asked to be excused. Taking Mother's arm, they walked some distance away. Martha saw Mother look up and nod her head to Mr. Emigh before he turned back. "I'll take it," he said.

With the assistance of the Indians, Mr. Emigh's two-wheel wagon was dismantled. It would take less room than the Burt's full-size wagon, leaving more space on the short raft for the contents of both wagons along with the horses and ox. Mr. Emigh planned to ride on the raft with the boys. The women were to ride in the long, cedar dugout canoe.

The Burt girls whispered their fears to each other, how uncomfortable they felt around the insolent staring Indians and the thought of riding in a canoe with these men. They had no choice, under the circumstances, but to ignore the insufferable savages.

Good-byes were said. Mother and Mrs. Crawford embraced, promising to find each other in Oregon City. The Burt girls returned hugs with Lizzy and promised to get together, as they climbed into the waiting canoe.

To Martha, the little family looked forlorn standing on the riverbank. Mrs. Crawford's impeccable white aprons had fascinated Martha from the beginning of the journey; she watched Mrs. Crawford use one end to dab at her eyes.

Louie shifted from one foot to another, aloof and bored. He'd showed little sentiment during the long journey and at the farewells between the families.

A sensation of melancholy took hold of Martha's spirit at leaving these folks behind, but there wasn't time for nostalgia, as one of the Indians impatiently hurried her into the canoe and shoved it out into the swift river.

Martha turned to face the shore one last time, and caught a glimpse of the only remaining provisional box of the four Papa had built for the journey. This one contained all the worldly possessions they owned. Mr. Emigh was attempting to cover it with the canvas from the big wagon. Her heart leaped at the sight of the little rocking chair sitting on top the provisional box. Mother's little chair was still with them.

The women bravely bore the river ride; it was a terrifying experience with the canoe laden down, sitting deep in the water, skimming along so swiftly.

Martha observed how green vegetation clung to every nook and cranny of the gigantic rocky cliffs on one side of her. On the other side of the river, steep cliffs ascended above to grassy plains; she inhaled the fragrance of cedars, pines, and firs they were now coming into. The numerous pristine waterfalls cascading down onto the river fascinated her as they swept past them.

Bertha and Ruthie squealed when they discovered the river was full of big, red-colored salmon floating upriver close enough to reach down and touch as they swam on either side of the canoe, while the Indians, silently with expertise, paddled around vessels sharing the river.

363

The rafts loaded with families and their belongings stayed close to the river's edge, for the most part, out of the swift current.

Martha wondered if Neil would be watching for their arrival. It would be good to see him. She wished he was here to share these sights with her.

It suddenly occurred to her that when she climbed out of this canoe, it would signify the end of her long journey. She'd long ago left Granny, Kohee, and apple blossoms. She'd had papa then too. She'd traveled each day with its endless walking, through dirt, mud, and sand, in all kinds of weather, through mountains, and across prairies, always moving further away from all she held dear.

She'd had to overcome fear and endure hardships, and death, that were shared with her family and the extended family, who she'd come to care for and depend on their companionship.

She admired the wagon master and his brave men, who gave them faith at times when they'd lacked for it, offering them encouragement when they were tired and hope when they'd felt defeated. Dear little Cookie, who could make them laugh. She'd traveled with so many strangers who were now friends, though they parted to move their separate ways.

Papa should be here with us. He'd be so proud of Mother, forging ahead, out of her love for him, to complete his dream. Tears stung Martha's eyes; quickly she blinked them away before mother and her sisters could see them. They too were quiet; perhaps they were in touch with their thoughts as the canoe rode the swift current.

Lost in reverie, it startled her when the canoe gliding around a bend in the river brought an exclamation from Ruthie "Look!" she shouted, pointing to a large settlement coming into view.

Martha remembered another time when Stephen had shouted with excitement to see the big wagons waiting for them at the beginning of their journey.

There was a softness to Bertha's husky voice as she called attention to the beauty of snow-capped Mount Hood hovering over them.

"Oh, my—isn't it spectacular?" Mother murmured softy, holding her hands to her breast as she gazed with reverence towards the lofty, impressive peak. "It looks like we an reach out and touch it."

"Look, Mother, there's two more of them. Over this way." Ruthie excitedly pointed at two more snow-capped mountains to the north of them.

"Oh—the wind's picking up. I'm getting chilled." Martha wrapped her arms around herself first, then searched for a quilt to wrap around her.

"I'm sure there's a storm coming; there's a change in the weather all of a sudden." She noted it had become overcast, and the sun had suddenly vanished. To the northwest, black clouds loomed menacingly.

The women looking ahead saw weather-beaten shacks and houses, with chimneys emitting blue smoke, come into view. The smell of burning wood, combined with the fragrance of new lumber and sawdust, all intermingled with the stench of dried fish.

At first the sounds were faint, but grew as barking dogs, children's squeals, and laughter floated out to them.

They could see a busy, bustling, active settlement, noisy voices were heard and the sound of traffic made by horses, buggies, and wagons.

The Indians skillfully guided the canoe left to the river bank white with discarded oyster and clam shells.

A variety of sailing vessels were tired up to the pier ahead, and across the river the scene was duplicated.

Mount Hood, in her majectic beauty, reigned supreme above the darkned evergreens that created a natural barrier for the settlement.

The Willamette Valley, to the weary women coming in from the river, offered a heaven of peace and traquillity.

The Indians pulled the canoe up a short distance from the river bank. The women, indecisive of what they were expected to do, waited for assistance but quickly realized by the men's silence, they were expected to climb out of the boat and wade ashore, with their belonging.

A muddy road ran adjacent to the river where horses hooves and wagons wheels had churcned through it. Raw sewage, and the rank swamp odors assaulted the women, but a darkened sky gave them reason to hurry.

For Martha, the greatest gift of all, was the sight of Neil, waiving his hat like a beacon to them. *No matter how crude or unrefined this settlement.* Martha vowed, *this is where I intend to make my home with Neil. Wherever Neil settles, I will be beside him..*

She resisted the urge to jump from the canoe and make her way to him. Instead she looked past her anger at the arrogance of the Indians in refusing to assist her Mother and sisters, in the challenging, clumsy, awkwardness it took to alight from the boat, tipping precariously to one side.

It amused Martha how the the Indians frantically use their paddles to stabilize and keep the canoe afloat.

Those, who caught sight of the women, stopped to watch them struggle in their long skirts and step down into the knee deep, cold water with arms laden to make their way over slippery river rocks toward Neil, who came wading out to meet them.

It was through steadfast determination, the Burt women had survived the long journey, with its test to their hopes, of their faith, and dreams,

With dignity and courage Martha, her mother, and sisters made their way towards the new land, with its promise of abundance awaiting them.

About the Author

Sustenance of Courage is my first historical novel, completed at seventy-one years of age, and after years of creative writing. I won an award for a historical document from the California Genealogical Society in 2003.

My story was written at the inspiration of a University of Washington college professor who desired a history of the early West told in story form to interest young people, the illiterate, and foreign students.

I'm retired from a career in the medical field, have raised four children as a single parent, and now reside with my West Highland-terrier, Tuppence, in Bellevue Washington.

Printed in the United States
63755LVS00001B/1-78

9 781420 872415